Praise for the novels

"Novak elevates mystery elements that will appeal to readers of Colleen Hoover."
—*Booklist* on *Tourist Season*

"Filled with mystery and drama, coupled with themes of family ties and secrets. This page-turner will not disappoint."
—*Booklist* on *The Seaside Library*

"*The Bookstore on the Beach* is a page-turner with a deep heart. You'll cheer for these admirable, complicated women. You'll be breathless (and smiling) when you read the surprising end. (Don't peek!)"
—Nancy Thayer, *New York Times* bestselling author of *Girls of Summer*

"Novak handles difficult topics with sensitivity, making for a heart-tugging romance. Readers are sure to be sucked in."
—*Publishers Weekly*, starred review, on *The Bookstore on the Beach*

"The prose is fast-paced and exciting making this a breathless page-turner with the conclusion proving no problems are too difficult to solve."
—*New York Journal of Books* on *The Bookstore on the Beach*

"This heartwarming story of sisters who bond as adults is sure to please the many fans of Novak as well as those who enjoy books by Susan Mallery and Debbie Macomber."
—*Library Journal* on *One Perfect Summer*

"I adore everything Brenda Novak writes. Her books are compelling, emotional, tender stories about people I would love to know in real life."
—RaeAnne Thayne, *New York Times* bestselling author

'Heartwarming, life-affirming, page-turning... I can always count on Novak to make me weep, laugh and fall in love!'
—Jill Shalvis, *New York Times* bestselling author

"Brenda Novak is always a joy to read."
—Debbie Macomber, #1 *New York Times* bestselling author

Also by Brenda Novak

THE MESSY LIFE OF JANE TANNER
THE TALK OF COYOTE CANYON
TALULAH'S BACK IN TOWN
TOURIST SEASON
THE SEASIDE LIBRARY
SUMMER ON THE ISLAND
KEEP ME WARM AT CHRISTMAS
WHEN I FOUND YOU
THE BOOKSTORE ON THE BEACH
A CALIFORNIA CHRISTMAS
ONE PERFECT SUMMER
CHRISTMAS IN SILVER SPRINGS
UNFORGETTABLE YOU
BEFORE WE WERE STRANGERS
RIGHT WHERE WE BELONG
UNTIL YOU LOVED ME
NO ONE BUT YOU
FINDING OUR FOREVER
THE SECRETS SHE KEPT
A WINTER WEDDING
THE SECRET SISTER
THIS HEART OF MINE
THE HEART OF CHRISTMAS
COME HOME TO ME

TAKE ME HOME FOR CHRISTMAS
HOME TO WHISKEY CREEK
WHEN SUMMER COMES
WHEN SNOW FALLS
WHEN LIGHTNING STRIKES
IN CLOSE
IN SECONDS
INSIDE
KILLER HEAT
BODY HEAT
WHITE HEAT
THE PERFECT MURDER
THE PERFECT LIAR
THE PERFECT COUPLE
WATCH ME
STOP ME
TRUST ME
DEAD RIGHT
DEAD GIVEAWAY
DEAD SILENCE
COLD FEET
TAKING THE HEAT
EVERY WAKING MOMENT

For a full list of Brenda's books, visit www.brendanovak.com.

Look for Brenda Novak's next novel
available soon from MIRA.

THE BANNED BOOKS CLUB

BRENDA NOVAK

/ll MIRA

//|MIRA™

ISBN-13: 978-0-7783-6959-2

The Banned Books Club

Recycling programs
for this product may
not exist in your area.

For questions and comments about the quality of this book, please contact us
at CustomerService@Harlequin.com.

TM is a trademark of Harlequin Enterprises ULC.

Mira
22 Adelaide St. West, 41st Floor
Toronto, Ontario M5H 4E3, Canada
MIRABooks.com

Printed in U.S.A.

To Sheila Chin, a reader and member
of Brenda Novak's Book Group on Facebook.
I'll never forget you coming to see me in Dallas while I was
on my big Bookstream (vintage Airstream turned traveling
bookstore/coffee shop) tour for *The Seaside Library*. There were
so many incredible moments on that two-month cross-country
odyssey, but your appearance stands out even still. You showed
up with boxes and boxes of my books, some of which contained
several brand-new copies of my latest releases (fifteen copies of
The Bookstore on the Beach!). You were giving them back to me
so I could use them for giveaways and other things in our book
group, and when I asked why you'd purchased so many, you said,
'Well, there's this certain author I've been trying to support...'" It's
one of the most generous things anyone has ever done for me,
and I was—and still am—completely blown away!
Thank you from the bottom of my heart!

1

"Wait...you're not still running that book club you started in high school, are you?"

Gia Rossi had been shopping at her local grocer when her sister called. "I've never really stopped. Not completely." She switched her phone to her other ear, so she could use her more dexterous left hand to steer her empty shopping cart across the parking lot to the reclamation point.

"Most of the members weren't your friends. They were just people who blindly followed you no matter what you did," her sister pointed out dryly.

Was there a hint of jealousy in that response? Margaret, who'd been known as Maggie when they were kids but now called herself a more distinguished Margot, was only thirteen months younger than Gia, so just one year behind her in school. Margot hadn't been nearly as popular—but it was because she'd never done anything exciting. She'd been part of the academic group, too busy excelling to be going out having fun.

"A few of them were close friends," Gia insisted. "Ruth, Sammie and a handful of others are still in the book club with me, and we rotate picking a read."

"*Seriously?* It's been seventeen years since you graduated. I thought you left them and everything else behind when you dropped out of college and took off for Alaska."

Her sister never would've done something that reckless, that impulsive—or that ill-advised. Gia had walked away from a volleyball scholarship at the University of Iowa, which was part of the reason her family had freaked out. But she was glad she'd made that decision. She treasured the memories of freewheeling her way through life in her twenties, learning everything she could while working on crabbing and fishing boats and for various sightseeing companies. She wouldn't have the business she owned now, with a partner, if not for that experience. "No. We fell off for a bit, then we went back to it, then we fell off again, and now we meet on Zoom to discuss the book we're reading on the fourth Thursday of every month." She lowered her voice for emphasis. "And, of course, we make sure it's the most scandalous book we can find."

Margot had never approved of the book group or anything else Gia did—and that hadn't changed over the years, which was why Gia couldn't resist needling her.

"I'm sure you do," Margot said, but she didn't react beyond a slightly sour tone. She'd grown adept at avoiding the kind of arguments that used to flare up between them, despite Gia sometimes baiting her. "So seven or eight out of what…about sixty are active again?"

"For one month out of the year, the ratio's quite a bit better than that," she said as the shopping cart clanged home, making her feel secure enough to walk away from it. "The rest of the group gets together for an online Christmas party in December."

"How many people come to that?"

Margot sounded as if she felt left out, but she'd never shown any interest in the book group. "Probably fifteen or twenty, but it's not always the same fifteen or twenty." She opened the door to her red Tesla Model 3, which signaled the computer to start the heater—something she was grateful for since she hadn't worn a heavy enough coat for the brisk October morning. Coeur d'Alene, Idaho, didn't usually turn this cold until November or December.

The car's Bluetooth picked up the call as Margot asked, "Why haven't you ever mentioned it?"

Now that they lived thirteen hundred miles apart, there were a lot of things she didn't tell her sister. It wasn't until she'd left her hometown behind that she'd felt she could live a truly authentic life—one without the constant unfavorable comparisons to her "perfect" sibling.

But that wasn't why she hadn't mentioned the book group. She'd assumed her sister wouldn't want to hear about it. Margot had been mortified when Gia challenged the gaggle of well-meaning but misguided women from the PTA who'd descended on Room 23 on Back-to-School Night, insisting Mr. Hart, head of the English department, drop *The Catcher in the Rye*, *The Outsiders* and *The Handmaid's Tale* from the Honors English reading list. Gia had expected her favorite teacher to stand up for the books she loved by explaining why they were so important. She'd known how much he'd loved those books, too. Instead, just to avoid a fight, he'd caved in immediately, which was what had incited her to start a club that championed the books they'd targeted—as well as others.

That was the first time Mr. Hart had let her down, but it wouldn't be the last. "If you'd ever joined the club, you'd be on the email list," she said as she backed out of the parking space.

"I would've, but you know me. I don't really read."

Her sister would not have joined. The Banned Books Club was far too controversial for Margot. It would've required a bit of rebellion—something she seemed incapable of. And maybe she didn't read much *fiction*, but Gia knew her to consume the occasional self-help tome. That was probably how she reassured herself she was still the best person she knew, because if there was anyone who *didn't* need a self-help book, it was Margot. Their parents' expectations were more than enough to create her boundaries.

"You should try reading along with us now and then. It might broaden your horizons." As good as Margot was, she had a mind like a steel trap—one that was always closed, especially when faced with any information that challenged what she already believed. She lived inside a bubble of confirmation bias; the only facts and ideas that could permeate it were those that supported her world view.

"I'm happy with my horizons being right where they are, thank you."

"You don't see the limitations?"

"Are you *trying* to offend me?" she asked.

Gia bit back a sigh. That was the difference between them. Margot would sacrifice anything to maintain her position as their parents' favorite child, to gain the approval of others, especially her husband, and be admired by the community at large. Growing up, she'd kept her room tidy, gotten straight As and played the piano in church. And these days, she was a stay-at-home mom with two children, someone who made a "hot dish"—what most people outside the Midwest would call a casserole—for any neighbor, friend or acquaintance who might be having surgery or suffering some kind of setback.

Her conventionalism was—in certain ways—something to be admired. As the black sheep of the family, Gia knew better than to try to compete with Margot. That wasn't possible for someone who couldn't take anything at face value. She had to question rules, challenge authority and play devil's advocate at almost every opportunity, which was why she was surprised that her sister had been trying, for the past two weeks, to convince her to come home for the winter. Their mother's health had been declining since she'd been diagnosed with breast cancer.

It was at stage four before they discovered it, and the doctors had done what they could, but Ida hadn't responded to treatment. Margot claimed their mother wasn't going to last much longer, that Gia should spend a few months with her before it was too late. But Gia was surprised Margot would risk the peace and contentment they all seemed to enjoy without her.

Gia wasn't sure she could go back to the same family dynamic she found so damaging, regardless. She and her business partner ran a helicopter sightseeing company for tourists and flew hunters and fishermen in and out of the remote wilderness—but Backcountry Adventures was closed during the coldest months, from November to February. She would soon have the time off, so getting away from work wouldn't be a problem. It was more that when she was in Wakefield, the walls seemed to close in around her. It simply got too damn hard to breathe. "Fine," she grumbled. "Don't answer that question. But speaking of limitations, how's Sheldon?"

"Seriously, Gia? I'm going to assume you didn't mean to ask about him in that way," her sister stated flatly.

There was no love lost between Gia and her brother-in-law. She hated the way he controlled Margot, how he could spend money on hunting or fishing or buying a new camper, but her sister had to scrape and bow for a new pair of jeans. Margot explained it was because he earned all the money, that he was trying to be a good "manager" by giving her such a tight budget so the business would be successful and they'd have money to retire in old age, but to Gia, it seemed that Margot was making all the sacrifices. Stingy was stingy, and yet *he* was the one who wanted Margot at home, waiting for him with a hot meal at the end of the day. Their boys, Matthew and Greydon, were eight and six, both in school. Margot could work part-time, at least, establish something of her own, if Sheldon wasn't calling all the shots.

"It was a joke." Gia really didn't want to cause problems in her sister's marriage. Margot insisted she was happy, although if that were *her* life, Gia probably would've grabbed her kids and stormed out of the house—for good—long ago.

"He's doing great. He's been busy."

"It's deer hunting season. I assume he's going."

"Next week."

And what will you do—stay home and take care of the kids and the house while he's gone? Gia wanted to ask, but this time she managed to bite her tongue. "He's going to Utah again?"

"Yeah. They go there every year. One of his buddies grew up in Moab."

"Last winter, Sheldon's business slowed down a bit, so I'm surprised to hear you say he's been busy."

"That was the economy in general. All trucking companies took a hit. I don't think the same thing's going to happen this year, though. He just bought two new semis and is hiring more drivers."

"He's quite the businessman." Gia rolled her eyes at her own words. He hadn't built the trucking business; he'd inherited it from his parents, who remained heavily involved, which was probably what saved it from ruin. But thankfully, Margot seemed to take her words at face value.

"I'm proud of him."

He was proud of himself, could never stop talking about his company, his toys, his prowess at hunting or four-wheeling or any other "manly" pursuit. Gia was willing to bet she could out-hunt him if she really wanted to, but the only kind of shots she was willing to take were with her camera.

Still, she was glad, in a way, that her sister could buy into the delusion that Sheldon was a prize catch. "That's what matters," she said as she pulled into the drive of her two-bedroom condo overlooking Mill River. The conversation was winding down. She'd already asked about the boys while she was in the grocery store—they were healthy and happy. She was going to have to ask about Ida before the conversation ended, so she figured she might as well get it over with. "And how are Mom and Dad?"

Her sister's voice dropped an octave, at least. "That's actually why I called..."

Gia couldn't help but tense; it felt like acid was eating a hole in her stomach. "Mom's taken a turn for the worse?"

"She's getting weaker every day, G. I—I really think you should come home."

Closing her eyes, Gia allowed her head to fall back against the seat. Margot couldn't understand why Gia would resist. But she'd never been able to see anything from Gia's perspective.

"G?" her sister prompted.

Gia drew a deep breath. She could leave Idaho a few weeks before they closed the business. Eric would cover for her. She'd worked two entire months for him when his daughter was born. She had the money, too. There was no good excuse not to return and support her family as much as possible—and if this was the end, to say goodbye to her mother. But Gia knew that would mean dealing with everything she'd left behind.

"You still there?"

Gathering her resolve, Gia climbed out of the car. "Sorry. My Bluetooth cut out."

"Did you hear me? Is there any chance you'd consider coming home, if only for a few weeks?"

Gia didn't see that she had any choice. She'd never forgive herself if her mother died and she hadn't done all she could to put things right between them. She wished she could continue procrastinating her visit. But the cancer made it impossible. "Of course. Just...just as soon as I finish up a few things around here."

"How long will that take you?"

"Only a day or two."

"Thank God," her sister said with enough relief that Gia knew she couldn't back out now.

What was going on? Why would having her in Wakefield matter so much to Margot?

"I'll pick you up from the airport," her sister continued. "Just tell me when you get in."

"I'll get back to you as soon as I've made the arrangements."

Margot studied the guns neatly lined up in her husband's locked cabinet in their bedroom. He had several rifles—a .30-30 Winchester, a Remington Model 700, a .375 H&H Magnum, a .22 and what he called a "varmint" rifle—as well as a twelve-gauge shotgun. He also had a 9 mm Glock up high in their closet for home defense. That was what he'd leave behind when he went hunting. She'd have easy access to it, but it was the shotgun she coveted. She'd feel safest with the shotgun. She'd heard her husband say that pistols and rifles almost always take multiple shots to hit a target. They'd visited the gun range together, but because of the recoil and the deafening noise—and her fear of guns in general, especially having them around the children—she'd only practiced shooting once or twice. After that, Sheldon had deemed her a "nervous Nellie" and given up trying to share his love of firearms with her. But she'd learned enough to know she wouldn't have to worry too much about aiming a shotgun.

Did she dare hide the shotgun so he couldn't take it with him when he went hunting? She could act as though someone had broken in and taken it, say she'd left the house unlocked for a short, fifteen-minute interval while picking up the boys from school, and it was gone when she returned...

No. That would raise his suspicions. He'd wonder why that was the only thing missing, and she didn't dare try to stage a full-fledged robbery. It would be too easy to get caught doing something like that. Sheldon was naturally suspicious—always looking out for how someone might put one over on him. With any luck, he wouldn't see *this* coming, but she could only count on having one chance, which meant she had to craft the perfect plan, and that included providing for every eventuality.

Maybe she should forget about the shotgun and the Glock and settle for pepper spray or mace—something she could buy over the counter at Walmart. Then she wouldn't have to worry about gun safety and would never be faced with the decision of whether or not she'd have to shoot her own husband...

"Margot? What the hell are you doing?"

Sheldon's sudden appearance in the doorway sent her heart slamming against her chest. She was standing in the middle of the floor not far from the bed, which, fortunately, didn't incriminate her in any way. She just had to hope she didn't look as guilty as she felt. "I was...trying to remember why I came in here."

He rolled his eyes. "Sounds like you. I swear, I have no idea how you graduated from college. Most of the time you're dumber than dirt."

Normally, Margot flinched at the insults he lobbed so casually, usually with a laugh so that if she took umbrage he could say he'd been joking. Today, she merely studied him for any evidence in his ice-blue eyes that a bigger argument was brewing. "What are you doing home?" she asked, checking her watch. These days, she lost minutes, even hours, ruminating over her future—and that of her children. But it *couldn't* be late enough for Sheldon to be home from work. She'd never lost an entire day.

"Forgot my lunch. I've been trying to call you to have you bring it to me but couldn't get an answer. Why the hell do I pay for you to have a cell phone if I can't even reach you on it?"

"I–It's in my purse," she said lamely. "From when I took the boys to school."

A disgusted huff revealed his irritation. "Of course it is. You never have it when you need it."

"I usually have it," she said in her own defense, but she was

careful to keep the pique out of her voice. She knew how easily they could wind up in a fight if she didn't.

He ignored her response. "My lunch isn't on the counter.
What'd you do with it?"

When he left it behind, she'd assumed he was going out with
his friends. Although he'd gained quite a bit of weight over the
years and made an occasional, half-hearted attempt to lose it,
his diets never lasted. She'd assumed he no longer wanted the
carrot sticks and other healthy food he'd directed her to start
packing for him. "When you didn't take it, I assumed you had
other plans and—and put it in the boys' lunches."

His eyebrows snapped together. "So you wouldn't have to
make more? Jesus, woman! Why didn't you just call me?"

Because she hadn't wanted to hear his voice. The only peace
she had was when he was at work and too caught up in being
the "boss" to check in with her. "I didn't want to bother you
if you were busy."

Lifting his Wakefield Trucking ball cap, he scratched underneath it before mumbling something she couldn't quite make
out—probably "stupid bitch"—as he trudged back down the
hall. "Now what am I going to eat?" he called back to her
when, judging by his voice, he'd reached the kitchen.

Margot curled her fingernails into her palms. She was having *terrible* thoughts lately—of wanting to put something gross,
like a spider or dirt, in his sandwich, or something dangerous,
like antifreeze, in his tea. She knew that was downright evil.
Her upbringing and her belief in God had stopped her so far—
that and she didn't want to be yanked away from her children
to spend the rest of her life in prison.

But the desire to hurt him in return was growing stronger by the day. That she could even consider such things—
Margaret Rossi, salutatorian of her high school class and daughter of two loving parents who'd raised her to be much better

than that—was shocking. It certainly wasn't something she'd anticipated before she got married.

But was it really her fault? Sheldon was like a girdling tree with roots that had slowly wrapped around her over the years, trapping her and holding her in place while squeezing the life from her...

"Dammit, Margot! Didn't you hear me? Get your ass out here and make me another lunch! I've got work to do!"

She wanted to scream *Make it yourself!* and slam the door. The anger simmering inside her was like bile rising in her throat. Sometimes it was all she could do to choke it back. But she knew what would happen if she let loose. He'd never struck her; she couldn't claim that kind of abuse. But his fits of rage were getting worse—bad enough that she believed it was possible he might completely unleash one day.

Even if that didn't happen, what he did was almost as bad. His words slugged her like fists. He belittled her to the point that she was afraid to say or do anything for fear of reprisal. And he made her feel as though she deserved every cutting remark.

That she was beginning to believe she wasn't worthy of being treated any better created a panic that gnawed at her soul. If she didn't do something soon, she was afraid the old Margot— the happy, well-adjusted Margot she was struggling to hang on to—would disappear for good.

It won't be long now, she promised herself, and cast his guns a final glance as she forced her feet to carry her back to the kitchen. "I'm here," she said woodenly. "What would you like?"

2

Most of the people Gia associated with were men. There were a lot more of them in her business—both as competitors and clients—and there'd been more men than women in Alaska, where she'd spent ten years before moving to Idaho. But as the men she knew got married, she had the opportunity to meet their wives—and then their kids—which was nice because it broadened her social circle. Eric Cheung, who'd learned to fly in the military and been her flight instructor in Alaska before becoming her business partner, had met and then married his wife only six months after they'd moved Backcountry Adventures to Coeur d'Alene, so Gia was coming to know Coty well.

"I thought we were going to head back to Glacier once the season ended," Eric said as they sat huddled around the fire pit he'd built in his backyard, holding a drink.

"I was looking forward to focusing on our photography, but—" Gia frowned up at the night sky "—who knows if the weather would even allow a trip to the park. Winter seems to be coming early this year."

"That's good," he clarified. "We were after *snow* shots, remember?"

She *did* remember and regretted that she couldn't follow through with their plans. He'd recently convinced a local gallery to carry his work and said he could probably get her in. But she couldn't ignore what was going on in the rest of her life by heading to Glacier National Park on November 1 as they'd discussed. "I know, but...my mom's taken a turn for the worse."

He sobered instantly. "I'm sorry to hear that. I've been meaning to ask about her, but I didn't want to keep probing that sore spot. The treatments aren't working, then?"

"I think they've done all they can."

Coty came out of the house after putting their daughter to bed. "What did I miss?"

"My mom isn't doing well."

"That's terrible news." She frowned as she sat down next to her husband, who shifted to put his arm around her and help keep her warm. They could've gone inside, but the one thing Gia had in common with the men she associated with was a love for the outdoors.

"It is. I wish that wasn't the case, but..." Gia let her words trail off before taking the last sip of her beer.

"How long will you be gone?" Eric asked.

"I'm not sure. Shorter would be better. I have so much history there. But it'll depend on how things go with my mom."

Coty leaned forward to reclaim the wineglass she'd set aside when she left. "What kind of history are you talking about?"

That was hard to explain. Even Eric didn't know. "Just people I'd rather not see and things I'd rather not remember."

Coty's forehead creased. "How long's it been since you were there?"

"About six months. I can handle a short visit over the weekend here and there—one where my family is all I see. But this could be for the entire winter, until I have to return to help open Backcountry Adventures."

"If you need to stay longer—" Eric started, but Gia cut him off.

"I'm hoping that won't be necessary. You're doing enough covering the rest of October. But...we'll cross that bridge when we come to it, I guess."

"Well, if your mom needs you, you'll be glad you went," he said.

"I don't know that she *needs* me. She has Margot. They've always been close, understand each other a lot better than she and I do. But..."

"Your mom's your mom," Coty said gently.

Gia nodded and got up to toss her can in the recycle bin a few steps away.

Eric followed her lead, the *chink* of his can hitting only seconds after hers. "Have you told Mike?"

Gia shifted on her feet, feeling awkward and uncomfortable. Mike was an aviation maintenance technician—he serviced and repaired helicopters. She'd met him when he did a thorough inspection of their craft right after she moved to Coeur d'Alene, but it had only been lately, after his divorce, that they'd started dating. "Not yet."

"He'll be heartbroken," Eric predicted.

"No, we're not that far along in our relationship." She'd been ready to bail out, anyway. She liked Mike as much or more than some of the other men she'd dated over the years. They both enjoyed flying and had a good time together. But she had a problem with intimacy. Getting close to someone required too much trust—more trust than she seemed capable of cobbling together. So whenever a romantic relationship began to grow serious, she'd break away and move on, and that usually only took a few months.

"Does *he* know that?" Eric asked wryly.

"I told him from the beginning that I'm not looking for anything serious, Eric. Believe me, he was warned."

Eric laughed. "All that does is create a challenge, G. I'm sure he's hoping he'll be the one to change that."

She settled back in her seat while Eric remained standing. "I don't think anyone can change it. It's just...me."

"When will you be leaving?" Coty asked.

"As soon as possible. Margot's in a panic, acts like she can't wait for me to get there."

"I bet she needs your support as much as your mother does," Eric said.

Gia pursed her lips. "That could be true. She has such a crappy husband. I doubt he gives her much of anything."

"You've talked about him before," Eric responded with a laugh.

Gia crossed her legs. "I don't understand why she doesn't demand more from him."

"I know Eric's heard this, but I haven't," Coty said. "Why don't you like him?"

"He's an arrogant asshole," Gia replied. "Thinks the world revolves around him."

Eric moved closer to the fire and held his hands over the warmth. "He was raised with money. Isn't that what you told me?"

"I wouldn't define his parents as mega-wealthy, but his family was one of the more prosperous in town."

"So he was spoiled?" Coty guessed.

Gia confirmed with a nod. "His parents *still* baby him."

Eric cracked open another beer before sitting back down with his wife. "Surely there are people in your hometown you'd *like* to see."

"My old friends and the people in my Banned Books Club." She'd liked a lot of them, but it'd been seventeen years since high school and most had drifted away. She'd probably see those who remained—Ruth and Sammie at least.

"Coty's been thinking about joining your club," he said, once again slinging an arm around his wife.

"I'm always down for flipping off people who are trying to

push their attitudes and opinions on others," Coty said with a laugh. "What are you reading this month?"

"We've been picking from a list of books that were banned in the nineties, simply because there were so many back then. It was my turn this month, and I chose *Cujo*."

"What's that?" Eric said.

Gia chuckled. He'd never been a reader. "A horror novel by Stephen King."

Tucking her feet underneath her, Coty leaned into her husband's body. "And how's that going for you?"

"It's good. It's about a dog who turns into a killer after being bitten by a rabid bat."

"Not sure I'd find that interesting," Coty said with a scowl.

"A killer dog's not for everyone. But you can always start next month. We'll be reading *We All Fall Down* by Robert Cormier."

"What's that about?"

"A gang of teenage boys who get into all kinds of trouble…"

"I bet that book's going to be pretty disturbing," she said, wrinkling her nose as if she wasn't thrilled by that idea, either.

"Most banned books are pretty…*something*," Gia said. "Scary. Thought-provoking. Challenging to the power paradigm—or the way things have always been. That's why they get banned."

Eric spoke up. "I read not too long ago that the Harry Potter books were banned."

Gia considered opening another beer. The more she drank, the less she dreaded going home to Wakefield. Eric and Coty lived only a few blocks from her condo; she didn't need to drive. But she decided against it. She wanted a clear head when she got back to her place so she could make her travel arrangements. "That's right. In some places, anyway."

"What could be wrong with Harry Potter?" Coty asked.

"Apparently, several exorcists weighed in," she replied flippantly.

Coty looked confused. "Did you say *exorcists*?"

"I did. They recommended the books be taken off the shelves." Gia grinned as she added, "Wizardry and magic are Satanic. Didn't you know?"

Coty rolled her eyes. "You've got to be kidding me..."

"Nope. Now you understand why I started the group. Some of the books that have been denied were targeted for ridiculous reasons."

"I love the way you're willing to challenge authority," she said.

Gia made a face. "My parents aren't so excited about it. They never have been."

"I bet." Coty stared into the flames as she continued, "To be honest, I'm not sure I'd want Ingrid challenging authority. What I do is one thing. But what she does—"

"I'd be proud of her," Eric broke in. "We might not always agree with the stances she takes, but there has to be *someone* willing to fight people who ban good books and do other stupid things."

Coty didn't look convinced. "But think of the backlash that goes with being the one to stand up and fight..."

"Maybe that's what your parents were worried about," Eric said to Gia. "The pain it might cause *you* to make yourself a target."

Gia thought it was more about their desire to see her conform, to avoid making waves. They'd always wanted her to do what girls were "supposed" do to and quit drawing so much attention. But she didn't want to go that deep tonight, so she simply said, "Maybe."

Pulling his wife closer, Eric spoke over her head. "I hope you can finally resolve a few things."

Gia doubted that was possible. She'd never been what her parents wanted. But, again, she didn't care to explain. "That would be nice."

"Well, you don't have to worry about Backcountry Adventures while you're gone," he added encouragingly. "I've got that. And a lot has probably changed at home over the years—more than you realize. As hard as it will be to see your mother in such poor health, I bet this trip will be good for you."

"I can't imagine that." As far as she knew, Mr. Hart, her old English teacher, still lived just a few houses down from her parents. And she'd be staying, possibly for weeks or months, in her old room.

Margot circled the airport again as she waited for her sister to emerge with her luggage. Gia's flight had been delayed. At this rate, they'd be late getting home, which would put off dinner and create a more difficult evening with Sheldon. He'd been so agitated lately, so irritable. If she had to call him and ask him to leave work even a few minutes early, so he could pick up the boys, it would trigger a fight. Matthew and Greydon were each playing at a friend's house, but she'd promised both mothers she'd return by six.

Growing more and more anxious, she pulled over to text Gia again. Earlier, when her sister sent a message to say she'd be getting in at four and Margot had arranged playdates so the boys wouldn't have to sit in the car for two or three hours, she'd never dreamed she might not be able to make it back in time. The Sioux Gateway Airport was only fifty miles from Wakefield.

At least the plane had finally landed. That was the last she'd heard from her sister. Any sign of your luggage?

Just grabbed it, came Gia's quick response.

Margot breathed a sigh of relief. I'll be right there.

With a glance at the clock on the dash—it was 4:50 p.m., which meant she *might* make it back in time if they didn't get behind a tractor or something else that would slow them down—she merged back into the flow of traffic streaming toward the terminal and began to search for the rather tall figure of her sister. Although Margot was only five foot two, Gia was five foot ten. They were opposites even in that.

Gia waved as soon as she spotted Margot's Subaru, and Margot eased over one lane at a time until she could reach the curb.

"How was the flight?" she asked as soon as she'd flung open her door and hurried to release the hatch for Gia's suitcase.

"Long and miserable," Gia replied, giving her an obligatory hug before loading up. "Is any flight enjoyable these days?"

"Not since 9/11." Margot slammed the hatch before returning to the driver's seat.

"Thanks for picking me up," Gia said as she climbed in.

"Of course. I'm glad you're here." Gia looked good, Margot realized. Much better than she did. These days when she peered into the mirror, all she saw was a tense, troubled expression and dark bags under her hazel eyes.

But Gia... Although summer was over and had been for several weeks, no one would be able to tell by looking at her. Her skin still held a warm glow, and her strawberry blond hair had lighter streaks going through it from all the time spent in the sun. The sprinkling of freckles across her nose made her appear younger than her thirty-five years. And she was well-toned with a broad, engaging smile.

Margot did what she could to be attractive, scrimping on the grocery budget to be able to get eyelash extensions and fake nails. Sheldon expected her to look good, even though he'd have a fit if he knew how much those appointments cost. Gia didn't bother with that kind of enhancement. She was too much of a natural, outdoorsy person. She looked wholesome, healthy and strong.

She *was* strong. Always had been. Margot envied her forthright manner, the way she tackled any obstacle in her path and overcame it. It was a relief to have her in Wakefield. Margot couldn't escape her situation without her sister being around to support their father and help care for their mother. She'd been trying to muddle through the way things were, at least until Ida's death, as sad as that would be. But no one could predict when their mother might pass, and Margot couldn't bear her current situation any longer.

Besides, maybe she'd be smarter not to wait. She was afraid Ida's death would pile so much grief on top of what she was already dealing with that she wouldn't be able to overcome it. Her mental health wasn't what it used to be. Recognizing that and acting before it was too late to recover from the long downward spiral that'd begun shortly after the birth of her second and last child, when her marriage had *really* begun to fall apart, was the best she could do.

So far, she'd mostly lived her life for other people. It was time she grabbed hold and started living for herself. And with her sister here, she had a better chance of doing that. Gia would take on Sheldon, if she had to. Gia would take on anyone.

"Do Mom and Dad know that I'm coming?"

Margot looked over at her. "You didn't call them?"

"I haven't had time," her sister replied vaguely.

"To *place a call*?"

"It's only been two days since I agreed to come! I was in a hurry, trying to take care of things so I wouldn't leave Eric in the lurch. I had to prepare my condo for the winter, pack my bags and get a ride to the airport in Spokane. Every time I thought about calling them, it was night, and then I was afraid they'd be in bed asleep. It's an hour later here than in Idaho, you know."

That was sheer avoidance, and Margot knew it, but she didn't care. Reinforcements had arrived. That was all that mattered. "Why didn't you have Eric fly you over?"

"Because it was a lot easier to catch a commercial flight. I didn't want to take up his time when he'll be filling in for me as it is. And our helicopter only flies three hundred miles on a tank of gas, which means he'd have to find several places to refuel."

"Makes sense," Margot said.

"So...do you think Mom and Dad are going to be upset having me drop in on them?"

"Of course not," she replied. "I'm sure they've been wondering why you haven't come home before now."

Her sister grimaced. "You'd think they'd know."

Margot gripped the steering wheel tighter. "What's going on is bad enough, G," she said in the same placating tone she had to use with Sheldon. "Can we just...leave the past in the past? Please?"

Gia shot her an aggrieved look. "*I'm* perfectly willing to do that. It's them, not me."

"Even if that's normally true, their minds are on something else these days. And I, for one, am relieved to have you."

Loosening her seat belt, Gia twisted to face her. "The question is why, Margot? Why were you so determined to have me come home right now? In less than a month, my business will be closed for the winter. You don't think Mom's going to make it that long?"

Margot wished she could tell Gia the truth, but she was afraid of what her sister would do if she learned what Sheldon had turned into. She had no doubt Gia would confront him. She didn't know how to be anything but direct, and Margot couldn't see where challenging Sheldon would end well. "Maybe not. That's the problem. They need you." She glanced over to see how her words were being received. "And so do I," she added more softly.

Gia must've heard the honesty in her voice, or something else defused her sister's antagonistic feelings, because she seemed resigned when she responded, "I can't imagine any of you need me, especially you. You've always done everything right."

It was true. Margot had gotten good grades, graduated from college and chosen a man her parents approved of—someone she'd known in high school and then dated in college. A lot of women had wanted Sheldon, but she was the "lucky" girl he'd chosen. So how was it that she found herself in a marriage that seemed to be burning down around her and felt so miserable and hopeless all the time? "Shows what you know," she muttered.

"What does that mean?" Gia asked.

Margot checked the clock against her speedometer, and succumbed to the pressure she was feeling by giving the vehicle more gas. "Just...help me out by taking care of Mom and Dad for a while, okay? You have to admit it's your turn."

At least Gia had the good grace not to argue that point. Margot *had* done a lot more for their parents. She was the one who'd stuck around for the past seventeen years while Gia had run off on her wild adventures. "That's what I'm here for," her sister said matter-of-factly and straightened in her seat.

When they reached their parents' house, Gia was surprised Margot didn't want to come in and say hello. She stopped just long enough to let Gia grab her suitcase before tearing out of the drive. Gia knew she had to pick up the boys, but would being five minutes late be *that* big a deal?

Maybe Margot wanted to avoid the awkwardness Gia herself was dreading as she approached the sliding glass door that looked in on the addition her father had built when they were kids.

She could see her parents sitting at the table eating dinner as she reached for the door handle—and braced for the moment they saw her. Part of the reason she'd been putting off coming home was facing her mother's illness. It was one thing to hear about what Ida was going through; it was another to look her in the face during these final months, weeks or days. The reality of the situation hit Gia like a right hook as she noticed her mother's dramatic hair and weight loss. Ida had never been a big person, but to see her so diminished...

A lump rose in Gia's throat, threatening to choke her. It

didn't matter how difficult and complicated their relationship had been; seeing her mother like this was even worse than she'd anticipated. She realized she'd been stoking the fire of her anger and resentment as a defense mechanism to ward off the pain of Ida's illness—but by doing that, she'd abandoned her mother to face cancer without even the limited support she could give. A very brief trip now and then just wasn't enough.

"Dammit," she muttered, squeezing her eyes closed and hanging her head. Her sister was right. She was a terrible person, had let them all down—and it was because she couldn't bear to see what was happening.

Her father glanced up and the next thing she knew he was walking toward the slider with a shocked expression on his face. "Gia?" she could hear him say through the door.

She yanked on the handle to open it and forced a smile. "Hi, Dad."

"What are you doing here?"

The lump in her throat would not recede no matter how many times she swallowed. She blinked, trying to hold back the tears that were filling her eyes. "Just...decided to come home for the winter."

"For the *winter*?" her mother echoed. Ida was moving more slowly, but she was now on her feet, as well, and coming to the door.

Gia had planned on saying she'd only be home for a week or two. She'd wanted to set their expectations low, so she'd have an escape if she needed it. But the sight of her parents, who'd aged more than she'd realized, and just the smell of home, had changed her mind. In that moment she knew she'd stand by her family until the bitter end, no matter what it cost her. "If you don't mind me moving back into my old room," she said with what she could manage by way of a chuckle.

She tensed as she waited for their response. There was a chance they wouldn't want their lives disrupted at this vulnerable time. But her father seemed relieved to have her home. No doubt the past two years had been a nightmare for him, watching the slow demise of the woman he loved. Her mother just seemed grateful.

"Really?" Ida said. "Well, isn't that nice! If I never dreamed you'd be able to do that."

"What about your business?" her father asked as a rapid follow-up.

Gia bent to pick up Miss Marple, her mother's gray-and-white cat, who'd roused herself from a nap on the other end of the sofa to jump down and say hello. "Eric will cover the next few weeks. Then it'll be closed for winter."

"But your photography," he said. "Last we heard you were going to Glacier National Park to take some photographs."

She'd sent them some of her work, knew they both liked it. "Eric can do that on his own for now," she said as she put Miss Marple back down. "He's a great photographer."

"That's wonderful!" her father exclaimed. "Of course you can have your old room. It's still filled with all the stuff you left behind. We haven't touched it."

Her mother felt like a bag of bones as Gia embraced her.

"Does that mean you'll be here for Christmas?" she asked.

"It does," Gia replied. The question was whether *Ida* would be there for Christmas.

"Come in." Her father gestured toward the kitchen. "We've got dinner on the table. You want some spaghetti?"

The menu meant her father had cooked. Spaghetti had been his one and only dish when she was growing up. "Are you sure you have enough?"

"We have plenty," he replied. "Your mother hardly eats these days."

Again, Gia felt like crying. All the defenses she'd worked hard to erect had crumbled in an instant. Seeing her mother so frail and wasted was just too heartbreaking. The last six months especially had taken a toll. "Well, we'll see what she thinks of some of the things I make."

Suddenly moving with more energy, her mother hurried back into the kitchen to set another plate.

As Gia started to follow, her father caught her arm. "Thank you for coming," he murmured, which made her hate herself all the more for not being there sooner.

"Of course," she said, suddenly grateful to her sister for pressing her. "I'll do whatever I can."

3

Dinner was late, but it wasn't Margot's trip to the airport that caused it. The mother of Matthew's playdate had wanted to show her a quilt she was making and was so eager to chat that Margot couldn't get away. Panic had risen inside her as the other woman continued to drone on about the various kinds of patterns she used and how she was thinking about selling her work online, but Margot had learned not to let on that she was under so much pressure. Someone who wasn't in her situation wouldn't understand, and making Sheldon "look bad" was a cardinal sin.

Fortunately, Sheldon arrived home even later than she did. He said "someone" had dropped by the office and held him up for a few minutes. He didn't say who, which was what made her guess.

"Was it Cecilia Sonderman?" she asked.

He was washing his hands in the kitchen sink—something she'd asked him not to do many times.

"Yeah." He sent her a sharp glance. "How'd you know?"

Cece had been sniffing around for a couple of months now, and Margot could tell Sheldon was flattered by the attention.

She suspected he also enjoyed the opportunity to try to make her jealous, because *he* was the one who'd let on that Cece was still interested in him. He threw it at her whenever he did something that upset her—to let her know there were other women waiting in the wings, she supposed. It should've galled her that his high school sweetheart, who'd only recently divorced her husband and moved back to town, was seeking him out. But as far as Margot was concerned, they couldn't fall in love fast enough. Then maybe he'd be distracted when she left. Perhaps Cece would even be decent enough to try to talk some sense into him. *Let her go. Let her live her life. You've got me...*

Or maybe Cece would become the next victim of his demanding and controlling nature. Margot was tempted to warn her that he wasn't what he appeared to be—she felt bad for any woman who might fill her shoes—but she couldn't take the risk. Not when it could get back to him and blow her chance to leave.

Cece would have to look out for herself; she had no business making a play for a married man in the first place.

"Just a guess," she said mildly.

"We're friends. That's all. Nothing's going on." He sounded defensive even though there'd been no accusation in her voice.

"Of course."

He gave her a funny look. Maybe he was surprised by her naivete. Or maybe he could tell it wasn't naivete—that it was absolute indifference. But she'd done nothing to make an issue of his tardiness or the reason he'd been late, so even he seemed hard-pressed to find a reason to get angry over their latest exchange.

"Are you hungry?" she asked.

"Starving."

"Good. I've made your favorite meal."

He seemed slightly perplexed again; no doubt he knew he'd

been awful to her of late and didn't deserve special treatment. "Shepherd's pie?"

She'd also made a pot roast. He liked both. Had he said pot roast, she would've served it to him and saved the shepherd's pie for tomorrow. The past two days she'd been doubling up on the cooking and planned to freeze the extra. She was trying to get ahead so she could spend some time with her family, especially her mother, before she had to escape and eke out a new life. "Yep."

"Sounds good." He sat at the head of the table and read the news on his phone while she got the kids in their seats and the food on the table.

"How was work today?" she asked as she took his plate and dished up a generous portion of shepherd's pie—originally her mother's recipe.

Sheldon barely glanced up from his phone. "It was okay."

"Anything happen?"

Irritated that she continued to interrupt him, he scowled. "Was something *supposed* to happen?"

She'd been looking for an opportunity to tell him Gia was in town, but he'd only complain about the gas money she'd spent driving to Sioux City, so she wasn't planning to volunteer that she'd been involved unless he specifically asked. Let him think their father had picked her up—or that she'd taken an Uber. "No," she said, backpedaling. "I was just…asking about your day."

"I got to go to Nathan's!" Matthew piped up, eager to talk even if his father wasn't.

Not to be outdone, Greydon joined in, "And I got to go to Jimmy's!"

"Great. I'm happy for both of you." Sheldon pointed at their plates. "Now quit playing with your food and eat."

Matthew scowled at the small mound of pie Margot had dished up for him. "I don't like this."

"It's good for you." Sheldon shoveled another huge bite into his own mouth. "Eat it."

Their oldest son slumped in his seat. "I hate green beans!"

The look that entered Sheldon's eyes caused the hair on the back of Margot's neck to stand on end. So far, he hadn't treated the boys too badly. Although he was stern and demanded to be obeyed, he reserved the worst of his temper for her.

But as Matthew got older and tried to establish his own will, she could see that changing. It was one of the things that gave her sufficient motivation to leave, despite the sacrifices she'd have to make. Sheldon refused to be challenged by a woman or a child. If she didn't do something to change the future, she could see Matt one day being on the receiving end of the badgering and belittling she had to endure—and that was if Sheldon didn't break down and do worse.

"There are kids just like you starving in Africa," he said. "Be glad you got something to eat."

"Just eat everything around the beans," Margot muttered, hoping to defuse the situation. But all that did was draw Sheldon's attention to her.

"Don't undermine my authority," he snapped. "If I tell him to eat something, he'd better do it."

Matthew flinched at his father's steely tone. "What happens if I can't?" he asked, worry filling his eyes.

"You'll sit there until you do," his father pronounced.

"*I'll* eat them for you!" Greydon, who looked almost like a clone of his older brother with thick dark hair and big brown eyes, demonstrated how much he liked them by picking one out of his mashed potatoes and stuffing it into his mouth.

Sheldon arched an eyebrow at Greydon. "Matthew will eat his own."

What Sheldon was demanding wasn't exactly Machiavellian. There were worse punishments than sitting at a table until you'd consumed four green beans. Knowing it was best to support her husband when she could, Margot nodded. "Your father's right, Matt. It can't be that hard to choke down a few beans."

"If I throw up, it's not my fault," he grumbled.

Margot hoped that wouldn't happen. Sheldon would interpret it as a voluntary act—a refusal to obey—and punish him by taking away something he loved, like saying he couldn't play baseball this year. She and the boys wouldn't be around long enough for baseball season, but Matt didn't know that, so it would definitely upset him.

Hoping to give her son a chance to come to terms with eating all his dinner, she reached over and smoothed the hair out of his eyes while changing the subject. "I was thinking we'd have pot roast tomorrow. Does that sound good? Everyone likes pot roast."

Her husband was once again focused on his phone and didn't seem to hear her. At least, he didn't respond—but then he jerked his head up and pinned her to her seat with a baleful glare. "Did you know your sister's in town?"

Margot lowered her eyes to her plate as though intent on taking her next bite. "She let me know she was coming. Who told you she was already here?"

"My mother has a friend who quilts with her. She stopped by your folks' place to drop off a pumpkin pie. Said Gia was there."

"It's about time Gia came home," Margot said, mostly as a deflection. "I've been after her for months."

"*Aunt* Gia?" Matthew perked up, but Sheldon didn't give her the chance to respond.

"She thinks she's pretty cool flying that helicopter into the wilderness," Sheldon said. "She loves her business so much I'm surprised she'd leave it."

"Backcountry Adventures closes for four months every winter," Margot explained.

"Not during hunting season, it doesn't."

"She has a partner, right? He must be covering for her until the first of November."

"That means she might be here for a while? A couple of weeks, at least?" He didn't sound pleased.

"I'm not sure what her plans are, exactly. You know Gia. She hasn't spent much time in Wakefield since she left—just a few days here and there a couple times a year. But with Mom being sick...that could change things."

"She doesn't care about your mom or she would've been here a lot more over the past months," he said matter-of-factly. "I bet she doesn't stay a week."

Margot hoped her sister would stay a lot longer than that. She couldn't disappear if Gia didn't stay, and that worried her. Gia could be so mercurial. She refused to be caged in by the expectations of others—by anything, really. Margot had always envied her that and wondered why she was built so differently. "You could be right."

"Knowing her, she has plans to go skiing in Canada or to take pictures of the North Pole next week," he said.

Sheldon had never liked Gia. Their first argument had taken place at the wedding, because he'd gone to the barn with his friends and gotten drunk instead of showing any interest in his bride. Gia had taken one look at Margot's tear-streaked face and marched outside to tell Sheldon he was being an insensitive jackass, that he should come in and whisk his new wife away so they could get on with their honeymoon, and that had turned into a shouting match during which Gia had said a bit too much.

His family still blamed her for "ruining" the wedding. Even Margot had bought into that argument—to a point. She hadn't wanted Gia to make a scene. But Gia was Gia. And it had really been Sheldon who'd ruined the wedding. Had he been treating her right, Gia wouldn't have felt the need to get involved.

Margot carried some resentment over how unconcerned he'd been with making their wedding special. It should've been the one time she came before his friends. She wished she'd paid more attention to the warning that night turned out to be. She and Sheldon had muddled through their first two years, trying to figure out how to get along. He'd had a temper even then, but Margot had blamed most of their problems on the stress he was under. Since he was determined to live a very traditional life, he refused to let her go to work, which meant he had to make a living on his own. And his parents had started demanding more and more of his time as he took over the business.

Their relationship did get better while she was going through the fertility treatments that had eventually given them two children. But after Greydon was born, Sheldon grew busier and busier—and more successful at work. Soon, his parents' opinion began to matter a lot more to him than hers, and not long after that, he seemed to quit trying to be a good husband altogether. Now when she suggested marriage counseling, he shut her down immediately. He claimed counseling was bullshit and never worked.

Margot believed he just didn't want to hear anyone else, especially a professional, tell him he was in the wrong. He wasn't willing to change.

Margot took a drink of her water. "We'll have to see."

"I hope you don't plan on spending too much time with her," he said. "I certainly wouldn't want you acting the way she does."

A shot of adrenaline brought up her heart rate. "People will think it's weird if I'm not there for my mother. She's dying of cancer, Sheldon. And I can't stipulate that Gia not be around when I go over."

He rolled his eyes. "I'm not saying you can't visit your dying mother," he said, his voice oozing irritation.

Margot reiterated the most salient part of what she'd said. "But Gia will be there."

His chair scraped the floor as he stood up to help himself to seconds. "Like I said, probably not for long."

Gia could be pretty protective. She was the fighter in the family. And that was exactly what Margot needed right now. Hopefully, her sister wouldn't let her down. "I'm sure you're right," she mumbled, and was relieved when Sheldon got a call. Although he didn't leave the table—he didn't care if they had to sit and listen to his conversation—he sat with his head hanging down over his food, kneading his forehead while he talked. Then Greydon dropped his fork and scrambled off his chair to get it, so she popped Matthew's green beans into her mouth.

"Mom!" Matt whispered, shocked by this tiny defiance.

She smiled as she pressed a finger to her lips—and he shot her a relieved smile in return.

When her parents turned in—her mother needed all the rest she could get—Gia wasn't ready for bed. It was only nine o'clock, eight o'clock in Idaho, and she didn't usually go to bed until eleven or twelve.

She spent some time planning out the meals she wanted to cook to give her father a break and provide her mother with a more varied menu. Then she logged on to social media because she was interested in catching up with some of the people she'd known in Wakefield. Usually, she was too busy and too far away to be concerned with what her high school friends and former classmates were doing, but now that she'd be here for a while, she wanted to let Ruth and Sammie and any other members of the Banned Books Club who were still in town know she was visiting. The next few months were going to be rough; she needed to figure out a way to give herself a break now and then and provide relief from the heartbreak that lay ahead.

She hoped to spend some time with Margot, too. Her sister had seemed different today, more open and reachable than ever before. But if being with Margot meant seeing much of Sheldon, Gia knew she wouldn't be able to bear it.

A ding signaled that she'd received a text. Sammie had responded to her message of a few minutes earlier.

I'm so sorry about your mom.

It was painful seeing her tonight. So much has changed since I was here last summer.

I've noticed that Margot has been pretty subdued lately. I was afraid that meant things weren't going well.

My mother being so sick has been hard on her.

Gia had already figured out that having a front-row seat to her mother's illness wasn't going to be easy on her, either. It might even be more excruciating for her than it was for Margot. Margot could at least feel good about her relationship with their mother. Gia had never been able to connect with Ida in a meaningful way, and it made everything worse to see the opportunity to build a stronger relationship in the future disappear.

I feel terrible for both of you.

Thanks. Want to get together for lunch or dinner tomorrow?

That sounds good.

Should we have Ruth join us?

I bet she'd love to come. I see her at spin class. I could talk to her tomorrow morning.

I can text her. She shouldn't be in bed yet. But if she comes, we'll have to make it dinner or drinks after. I don't think schoolteachers get much of a lunch, do they?

If we want to do lunch, we'd probably have to go there and eat in her classroom.

Not quite what I had in mind.

To avoid the clumsiness of continuing to text, Gia called Sammie, and they decided on drinks so Gia's parents would be in bed before she left the house. Then Sammie asked if she was currently seeing anyone, and she said she wasn't, even though Mike had talked her into waiting until she got back to make a final decision about their relationship. He was hoping she'd miss him and change her mind, of course, but she already knew she was more comfortable backing away.

Sammie indicated she was dating the same on-again, off-again boyfriend she'd had for years—a concrete contractor—and said her only sibling, a brother whom Gia had briefly dated in high school, had moved to Hawaii to become a surf instructor. Sammie was a little disgruntled that he was so far away because their father had shingles, and she'd had to take several months away from her own job working as a paralegal for two attorneys in town to help him keep up with his soybean farm.

"What do you think of getting the Banned Books Club together while you're here?" Sammie asked as the conversation was winding down. "We could meet at the elementary school in Ruth's class."

"The chairs there are tiny—for third-graders," Gia replied. "We should plan a night out at a restaurant or something."

"Want me to send a group email inviting everyone to The Jukebox for a meal and drinks?"

"That sounds like fun."

They decided on a week from Saturday to give everyone enough notice so that even some of those who'd moved away might be able to come back.

"You've got the list?" Gia asked, making sure.

"The one I've been using every Christmas, but—" there was a slight pause "—what about Cormac Hart?"

"What about him? We haven't been inviting him to our Christmas parties." Gia had taken him off the list long ago. She knew there was no way he'd ever want to hear from *her.*

"I know, but he still lives in town and might hear about this one. Seems kind of mean to leave him out. I mean…*he* didn't do anything wrong."

Gia gripped her forehead as she talked. "He hates me, Sam. He thinks I was lying."

"But you weren't. Maybe he's come to realize that."

"I doubt it." Gia would never forget the day Mr. Hart was fired. Cormac had approached her right after, at her locker, red-faced, red-eyed and livid. He'd said some terrible things and hadn't spoken to her directly since, but she could remember his smoldering gaze as she sat in the witness box, testifying against his father…

"What's he doing these days, anyway?"

"Mr. Hart or Cormac?" Sammie asked.

Just hearing the name of her former teacher made Gia's stomach churn. She'd thought so highly of the handsome, distinguished English chair. Generally, she refused to talk about him, tried not to remember how everything had been turned on its head. But if she was going to be in Wakefield for any length of time, she figured she should find out for sure if he was still around. "Let's start with the father."

"I don't think you were here long enough to see all the fall-out after the trial. I assume your family told you, though."

"We don't talk about it." They did even more than not talk

about it—they studiously avoided any mention of the parties involved, which was why Gia knew absolutely nothing.

"Got it. Well, I'm sure you remember that he was sentenced to quite a bit of community service, and he also had to register as a sex offender? That made it pretty hard for him to get another job."

Gia flinched. "That wasn't my fault."

"I'm not saying it was—just letting you know why it is that nowadays he runs the tractor store at the far end of town."

Mr. Hart was capable of doing so much more. He'd been one of the most intelligent people she'd ever met. He'd been an excellent teacher, too. Which was part of what made the whole situation so sad.

But she wasn't the one who'd betrayed *his* trust. "Does he still live down the street from my parents?"

"You've never asked them?"

Gia could hear the surprise in Sammie's voice. "I told you—we don't talk about him. I wouldn't be talking about him now except I need to know what land mines remain—and where those land mines might be." She also didn't want to remind her parents, who she felt hadn't supported her the way they should have.

"He's no longer down the street. He and his wife lost that house about a year after you left."

It'd been repossessed? Gia was glad she hadn't heard that. Over the years, she'd felt bad enough about what had happened. It wasn't as if Mr. Hart's wife or children had deserved any punishment.

"Some other family lives there now," Sammie was saying. "But Cormac lives right behind you."

Gia had been lounging on her bed while she talked, but at this she sat up. "What'd you say?"

"Cormac bought the house right behind you."

She blinked, staring at nothing, remembering the house

Sammie was referring to. She knew it almost as well as her own. Leslie, her childhood bestie, had lived there until she and her family had moved to Des Moines when she was in the fourth grade. Gia and Leslie had been so close Leslie's father had installed a gate so they could go back and forth between the two houses without having to walk all the way around the block. "But…how could Cormac afford a house like that?" she asked. "It's nice. I mean, it doesn't have a pool and hot tub like this one, but…it's almost as big."

"The same way you own a helicopter, I guess," she said with a laugh.

"I have a loan on that. And I have a partner who helps make the payments."

"I'm sure Cormac has a loan on his house, too. No partner, though—of the personal *or* business kind. But I doubt he needs any help. Since old man Tomlin retired, Cormac's the only veterinarian in town. I think he does pretty well for himself."

"He never married?"

"Not yet, despite a string of girlfriends in his twenties and one or two—so far—in his thirties. There isn't a single woman in town who doesn't have her eye on him."

"Including you?" Gia was mostly joking, so she was surprised by Sammie's response.

"Including me," she admitted with a laugh. "You should see what he looks like these days. He's freaking hot. And he's nice, too."

Gia bit her bottom lip as she considered this information. She didn't want to think about the good-looking or nice parts. She was focused on his close proximity. "Is he with anyone now?"

"No. He hasn't had a girlfriend for a couple of years, at least. As I said, a lot of women have tried to change that, but he seems to be too preoccupied with his clinic, his dog and enjoying the single life."

She got up and peered out her window. There were a few

trees in both yards that'd grown enough to partially obstruct her view, but she could see light spilling around the blinds on the ground floor and found it odd to think that Cormac was in Leslie's old house, watching TV or working on his computer before bed. "What made him buy the house right around the block from my parents?" she asked. She was mostly talking to herself, but Sammie attempted to answer.

"Maybe he got a good deal."

A shadow passed in front of one of the blinds, causing Gia to step back. Unless he had a guest over, that was him right there. But just because he lived so close didn't mean she'd bump into him, she told herself. Having him around the block was far better than having him down the street where she'd be more likely to drive past while he was pulling in or out of his drive-way, doing yardwork, washing his vehicle or whatever. Chances were he wouldn't even realize she was back.

Except that someone would probably tell him. The scandal that had erupted her senior year, his junior year, had shaken up the whole town…

"G?"

Gia drew her mind back to the conversation. "What?"

"Do you want to invite him to the Banned Books Club get-together or leave him out?"

Gia sank onto her bed. She understood that Cormac wasn't responsible for what had happened. He and the rest of his family were victims of what his father had done as much as she was. But with her mother so ill—and having to face more than enough as it was—she preferred not to have any interaction with him. "Leave him out."

4

Cormac gentled his voice and, with what he hoped was a patient smile, once again tried to explain to Mrs. Wood—who'd brought her golden Labrador in for the second time in as many weeks because he was listless—why she couldn't continue to overfeed her dog. "Animals are like humans," he said. "It's not healthy for them to be overweight. It increases the chances of cancer, diabetes, heart disease, high blood pressure—a whole host of problems. You don't want to see Astro deal with such serious health issues, do you?"

She looked suitably horrified. "Of course not! But...he's not *that* overweight, is he?"

"Like I told you last Wednesday, he's *a lot* overweight," Cormac replied. "He just weighed in at ninety-two pounds."

She looked as though she was about to burst into tears, and he knew after what she'd been through, that was a real possibility. "Aren't a lot of Labs on the heavy side?"

The last time she was in, Cormac had been a little too careful not to say anything upsetting, which was probably why she hadn't taken his advice to heart. "Labs have a genetic tendency to be overweight, yes, but Astro should still be closer to seventy pounds. That means he has twenty-two pounds to lose—or twenty-four percent of his body weight. That's a lot," he emphasized so she'd finally understand the gravity of the situation.

"But to get him to lose that much, I'll practically have to starve him! He'll be miserable."

Cormac surreptitiously glanced at the clock hanging on the wall. He'd given this poor woman and her dog his lunch hour but thanks to an early-morning surgery that ran long, he was still behind schedule. He didn't want to push them out the door, though. "Dieting isn't fun for anyone. You told me he's listless. He doesn't feel good—physically or emotionally. But I promise he'll feel much better once he gets the weight off."

"Emotionally? Are you saying he's *depressed*?"

"That's a very real possibility."

"Won't cutting back on his food only make that worse? He lives to eat!"

"He'll feel better if you'll listen to me. He should get about three cups of kibble per day. That's all. Don't give him any more. And lay off the treats for a while."

She put a hand on her dog's head and the two of them exchanged a mournful look. "This is going to hurt me more than you," she told him.

"A lot of people show their love through food," Cormac said. "I can see why you have a hard time restricting his diet. But there are other ways to be good to your dog. Why don't you take him out more, get him moving? I bet he'd like that." Cormac couldn't say it, but he thought the exercise would do her as much good as the dog. He guessed she was depressed, too, and had even more weight to lose.

In her defense, she'd had a rough couple of years. About ten months ago, her beloved cat had run into the street and been struck by a car. Cormac had had no choice but to put Mischief down. Then, right after that, her husband of more than fifty years suffered a debilitating stroke and passed away. Since they had no children, Astro—named because Mr. Wood had been an astrophysicist—was all she had left. It was natural that she'd indulge him.

"With winter coming, it's going to be hard to get out very often," she said in despair.

He could hear voices in the waiting room, knew his next appointment had to be getting restless. But when Mrs. Wood had called in this morning, claiming her dog had an emergency, he'd told her to bring Astro to the office right away. He'd been afraid he'd missed something serious. He knew she couldn't sustain another loss in her life.

But Astro was fine—other than the fact that he was too fat.

"I'll tell you what," Cormac said. "I take my dog and jog around the park every morning at six. Why don't I come by and get you and Astro, and you can walk while I run? A standing date might keep you motivated, you won't have to drive yourself, which means you won't have to worry about taking the car out when it's snowy and cold, and you'll have someone to watch over both of you while you're there."

He glanced away as tears filled her eyes. Large displays of emotion made him uncomfortable. "You're too important a person to go to all that trouble for me." She lifted an arthritic hand. "I'm just an old woman."

"People matter at every age," he said. "Let's do it. We can start tomorrow."

Obviously reluctant to commit herself to such a rigorous routine, she hesitated. He knew she'd been mired in grief since she lost her husband. But she had to do this for herself and her pet. Cormac could only hope making it as easy as possible would be the catalyst she needed.

"Really, that's too much trouble..." she said.

"I don't mind," he insisted. "Statistics show that being accountable to a buddy makes it easier to work out each day."

A tear caught in her bottom eyelashes before she wiped it

away with an air of impatience. "Well, how can a woman—even an old one—refuse a standing date with the most eligible bachelor in town?"

His sister Louisa, who ran the front office, poked her head into the room just then, and his rottweiler, Duke—named for where Cormac had done his undergrad years before going to North Carolina State University's College of Veterinary Medicine—pushed past her to say hello. "Is everything okay in here? Is there anything I can do to help?" she asked.

Obviously, he wasn't the only one getting anxious about the people gathering in the waiting room.

"No, I was just leaving," Mrs. Wood replied and called her dog, who eagerly jumped down off the examination table.

"See you tomorrow morning?" Cormac said as he crouched to pet Duke, who liked to lie around the front office near the windows, where he could see what was going on outside.

"Any chance you'd be willing to go at a more decent hour?" she asked with a hopeful wince.

"Sorry, it has to be six, or I won't be able to keep up with things around here," he responded with a chuckle. "But nice try."

"Okay," she relented. "I'll be ready."

He gave Duke a solid pat before standing. "Dress warmly," he told her as she went out. "It's chilly in the mornings."

Louisa closed the door and dropped the polite expression she'd been wearing throughout the exchange. "What was that all about?" she asked.

"Thankfully, nothing."

"Astro's okay?"

"He will be once we get his weight under control."

His sister's face revealed her confusion. "So…what was the emergency?"

"Fear."

"Fear?" she echoed.

He set about cleaning the room in preparation for his next four-legged patient and had to dodge Duke, who kept getting in the way. "Yeah. She's already lost too much, can't bear the thought of saying goodbye to another member of her family, so she tends to panic if Astro shows any signs of slowing down. But they're both going to be fine."

She shook her head as if she still didn't understand why he'd had to jeopardize their entire schedule to see Astro *immediately*. "Okay, well, we'd better get moving, or we're going to have some very disgruntled patients this afternoon."

He put away the antiseptic he'd just used. "I'm all set."

She started to open the door but, before Duke could even walk out, closed it again. "I almost forgot what I came in to tell you."

"What's that?"

"Edith texted me while you were with Mrs. Wood."

Edith was his other sister, the baby of the family. Although Louisa and Edith were younger than he was, they were both married with children. At thirty-four he was definitely behind the curve on starting a family—which was probably why so many of the pet owners he dealt with tried to set him up with various women. "What'd she want?"

When Louisa seemed reluctant to say, he got the impression it wasn't good.

"Don't tell me something's wrong with *her* dog." His youngest sister's Corkie was getting old. Cormac had been doing all he could to prolong the dog's life while keeping him comfortable.

"This has nothing to do with Malone."

"Thank God."

"I'm not sure you'll be so relieved once you hear what she had to say."

This must have something to do with their father. Evan had been a mess ever since Cormac was a junior in high school. He couldn't keep up with his bills. His last wife—the fourth in a succession of marriages since their mother left him seventeen years ago—was hounding him about some charges he put on her credit card after they split up. The next-door neighbor was complaining that Evan wasn't keeping the grass in his yard cut. Evan's boss was threatening to fire him for having alcohol on his breath when he came to work. The list went on. "So... was it about Dad?"

"Sort of." She lowered her voice. "Gia's in town."

"Gia Rossi?"

"Yes, Gia Rossi."

The girl who'd nearly destroyed his family. The horror and humiliation he'd experienced when she'd accused his father of inappropriate sexual conduct nearly two decades ago washed over him again. "She won't be here long," he said to battle the rising tide of his own resentment. "She never is." That, in his view, served as proof that she didn't want to face the repercussions of her lies.

"Apparently she's staying months, maybe the whole winter," Louisa informed him.

He suddenly felt scorched, as though he'd been shoved inside an oven beneath the broiler. "How do you know?"

"One of Edith's best friends—I think it was Janet Robel—got an email this morning saying Gia's starting up in-person meetings for the Banned Books Club now that she's back in town. The email was an invitation to the launch party."

Had *he* received that notice? He hadn't been on the computer to check. Usually, he handled emails while he ate lunch, but today he'd given up that time to squeeze in Mrs. Wood and Astro.

He couldn't believe there'd be anything about the club in *his* inbox, however. Gia wasn't that obtuse. "She's probably here because of her mother," he said. "I've seen Mrs. Rossi around town, at the bank and grocery store. She looks very frail. I bet she doesn't have much longer."

"That's unfortunate—not only for everyone in their family but for us now that Gia's back. How will we deal with having her around? I can only imagine how Dad's going to react. He's been struggling enough as it is. I can't take another call from him for help."

Cormac tried to picture what the next few months might be like. He knew Gia had visited Wakefield since she left, but as far as he could tell, she did it ninja-style—stealing into town after dark and leaving fairly quickly, without anyone other than her sister and parents seeing her. "Maybe their paths won't even cross."

She gaped at him. "I get that you're basically an optimist, but even you must know that if he finds out she's this close, he'll track her down and try to set the record straight. You've heard him talk about how much he longs for that opportunity. And in a town this size, *someone's* bound to tell him she's here."

Protecting his father was a role Cormac was very familiar with. After all, he'd been doing it for years. His sisters had been doing the same. "I can understand why he'd be dying to confront her," he said. "When she was seventeen, he couldn't go anywhere near her, not without making himself look even worse. But now that she's an adult and it's been so long, he'd like to have a conversation with her, see if he can talk some sense into her and finally get her to come clean and admit the truth. That's the only way he'll ever be able to remove the stigma he's lived with for so long. Without a retraction that comes directly from her, everyone will continue to believe what they've believed since it happened."

Louisa nibbled on her bottom lip. "Mom thinks he did it. That's why she divorced him."

Cormac had met their mother for dinner last night after he got off work. She'd lost quite a bit of weight, was obviously working out and looked better than she had in ages. She'd been wearing a pricey sweater dress with a long leather coat and had a handbag that was so expensive he'd nearly choked on his drink when she told him how much it cost. As a nurse, she made a decent living, but she certainly wasn't wealthy. The way she'd been spending lately, she often had to borrow money from him just to get through the month.

"I know, but Mom's wrong, okay? Dad had a great career going, an impeccable record of working with children and young adults, and Gia took that from him. Not only did they fire him, they prosecuted him—all because of what she *said* he'd done. There was no evidence whatsoever. It was her word against his. That was all it took."

They'd had this conversation a million times, but he assumed they'd have it a million more—unless they could finally achieve some resolution. It was impossible to get over the injustice of it.

"Maybe for Mom it wasn't about guilt or innocence as much as embarrassment," Louisa said. "She couldn't live with the humiliation. She said people in town looked at her like she couldn't keep her man satisfied, as if they were thinking, 'Why wasn't he getting what he needed at home? Why would he ruin his career and his reputation going after a high school girl?'"

Cormac wished their mother hadn't folded on Evan. The fact that she'd defected to the other side made her husband look even guiltier. "The lies Gia told back then changed the trajectory of all our lives."

"And yet *she* was able to go on as if nothing ever happened," Louisa said bitterly. "It's not fair."

Duke's tail was thumping the floor as he waited patiently by the door to be let back out. Cormac wasn't feeling quite so patient. He was conscious of all the people waiting to have their animals seen and felt pressure to get back to work. But having Gia in town made it hard to focus. "Maybe *I* should talk to her..."

"And say what?" his sister gasped.

"See if I can convince her to tell the truth. Apologize. Right the record. If I do it, Dad won't have to, so she won't be able to claim he came after her again."

Skepticism descended on Louisa's face. "You'd rather she told people *you* came after her? No way. I won't have her maligning you next. Besides, have you forgotten what happened the last time you confronted her?"

"That got a little out of control," he admitted. "But I was young, and I'd just found out what she was saying about Dad. I've had to live with the situation long enough that I've gained some perspective—at least on how *not* to approach her."

"Any way you approach her would not be good," Louisa insisted. "Even if it doesn't get as explosive as it did before, she can't take back what she's done. There's been too much fallout. So what would be the point?"

"The point would be closure," he argued. "Don't you want the truth to finally come out? To feel vindicated for remaining loyal to a man who was a good teacher, a great father and an upstanding citizen—instead of continuing, like we have for seventeen years, to deny that any impropriety took place? So many people are convinced Dad did it. I'm tired of all the doubt, would love to show them how wrong they've been."

"So would I. There hasn't been one other girl, *ever*, who has accused Dad of anything even remotely like what Gia said he did to her." Louisa shook her head. "It doesn't make sense that he would have done that to her."

Actually, it sort of made sense to Cormac. Gia had been unlike anyone he'd ever met. Vital. Full of life. Confident. And sexy as hell. He could easily see a man wanting her. Although he wasn't about to admit it, he'd once wanted her himself. That was why he'd joined her Banned Books Club. At that age, he hadn't been much of a reader—or even an advocate for books. He'd just wanted to see her, be near her. Although he'd never held out much hope that she'd be interested in him—he was a year younger—her sex appeal had been *that* potent.

But the false claims she'd made had essentially tossed a hand grenade into his family's living room. Once it exploded, the pieces of their lives flew in every direction. "She was attractive. I can't deny that," he said, admitting only to a watered-down version of the truth. "But Dad wouldn't lie to us. He wouldn't let us make fools of ourselves standing up for him all these years if he'd done such a terrible thing. He was nothing but kind and fair—completely consistent—all the time we were growing up. If that doesn't earn him a little loyalty and trust, what will?"

"Exactly! The way so many people turned on him was gut-wrenching. I've seen him cry over this, cry so hard his shoulders were shaking!"

Cormac had seen his father break down, too. It made him hate Gia Rossi even more—for costing Evan his dignity along with everything else.

"So are you going to try to talk to her?" Louisa asked, seemingly warming up to the idea.

A knock interrupted them. "Dr. Hart?"

Louisa barred Duke's exit with one leg while she cracked open the door to find one of Cormac's next appointments—Venice Gomez, a middle-aged bank teller with purple hair who had a labradoodle on a leash.

"I'm sorry to interrupt, but—" Venice lifted her arm to indicate her watch "—I need to be back at work in fifteen minutes. Are we going to have to reschedule?"

"No," Louisa said. "I'm sorry for the wait. We...we ran into an issue, but Dr. Hart can see you and Trixie now."

"Thank you," Venice said, and his sister cast him a final worried glance that indicated they'd have to finish their Gia Rossi conversation later.

5

Once she was parked at the grocery store, Gia called Sammie for moral support. "I'm at Higgleston's and there isn't a Hart in sight," she said as she got out of her father's SUV, dropped the keys in her purse and gazed furtively around the parking lot. She had a list of items she wanted to pick up for the meals she'd planned last night, but she could wait if she happened to spot someone she'd rather not see. According to Sammie, Mr. Hart—Evan, she reminded herself, even though he'd only ever been Mr. Hart to her—still lived in town. So did Sharon, the woman he'd been married to when she was in high school, and all three of his children, two of whom were married. She didn't want to bump into any of them.

"I told you I'd pick up what you need," Sammie said.

Gia hitched her purse higher. "You're at work."

"I get off at five."

"I appreciate the offer, but I hope to be making dinner by then." Gia paused to let a vehicle cross in front of her. "I can't hide in my parents' house all winter. Even if I could, I refuse to. I'm just…trying to ease into life here in Wakefield without making too many waves."

"Considering how fast gossip travels in this town, that'll be impossible," her friend responded.

Gia feared Sammie was right, but she was still raw from seeing her mother in such feeble condition. Knowing she was losing Ida—and in one of the worst ways—was bad enough. She didn't need anything else to upset her. "You said I probably know one of Mr. Hart's sons-in-law," she said as she approached the entrance.

"Victor. He was two years behind us in school. He's married to Louisa."

"I don't remember a Victor."

"Your parents would know him. He worked for your dad after high school—until he saved up enough to start college."

"Running the office?" She'd almost always had sports after school, so Margot had been the one to help their father with the paperwork at his small agency on a regular basis. Victor must've stepped in after Margot left.

"I think he was selling insurance, but you'll have to ask your father."

She wasn't going to mention the Harts to Leo or Ida. Her parents didn't even like to be reminded of what'd happened during her senior year. It was partly how they'd reacted, as if she should've somehow expected—and avoided—what Mr. Hart had done that'd cut her so deeply. She'd felt as though she'd had to convince them she'd been victimized, that they'd been tempted to believe their wild daughter must've been culpable in some way. "Doesn't matter. I was just wondering why I couldn't remember him."

"He was a bit of a nerd—a gamer. These days he does computer programming, builds websites, that sort of thing."

"And yet he once sold insurance for my father?"

"I think he was trying to get enough money to start college. Or his parents were tired of having him hole away in his bedroom and made him get a regular job. I don't know. Anyway, he works out of the house and takes care of the kids while Louisa runs the veterinary office for her brother."

Gia grabbed the closest shopping cart. After a few steps she realized it had a wonky wheel, but she didn't bother going back to get a different one. She was hoping to make this as quick as possible. "How many kids do they have?"

"Two. A boy and a girl. They're both in elementary school."

The automatic doors whooshed open as she entered the store. "And Edith?"

"Edith married Dan Mudrak and they have one little boy."

"Dan Mudrak," she repeated, searching her memory.

"He moved here after you left," Sammie said.

"What does he do?"

"Sells farm equipment."

"And Edith?"

"She edits out of her home."

"Edits what?"

"Manuscripts for writers—or anything people need her help with, I suppose."

Keeping her head down, Gia wrestled her difficult cart into the produce section, where she started loading up on peppers, onions, cilantro and the other ingredients for fresh salsa. "Where did she get the experience to do that?"

"She majored in English. Maybe she worked in that field for a bit after college, too. I don't know her all that well, to be honest."

"Sounds like everyone in the family's doing okay. Maybe they've moved on with their lives and won't care that I'm back."

"Do you really believe that?" Sammie asked dryly.

"No." Gia felt the avocados, looking for the slight give that indicated she'd found a ripe one. But they were all hard as a rock. Giving up on them, she forced her cart into the dairy section. "But I have the right to be here as much as they do."

"Exactly. So forget about them. What happened wasn't your fault."

They didn't believe that, but Sammie had to be tired of hearing about her problems, so she changed the subject. "Did you get the email out this morning to the Banned Books Club?"

"I did. I've already heard back from a few people."

"What're they saying? Anyone coming?"

"A few said they were. Most of them have written back to ask if Cormac knows you're in town."

Gia stopped forcing her recalcitrant cart. "What are you telling them?"

"That you have no beef with Cormac."

"That's true. And how are they responding?"

"They're saying they support you and want to see you."

A brief injection of hope made Gia feel infinitely better. But that faded as fast as it had arrived when she guessed her friend was just trying to save her feelings. "No, they didn't…"

"Some did," she said sheepishly.

"And the others?" When Sammie didn't answer right away, Gia spoke a little louder. "And the others?"

"They said you'd better watch out for Cormac, because what he said to you in the halls in high school will be nothing compared to what he'll say to you now that the whole family's been living in the rubble you created before you left."

"*I* created!" she nearly yelled, causing a woman half an aisle away to startle and look back at her.

"They're idiots," Sammie was quick to say. "Ignore them."

That was impossible. The subject matter was too sensitive. But she listened to Sammie offer a few more platitudes before telling her it was too difficult to push her broken cart and hold her phone at the same time—that she had to go.

She hung up feeling self-conscious and uncomfortable instead of reassured, especially when the woman she'd surprised a moment earlier kept turning around to see what had made her cry out. Gia was about to tell her to go on about her business when she heard a voice behind her.

"Excuse me. Aren't you Gia Rossi?"

Gia froze. Was it Sharon Hart? Or one of Cormac's sisters? Someone else who would have something to say about the scandal she'd caused when she was in high school?

At least it was a female voice, which ruled out both Cormac and his father.

Forcing a smile, she turned and let her breath seep out in relief when she recognized Mrs. Milton, who'd been her Advanced Math teacher in the tenth grade. "Yes, it's me," she said.

"Look at you! You're even more beautiful now than you were when I knew you before."

Gia felt the tension leave her body. This was a friendly conversation. "Thank you. You look great yourself."

"No, I don't," she said with a knowing chuckle. "You're just being kind."

"You do! Are you still at the high school?"

"No. After teaching for more than four decades, I retired three years ago."

"You must've had fifteen hundred or more students over such a long career. I'm shocked you recognized me, especially since I've been gone for so long."

"I might not have realized it was you, but I was just at the pharmacy, where someone mentioned you were in town."

Of course. It wouldn't take long before everyone knew. But she wasn't doing much to go unnoticed having Sammie send out that email to all of the book club members. She probably shouldn't have done that—not so soon—but she needed to establish some sort of life here.

"How's your mother?" Mrs. Milton asked.

"Struggling." Gia didn't see any point in claiming Ida was "fine." Nothing could be further from the truth.

"I'm so sorry." Mrs. Milton nudged her own cart a bit closer. "I'm glad you can have this time with her."

Deluged by an onslaught of guilt for not returning sooner, Gia nodded. "Me, too."

"I was afraid—" she lowered her voice "—I was afraid that what happened before you left might be keeping you away. But I should've known you're too strong to let a few naysayers have the last word."

"I wasn't out to hurt anyone," she said. "I just…didn't know what to do. Mostly, I wanted to be taken out of Mr. Hart's class. That was all I was expecting when I told the principal about what he'd done."

"You were seventeen, Gia. You did exactly what you should've done. The rules are there to protect students. He was the one who broke them."

"But it's hard to know you've ruined someone's life," she heard herself saying. "Then there's Cormac and the girls…"

"If they're not over what their father did yet, I hope they will be soon. Like you, I feel bad for them. But they were never your responsibility. Evan Hart's the one who let them down. He needs to apologize and make things right—for the sake of everyone involved."

That'll be a cold day in hell, Gia thought. After seventeen years of telling the same lie, what would be his motivation? He obviously didn't have a conscience. "I doubt he'll ever do that," she said. If only he'd owned up to what he'd done instead of claiming she was out to get a better grade, maybe she wouldn't carry such a deep scar herself.

"It's never too late to right an old wrong," Mrs. Milton responded. "Now that you're back and he has the chance to apologize to your face, I hope he'll do exactly that."

Gia had been so defensive when she walked into the store, so primed and ready to encounter hostility, that Mrs. Milton's kindness had completely disarmed her. "Thank you," she said.

"I—I can't tell you how much this means to me. What he did was bad enough. But then... Not to be believed..."

The incident with Mr. Hart had lasted only a few minutes. It'd certainly upset her—thrust her into a tailspin—but after she'd come to terms with all that, the doubt and suspicion she'd faced, at least from certain parties, had lingered.

It was still there; maybe it always would be.

Mrs. Milton's eyes filled with sympathy and concern. "*I* believe you," she stated unequivocally. "And I know there are many others."

But Mrs. Milton and anyone else who believed her had to go on faith—they couldn't *know*. Mr. Hart had used his charm and persuasiveness, not to mention his sterling reputation, to make himself look like the victim, dividing the whole town. The fact that anyone could think she'd lie about something that serious ate Gia up inside. That was why she'd tried so hard to distance herself.

For the most part, when she was in Idaho, working and busy, she managed to forget—except on the odd night when she drank too much or lay awake, staring at the ceiling. Then she could get caught up in the past. But those moments had been limited, especially in recent years. It was returning to Wakefield that dredged up that incident, put it front and center and made it inescapable again.

She wanted to head back to Idaho right away—leave her hometown in the dust as she had before. But she couldn't. She wouldn't abandon her mother, no matter what. She'd never forgive herself if she did.

His father was calling. Cormac had just finished with his last patient and was turning off the lights when his cell phone went off. Even Louisa had gone home. She'd brought up the subject of Gia again before she left, but they hadn't had the chance to say much more. It was getting so late by then that her husband was pushing her to get home. Victor was on a tight deadline and needed her help with the kids.

Cormac stared at his phone, trying to decide whether to answer. He had to talk to his dad at some point; he just wasn't sure he wanted it to be now. He was starving—eager to get home and have dinner. And Duke was just as excited to escape the office.

He could call his father back in an hour or two, once he'd had a chance to unwind and consider the situation without having to focus on so many other things at the same time. He almost shoved his phone into his pocket. But then he realized that his father couldn't be trusted not to do something stupid, especially when he was upset, and Gia's return would definitely upset him.

Hoping to talk him down, if necessary, he answered the call. "Hello?"

"Have you heard?"

Had this been an ordinary conversation, Cormac would've taken his dog to the truck, loaded him up and headed home while he talked. But this wasn't an ordinary conversation, so he remained rooted to the spot. "About Gia Rossi?"

"She's back. Ever since her mother got sick, I knew it was only a matter of time."

"If it's any solace, I don't think she'll be here for long."

"I can't imagine she'll leave before her mother dies. That isn't what you mean, is it?"

"No, but it doesn't look like her mother has much time."

"Don't kid yourself. Ida could hang on for months."

Cormac winced at the callous way they were talking. As much as he held against Gia, they were speaking about a woman's life— a woman who'd had no part in what had happened, a wife and a mother. "I wish her the best," he clarified.

"So do I. It's just unfortunate that her poor health impacts *my* life, too."

"I'd say she got the worst of it."

"We're talking about Gia, not her mother," his father reminded him.

Cormac began to pace in his own waiting room, and Duke, who'd been standing by the door, sat down as if he'd seen this kind of agitation before and knew it wouldn't result in getting him what he wanted. "I've been thinking about it all day, and I've decided there's nothing we can do about her being here except…grin and bear it. Say nothing. Do nothing. Act like we don't even know she exists."

"What about getting a retraction? What happened back then wasn't as she portrayed it. *She* was the one who was trying to get something out of *me*—a grade she didn't deserve."

Cormac had already heard how upset she'd been that she hadn't done well on her big research paper, how she'd been pressing his father to change her grade and how important that grade had been to her, since she hadn't been doing as well as usual in her other classes and so everything had come down to her English grade. She'd been anticipating a college scholarship for volleyball, so she'd had that going for her, but even student athletes had to maintain a certain GPA. From what his father said, if she didn't get an A in English, her college career would've hung in the balance. That would certainly motivate a student to press harder than usual. But it enraged him to think any young woman would use her sexuality to improve her report card. And then to annihilate the teacher who refused to cooperate with something like that?

"I know," he told his father. "It's terrible, but I don't think we can get a retraction. If she was sorry for what she did, she would've spoken up by now."

"No doubt she's too embarrassed."

"Or she's convinced herself it's true. That happens to people, you know. Especially after the passage of so much time—so many years spent convincing themselves they didn't do anything wrong. Regardless, we need to leave the past alone and move forward."

"So…you're not going to confront her?" his father asked.

"Why would I do that?"

"Louisa said you were thinking about it, thought it might help."

"I was just saying I'd *like* to confront her. And it would be better for me to approach her than for you to do it."

"You're right about that. I'm afraid to so much as bump into her for fear of how she'd construe the encounter. Once you've been falsely accused, you get paranoid."

Cormac couldn't even imagine how terrible that would be. "Like I said, it's in the past. We need to leave it there."

"I think you're right. The more we stir things up, the worse it could get. What she did has taken enough of a toll. I don't want to be forced to defend my integrity a second time."

Cormac opened his mouth to continue to commiserate, but then closed it. He was having an odd reaction to his father's words. They made him so defensive that he was once again dying to approach Gia, if only to let her know what a terrible person she was. And yet he was also surprised that, after years of saying how he'd confront her if he ever got the chance, Evan was backing off so easily.

But maybe that didn't mean anything. These days, Evan talked a big talk but rarely followed through with anything. He was too beaten down. And Cormac blamed Gia for that, too. "Just go on with your life and try to ignore that she's here."

"It won't be easy when everyone I meet is talking about her."

"The talk will die down soon enough."

"I hope so," his father said.

Finally settled enough to leave, Cormac dug into his pocket for his keys. "So you're going to leave her alone?"

"I will if you will."

"Yeah, I've decided not to approach her." Her mother was

so sick that he'd be a callous asshole not to take that into consideration. He didn't want to do anything that would hurt the
innocent people around Gia—people who were already going
through hell.

But he knew all he'd be able to think about tonight—and
maybe every night while Gia was in town—was the fact that
she was staying in the house right behind him.

There was even a gate between the two yards...

6

"I *loved* this book," Ruth said, a worn copy of Stephen King's *Cujo* at her elbow.

Gia would've preferred to have snagged a table on the upstairs patio of Harmony House. In the warmer months, it was fun to hang out there in the evenings, where you could look down on the main drag and watch the activity on the street. But the patio was already closed for the season. When they met up at the entrance of the restaurant after Ida and Leo had gone to bed, she and her friends had found a booth on the first floor, where they could listen to the music—which wasn't live on Thursdays but was still a good mix of everything from the eighties to present day—and order a few "small plates" and some drinks.

"I guess I'm not much of a horror reader." Sammie, who was sitting on the same side as Ruth, was notably less thrilled with their most recent read. "If you'd told me before I read it that I'd ever find a Saint Bernard frightening, I wouldn't have believed you. But holy hell! I'll never look at that breed the same way again. This book *totally* freaked me out."

Gia finished off the last of the sliders. "It was supposed to freak you out. That's the whole point of a horror novel."

Ruth sipped her old-fashioned. "My only complaint was that the whole thing felt a bit...dated."

"Well, it *was* written in 1981," Gia pointed out, "before cell phones and the internet. I was amazed by how well it withstood the test of time."

"I wonder where Stephen King got the idea for this book..." Sammie said.

"He had to visit a mechanic one night in rural Maine," Ruth told her. "It was in the middle of nowhere, and when he got there, he was greeted by a Saint Bernard who did *not* take a liking to him."

Sammie dipped a French fry in ketchup. "No kidding?"

"No kidding. I looked it up."

"You didn't find the story upsetting?" Sammie asked. "I mean... I could see why some people would want to have it banned. Especially back then. What message could there be in it?"

"I don't think there needs to be a message," Gia replied. "A horror novel is simply meant to entertain. But it could be that King was trying to say that the greatest thing to fear is fear itself."

"Is that what Mr. Hart told you when we were in high school?" Ruth asked.

Surprised by the mention of their former teacher, Gia, who'd just picked up her drink, set it back down. She couldn't remember discussing this particular book with their old teacher. But he'd also loved Stephen King, so maybe he'd told her about it. "I don't think so. Franklin D. Roosevelt said it during the Great Depression."

Sammie shot Ruth a dirty look, no doubt for bringing up Mr. Hart, and Ruth covered her mouth. "I'm sorry. I don't know why I said that. I wasn't thinking."

Although Ruth was claiming it was merely a gaffe, Gia suspected it wasn't. That she was back in Wakefield made what'd happened their senior year top of mind, so she couldn't really blame Ruth for addressing the elephant in the room. "It's fine." She waved away the apology. "The dude wasn't *all* bad."

As a matter of fact, in many ways Mr. Hart had been very good. That was the worst part. She'd loved him as a teacher—admired him, trusted him and listened to what he had to say.

Sammie looked concerned. "What do you think he's going to do when he learns you're in town?"

"What can he do?" Gia asked.

Ruth toyed with the condensation on her glass. "I bet he feels bad for what he did."

Gia wasn't convinced. If he felt any remorse—true remorse—he wouldn't have tried to make her look like a vengeful liar. "If he feels bad, it's only because he got caught."

"He still claims he didn't do anything wrong," Ruth said.

The memory of him inviting her to walk down to his house when his family was at the high school baseball game—and what he'd done while she was there—made Gia slightly nauseous. Unable to continue eating, she pushed her plate to the side. "How do you know? Do you ever talk to him?"

"Not more than a hello or a nod in passing," Ruth told her. "But his youngest daughter—Edith—is in our spin class."

Gia shifted her gaze to Sammie. "You didn't mention that."

"We just work out together," Sammie was quick to say. "We don't ever really have a conversation."

"Apparently, she talks to Ruth." Gia used her straw to stir her spicy jalapeno gimlet. "What has she been saying, Ruth?"

Ruth cleared her throat. She'd obviously been dying to broach the subject, or she wouldn't have dropped Hart's name into a conversation about the book they were reading. But it was easy to tell she was having second thoughts. "When I told her you were in town, she got a little upset. She's been adamant since the beginning that her father is innocent."

Gia got the distinct impression they'd become friends. Maybe even *good* friends. She hadn't anticipated that. Edith was five years younger than they were, and Ruth hadn't mentioned her when they'd caught up now and then or used Zoom for their book group meetings.

But there'd been several long lapses in the Banned Books Club—some lasting years. Edith and Ruth lived in the same small town. And Gia had been gone a long time. She supposed she shouldn't be *too* shocked that Ruth would suddenly find her loyalties split. "How would she know?" Gia asked.

Ruth signaled to the waitress that they were fine when she came by to ask if they'd like anything else. "She told me that if he was the pedophile you made him out to be, there would've been other girls claiming the same kind of inappropriate behavior—and there's been no one."

Did Ruth agree with Edith? And was Sammie of the same mind? When neither of them would meet her gaze, Gia began to realize a lot more had changed in her hometown than she'd thought. "I never called him a pedophile. He… What he did was inappropriate, but…" She let her words trail off. "Never mind. I don't want to talk about it."

Gia had never believed he'd been out victimizing girls. But that didn't change what he'd done to her. *He* had been the adult—and her teacher. That'd given him more power in the relationship. It'd also screwed with her ability to trust. Although she often wondered if she'd done the right thing in coming forward, she knew in her heart that if she *hadn't* spoken up, he probably would've continued to pursue a sexual relationship with her.

"I shouldn't have brought it up," Ruth said. "I just…feel bad for Edith. I mean, it split up her family, made it almost impossible for her father to earn a living—"

"I'm out of here." Gia shot to her feet just as Sammie reached out to grab Ruth's arm, presumably to get her to shut up.

"Can't we talk about it?" Ruth asked plaintively. "My God, G, what happened to his family was terrible!"

"I'm glad you feel so sorry for *them*," she said and threw a couple of twenties on the table to cover her food and drink before walking out.

Gia had to get out of the house. She was feeling claustrophobic again, just like she always did when she visited Wakefield. And yet this time she couldn't escape. Her mother's cancer held her more securely than any prison. Today, she'd done the grocery shopping, played cards with her parents, picked up her mother's medication and cooked supper before meeting Ruth and Sammie once her parents had gone to bed. She'd been feeling good about doing her part for her family.

But her night out certainly hadn't provided the social relief she'd been looking for. Because the Harts hadn't left town the way she had, and they knew so many people, even her closest friends were becoming more sympathetic to them. How was she going to get through the coming months? And would the rest of the people in the Banned Books Club react the same way?

Maybe it wasn't wise to get the group going again. She'd been trying to hang on to *some* part of her past, hadn't wanted to let Mr. Hart take *all* her friends from her.

Turning her face up to the moon, she pretended she was on her own deck in Coeur d'Alene, staring up at the sky. Her stay in Wakefield wouldn't last forever, she told herself.

But it would end with her mother's death, which wasn't what she wanted, either.

"There's no way to win," she muttered and was about to get up and go inside when her phone buzzed with a text from Margot.

Everything go okay today?

What did her sister think? That she could come back to town and the past would be erased? That her detractors would forget the animosity they felt toward her?

Did Margot even realize how difficult this was for her?

Perfect.

She preferred to lie rather than reveal her vulnerability.

I meant to come by today, but I've been swamped helping get the food and other stuff ready for Sheldon to go hunting.

No worries. I've got this.

That wasn't remotely true, but Gia would be damned if she'd admit she didn't, especially to Margot, who'd always made doing the right thing look easy. Although fulfilling her husband's expectations took a lot of time and effort. Margot served him more like a slave than a partner.

You're the strongest person I've ever known.

Gia blinked at her sister's response. Read it twice. Was there a barb in there somewhere?

If so, she couldn't find it. It felt…sincere. She had to chuckle at the irony. Part of the reason she didn't like coming back to Wakefield was because it made her feel so fragile—as if the slightest thing would cause her to shatter. "Strong," she muttered with a humorless chuckle.

That's what I've always thought about you.

Thanks. I'll be over tomorrow.

She remembered her sister alluding to the fact that it was her "turn" to take care of their parents and decided she'd fulfill that debt without leaning on Margot any more than she already had.

Setting her phone aside, Gia drew a deep breath and turned her face back up to the sky. She'd battle the whole damn town if she had to, but she wouldn't let something that happened seventeen years ago get the best of her now.

There she was! Cormac stood at his bedroom window, transfixed. Since learning that Gia was home, he'd looked out at her parents' property again and again—mostly in agitation. He was irritated that she was so close and couldn't help wondering what was going on in her mind. How it felt to be back. If she regretted the choices she'd made and the things she'd done when she lived in Wakefield.

And then, just as he was about to call it a night—the Rossi house was dark, so he'd assumed everyone there was already in bed—Gia had appeared in the yard and sat on a lounger near the pool and hot tub.

After racing down the stairs, he held Duke inside so the dog couldn't give him away, let himself out and crept around to the back.

He realized almost immediately that he should've grabbed a jacket. It was freezing. But Gia didn't seem to notice. Still in chinos, a button-up shirt and loafers from work, he was probably warmer than she was in her short-sleeved orange blouse and jeans, and yet she wasn't even shivering.

He could take the cold if she could, he told himself and refrained from going back inside. He was too curious to see what he could, too afraid he'd miss something if he left for even a few minutes. What was she like these days? How was she approaching her return? Boldly and unapologetically? Filled with remorse? Older and wiser and, hopefully, kinder?

There was no way to tell. Although she had a cell phone in

her hand, she wasn't on it, so it wasn't as if he was privy to any revealing bits of conversation. She seemed restless, troubled, and he could understand why. If it were anyone else, he would've had some compassion for what was happening in her family. But this wasn't anyone else. This was the one person who'd damaged his own family beyond repair.

When she turned her face up toward the sky, he caught his first clear glimpse of what she looked like these days. He'd been hoping she wasn't nearly as attractive as she'd been in high school. Then she'd have one less weapon to use against the unsuspecting men around her. His animal studies had taught him that certain predators employed aggressive mimicry—the use of signals or behaviors to draw their prey in close before pouncing.

When he'd first learned the term, he'd thought he finally had a way to describe what she'd done to his father, and felt sorry for any other men who might've been fooled by her since. So he was disappointed to see that she was more beautiful than ever with her long, strawberry blond hair, flawless skin and high cheekbones. She'd always had a particularly kissable mouth— even if she did have a sharp tongue when provoked. She definitely fit the feisty stereotype of a redhead. But her best feature was her clear green eyes rimmed with thick golden lashes. In high school, they'd held him spellbound whenever she looked at him...

But that was before he knew what she was really like, he reminded himself. Had she accused anyone else of improper conduct over the years? He wouldn't doubt it. She'd probably filed a sexual harassment complaint at every place she worked.

She stood and began to pace for a few minutes but instead of going inside, where it was warm, she sat back down on the chaise and began to cry. Several tears rolled down her cheeks unheeded and fell off her chin. Then she buried her face in her hands.

Shit. That wasn't what Cormac had wanted to see. That was

the *last* thing he'd wanted to see. There was no way he was going to allow himself to feel any sympathy for Gia.

Backing away, he slipped deeper into the shadows before making his way around to the front. In the past seventeen years, he'd only ever imagined her as she'd been right after she accused his father—stoic, tough, impervious to challenge. She'd stuck with her story in spite of all the pressure she'd been under to tell the truth—and some of that pressure had come from her own parents.

To tell a lie with that much resolve required nerves of steel.

Tonight, she was probably just grieving for her dying mother, he told himself. Someone would have to be a robot not to feel pain for a beloved parent suffering from cancer. But the vulnerable expression on her face had gotten to him, so much so that he spent the rest of the night trying to get that tragic image of her—a beautiful, forlorn woman weeping in the dark—out of his head.

When she pulled into her parents' drive, Margot felt the same relief she used to feel—before the cancer struck. Her childhood home was a safe haven, a place where Sheldon was more careful than anywhere else to keep up appearances—although lately, he typically chose not to accompany her here. He claimed he was too busy. But he had plenty of time for his own parents. He just didn't have any interest in hers, and she knew it.

She didn't mind, though. She preferred to come alone, always enjoyed the reprieve. Today, she didn't even have the boys with her, since they were both in school.

Although she had errands to run—some for Sheldon's business, and he wouldn't be happy if she didn't get them done—she'd gotten up early to be sure she could fit everything in and still have time to stop over for breakfast. Gia and their parents had always struggled to get along. Gia was too much like their mother—opinionated and headstrong—which meant they often clashed, and their father seemed to believe it was his duty to support Ida whether she was right or wrong, so he clashed with Gia, too.

But these days Ida was so sick. She probably didn't care about trying to keep her oldest daughter in line.

Margot hoped that meant she'd be satisfied letting Gia take care of her. It didn't hurt to check, though. Margot couldn't leave town if she felt her mother needed her to stay. And since she was dreading uprooting herself and her children and heading into the unknown almost as much as she was looking forward to it—even the thought of coming out in open opposition to Sheldon was frightening—she was sort of hoping for an excuse to stay.

"The devil you know..." she mumbled. There was undeniable comfort in the familiar.

As she got out of her Subaru and approached the house, Margot could see Gia through the window over the kitchen sink and felt a strange sort of nostalgia. As much as they'd bickered as children, they were family. She'd always secretly admired her courageous older sister—and often wondered why she didn't feel the same level of passion and drive.

Her father was watching the news when she opened the slider, so he saw her first. He got up to welcome her as she walked in and followed her into the kitchen.

"Smells good in here," she said.

Gia was frying potatoes in one pan and bacon in another, and there was a carton of eggs on the counter.

"Mom said she was craving eggs over easy." Gia used her spatula to motion toward the toaster. "Can you put the bread in? The bacon and potatoes are almost done."

Margot bent to pet Miss Marple, then washed her hands and did as Gia requested before crossing to the pink vinyl booth that had always served as their kitchen table. Their mother was sitting at one end of it in a purple sweat suit with a blanket wrapped around her shoulders. "How are you feeling today?"

Ida offered her a wan smile. "About the same."

Margot leaned in to kiss the papery skin covering her mother's cheek. "I'm sorry there's been no improvement."

"Everyone has problems," Ida said with a shrug.

Not like this one. Death was approaching—slowly but inexorably—and Margot considered knowing that time was running out to be both a blessing and a curse. Ida's diagnosis had given them the chance to get prepared before it was too late. But watching her suffer wasn't worth the trade-off.

Margot wondered, again, if she should wait to leave Sheldon— stick it out in Wakefield for a few more months.

Could she survive mentally and emotionally if she did? Would she have the willpower to start over somewhere else after Ida was gone?

She was afraid that if she didn't have such a good reason for visiting her family so often, he would only clamp down on her that much harder and she'd have even less freedom.

"You hungry?" Gia tossed the question over her shoulder as she cracked an egg.

"Not really," Margot said.

Gia turned to look at her. "Have you eaten? Because from what I can see, you've lost almost as much weight as Mom."

Margot shook her head. "I haven't lost nearly that much," she said, but during the past few months, the pounds had been melting off. It was the anxiety. Living with someone like Sheldon kept her constantly agitated. And since she'd decided to leave, she was always stewing about how she was going to get away from him, where she'd go and what she'd do once she left—and how she was going to protect herself and her children if he came after her legally or physically. "He's demeaning" wasn't a strong defense. Not nearly as strong as if she could claim physical abuse. He'd been careful not to go that far, and yet what he did was equally bruising, especially to someone as sensitive as she was. Just because no one could see those bruises didn't make them any less real. "I've been eating healthy, trying to cut out all the junk," she said, but she'd made no such concerted effort.

Fortunately, since most of the attention was focused on Ida these days, her own weight loss hadn't become a focal point, and she didn't want that to change.

"Well, sit down and have some eggs and toast, at least," Gia insisted. "Unless regular food is 'junk' to you now."

Margot figured it'd be wiser to try to choke down some breakfast than argue. She slid into the other side of the booth and all the way around to be able to take her mother's hand.

Ida smiled at the gesture. "How're the boys?"

"They're doing great."

"And Sheldon?"

She could no longer meet her mother's eye. Because of him, she was about to walk away without an explanation or a forwarding address. But she'd spent countless hours thinking it over and couldn't see a better way. Drawing them into her confidence would only make matters worse. She would not start a feud between the two families and have her parents try to defend her in the middle of all they were going through. "He's...busy."

"He works too hard," Ida said matter-of-factly.

"He's quite a guy." Margot had been saying such things for so long—without her parents picking up on the sarcasm belying those statements—that she felt a stab of alarm when her sister sent her a curious look.

"Was that sincere?" Gia asked, eyebrows knitted in confusion.

Margot conjured up an innocent expression. "Of course," she replied, but knew with Gia around, she'd have to be more careful. Her sister would quickly pick up on the clues her parents missed.

"I guess Sheldon didn't hear *I* was back in town," Gia said. "Or he would've made arrangements to be here this morning."

There was no missing *her* sarcasm. But then... Gia had never been subtle. She usually said what she felt—or her feelings were written all over her face.

"Gia..." their father gently chided.

No doubt Leo was hoping to get ahead of anything that might distress Ida. But their mother didn't react. She suddenly seemed so deep in her own thoughts Margot wasn't even sure she was listening to the exchange.

After a quick glance at their father, Gia returned to cooking. For once, her sister had chosen to back down. Margot was happy to see that. It meant she was finally learning some restraint.

Maybe, just maybe, Margot would be able to trust Leo and Ida to her sister's care. After her recent indecision, all the second-guessing, she decided that her plans were most definitely back on.

If Gia could learn to keep the peace, Margot thought *she* could learn to stand up and fight.

7

Gia was just reaching for the door handle of the bedroom, holding the green tea she was about to carry in, when she heard her mother answer a call that stopped her in her tracks. The surprise in Ida's voice tipped her off that something was up, which was what initially made her pause. It wasn't until she heard a bit more of the conversation that she realized the caller had to be connected to her former English teacher.

Instantly angry that anyone, especially someone from the Hart camp, would contact Ida about what happened seventeen years ago, Gia was tempted to barge in and grab the phone. But she was hesitant to give herself away so soon. She was keen to learn who it could be, what the person wanted—and to see how Ida would respond.

Although her mother's voice came through the wooden panel, it was muffled enough that Gia found herself leaning closer. "It's in the past...We didn't decide his fate, the judge did...I'm not sure what to tell you, Louisa. Your father had the chance to give his side...That isn't an easy thing to prove—it's darn near impossible...She wouldn't lie. Not for a grade...I'm not taking offense...Of course I appreciate the care you and your brother have given our cat. But there's nothing I can do for you when it comes to your father...You'll have to talk to Gia. But I can't guarantee you'll like how she responds. My oldest daughter speaks her mind...You, too...Thanks for calling."

Louisa Hart had obviously been trying to enlist Ida's help in getting Gia to finally "tell the truth about what happened," which made Gia want to scream.

The conversation revealed something else, too. It wasn't just Gia's old schoolmates who'd become friendly with the Harts. It was also her family. They'd all been living in Wakefield together since Gia left and had, apparently, figured out a way to get along.

Gia was pretty sure they even *liked* each other. Her mother would've been much harsher otherwise. Gia supposed that didn't constitute a betrayal exactly, but it sure as hell felt like one.

The sound of footsteps made her jerk her head up.

"What's going on?" her father asked, wearing a quizzical expression as he trudged toward her from the living room, probably on his way to the bathroom down the hall.

"Nothing, I... I was just taking Mom some tea," she said and opened the door.

When she entered the room, her mother looked up but didn't mention the call.

"I thought you might like some green tea," Gia said.

Ida's smile grew pained. "I hate green tea."

Gia had to be careful not to trip over Miss Marple, who'd gotten up to come toward her. "I'm not a fan of it myself, but..."

"I know," she said. "They say it fights cancer. Not nearly well enough, apparently, but—" a tired smile softened her expression "—I'll do my best to get it down."

Gia wanted to bring up Louisa's call. To reiterate that she'd been telling the truth all along. She had no idea how to convince everyone of that and was *so* tired of battling the doubt.

Feeling it was pointless to keep trying—she put the cup on the bedside table and started to leave.

Her mother's voice stopped her at the door. "The truth is the truth, Gia. You were right to stick to it."

This was the first time her mother had addressed the situation in what Gia interpreted as an authentic manner. After Evan Hart was sentenced to hundreds of hours of community service and had to register as a sex offender, Ida had said a few things, but they'd felt more like platitudes—a way to keep the peace between them because their relationship had become so rocky.

Gia held her mother's gaze. "What I told you back then went down exactly as I said it did."

"I know."

Ida's response caused Gia to blink in surprise. She hesitated to delve too far into this subject. It'd been such a source of pain through the years. The resentment she felt was bound to seep out in some way—and would probably start an argument. She didn't want it to come to that. She'd only been home a short while. And she was here to help—not put her mother through another emotional episode.

Still, she couldn't resist one final question. "So...why have I always felt as though you wished I'd never said it?"

Her mother removed her reading glasses and pinched the bridge of her nose for several seconds before putting them back on and looking up again. "Because I didn't want what you told me to be true. No mother wants to hear something like that has happened to her daughter."

Gia had expected Ida to insist she'd been as supportive as a parent should be. This far more honest answer took her off guard. "I didn't invite that...that sort of relationship, Mom. I admired him, yes. And I was stupid and naive enough not to see his interest changing. But...I was seventeen."

"It wasn't your fault."

In that moment, Gia should've felt she'd just been relieved

of a huge burden. Her mother had finally said the words she'd longed to hear ever since it happened. Ida didn't hold her responsible!

But the self-doubt was still there—what had *really* made the incident so difficult. If she'd never felt anything for Mr. Hart and could be totally convinced her admiration was just that—admiration of a student for a teacher—she could accept this as the absolution she needed. But she'd found it flattering that he'd liked her so much, especially because so many of the other girls had vied for his attention. She'd been excited to visit his house, too. She'd thought he was so handsome and smart.

Could it be that she was partially to blame, after all? Should she have seen it coming and done more to stop it? What had made her agree to go to his house that day instead of asking why they couldn't take care of the problem with her grade at school?

Those questions drove her nuts late at night. But *she* hadn't crossed the line. *He* had, she reminded herself. "I cared about him," she admitted, her voice almost a whisper.

"Which makes what he did even worse," her mother said.

Gia wished she could kneel in front of her mother and sob into Ida's lap—finally rid herself of the guilt she carried in addition to all the other emotions that'd plagued her since that long-ago evening.

But now she had to admit that it wasn't just her parents' doubt that'd been stopping her from letting go of the past.

It was her own.

Cormac was looking forward to the weekend when Louisa poked her head into his office. "You heading home?" he asked when he saw her.

She nodded, said good-night and started to leave—but then stuck her head back through the opening. "I called Gia's mom this afternoon," she blurted as if she just couldn't hold it in.

He'd been annotating the charts of the animals he'd seen today. At this, he shoved away from his computer. "You *what?*"

"I couldn't help myself." Leaving the door open, she came in and slouched into the chair across from his desk. "I know Ida Rossi. She's a fair and honest woman. She donates to the animal shelter every year. She brings her cat, Miss Marple, in for regular checkups and shots and is always friendly to us. I thought—"

"Ida Rossi is dying of cancer, Louisa," he broke in.

"I didn't mean her any harm. I just thought…maybe I could reason with her, get her to speak to Gia and convince her to have some compassion, before…before Ida isn't around to have any influence."

"Oh, my God!" He rubbed his forehead. "I hope you didn't say that."

"I didn't, but—"

"Don't tell me she hung up on you…"

"No. She was polite. She just wasn't interested in helping."

"Of course not. Gia's her daughter!"

"But I'm not sure she's entirely convinced Dad's guilty, Cormac. I feel like she would've shown more anger back in the day—and wouldn't have been so nice to us through the years."

"*We* didn't do anything."

"Even so, there's probably residual anger in that type of scenario."

Cormac jammed a hand through his hair. "I wish you hadn't bothered her. That was going too far. She's dealing with more pressing problems than something that happened seventeen years ago."

"What happened seventeen years ago is still very present in *our* lives. I'm desperate to dispel the black cloud that's been hanging over us for so long—for Dad's sake more than ours. I hate that he's had to live with the assassination of his character all these years. I keep thinking that if we can clear his name, he might be able to pull himself together and be the man he once was." She sighed. "But I agree that—"

The bell jingled over the door out front, causing Louisa to fall silent.

Cormac patted his desk, searching for his calendar. "Do I have another appointment today?" He'd thought he was done. He'd been planning to leave as soon as he finished updating his charts.

"Maybe we have a walk-in." She went out to see, and Cormac came to his feet as soon as he heard her exclaim, "Gia!"

"Did you call my mother today?" Her voice was filled with anger.

In his rush to get out of the room, he whacked his thigh on the corner of the desk. Limping for one or two steps, he hurried to where his sister was squaring off against Gia Rossi.

His first thought was that it was after their normal business hours. Louisa should've locked the front door when their last patient left. Then Gia couldn't have gotten in. But Louisa typically didn't lock up until *she* left. As a small-town vet, Cormac tried to offer some of the more personal care shown by regular doctors in the old movies his parents had watched when he was a kid. That sort of approach had always appealed to him. Taking satisfaction in his work meant it couldn't all be about the money.

"What's going on?" he asked, even though it was obvious that Gia was furious her mother had been disturbed at such a difficult time.

"Your sister called my house this afternoon and brought up what happened when we were in high school. She thought she could turn my own mother against me and...what?" She yanked her attention back to Louisa. "Get her to convince me that what happened wasn't what happened, after all?"

"It *didn't* happen!" Louisa insisted. "When will you finally admit that?"

"You weren't there!" Gia cried. "*I* was."

"If my father said he didn't do it, he didn't do it," Louisa fired back. "Why would he risk his family, his career, his reputation—to touch a seventeen-year-old girl?"

"I don't know what he was thinking!" Gia said. "I only know what he was doing. And he was hoping to do a lot more than cop a feel!"

"You're just trying to save face, and you know it!"

Cormac couldn't get the vision of Gia crying at the pool last night out of his mind. Seeing her in such a vulnerable state had messed with his impression of her as a hard, lying bitch. But regardless of how he felt personally, he had to make sure this confrontation didn't get out of hand. He had his business and reputation to worry about. "Look, I'm sorry Louisa called your mother," he said, stepping between them. "She shouldn't have done that, okay?"

Gia's eyes were riveted on him. He saw anger flashing in them, but he thought he saw hurt, too, which took even more fire out of his reaction. It undermined his conviction, too. He also had that call with his father working against him, when Evan had backed away—far too easily—from challenging Gia about her lies. It'd felt almost as if he'd called because he was afraid Cormac *would* approach her, and he was worried about how that might go. Was it because he just wanted Cormac to continue to accept his version of events?

If there was a chance, even a remote one, that Gia could be telling the truth, Cormac and Louisa—Edith, too—had done her a grave injustice. He hated the thought that maybe they'd only made things harder on a girl who really had been molested.

He couldn't bear to even consider that possibility. It was easier to stubbornly believe what he'd always believed. But he couldn't help asking himself…*what if?* His mother must've asked herself the same question. And she must've arrived at a very different answer, or she probably wouldn't have left Evan, at least not when she did.

He should've asked—with a much more open mind—why she'd doubted her husband enough to leave him. Did she know something they didn't?

He hoped it was only the humiliation that'd caused the divorce, as Louisa claimed. Because calling Gia a liar and sticking with it all the years since would be—

Blocking the rest of that thought, he cringed. "We won't try to contact her again," he told Gia. "I apologize on behalf of my sister. We're sorry. Truly."

Tears welled up in Louisa's eyes. "You're *apologizing* to her?"

"Louisa, stop." He sent his sister a sharp look before addressing Gia again. "There's no fight here. You can go on your way."

He thought Gia might continue the argument. How well he remembered the argument he'd had with her in the hallway of the high school way back when. She hadn't backed down one inch. She was even more formidable as an adult. She came off as strong, confident.

But she glanced between them, made a sound of disgust and rolled her eyes before turning on her heel and marching out.

"What the hell, Cormac?" Louisa dashed a hand across her cheeks as soon as the door swung shut. "So much for confronting her and getting a retraction!"

"Do you think what *you* did has helped our cause?" he asked.

"I'm sick of it," she said, amidst fresh tears. "What she claims happened paints such a terrible picture in my mind. It turns my stomach. And I've had to live with that for almost half my life!"

He almost said, *That might not be* her *fault*, but bit his tongue. He couldn't start to doubt their father at this late date. That would open up a whole realm of unpleasant possibilities—including the idea that he and his sisters had made a bad situation even worse.

8

Margot found herself humming while she was doing the dishes. Just having Gia in town was enough to buoy her spirits. It was her sister who was going to make it possible for her to get out of her current situation, and seeing the way out was almost as exhilarating as actually running through the door. She wanted to spend time with Gia and her parents while she could, so that tempered some of her impatience to get away, especially because she was finding that Gia's confidence—or at least a little bit of it—had a way of transferring over to her when she was around. Margot knew she was taking a big gamble leaving her husband. She'd never been in the workforce, wasn't sure her business degree would afford her much after so long, but she'd find a way to pay the rent. She'd do whatever she had to for the sake of her children. Besides, she had no choice. She'd become smaller and smaller and would disappear entirely if she didn't do *something*, and there were no half measures with someone as controlling as Sheldon.

"Could it take you any longer to do a few dishes?" Sheldon demanded, coming into the kitchen.

He'd been cleaning his guns in the living room while watching an old Liam Neeson movie. After putting the boys to bed,

Margot had assumed he'd be occupied for the rest of the evening and was taking her sweet time, enjoying being alone in what had become her sanctuary. Since he left all the grocery shopping, cooking and cleaning to her, the kitchen was the best place to retreat when she wanted to avoid him.

"I decided to wash down a few cupboards," she said. But that wasn't true. She didn't plan to be living in Wakefield long enough to make such an effort worthwhile. She was leaving him the house. If he wanted clean cupboards, he could handle that himself.

Or Cece could do it...

"Really? You gotta wash cupboards on a Friday night when I'm home?"

Just the sound of his voice made her cringe inside. Apparently, this wasn't going to be the easy Friday night she'd hoped. The realization dragged her spirits down considerably. "You were busy," she said. "Talking to your friends on the phone, watching TV, cleaning your guns..."

"I gotta get ready for the trip, don't I? What do you expect me to do?"

She hadn't complained about what he was doing. *He* was the one complaining about what *she* was doing. "Nothing," she replied. "I was just making myself useful while you were occupied with other things."

Coming up behind her, he slid his arms around her waist, pulling her back against him, and it was all Margot could do not to stiffen.

"I'll finish cleaning my guns in the morning," he said. "I can think of a lot better things to do now that the kids are asleep. Why don't we go back into the bedroom?"

He demanded sex almost every day, but Margot couldn't remember the last time she'd enjoyed it. He didn't treat her like he cared about her; he was simply using her for pleasure the way he used her to fulfill his other demands.

She was grappling for the self-control to dry her hands and let him lead her down the hall, when he added, "I'll be gone for a whole week. Might as well stock up while I can, right? I wouldn't want to leave my wife at home alone, hungry for a man."

He thought he was so funny. But it was beyond her to laugh. Gritting her teeth, she steeled herself for the next fifteen or twenty minutes. "Sure, no problem," she said.

Apparently, acquiescence wasn't enough, because she saw his expression change almost immediately in the reflection in the window over the sink. "God, you don't have to act like it's such a chore!"

She must not have kept the dread completely out of her voice. But it wouldn't be a chore if she had any desire for him, any love left. *He* was the one who'd destroyed those things, and now he held *her* accountable for it. "I didn't say it was a chore."

"You don't act very excited."

"I— You caught me at a bad time." It was an excuse. But she'd found he usually believed what he wanted to believe— otherwise he'd know how much she hated him—so she wasn't too worried that he'd challenge her statement.

He dropped his hands. "Jesus. Being with you is about as exciting as watching paint dry." He opened the fridge and helped himself to another beer. "Are all wives this bad? Because if they are, it's not hard to understand why men cheat."

"Are *you* cheating?" The words came out before she could stop them. An affair could prove helpful, grant her more understanding from his parents and hers—or just ease the guilt she felt for being unable to fix her life in any other way. Cece was contacting him, after all...

His eyebrows snapped together. "Are you accusing me?"

He acted outraged, but for a split second she thought she spotted a flicker of guilt in his eyes. There *was* something going on between him and his ex-girlfriend; she'd bet her life on it.

Margot drew a deep, steadying breath. "Just asking," she said and met his gaze without flinching for the first time in ages.

He popped the top off his beer. "You see why I don't like you hanging out with your troublemaker sister?"

He hadn't answered her question. He was deflecting it instead. *"Hanging out with her?"* she echoed. "Today was the first time I've been able to spend any time with Gia in months. And it was only breakfast! You can't blame anything on her."

"Just seeing her makes you different, changes you for the worse," he insisted.

"Because I'm bolder? More willing to stand up for myself?"

He looked startled. "What do you mean 'stand up for yourself'? I'm not doing anything to you."

"You don't think so?"

"No," he said with a scowl. "It's *you*, not me."

She pressed a hand to her chest. "What have *I* done?"

"I told you, you're acting like your bitch of a sister, and you seem proud of it."

"I am, actually." She knew she was being reckless. She was drunk on the small amount of power she seemed to possess in this moment. But she knew how quickly that would change, that he'd get back on top somehow. He always did.

His eyes narrowed. "Be careful, or you're really going to piss me off."

Her heart felt like it was trying to claw its way out of her chest, but there was another force inside her, stronger than the fear, that was urging her on. She'd been dying to tell him *exactly* what she thought of him for so long... "What if I don't care?"

His jaw dropped. "What the hell, Margot? You see what Gia does? Maybe it's a mistake to go hunting while she's here. If I let her have that kind of influence, there's no telling what I might come home to."

Margot had expected him to get mad and start a blistering argument. She was suddenly spoiling for a fight—if only to avoid having sex with him tonight. But this... No, he had to go to Utah. Everything she'd planned depended on having that time before he learned what was happening.

Praying that the panic she felt at his last words hadn't already revealed itself on her face, she shrugged and turn back to the dishes. "That'd be nice, actually. I could use your help with the boys while I deal with my mother."

"What do you mean...deal with your mother? There's nothing more you can do for her," he said as if she shouldn't still be whining about it.

"Losing your mother is...is heartbreaking and...and traumatic, especially in this way!" she said through gritted teeth.

"I have no doubt that's true, but...let's be real," he said. "Everyone's going to lose their mother at some point. That's life."

Shocked that he could be so callous, she turned to face him again. "Are you serious right now? What if it was *your* mother?" She almost said "sainted" mother, because he was such a mama's boy, but she'd already caused enough trouble for herself for one night.

He studied her for several seconds. "Forget it," he snapped and walked out.

"So you're staying? You're not going hunting?" she called out as he disappeared into the other room. The only way to convince him to go was to make him think she preferred that he stay. Reverse psychology worked on him better than most people. But there was always the chance he'd surprise her, especially if he was growing suspicious.

"I'm thinking about it," he yelled back, and Margot dropped her head in her hands. What on earth had she done?

There were books all over Cormac's father's house, but they weren't neatly organized like they'd been before Sharon had forced him to take his stuff and move out. They were piled on every horizontal surface, even on the kitchen counter—too close to the stove, but his father refused to listen. There were papers and bookmarks sticking out of them, too. Or they were lying face down, creased at the spine where Evan had left off reading to pick another book or go to work.

Reading had always been a passion for him, so much so that he'd named his three children after American writers—Cormac McCarthy, Louisa May Alcott and Edith Wharton. But these days he'd sunk so deeply into the imaginary worlds these authors and others had created, he wasn't doing much real living. Cormac was glad Evan hadn't lost his love of the written word. At least he still had that. But he wished his father could get some balance in his life and take care of a few other things—like mowing the yard so the neighbors would quit calling to complain.

"Hey, it's me! You here?" Cormac yelled, confronting the mess while pocketing his keys and slamming the door behind him.

It took a few minutes before his father finally appeared from the back bedroom, looking tired and rumpled. Cormac had found him passed out drunk so many times that he had a spare key. Whenever Evan didn't answer the door, he let himself in, as he had tonight.

Discouragement settled on Cormac's shoulders like a heavy rucksack. "What's going on? Didn't you go to work today?"

"No, I didn't make it today. I… I wasn't feeling well."

Because he had a hangover? It looked like that might be the case. He hadn't even shaved or combed his hair.

Or was it that he'd been too immersed in whatever book he was reading? Lately, he'd been on a fantasy kick. "How many sick days have you taken this year?"

"I don't know," his father replied.

Cormac was willing to bet he had some idea—and that it was too many. "You're going to lose your job. You know that, don't you? And then where will you be?"

"I haven't missed *that* many days," he said with a scowl. "I didn't want to be out and about, not with Gia in town. You think I want her to see me working at a tractor shop?"

Cormac's head was beginning to hurt. He'd probably let himself get dehydrated since he took Mrs. Wood and Astro to the park this morning. He needed to remember to drink more water. But it was also his father. "I think you need to go on and live your life and forget about her—I mean *completely*. I've decided we all need to do that. Who cares if she's in town? Getting fired will only…" He'd been about to say, *Getting fired will only allow her to take more from you than she already has.* But he could no longer bring words like those to his lips, which said something about the doubt that'd crept in over the last twenty-four hours. "Getting fired will only put you in a worse position," he finished instead.

"Cliff's not going to fire me," his father said, grimacing to show his skepticism. "He and Marilou are lucky to have me down there. I'm way overqualified for the job."

And yet he'd been a terrible employee. Didn't he understand that his qualifications didn't matter if he didn't actually apply himself? "It's a living, Dad. It pays your rent. You can't afford to lose it. And think about them. They're not babysitters. They're relying on you to help with their business."

His father raked his fingers through his hair, which had grayed and begun to thin in front. His beard growth, which was so prominent today, was gray, too, and he had deep lines in his face. "Don't be a judgmental ass. I know what my responsibilities are. I was sick. I'm sure I'll be fine tomorrow."

Cormac was willing to bet he'd been well enough to work *today*. But he hadn't come over to try to police his father's lazy approach to his job. As much as Cormac was afraid to learn the answer, he wanted to know if Evan had been lying about what happened with Gia that long-ago night.

"What are you doing here, anyway?" Turning his bloodshot eyes toward the clock, Evan yawned. "It's Friday night. I rarely see you on a Friday."

Because Cormac usually went out with his friends—or had a

date. After a long week at the clinic, he took Saturdays off, wasn't even on call thanks to a deal he'd made with Vinny DiVincenzo, the vet in the next town over. Vinny covered both offices on Saturday, and Cormac covered both offices on Sunday. That way they each had one day a week they weren't going to get called out on an emergency. "I'm on my way home from the clinic and have Duke in the truck, so I can't stay long, but I came to tell you that Gia showed up at my office a few minutes ago."

His father dropped his hand from his hair. "She...what? Why? She's never approached you before."

"It was Louisa's fault. She called Ida today."

"What for?"

"Because she wants what you want, Dad. What we all want. A retraction."

"Gia won't give us one. Not after all this time."

Cormac studied his father, wishing he could see what was going on behind his eyes, because there were no telltale signs he was lying. Had that been the case, had there been the slightest hint of dishonesty, Cormac would've stopped believing him years ago. "You've been talking about confronting her for so long. I guess Louisa couldn't stop herself from stepping up to say something."

His father seemed thoughtful. "How'd Ida respond? She and I are friendly, you know."

"Actually, I didn't know. She speaks to you?"

"Not exactly. We don't have any business that's brought us together. But she treats me kindly enough when we pass on the street."

"That doesn't mean she's going to take up your case against her own daughter, Dad," Cormac said. "She's not interested in getting involved. For one thing, she's probably too sick. It was insensitive of Louisa to even contact her."

Evan didn't say whether he agreed with that assessment or not.

He seemed to think it over for a few minutes. Then he scratched the back of his neck and said, "What'd Gia have to say?"

"She was mad as hell that Louisa had bothered her mother, and I can see why."

His father walked around the counter and into the kitchen, opened the fridge and pulled out two beers, one of which he offered to Cormac.

Cormac shook his head. He wasn't in the mood to relax with his old man and have a cold one. He was irritated by the way Evan lived his life, and he was no longer sure he could blame Gia for it. The cognitive dissonance he was beginning to experience was bringing a whole new kind of discomfort; he just wanted to be put out of his misery. And he hoped his father could make that happen by convincing him that what he was beginning to suspect wasn't the actual way of things.

"Did you talk to her?" Evan asked.

"I did. I had to act as referee so the situation wouldn't get out of control. Louisa was freaking out."

Cormac heard the release of the pressure in the can when his father popped the top. "So...how'd it end?"

"You were right—Gia won't back off on what she said."

He raised his eyebrows before taking a big gulp of his beer. When he didn't reply, Cormac looked around at the kitchen. There was food stuck to plates sitting between and on the various stacks of books, trash overflowing the wastebasket, milk that'd been left out to spoil... "Have you had anything to eat today?"

"Had a sandwich earlier."

"You've got to clean this place up. It's not healthy in here. It's been seventeen years since Gia accused you of molesting her. It's time to put that behind you whether it happened or not."

His father's head jerked up. "Whether it happened or not?"

Cormac had just inadvertently revealed his doubt, but he'd

been planning to steer the conversation in that direction, anyway. "That's right. Why would she say it if it isn't true?"

"We've been over this! She wanted me to raise her grade!"

"She claims you invited her to the house to talk about her grade. And that's when it happened."

Suddenly, his father crushed the can even though it was still full, causing beer to run out onto his hand as well as the floor. "Are you kidding me?" he yelled, throwing it against the wall. "I'm getting this from you now, too? *You* of all people, Cormac?"

Cormac stared at the beer running down the wall and the can that'd landed on the floor. Evan didn't raise his voice that often. Cormac had obviously touched a nerve. He'd always been so careful not to look too closely for fear he might lose something even greater than he'd lost so far. But the need to know the truth was growing and so was the desire he felt for that incident to be resolved in his mind at last. "She's always been beautiful," he said, keeping his voice low but insistent. "Appealing. Engaging. *Sexy* as hell. I remember her clearly and can see why you might've found her attractive. She was almost an adult. It wasn't as if she was a little girl. You were a popular teacher. Maybe you thought her feelings mirrored your own or…or you thought she was coming on to you? Just tell me the truth, Dad! Did you do it? Because I don't want to continue to defend you if you're the guilty party. It's not right. It's not fair. Especially to someone who's been victimized."

"I didn't do it!" he yelled. "How many times do I have to say it? *I didn't do it!*"

Cormac closed his eyes against the echo of his father's voice. He'd been hoping for some clarity. But he didn't know any more now than when he'd driven over here, intent on *finally* pressing Evan. He couldn't say if he'd ever *know*.

Evan was adamant.

But so was Gia.

9

Ever since he'd seen Gia by the pool on Thursday night, Cormac had been inexorably drawn to the windows of his house that overlooked the Rossi yard. She hadn't appeared on Friday night; he'd assumed that maybe she was out with friends. But she'd sat by the pool for over an hour on Saturday and walked out again on Sunday just before Cormac was about to go to bed, which held him transfixed at the window in his room, despite the fact that he had to be up early to take Mrs. Wood and Astro to the park.

This morning he'd pulled out the transcript of his father's trial he'd originally gotten online and stored in a box in his closet. He'd been poring over it on and off as he went through his day. Not only did he want to know whether she was lying, he was interested in how she might've gotten beyond the incident if she'd been telling the truth. The pushback and skepticism—from him and others—couldn't have been easy to endure.

He'd never forget seeing her sitting in the witness box, pale but resolute, in a pretty pink dress that made her look young and sweet. She must've been instructed to wear something like that, because he'd never seen her in anything like it before. She'd probably been coached on how to answer, too, as the district attorney led her through a recounting of the events in question. Although Cormac had read it once today already, he took the transcript off his nightstand, where he'd left it last, and sat on the bed to go over the part again where the district attorney, a man named Brindley, had Gia on the stand.

To get through the trial as quickly as possible and put it behind him, his father had elected to forgo a jury. The defense attorney they'd hired had suggested a bench trial might be the smarter route, because it would preclude the prosecution from being able to stack the jury with mothers who'd likely be more susceptible to the emotional pain Gia would, no doubt, claim she suffered.

So the jury box had sat empty but the gallery was full.

MR. BRINDLEY: *How were you doing in school generally?*

GIA ROSSI: *Not the best. I was too caught up in socializing.*

MR. BRINDLEY: *But you loved English. You usually did well in that subject. Am I right?*

At that point, the defense attorney had jumped to his feet.

MR. JACOBS: *Objection, Your Honor! Leading statement.*

THE COURT: *Immaterial. The witness may respond.*

Gia had looked a little shaken by the fervor of the objection, but she'd gathered herself and said, *I've never gotten less than a B in English.*

MR. BRINDLEY: *And we have your transcripts right here to prove it. Let the record show that Gia's previous report cards reflect this.*

The prosecutor had lifted a file, which he'd entered into evidence before proceeding.

MR. BRINDLEY: *How were you doing in Mr. Hart's class?*

GIA ROSSI: *Fine. I turned in all my work on time. I had good marks up until that point.*

MR. BRINDLEY: *Then you weren't worried about your grade.*

GIA ROSSI: *I was a little worried. Only because I needed to get an A in English to keep my volleyball scholarship to the University of Iowa. I assumed it'd be easy enough to do, since I'd never had a problem before. But then Mr. Hart gave me a D on my big research paper.*

MR. BRINDLEY: *Why do you think he gave you such a low grade?*

GIA ROSSI: *At the time I didn't know.*

Cormac remembered her voice dropping dramatically at that point.

GIA ROSSI: *Now I think I do.*

MR. JACOBS: *Objection, Your Honor! Conjecture!*

THE COURT: *Please, just answer the question.*

After that, Mr. Brindley had tried to gain Gia's attention right away so she wouldn't falter.

MR. BRINDLEY: *You're telling me you don't think you deserved a D on your research paper?*

GIA ROSSI: *Not at all! Why would I go from making almost all As in his class to almost failing such a major assignment?*

MR. BRINDLEY: *Maybe you were falling off in English like you were in your other subjects. Senioritis gets the best of a lot of kids.*

Cormac chuckled humorlessly as he read that. Brindley had obviously been trying to neutralize some of the claims he'd known would arise from the defense.

GIA ROSSI: *That's not the case here. You can read my paper yourself and compare it to what the other kids turned in—kids who got a much better grade from Mr. Hart. You can talk to my friends, too. They'll tell you I was taking the assignment seriously. I even stayed home and missed a party I really wanted to go to so I'd have enough time to get it done right.*

MR. BRINDLEY: *Can you tell us what Mr. Hart didn't like about your work?*

GIA ROSSI: *I went up to his desk after class to ask, but there were a lot of kids around, trying to talk to him, too, and he just said he expected more from me.*

MR. BRINDLEY: *He didn't tell you what you did wrong?*

GIA ROSSI: *He said we'd talk about it later.*

MR. BRINDLEY: *Did you ever have the chance?*

GIA ROSSI: *I assumed I was going to when the bell rang and he handed me a slip of paper telling me to come by his house after volleyball practice that afternoon.*

MR. BRINDLEY: *Isn't it unusual for a schoolteacher to have a student come to his house? Had Mr. Hart ever asked you to come over before?*

GIA ROSSI: *No, but he lives just down the street. Since he's my neighbor, I didn't think it was all that unusual.*

MR. BRINDLEY: *And did you go to his house?*

GIA ROSSI: *I did.*

MR. BRINDLEY: *Is that when you pressed him to give you a better grade?*

Again, Cormac could tell, especially as an adult, that Brindley had been trying to preempt the defense by getting ahead of the story that she was so disappointed with her grade she was smearing her teacher's reputation as a form of revenge.

GIA ROSSI: *I didn't press him to give me a better grade. I was hoping he'd allow me to rewrite the paper. He sometimes did that when he knew a student could do better.*

MR. BRINDLEY: *You're saying he allowed his pupils to redo an assignment and they could still get an A?*

GIA ROSSI: *No, the highest he'd give on that type of thing was a B, but a B was all I needed on this paper to get an A in the class.*

MR. BRINDLEY: *Were his wife and children at home the evening you were there?*

GIA ROSSI: *No.*

MR. BRINDLEY: *Did he tell you where they were?*

GIA ROSSI: *He might have. I don't remember. I know now that they were at the high school watching Cormac's baseball game.*

Cormac had been a decent pitcher—nothing for the major leagues, but he'd earned a baseball scholarship at Duke, where he'd gotten his bachelor's in animal science. Wakefield had been playing their biggest rivals that night, so even his sisters had attended. Only his father had missed the game, saying he had papers to grade. The end of the year in Honors English always required a great deal of his time.

But if what Gia said was true, Evan hadn't begged off because of work; he'd been planning to spend those hours having sex with a student he'd become infatuated with.

MR. BRINDLEY: *Did you have your paper with you?*

GIA ROSSI: *I brought it, yes. But he had me set it aside, said we'd get to it later. First, he wanted to give me some suggestions for my Banned Books Club and asked me if I wanted a drink.*

MR. BRINDLEY: *He offered you something like a Coke? Maybe iced tea?*

Cormac remembered her gaze darting self-consciously in the direction of Cormac's father.

GIA ROSSI: *No. Alcohol.*

The DA's eyes had gone wide as he pandered to the judge.

MR. BRINDLEY: *But you're only seventeen. What would make a teacher give an underage student alcohol?*

GIA ROSSI: *He said I probably drank with my friends already, and it wouldn't hurt to have a little rum and Coke.*

MR. BRINDLEY: *Did you drink with your friends?*

She'd hung her head.

GIA ROSSI: *Sometimes.*

MR. BRINDLEY: *And did you drink that night with Mr. Hart?*

She'd looked up again, long enough for Cormac to see her face turn bright red.

GIA ROSSI: *A little.*

Cormac remembered the murmuring that rose in the gallery—it would probably always stay with him—and the frowns that'd creased the faces of her own family, all of whom were sitting on the opposite side, across the aisle. Obviously, they hadn't liked the idea of her accepting alcohol. That besmirched *her* reputation, made her something slightly less than an innocent victim.

But that had probably been orchestrated. Admitting to doing *something* wrong gave her more credibility. It would be logical for the judge—for anyone—to think, if she'd tell the truth about that, she must be telling the truth about all of it.

Cormac hadn't let it sway him, though. There was no way his father would offer alcohol to any of his students. That right there would risk his job.

The DA had spoken above the noise.

MR. BRINDLEY: *Then what happened?*

Gia's face had gone from red to slightly tinged with gray, as if it made her nauseous just to retell the story. To that point, she'd been putting on a stellar act. His sisters had been sitting on either side of him. He remembered Louisa leaning over to whisper that Gia deserved an Oscar for her performance.

But now he had to wonder if it'd been an act at all.

GIA ROSSI: *He took off his shirt.*

The embarrassment that'd hit Cormac when she made that statement had been excruciating. But he'd insisted his father would not have done something so humiliating—just like he wouldn't have offered a student alcohol. This whole thing had been designed to punish a teacher for standing in the way of a volleyball scholarship.

MR. BRINDLEY: *He did…what?*

Cormac had squirmed in his seat as Mr. Brindley tried to make a bigger issue of her response—to be sure the judge heard it, no doubt.

GIA ROSSI: *He took off his shirt.*

MR. BRINDLEY: *Did you leave at that point?*

Cormac pictured her digging at her cuticles.

GIA ROSSI: *No.*

MR. BRINDLEY: *Why not? Surely, you must've found it strange that he'd disrobe.*

GIA ROSSI: *I believed he took it off because he was too hot. He said he was. Also, he was drinking, so I thought he might not be thinking straight. I was still hoping to talk to him about my paper. I wanted him to tell me why he thought it was so terrible. And what I could do to improve it. And…and he seemed to be more friendly the longer I stayed, which made my hopes go up.*

MR. BRINDLEY: *That's understandable. Doesn't sound too out of line to me…*

MR. JACOBS: *Your Honor, Mr. Brindley is inserting his own opinion into the witness's testimony!*

There'd been so many objections. Some the judge had supported; others, he hadn't. This objection had been sustained. But Mr. Brindley hadn't seemed to care. He'd smiled at his assistant when his back was to the judge as if he'd already accomplished his goal just by making sure everyone had heard what he'd said.

MR. BRINDLEY: *Did you ever get to talk to Mr. Hart about your grade?*

GIA ROSSI: *No.*

MR. BRINDLEY: *Can you speak up?*

Gia's answer *had* been barely audible. Cormac had been hanging on every word and still had to lean forward to catch it. But at the prosecutor's urging, a stubborn defiance had come over her face and she'd lifted her chin and spoken more loudly.

GIA ROSSI: *I said no.*

MR. BRINDLEY: *Why not?*

GIA ROSSI: *Because that was when Mr. Hart pulled me up against him and…and…*

Her words had faltered, and Cormac remembered hoping and praying she wouldn't be able to finish that statement.

MR. BRINDLEY: *I know this is difficult. It's got to be almost as embarrassing and hurtful to recount as it was to live through it. But I need you to tell the judge exactly what happened.*

By that point, Cormac had felt sick to his stomach. He'd told himself to get out of the courtroom before she could comply with the prosecutor's instructions. He'd known that the images her response put in his mind would never leave him. But he'd been unable to believe she'd lie about something so monumental and had to stay and hear it for himself. It'd been like watching a car wreck; as horrified as it had been to witness the carnage, he couldn't look away.

GIA ROSSI: *He kissed me.*

Given the number of times he'd dreamed of kissing her himself, Cormac had flinched.

MR. BRINDLEY: *Did you try to resist?*

She'd looked down for several seconds, kept digging at her cuticles while Cormac—and probably the rest of his family— held their breath.

MR. BRINDLEY: *Miss Rossi?*

Her eyes had been shining with tears when she looked up.

GIA ROSSI: *Not at first.*

While he'd heard the gasps and murmurs around him, Cormac had remained silent, his gaze on her face. She was doing the same thing here as she'd done with the alcohol—admitting to some small wrongdoing so that the rest of what she said would be more believable, he'd thought.

MR. BRINDLEY: *Why not?*

GIA ROSSI: *I was shocked...and...and overwhelmed, I guess. To be honest, I don't really know. I still thought I liked him, that...that he was a cool teacher... I don't know.*

She'd shaken her head helplessly as she'd repeated that she didn't know.

MR. BRINDLEY: *Then what happened?*

GIA ROSSI: *He pulled off my shirt, undid my bra and started kissing my breasts. That was when I pushed him away and said I wanted to talk about my paper.*

Cormac winced. Even now, he felt sick. At this point, Mr. Brindley had been forced to raise his voice to be heard above the noise.

MR. BRINDLEY: *And how did he respond?*

GIA ROSSI: *He said I didn't need to worry about my paper. It was one of the best in the class.*

At that point, the murmuring had crescendoed to the point that it nearly drowned out the prosecutor's next question, and the judge had to warn the gallery to remain quiet.

MR. BRINDLEY: *Yet he gave you a D?*

GIA ROSSI: *Yes. That made me so mad I pushed him away again. I knew then that…that there was nothing wrong with my work. He'd used my paper as an excuse to get me to come over.*

MR. BRINDLEY: *What happened next?*

GIA ROSSI: *He told me I was all he could think about. That he would give anything if only I'd go into the bedroom with him. But by then I was too grossed out by what was happening to even let him touch me—the bad grade I didn't deserve, the alcohol, the rest of it.*

MR. BRINDLEY: *So what did you do?*

GIA ROSSI: *I tried to wrench away. But he had hold of my arm and wouldn't let go. He kept telling me that I'd enjoy myself if…if I'd just quit fighting. That he'd be gentle with me, and I deserved some-one who was experienced for my first time. He said making love would be something we'd both always remember and not to worry about my scholarship because he'd give me an A in the class.*

Once again, the noise that'd erupted in the gallery had made it difficult to hear the prosecutor—and once again, the judge had warned everyone to pipe down.

MR. BRINDLEY: *Did he tell you he loved you?*

GIA ROSSI: *He did. I asked him about his wife, and he said he'd leave her if we could be together.*

Cormac had shot a glance at his mother when Gia had said that, but Sharon had sat, rigid and stoic, and hadn't returned his gaze.

Those words had cut him, too, though. That his father would walk away from the family for a student... It'd been unthinkable.

MR. BRINDLEY: *And do you feel as though you ever loved him?*

She'd hesitated as if she didn't know how to respond, before finally answering.

GIA ROSSI: *It wasn't love. I liked him. I thought he liked me. I trusted him. I couldn't believe he'd give me a D if I didn't deserve it. And I knew I didn't want him to keep touching me. It felt creepy, wrong.*

MR. BRINDLEY: *And did he stop?*

GIA ROSSI: *Not right away. He was trying to get inside my pants. He unbuttoned and unzipped them and jammed his hand down the front. I was trying to fight him off, but it wasn't until I started to scream for help that he realized my answer was really no. Then he let me go and stepped back as though he was shocked I wouldn't go into the bedroom with him.*

Tears had started rolling down her cheeks, which she'd quickly wiped away.

GIA ROSSI: *I told him I was going to tell the principal that he'd cheated me on my grade. Somehow, I was more concerned about that than anything else, since...since the physical stuff really hadn't gone that far, and I felt partially to blame for drinking with him. But then he started to threaten me, said that he'd fail me if I told anyone. He said I asked for what I got by flirting with him at school and that he held all the power, so no one would believe me, anyway.*

The silence that'd fallen over the court after that statement had been more deafening than the noise. Mr. Brindley didn't speak for several seconds. Cormac had known even back then that he'd been drawing out the moment for dramatic effect. He'd wanted everyone in that courtroom, especially the judge, to see that evening through Gia's eyes.

When Brindley finally spoke, he did so quietly.

MR. BRINDLEY: *How did it end?*

GIA ROSSI: *I did what I could to straighten my clothes and ran out.*

MR. BRINDLEY: *Did he come after you?*

GIA ROSSI: *No.*

MR. BRINDLEY: *What was he like the next time you saw him?*

GIA ROSSI: *When I got to class the next day, he acted as if it never happened—except he did change the grade on my paper to a B. My friend pointed it out to me almost as soon as I walked in. Our grades were posted on a chart on the wall.*

MR. BRINDLEY: *But you still went to the principal.*

GIA ROSSI: *I was torn about it, but I didn't want to be in his class any longer, so, yes, I went to Mr. Applegate, and he put me in Mrs. Summerfield's class instead. The funny thing is that they were a week behind us. People were just turning in their research papers, so I turned mine in right along with everyone else.*

MR. BRINDLEY: *You didn't change it in any way?*

GIA ROSSI: *Not one sentence.*

MR. BRINDLEY: *What kind of grade did you get from Mrs. Summerfield?*

GIA ROSSI: *An A minus.*

There'd been another collective murmur in the gallery then, after which Mr. Brindley had said, "No more questions, Your Honor."

Cormac set the transcript aside. After that, the defense attorney had had a chance to cross-examine Gia and got her to admit, once again, that she'd been drinking that night, which meant she might not remember it clearly. He'd pointed out that grading a research paper was often subjective, so getting two vastly different grades could happen even when there was no impropriety involved. And then his father had taken the stand and done an excellent job of presenting his side of the argument, which had made Gia look bad.

Bottom line, the whole thing had been a fucking nightmare.

Leaving the transcript on his nightstand again, Cormac got up and leaned against the wall of his bedroom as he went back to staring down at Gia. Although she had her phone in her hand, she wasn't using it. The fact that she'd come out so quietly, without turning on any lights, suggested her parents were asleep and she was enjoying a peaceful moment alone, just sitting in the lounger and staring up at the stars.

He wondered why the cold hadn't driven her back inside. But then he reminded himself that she'd spent considerable time in Alaska. Maybe the cold didn't bother her. Maybe she missed the wide-open spaces she'd enjoyed during those years enough that it was worth the chill. Wakefield wasn't exactly crowded—there were only five thousand people—but that was probably big compared with some of the places she'd lived since moving away from home.

After she'd first left, he'd been tempted to track her down.

His world had been crumbling around him, and he'd thought if only she'd listen to what was happening as a consequence of her lies and have some compassion, she might be willing to come forward with the truth, which could restore his father's reputation and save his job—as well as his parents' marriage. Cormac believed if she had a conscience, she'd have to right this wrong. But his father had villainized her to the family and anyone who'd listen to the point that he hadn't believed he could reach her no matter what.

And now, seventeen years later, she was becoming human to him again. Should he talk to her? If so, what would he say?

He'd be a lot less accusatory than he'd been before; he knew that. Judging by the way his father had lived his life—and what she'd accomplished since—*she* was the one who seemed more reliable these days. Even though Cormac wanted to blame what his father had become on her—and in all fairness that was still a possibility; there were men who couldn't get over the false accusations they'd endured—there was a small voice inside Cormac that said if his father's character had been what it was supposed to be, he would've figured out a way to live a life of integrity, nonetheless. A man like he'd once thought his father was would not want to be a liability to his family and friends...

He rubbed his temples as he tried to figure out a way to contact Gia that wouldn't involve anyone else and wouldn't become the subject of gossip around town.

They definitely couldn't be seen together...

Fortunately, their houses backed up to each other. There was even a gate between them. And she came out alone almost every night despite the cold. He could walk over there right now and interrupt her solitude, but he knew that wouldn't be a welcome surprise. She had to be willing to meet with him; he felt that was the only way they might have a civil conversation. And that meant he needed to give her the choice and hope she'd agree.

So he wrote a note asking her to come to his house tomorrow night—or suggest another private meeting spot if she wasn't comfortable doing that—and waited until she'd gone inside to leave it on the chaise under a rock so the wind couldn't blow it away.

10

Sunday had been torturous. Sheldon had been acting suspicious of every comment or expression, and he'd insisted they spend every moment together. When Margot had told him she was supposed to go to brunch with her parents and sister, he'd said they had things to do as a family.

While they drove to the sporting goods store in Sioux City, she'd wanted to ask if it meant he was going hunting, after all. She needed that reassurance. Thankfully, the cooler purchase signified he hadn't entirely ruled it out.

She redoubled her efforts to be the cowed, obedient wife—to act as though nothing had changed. But the arrival of her sister, together with the brief flash of defiance she'd shown in the kitchen on Friday night, seemed to have put him on high alert. He knew if she ever told Gia she was unhappy, he'd have a real fight on his hands. Margot finally had the possibility of some support—beyond two parents who tried not to get involved and couldn't now that they were dealing with the last stages of cancer.

She was folding the laundry on the couch after dinner on

Monday night while the boys were playing in their room and Sheldon watched golf on TV when she heard a knock at the door.

"Who's that?" he asked, but he didn't leave his recliner. Answering the door was apparently her job.

She set the T-shirt she'd just folded aside and went to find out. She could see her father's SUV in the drive through the front window, but when she opened the door, it was her sister standing on the stoop. "Hey, where's Mom and Dad?"

"Mom wasn't feeling up to coming over. She was ready for bed, and Dad stayed home with her in case she needed anything."

"Other than working a few hours a day—when he can—he's barely left her side, poor guy."

"He was able to work as long as he needed to today. So I think he's eager to tuck her in and spend some time alone with her." Gia lifted the sack she was carrying. "I brought the kids a present. Do you mind if I come in?"

Margot didn't want to let her. She couldn't afford a confrontation with Sheldon, and since Gia never curbed her tongue, putting them in the same room was a risk. But how could she turn her sister away? Gia hadn't seen the boys since she'd returned to town. "Sure. It...it would've been easier had you called. Then we could've arranged something—"

"*Arranged* something?" she broke in. "I didn't think it would be a big deal to stop over and see my nephews."

"It's not," Margot reassured her. "Of course not. I just meant... Never mind." Reluctantly, she stepped back to admit her sister and called out, "Matthew! Greydon! Your aunt's here to see you."

They came running from the back bedroom and threw their arms around Gia's legs, nearly bowling her over as she laughed. "Wow! You two have grown so much since I saw you last."

"I'm going to be bigger than my dad," Matthew announced.

"So am I," Greydon said.

Sheldon didn't so much as turn down the television. He eyed

Gia as if he was wondering whether he had to tolerate her presence, and it wasn't until the boys had ripped the packaging off the new Lego sets Gia had purchased for them and begun to build a Harry Potter castle that her sister looked up and addressed him. "Hey, Sheldon."

He merely grunted, which embarrassed Margot. Given what was going to happen in the very near future, she couldn't say why. Maybe it was because Sheldon's behavior was just more evidence that Gia was right about him—he was a subpar husband. She wondered why Sheldon didn't try to keep up appearances with Gia like he did with both sets of parents and everyone else in town and supposed it was just too difficult to do that with someone who'd already seen through him.

After reclaiming the sack she'd carried in, Gia reached inside it and brought out a pocketknife with Sheldon's name engraved on it. "Thought you might be able to use this when you go hunting next week," she said and crossed the room to give it to him.

He took it and studied it for a moment. "You got this for *me*?"

"Has your name on it, doesn't it?" she said jokingly.

"It does. And not many things do."

"Yeah, well, your name isn't a popular one in the hunting world. But a buddy I met through Eric does a lot of woodworking. He personalized it for me."

"Thank you," he said, his voice only slightly grudging. "Maybe you're turning over a new leaf, eh?"

"If you're asking if I like you now, the answer's still no," she replied, but she was laughing when she said it.

Margot could tell he couldn't figure out if it was a joke—and she certainly wasn't going to enlighten him that it was probably more of a peace offering for *her* sake than any real change in Gia's opinion.

"Yeah, well, I don't like you, either," he grumbled. "But I like this," he added with a grin, holding up the knife.

"Good." Gia shrugged. "Now you can't say I never gave you anything."

"That's true, but don't expect a gift in return." He laughed uproariously, as if his reply had been the wittiest thing ever.

Gia gave him a wry grin. "Considering how long you've been in the family, why would I expect you to start being nice now?"

Relieved that their banter was fairly friendly, despite the more serious undercurrent, Margot jumped in before it could turn to something worse. "I made a red velvet cake we had after dinner. Why don't you come into the kitchen, and I'll get you a piece?"

Gia insisted on playing with the kids first and helping them build the Lego sets she'd brought them. When it came time, she also put them to bed and spent at least a half hour reading them stories.

When she finally came into the kitchen, Sheldon had just turned off the TV and headed down the hall to get ready for bed.

Grateful for some quiet time with her sister, Margot cut a piece of the cake, added a large scoop of ice cream and set it on the table.

"Those boys are turning out great in spite of Sheldon," Gia said as she sat down and picked up her fork. "Must be our genes."

Margot started to laugh.

"What?" she said, obviously surprised. "You're not going to get mad at me for that comment?"

"No."

"Why not?"

"Would it do any good?"

"Probably not." Gia gave her a wicked grin but then sobered. "What's going on with you?"

"What do you mean?"

"With the weight loss. It seems kind of extreme. And there are dark circles under your eyes. I'm getting worried about you."

Margot sobered instantly. "It's fine. It's nothing. I just wanted to slim down."

"By eating red velvet cake?"

Margot laughed. "I didn't have any. I haven't had much interest in sweets lately."

"It's not just the weight. Tonight's the first time I've heard you laugh since I got home."

Margot lowered her eyes. "Mom has cancer, Gia. She's dying. What's there to be happy about?"

"What's happening to Mom is horrible," Gia said. "But… is that all of it?"

"Of course."

Gia took a bite before leaning in close. "You'd tell me if there was something else, if you were in financial trouble or had bad news about you or one of the kids, wouldn't you?"

Margot got up, covered the cake and straightened the counters. "The business is going well, and we're all healthy as can be."

Gia studied her closely. "Promise?"

Margot was dying to tell her sister the truth. She knew better than to do it, but she needed to talk to someone so badly. She opened her mouth to say something—she didn't know what—but then a noise at the edge of the room caused her to turn and see Sheldon.

"It's getting late," he said with a scowl. "Aren't you coming to bed?"

Margot's heart started to race. She'd almost blown everything, almost opened up.

Thank God she hadn't.

She cleared her throat as she tried to decide how to respond. She knew what Sheldon had said was more than a suggestion. There'd be hell to pay if she didn't come to bed because he'd interpret that decision as choosing her sister over him. "Yeah, um... I... We were just finishing up."

Obviously surprised by this sudden turn when they hadn't even had time for a full conversation, Gia looked from her to Sheldon and back again. Margot recognized the steely determination in her sister's eyes. Gia was tempted to tell Sheldon to mind his own business and leave them alone. But something about Margot's sudden panic must've shown in her face because Gia seemed to change her mind.

After shoveling the last bite of cake into her mouth—she probably did that to show she'd at least finish her dessert before she let him drive her away—she handed Margot the plate. "Cake was delicious. Thank you."

"No problem."

"I'm leaving," she told Sheldon in a voice that sounded like *Have it your way.*

Still trying to avert any problems, Margot spoke up before he could respond. "Sorry, we...we have to be up early."

Gia gave her a brief hug as she said goodbye but simply walked past Sheldon. That was much better than what Margot was afraid she'd been about to do, though.

After the door closed behind Gia, Margot held her breath for fear Sheldon would say he didn't dare go on his trip if her sister was going to be coming around, hanging out with her and the kids while he was gone. But he surprised her by handing her the knife Gia had given him instead. "Can you believe she brought me a present? That's a first, isn't it?"

Margot took it from him, turned it over and ran her thumb over the engraved letters. "Looks like a nice one," she said and wondered, knowing how much her sister disliked Sheldon, why she'd bothered.

"Must've cost her a pretty penny."

He seemed flattered she'd spend so much, so Margot couldn't

help taking some of that away from him. "Yeah, but I get the impression she makes good money."

"Since when did you start thinking your sister's all that?" he said with a scowl. "She might do okay for herself, but she doesn't make anything close to what I do."

Gia and her partner had built their business from the ground up. It hadn't been handed to them by someone else. That was worth noting. But she wasn't going to mention it. Sheldon didn't like having any competition—especially when it came to her sister. "There's no way she makes as much as you do," she concurred even though she had no idea whether that was true. She didn't care. She just wanted to be done with him, and if playing it this way made that more likely, she'd say almost anything.

"Do you think she's really going to stay for the whole winter?" he asked, somewhat speculatively, as she handed back the knife.

Margot needed and wanted him to leave town so badly, she couldn't give him a reason to stay. "Oh, no. Before you came in, she was already talking about going back."

"How soon?"

Margot wasn't a good liar, but she scrambled to come up with something that would make her comment completely believable. "She didn't say when. She just mentioned the pressures of work, since the business isn't quite shut down yet, and how she really hated to miss that photography trip she'd been planning with her business partner. I could tell it's only a matter of time."

He clicked his tongue. "Told you so."

"Yes, you did," she said and breathed a sigh of relief when he left the room, suddenly no longer concerned with whether or not she was coming to bed.

Something was wrong with her sister. The dynamic that Gia had just witnessed was…odd. Sheldon had always held more power in the relationship, and Gia had seen him abuse it over the years, but in subtler ways.

Now, the relationship was even more out of balance. Over a decade of working hard to please him, thinking he'd be happier and treat her better if only she could meet every demand, had obviously backfired. All he had to do was walk into the kitchen and suggest Margot come to bed, and her sister scrambled to obey, even though it'd looked as though she'd been about to confide something important.

What was it she'd wanted to say?

If Margot and Sheldon weren't getting along, Margot would've spoken up, wouldn't she? Why would she hold *that* back? She knew Gia didn't like him.

It was only nine fifty when she got home, but except for the kitchen light, which her father had left on for her, the house was dark and quiet. She figured she'd eventually get used to going to bed early, but if she tried to sleep now, with the anger and resentment she was feeling toward Sheldon boiling in her blood, she'd just stare at the ceiling for the next two hours.

She decided to pour herself a glass of wine, get in the hot tub and watch a movie on her laptop while she was outside. So she washed her face, brushed her teeth, piled her hair in a messy bun on top of her head, put on her bikini and searched Netflix for a series she wanted to watch. After deciding on the latest true crime offering, she took her laptop, a glass and a bottle of wine out with her.

After she removed the thick foam cover, steam roiled from the surface of the water and wafted toward the black expanse overhead, and a quick check showed the thermometer at a toasty 103 degrees. Relieved that she wouldn't be sitting out in the cold like she had on previous nights when she'd come out to get some air, she set up her laptop so she'd only need to press Play, pulled off her Alaska sweatshirt and kicked her flip-flops to one side before climbing in.

The heat felt so good, and she closed her eyes as she sank beneath the water and rested her head on the lip of the hot tub for a few minutes, relaxing. She'd just sat up and poured some wine when her gaze landed on the chaise where she normally sat.

There was a big rock on it, which was strange. Who would've put that there? she wondered. These days, her parents rarely came into the backyard. It'd gotten too cold outside. A professional handled the pool, and since her mother's diagnosis, a yard service had taken over the mowing and trimming from her dad. Gia had wondered why Sheldon had never offered to lend a hand. She knew Margot would've done everything she could to help if it'd been *his* mother who was battling a life-threatening disease. But maybe he was too busy.

Spotting something white sticking out from beneath the rock, she got out to see what it was.

Paper, she realized as she approached it. Someone had put a piece of paper on the chaise and secured it with a rock so it wouldn't blow away. But who would do that?

She looked back at the house. Every room was still dark, except the kitchen, which had the same light burning.

She peered over the fence, but Cormac's house was dark, too. There wasn't so much as a porch light on there. Either he wasn't home or, like her parents, he'd already gone to bed.

"Weird," she muttered and dried her hands on her cast-off sweatshirt, since she hadn't bothered to bring out a towel, before lifting the rock.

It was a note. And it was addressed to her.

Gia,

We've had to live with what happened in high school for nearly two decades. That's a long time. I remember confronting you over it at school and that memory makes me cringe. I acted so badly. If you didn't deserve what I said, I'm sorry.

But I'm not going to lie—I still find myself torn and confused as to who might be telling the truth. My father insists you were out to ruin him, and I don't have any real reason to doubt him. His story makes as much sense as yours does. Then there's love and loyalty, of course, and what I want to believe—and it certainly isn't that my father could do what you accused him of doing.

Will you take the time to talk to me now that I'm calm and will actually listen? I realize it must be a hard subject for you, especially now, with what's happening in your own family. But I don't know whether to hold my father accountable for that night or continue to pity him as someone accused of something he didn't do.

If you're willing, please come over—or suggest somewhere else we could meet—so we can have a few minutes to chat. I swear I won't mistreat you. I won't even raise my voice. And I won't keep you more than a few minutes. I just really want to talk.

Thanks for your consideration.

—Cormac

"Oh, God," Gia muttered. She didn't want to meet with Cormac. Why would she go over to his place—stroll into the proverbial lion's den—to discuss something she wished she could just block out of her mind? And if she didn't do that, where else could she even suggest?

She folded the note along the same crease lines. *Nope*, she told herself. It didn't matter how nicely he'd asked. She didn't have to do it, didn't owe him anything.

But would he interpret her refusal as guilt? Assume she was ashamed of her behavior?

She didn't care, she decided. There was no way to convince him of the truth. If he didn't believe her after sitting through the trial, he wasn't going to believe her now. He'd said it himself—he didn't *want* to believe her.

Except...the sympathy people in town were giving the Harts

was costing her friends. She hadn't spoken to Ruth since they'd had drinks together the other night, and Sammie had sort of tried to defend Ruth when she'd called the day after to smooth everything over. Gia could tell she was getting caught in the middle, but she felt Ruth would probably receive more of her loyalty in the end since she lived here and Sammie saw her so much more often.

Besides, Cormac had been young and emotional back when they'd had that confrontation at school. So had she. Maybe they *should* talk as adults and try to ease the pain Mr. Hart had caused so they could all find some type of closure. She'd never wanted his family to be hurt; she wished *someone* would understand that...

Gia put the note back under the rock so it wouldn't blow away or get wet while she went back to the hot tub, where—instead of watching the movie—she spent the next twenty minutes staring at it and going back and forth in her mind as to whether she should actually meet with him.

Fortunately, by the time she got out, it was too late to go to anyone's house, so she didn't have to wrestle with herself any longer tonight.

She'd put the onus back on him, she decided at last. If he really wanted to talk to her, she'd give him the chance. But she wasn't going to show up at his place, especially in the middle of the night. The only reason she was willing to meet him at all was because he'd shown so much restraint at his office. He could've piled on. Louisa had certainly wanted him to. And yet he'd apologized for her and treated Gia with respect.

After she got out of the water, she went inside and showered. Then she dressed in a warm pair of sweats, wrote a note of her own and used the same rock as an anchor when she left it on his back doorstep.

11

Cormac banged loudly on his mother's door. Now that she was dating, he rarely swung by unannounced, especially in the evening or early morning. He was afraid of what he might encounter. If she was sleeping with someone, he didn't want to know about it. That was her business entirely. But he'd just dropped off Mrs. Wood and Astro and had a few minutes before he had to hurry home and shower. Fortunately, his first appointment at the clinic had canceled; he didn't need to be at work until ten.

Finally, through the narrow side window, he could see his mother shuffling to the door while belting her robe, her short gray hair sticking up in back where her head had obviously been resting on the pillow.

"What is it?" she asked as soon as she let him in. "Is there some sort of emergency?" Her gaze swept over him in alarm. "Are you okay?"

He lifted his hands to signal that she could quit looking for injuries. "I'm fine. I just…wanted to talk to you."

Now that she knew her nursing skills weren't required, she

scowled at him. "And you couldn't have called me later? You had to wake me up at seven thirty in the morning?"

He gave her a sheepish look. "I've been up since five. Seven thirty isn't all *that* early, is it?"

"It is to me," she replied. "I worked late last night."

"I'm sorry. I should've waited."

She blinked at him. "But?"

But he'd looked out the window first thing this morning and noticed that the rock he'd left on the chaise in the Rossi yard was gone. Gia had probably gotten the note he'd written—or someone else in the family had—and yet she hadn't come by. Maybe it'd been too late. But he couldn't help being skeptical that she'd ever be willing to talk to him, which left him with no way to resolve the conflict inside him.

"I need to know something. Why did you divorce Dad? *Did* he molest Gia?"

Her jaw dropped. "What the heck, Cormac! You hit me with this at the crack of dawn seventeen years after the fact? Why'd you wait so long?"

He probably should've gone home and showered, then dropped by on his way to work. He was damp from running and getting a chill despite the well-worn Hart Veterinary Clinic sweatshirt he wore with his running shorts. "I..." He let his words trail off because he wasn't sure how to express that it was loyalty that'd stopped him. He felt guilty even now for trying to verify his father's story.

Besides, actually saying what he was thinking would identify him as a traitor, make it impossible to take back.

But the truth was the truth. He figured he might as well face it. "I was afraid of what you might say."

"And you're not anymore? What's changed? You're tired of putting up with the way he lives his life?"

"Yes, I'm tired of that. But it's more that my desire to know the truth is finally outweighing my love and loyalty. Or...not my love," he quickly corrected. "But you know what I mean. I'm finally willing to consider the possibility."

"*Really!* After defending him for so long?"

"That's the thing. I can't keep it up any longer unless… unless I feel more confident than I do at this moment."

"Okay." She gestured to his truck, where Duke was staring at them with his head hanging out the window of the driver's seat. "Will he be okay if you come in for a few minutes?"

"He'll be fine."

"Good." She waited for him to step inside before pushing the door closed behind him. "Let's go into the kitchen. I'm going to need a cup of coffee for this."

She was acting as if he'd asked her to open Pandora's box. Was this something he really wanted to do? After seventeen years, what did it matter what'd happened that night? Gia would probably only be in town for a few weeks or a couple of months, and then life in Wakefield would continue very much as it had before. He didn't *need* to know, did he? Why stare down that ugly possibility?

Because the truth mattered. Being fair to Gia mattered. He was late forcing himself to entertain the possibility. And it could be that his mother didn't know any more than he did. But he wanted to hear her perspective—at last.

"Sit down." She circled the island and went to the far counter— and that was when he noticed the new automatic latte machine.

"When did you get that?" he asked.

"A few weeks ago," she said nonchalantly.

"I saw that brand in Williams Sonoma when I was looking for your Christmas present. It was nearly four thousand dollars!" Which was why he'd chosen something else. No one who lived alone needed a four-thousand-dollar latte machine, especially when they weren't—by any means—rich.

"Good coffee means a lot to me," she said.

"Mom!" He was prepared to tell her she had to be more

careful with her money, but she sent him a look that warned him off.

"Don't start. We're talking about your father's problems today, remember?"

He sighed. He had a shopaholic for a mother and a reprobate for a father. Were either one of them credible? Or was this a fool's errand?

He supposed he wouldn't know until he learned what his mother had to say. Being irresponsible with money might indicate she wasn't perfect, either, but that sort of thing didn't make her a liar. "So...what do you have to say about Dad? Do you believe he did it? I mean...you left him right after the trial, so...you *must* think he was lying."

He wished she'd been more forthcoming all along, but she'd been so careful not to influence their feelings toward their father. She'd always said they had to decide for themselves.

"There are things you don't know about that night," she said as the latte machine began to hum.

He slid onto one of three modern-looking black bar stools. His mother might be a shopaholic, but no one could say she lacked taste. "What are they? And why haven't you ever told me about them?"

"Because you haven't asked. And I don't know anything for sure. Only he can tell you what really happened that night."

Gia could, too, of course. If only he could believe what she had to say.

"I just...had a few more pieces of evidence to consider than you and the girls had," his mother said.

"What are they?" he repeated.

"Subtle clues, for sure." She set a macchiato in front of him and returned to make herself a cup. "The way he was behaving that night. The things he said."

Cormac sampled his drink and was glad she'd decided to

make coffee. The hot liquid helped warm him up. "I'm afraid I'm going to need a more detailed explanation."

"When we left for your game that night, I asked him to come with us. I really wanted us to be there as a family to support you. But he said he had to work and insisted he couldn't take the time."

"That's plausible, isn't it? He was always busy the last couple months of school."

"Except *I* knew he'd finished grading the research papers, which is what took so much time. There could've been other stuff he needed to get done, which is why I relented, but... something about his excuse didn't ring true. I remember being frustrated that he wasn't more committed to watching you play. And he certainly didn't tell me he had a student coming to the house. I would've taken a strong stand against that."

"Because having a girl at the house leaves him open to accusation?"

"Even having a boy over would do that. If a student claims they were threatened or struck—or molested, as in this case—there's hell to pay, right? Believe me, after the years we spent in the school system, and the difficult students and even more difficult parents we encountered on occasion—not to mention the stories we read in the paper, which were even worse—we'd learned not to take chances. So I couldn't understand why he'd set himself up like that."

"The fact that he broke with protocol is what made you suspicious. But she was a neighbor, Mom. He claims she just walked over uninvited."

Sharon shook her head. "No. That didn't ring true, either. He was staying home that night for a reason, and I believe it was to see Gia."

"Women's intuition?"

"That and his growing obsession with her."

Cormac felt his eyebrows shoot up. "What do you mean?"

"Leading up to that night, I'd been treated to *so* many comments about this particular girl. How bright she was. How special she was. What a great student and writer and person and… you name it. He admired her for standing up to the women who forced him to ban the books he wanted to assign in class and was involved in helping with that renegade book club she started. In my opinion, it put them in too much contact."

"Gia was beautiful, too." She *still* was…

"He never came right out and said *that*, but I could tell he thought it. He was making me uncomfortable where she was concerned long before the accusations came out."

"Did you say anything to him before that night? That you could tell he was getting too caught up in Gia?"

"I once asked him if he realized how often he talked about her, and he said I was being ridiculous, that he had no interest in her other than to see her make it to college."

"Then why'd he give her a D on her paper, knowing she had to have a B to get an A in his class?"

"He claimed it was truly subpar. You heard him at his trial. But I read that paper. I'm not saying it was the best research paper in the world, but it wasn't a D. It was well thought-out, the right length, structured correctly, with footnotes and everything. At the worst, he could argue she deserved a B minus, but not a D. She was right about that."

His mother had hit a nerve because Cormac had read Gia's paper, too. Way back when, a photocopy of it had circulated around the school. But he'd been a year younger and hadn't understood what her research paper should've been like, so it hadn't been too hard to trust that it was lacking in some way, as his father claimed. He'd told himself he just didn't see it because he wasn't a teacher.

Since then, however, he'd realized it truly wasn't that bad and had relied on the fact that grading English papers could be very subjective to shore up his belief in his father. Besides, his father had admittedly high expectations for her. But a D? Ds were reserved for people who didn't put much effort into their work, didn't follow the syllabus, didn't turn in the assignment on time or turned in papers with huge gaps in logic, poor writing, grammar and punctuation—or a mixture of all those things. Gia's paper had none of that. "Did he mention he was disappointed in her paper before that night?" he asked, still looking for some way to cling to his conviction that Gia was lying.

His mother carried her own cup to the counter and stood opposite him instead of sitting down. "No. After everything else I'd heard about her, I would've thought he'd say something. But he never said a word." She took a sip of her coffee. "And the way he acted when we got home that night?" She grimaced. "He was so agitated. He couldn't sleep, made several comments about how students make things up and that even the best teachers can run into trouble when there was dishonesty involved. It was as if he was preparing me for what was about to happen, hoping to inoculate me against Gia's accusations."

Cormac frowned. "Is there anything else?"

"Gia," she said simply.

"Gia?"

"I hate to admit it, but she came off as more authentic to me. Could be that it was a trick of the prosecution, but the fact that she's stood by her story ever since—"

"Dad's stood by his story, too," Cormac interrupted. "I feel like they'd both have to—to save face."

"I realize that."

"And Gia was strong-willed, a free spirit who wasn't afraid to defy authority. I could see her trying to get away with something like...like making it all up to get a better grade."

"Which is why Evan might've thought he had a chance with her," she said softly. "Have you ever thought of it that way?"

When Cormac cursed under his breath, his mother came

around to squeeze his shoulder. "Don't let this drive you crazy, honey. It's water under the bridge. Regardless of what your father did or didn't do, it's all in the past. Just...forgive him and move on."

"Is that why you've never tried to persuade me or Louisa or Edith?"

"I didn't want to persuade anyone because I wasn't sure I was right. No one likes to accuse an innocent person. I just had enough doubt that I could no longer trust Evan. So, as much as I knew it would be difficult for you and the girls—and I still feel bad about how hard the divorce was on all three of you—I had to get out of the relationship and start over."

He couldn't accuse her of being selfish; she'd lived her life mostly for them for a decade or more after, when they were all well into adulthood. It wasn't until a few years ago that she'd started to date, and even more recently that she focused on herself with the weight loss and new wardrobe. "If that was what you needed for your own sanity and happiness, you did the right thing."

Her lips curved into a smile that was full of gratitude. "Thank you. I didn't want to be married to someone who could—"

"Take advantage of one of his students?"

"Yes, but for me it was more about the lies. That he could do that to Gia and then try to make her look so terrible to save himself. She was only seventeen."

"I'm sure she bears a few scars."

"I'm sure she does," his mother agreed. "So...what do you think?"

"I wish you had more of a smoking gun, that you could tell me Dad confessed to you or something like that."

"I'm afraid I can't make it *that* easy. But there is one other thing."

He'd just lifted his cup again; at this, he put it back down. "What is it?"

"It's...pretty personal, so hard to talk about, especially with you. I wouldn't mention it if...if you weren't struggling so much to figure this thing out."

"Just say it."

"Okay. In the name of full transparency, your father called me from school the next day to tell me what'd happened—that Gia claimed he'd acted inappropriately and he'd be home late because he had a meeting with the principal. I was so upset that I went through the entire house, searching for anything to prove her wrong." She took another drink of her coffee before adding, "Or right, as it turns out."

The acid in Cormac's macchiato was beginning to burn his stomach. He pushed it away. "And what did you find?"

"A new lubricant I'd never seen before hidden in his drawer."

"Oh, God," Cormac muttered. "Why didn't you say something at the trial?"

"That wasn't exactly damning evidence, you know? He could easily have bought it for me, so I didn't think I was holding back anything that would be important in that regard. I also wanted to give him the benefit of the doubt—mostly for the sake of you and your sisters. But finding that... Well, it said a lot to *me*, especially because I never saw it again."

"He got rid of it?"

"It wasn't in his drawer when I looked again. I think he didn't even try to pretend he'd bought it for me because he knew the timing would be weird."

"And by that point, it probably represented his guilt, so he was ashamed of what it signified."

"Exactly."

Cormac hung his head as he thought about what she'd told him.

"So...are you sorry you asked?"

He slid off the stool to go home and get ready for work. "Yes."

★ ★ ★

"You're late."

Louisa's curt response to his greeting caused Cormac to hesitate before continuing to his office. "I have ten o'clock on my calendar."

"That's our first appointment. We open at nine. What if there'd been an emergency?"

"You would've called me."

"People expect us to be open on time," she snapped.

Duke nudged him to the side so he could get through to his water bowl.

"Louisa, this is *my* clinic," Cormac reminded her. "I set my own hours."

"What would happen if *I* decided to treat my job like that?"

"What would happen to any other employee who didn't show up for work?" *He* covered her paycheck. Surely, she could see the difference.

"You'd *fire* me?" she challenged.

He sighed. "This is about Gia, isn't it?" He should've called his sister and tried to work through what'd happened in the office. He could've reassured her, convinced her to calm down and mitigated some of her anger. But he hadn't wanted to admit that he was becoming so conflicted. He'd hoped they could just leave it as it was, ignore that little blip in their day and pick up where they'd left off before Gia had walked in.

"You took her side over mine," Louisa said. "I never thought I'd see the day."

"I didn't take her side," he argued. "I was trying to head off an ugly confrontation. We run a business. We need to maintain a certain image in this town, be professional."

She sneered at him. "It had nothing to do with the fact that she's so pretty?"

He flung out his hands. "What are you accusing me of?"

"You think I don't know how you felt about her in high

school? That she was your biggest crush? I remember when you joined her stupid book club. You didn't even read back then. You were so caught up in baseball you were lucky to get your homework done."

"That was a long time ago."

"Are you saying you no longer find her attractive?"

"This is ridiculous. I haven't even talked to her, other than when I tried to stop what was happening here in the office. She's tough. You don't want to mess with her." *He* should know. She certainly hadn't backed down from arguing with him the day their dad had been fired. Most of the school had been privy to that shouting match.

"I can handle Gia," she said. "Or I could have, if only I'd had a little support!"

He walked down the hall to his office, but once he swung the door open, he turned back. "I'm not going to gang up on her with you or anyone else. At some point, it has to be between her and Dad. I say we leave it there."

She followed him into the room. "Why now? That's the question. You know what she did to Dad. You've hated her right along with us for seventeen years."

"*Hate*'s a strong word, Louisa."

Her jaw dropped. "Oh, my God! What's gotten into you?"

"Doubt!" he finally shouted. "Don't you ever wonder if *she's* the one who's been telling the truth? Especially after the way Dad's lived his life?"

"He's lived his life the way he has because of her! She took everything he had. She broke him, Cormac. That's why I'm so angry. That's why *you* were angry, too."

Cormac shoved a hand through his hair. "But is that the truth—or is that only what we want to believe?"

"You sat through the trial with me."

"I did. But there's such a thing as confirmation bias, which might be why we never changed our minds, but the judge, whose job it was to be impartial, came to the conclusion Dad was guilty!"

"That doesn't mean the judge got it right. The benefit of the doubt often goes to the woman these days. You heard Dad's attorney. After the verdict was read, he said that ten or fifteen years earlier, the result would've been completely different."

"That may be the case, but that's because the courts are finally giving victims the consideration they deserve. The fact that he was found guilty should at least make us examine the possibility that *we* could be the ones in the wrong."

"No," she said, adamant. "I won't let Dad down."

"Dad is the one who's let Dad down," he said. "At least since this happened. And it could be that he was the one who let us all down from the beginning."

She threw up her hands. "I don't know why you're second-guessing everything. Have you talked to Dad?"

"I have."

"And? Did he change his story?"

"No, but neither did he do anything to convince me. I've also talked to Mom. That's what made me late."

She froze. "What'd *she* say?"

Cormac had to be careful. The last thing he wanted was to further damage his family, especially his father, who was barely hanging on to a productive life as it was. "Nothing new. She has her doubts. That's why she left him."

"But...how convinced is she?"

"Enough that she couldn't continue to live with him but not enough to try to convince *us*." And neither was he in a position to try to convince Louisa or Edith or anyone else. He had no answers, just more questions. And if they were at peace with the opinions they held, so be it. They could easily be right; why challenge them?

The bell rang over the front door in the lobby. Louisa looked back when she heard it, then lowered her voice. "You're wrong, Cormac. You're making a big mistake."

He wished he could be that confident. Instead, he found himself in no-man's-land—suddenly on neither side. He was doing his best to regain his conviction, but the more he dug into the problem, the more uncertain he became. "Maybe that's true," he said. "But I have to be honest with myself and everyone else."

12

Gia hadn't heard from Sammie since that call the day after they'd had drinks together. She hadn't heard from Ruth, either. She kept thinking one of them would reach out, but she understood what was keeping them away. Ruth would feel disloyal to Edith, and Sammie would feel disloyal to Ruth, and since Sammie and Ruth had to live with each other—and the Harts—on a day-to-day basis, they were probably more concerned with protecting those relationships.

Evan Hart had maintained the same narrative for so long, the people in Wakefield had begun to accept his version of events, and any doubt or sympathy that'd once favored her was gone. Maybe that didn't matter so much when she was in Alaska or Coeur d'Alene, doing her own thing. Then she could talk to Sammie and Ruth, and any relationship they had with Edith and Louisa didn't play a role. But it was a completely different story now that she was back in town. They felt torn, as though they had to choose.

"You're quiet today," her mother commented as they played a game of gin rummy. Her father had gone to the office after breakfast and probably wouldn't be back until dinner. He seemed grateful for the chance to take care of the things he'd had to let languish. It was about time she came through, but the fact that she *should* be here didn't mean it was easy to stay.

"Just worried about Margot," she said. The dynamic she'd witnessed in her sister's kitchen last night had been curious. Margot had seemed so eager to talk to her about something—and yet she'd immediately sided with Sheldon when he'd entered the kitchen and made it clear he wanted Gia to leave. But Gia was also feeling bad about losing her oldest friends over an incident that wasn't even her fault. Although she'd kicked herself for years for ever going to Mr. Hart's house, there was no way she could've foreseen what he was going to do. Yes, she'd been aware of his partiality and was flattered by it. She and her friends had long talked about the cutest teacher in school. But she'd never dreamed of getting physical with him. He'd done so much to support her book club that she'd trusted him even more than her other teachers. And he'd betrayed that trust.

When she was in therapy—before she'd quit college and gone to Alaska to try to heal herself with freedom and time away—her psychologist had told her, again and again, that Mr. Hart was the one to blame. Her English teacher had set her up. He'd given her a low grade on purpose, had known it would drive her right into his trap. She needed to forgive herself for being so gullible.

But she couldn't tell her heart how to feel; it just felt what it felt, and what it felt was regret. She could've avoided all the trouble and the pain she'd been through—and the trouble and pain so many others had been through—if only she hadn't gone to his house that night.

"I've been worried about her, too," Ida admitted. "The light's gone out of her eyes. She's preoccupied, nervous, always keeping one eye on her phone or the clock when she comes over."

"You've noticed?" Gia said.

Ida nibbled thoughtfully on her bottom lip. "How can I miss it?"

"And you haven't asked her what's wrong?"

"I've tried. She insists it's nothing."

"It seemed as if she was going to tell me something last night, but then Sheldon came into the room."

Ida frowned.

"What is it?" Gia asked.

"I think he's having an affair," she replied while stroking Miss Marple, who rarely left her side and had crept into her lap while they were playing.

Gia lowered her cards. "Are you serious? He'd risk losing Margot by getting involved with another woman?"

"I don't know. I hope not."

"What makes you think he's cheating?" Gia asked, leaning forward.

Ida played a card. "A couple of things."

"Like..."

Her mother sighed. "He's become sort of...distant—rarely comes over these days. And the way he and Margot act when they *are* here together is... I don't know how to describe it. Cool. Strained."

It was Gia's turn. She played, then chose her discard. "Who could he be cheating with?"

"His old girlfriend."

"Cece?"

Ida nodded. "You remember her?"

"Of course. They were an item all the way through high school. I've often wished they'd gotten married."

Her mother scowled, but she didn't warn Gia to be careful of what she said as she normally would have. "Cece's divorced and back in town—has been since last spring—and your father and various other people have seen them together here and there."

Gia took a drink from her water bottle. "You mean...just the two of them?"

"Just the two of them," she confirmed.

"What were they doing?"

"One day last month, your father drove past the park and saw them sitting at one of the tables in the picnic area, talking so earnestly he's pretty sure they didn't notice him. My hairdresser mentioned that she saw them both leaving Sheldon's office last week—she couldn't remember exactly what day. And when Roberta Peden, from church, called to check on me this morning, she said she's seen his truck parked in front of Cece's house a number of times. She lives on the same block."

"That certainly sounds suspect to me..."

"Maybe that's what's wrong with Margot..." her mother suggested.

"I don't think so. She would've told us if that was the case."

"I'm not convinced she would," her mother argued. "I'm guessing she doesn't want to upset us."

Given Ida's health, Gia could see that and backed off a little herself. "It could be that they're just friends," she said. "There's no law against being friends with a former boyfriend or girlfriend. I've asked Margot how she and Sheldon are doing, and she insists they're fine."

"How do you know she wasn't going to tell you about Cece last night?"

"Because if she thought Sheldon was cheating, she would've told me that already."

Her mother didn't look convinced, but her phone rang before she could argue. She'd left it in the home office, so Gia jumped up to get it for her. "It's Dad," she called back and answered so that her father wouldn't be transferred to voicemail. "Hey, Dad."

"How's it going?" he asked.

"Good. Mom ate almost a whole tuna-and-pickle sandwich

for lunch, so that's good. And she had quite a few of the date bars I made for dessert."

"She loves those things," he said. "I can't thank you enough for what you're doing."

His gratitude was nice but also made her feel guilty. "I'm glad I came home."

"I'm happy to hear you say that, especially because...well, I know you have good reasons for wanting to be anywhere else."

"I'm an adult now. I'll get through it," she said, even though there were moments when the anger and outrage welled up and it was so strong she wondered how long she could truly last.

"Do you need me to stop by the store and pick up anything for dinner? I'm on my way home..."

"No, I'm planning to make a chicken pot pie, and I already have everything."

"Sounds delicious. It's great to have some different meals than what I was preparing."

"I'm happy you're enjoying them. Here's Mom," she said.

While her parents talked, she walked into the backyard to peek over the fence. She'd done that periodically throughout the day, hoping to see the rock she'd left on Cormac Hart's back porch gone, so she'd know her message had been received. But it was still there, with the paper sticking out underneath.

"Damn," she muttered. She should've put the note on his front porch. Then he would've seen it when he went to work.

She considered going over to move it. But she was afraid he'd pull up right when she was on his front stoop. Or that he'd bring his sister or someone else home with him, and they'd discover her note together. She was feeling defensive enough that she preferred her message to be private.

Deciding he'd find it whenever he found it, she turned to go back to the kitchen. But then she noticed the darkening sky, pictured it getting wet and falling apart and hurried over to grab it.

She didn't need to talk to Mr. Hart's son. She wasn't sure why she'd agreed.

And yet, later that night, after Ida and Leo took Miss Marple with them and went to bed, she found herself obsessed with the house behind her—couldn't stop watching it from her bedroom window since the weather was too bad to go outside. She wondered what Cormac was thinking about finding his message gone and no response. Was he assuming she must be as bad as he'd always believed?

Why did she care? she asked herself. He was never going to be her friend. They'd known each other but never really been friends even back in high school. And that encounter at her locker when his father was fired loomed large in her memory.

But she knew he'd been reacting out of his own pain. Maybe if it was *her* father who'd been accused of something that heinous, she would've reacted the same way.

She thought again of the note Cormac had left. He seemed sincere in wanting to talk. Certainly she could give him an audience, couldn't she? Some kind of resolution could make her presence in Wakefield easier on both of them. Then maybe she could set the past aside, at least to a degree, and focus on getting through her mother's illness...

Gathering her courage for what would undoubtedly be a difficult conversation, she threw on a pair of sneakers and ran through the backyard, trying to block what she could of the rain with one hand.

Cormac had reconciled himself to the fact that Gia wasn't interested in talking to him. It'd only been twenty-four hours since he'd left her that note—not long enough to truly decide which way she'd go—but he'd expected rejection from the beginning and believed he was getting it. So he was surprised when she showed up at his door, soaked, just before he went to bed. With the storm, he hadn't even looked outside to see if she'd appear by the pool.

"Wow, it must be raining even harder than I thought," he said as he took in the water dripping from her hair and the white long-sleeved T-shirt that was plastered to her body, along with a pair of blue leggings.

"I've been out here a while," she admitted. "I went back to my house twice before I actually knocked."

He eyed her, trying to gain some idea of what he should expect in the next few minutes. "Couldn't make up your mind whether to come?"

"Wasn't sure it would do any good."

She wasn't giving much away, except a general sense of fatalism, which he supposed he could understand, given the longevity of the feud between her and his family. That didn't mean she wasn't up for a fight. But he'd asked for this audience; he needed to take his chances. "Please, come in," he said, holding Duke out of the way and stepping back at the same time. "I'll get you a towel."

Leaning to one side, she tried to peer around him. He got the impression she was checking to make sure he was alone, that she wasn't about to walk into an ambush. The fact that she felt the need to be so cautious made him feel sorry for the way he and his family had treated her in the past; it also made him admire her for being brave enough to come over, despite their history. "We can talk right here," she said.

She didn't trust him. That was obvious. But he was the son of the man who, according to her, had betrayed her trust seventeen years ago, so it made sense. "It's freezing outside," he said. "And I'm harmless. I promise. I have a business here in town. The clinic is everything I've worked to achieve in the years since high school. I wouldn't jeopardize what I've built, wouldn't want to lose everything like my father did."

Her gaze swept over him and his dog as if she was trying to

size them both up. They must not have seemed too threatening, because her chest lifted as though she was drawing a deep breath. Then she stepped inside.

He closed the door to keep his dog in and the cold out and went to the linen closet to grab a towel. He'd already started back to where she was waiting in the entryway, dripping on the hardwood floor, when he realized he should also get her some dry clothes and ran upstairs to his room.

"Here. You can towel off in the bathroom and have something to put on afterward," he said when he returned and handed her a sweatshirt with the towel.

She lifted the sweatshirt as if she wasn't convinced she should even be touching it.

"You'll be more comfortable," he said by way of enticement. "And you won't have to worry about changing back before you go. You can just leave it on the fence, and I'll grab it when I see it." He raised his eyebrows. "Unless you'd rather stay wet and cold..."

She must've decided that she *didn't* want to remain wet and cold, because she took it into the bathroom he pointed out to her and emerged a few minutes later with it on. For the time being, she must've left her own shirt behind with the towel.

He'd just finished wiping up the floor in the entry. "Can I get you a cup of hot chocolate?" he asked.

"Hot chocolate?" She bent to pet Duke; apparently, she didn't hold anything against him.

"I can make coffee if you'd prefer, but I figured you probably wouldn't be too keen on drinking caffeine this late."

"And that would be true," she admitted as she straightened. "It's been hard enough to sleep."

Because... He wished she'd elaborate, but she didn't, and he didn't want to scare her away by pressing her for answers too soon. He felt it would be wiser to ease into it. "I have wine, whiskey, other things that might also warm you up..."

"I'll stick with hot chocolate."

Relieved she didn't make a joke about being poisoned by him, he gestured toward the kitchen. "Come on. You can have a seat in here."

She followed, albeit slowly. He could tell she was taking in everything she saw in his house and drawing whatever conclusions she could.

"So?" he said.

She slid onto a seat he'd pulled out for her as he rounded the island in the center of his kitchen. "So...what?" she replied in confusion.

He tossed the dirty towel he'd used to wipe the floor into the laundry room. "What does my house say about me?"

"That you're not much of a decorator," she replied, which made him laugh. He'd bought only the most functional furniture, hadn't done anything to dress up the place. One, he didn't have the cash. He was still making sizable payments to the veterinarian he'd purchased the practice from, not to mention his student loans. And two, he didn't have the time. He was either running at the park or working at the clinic and didn't want to dedicate his days off to anything other than rebuilding the vintage motorcycle in the extra stall of his garage.

He supposed that indicated he didn't really have any interest in decorating, either. "I have a TV, a bed and a couch. What more does a guy need?" he asked with a grin to show he thought he had his priorities straight.

"Do you really want me to tell you?" she asked, but she was trying to resist a smile, so he could tell she was only joking.

It was good to see that she had a sense of humor. And she seemed to like Duke, who'd followed them and was sitting dutifully at her side. Maybe they could find some common ground, after all. "Wow, and here I thought you'd come over to help me call a truce."

"We haven't been fighting. It was your sister who had the nerve to call my mother."

"Something I'm embarrassed about," he said. "But still, there's work to be done. We definitely haven't been friends."

Her eyes narrowed. "Is that what this is about? Becoming friends?"

He pulled the mug he'd filled with milk from the microwave and added a packet of hot chocolate mix. "It's about conflict resolution."

"You hate me for ruining your father's life. How are we ever going to resolve that?"

She scratched Duke behind the ears, and the dog moved even closer to her. Apparently, he didn't understand she wasn't to be trusted.

"Traitor," Cormac grumbled to Duke and saw Gia's lips twitch, as if she wanted to smile again.

"Apparently, he's a better judge of character than you are," she quipped.

He arched an eyebrow. "He likes my dad, too."

"Never mind," she muttered.

He chuckled. "Actually, Duke's not that keen on him," he admitted. "And if my dad did what you claim he did, he ruined his own life, right?"

"Whoa! Those are words I never dreamed I'd hear *you* say," she replied. "But that was my therapist's take on it, yes. And he was a professional."

She'd had to go to a therapist? He was beginning to feel even worse about what he'd believed—or chosen to believe—in the past. "That would be my take, too," he said. "Even though I don't have the same credentials as a therapist."

She frowned. "Problem is…you're still using 'if,' and I don't know how to convince you that it really happened."

The levity he'd felt drained away as he stirred her hot chocolate before sliding it across the granite countertop. "I'm afraid you already have."

She sat up taller in her seat. "How'd I do that—after so long?"

Feeling like a traitor simply for admitting what was going through his mind, he blew out a sigh. "I think I was afraid of it almost from the beginning. Well, not in high school, of course. I was as shocked and outraged as anyone—"

"I remember," she broke in, sending him a sulky look.

"I'm sorry I… I verbally attacked you at your locker. Especially because the way my father's lived his life since then hasn't built much credibility."

"Wait. You're not blaming me for the way he's lived his life since then, too? Your sisters think I broke him, that he would've continued to be a stellar husband, father and teacher had I not 'lied' about him." She used fingers to make quotation marks around "lied."

"I know. But the more I've watched him, the more I've had to face the fact that he isn't the man I once believed him to be. Maybe if he'd never met you—"

"Met me! I was his student!" she cut in.

He lifted a hand to signal he wasn't finished. "I was pointing out that part of it might simply be bad luck. He ran into someone he craved badly enough to break every rule in the book."

"I was his student," she repeated. "And you're blaming it on bad luck instead of his character."

"I'm saying you were young and beautiful, and I believe he fell in love with you. That would explain why he never did that kind of thing to anyone else. It's not an excuse, it's—" he shook his head "—it's just trying to understand how it occurred."

"You mean how he could do what he did?"

He nodded. "I guess that's what I mean."

"So you invited me over to apologize?"

He watched as she took a tentative sip of the hot chocolate he'd made and couldn't help noticing the subtle changes in her face and body since he'd first known her. He'd already admitted to himself that she was even more attractive these days, but now he had the chance to study her long enough to decide why. Her face had thinned slightly, making the most of her high cheekbones. She hadn't lost that dusting of freckles across her nose, which he hadn't been able to see from his window. And her eyes, while wary and distrusting, also seemed...hopeful, and he found that incredibly appealing—that she hadn't become a total cynic.

If she were any other woman, he knew he'd go to bed dreaming about those eyes. "If I'm being honest, I invited you over hoping there would be something about you—or something you said—to shore up my belief in my father. Ignorance is bliss, right?"

"The truth is the truth," she replied.

He nodded. "I know. And hiding from it doesn't help."

For a moment, his honesty seemed to take her aback. She'd barely drunk any of her hot chocolate, but she shoved the cup away and got off the stool. "It's not your fault. None of it was ever your fault. I'm sorry you were hurt by it, too. I feel terrible your whole family was hurt. That was never my intention when I came forward. I just... I wanted to get out of his class and be able to go to college."

Of course. Anyone in her shoes would want the same thing. He believed her. Everything—her tone of voice, her approach to the subject, the sincerity in her expression and body language—suggested *she* was the one telling the truth. If he'd ever been willing to hear her before, *really* hear her, he might've come to the same conclusion. But it'd been too awful a reality to face.

It wasn't easy even now.

"Shit," he said, coming around the island to sink into a chair.

She'd started to leave, but seeing this, she hesitated. "What is it?"

"I wish you were lying. I wish...I wish he didn't do it."

The empathy in her expression when she briefly touched his shoulder surprised him, because it let him know that they really had been victimizing an innocent person. A *caring* person. "It's in the past, Cormac. Let it go," she said and showed herself out.

But she didn't understand. He *couldn't* let it go. His father was still perpetuating a fake story, still refusing to take responsibility—still hurting Gia by calling her a liar.

13

Cormac believed her. Gia never thought she'd see the day. Neither could she have anticipated the feeling of relief it would bring. She knew she shouldn't care what anyone else thought, least of all Mr. Hart's family. The therapist had emphasized that over and over. *You know the truth. That's all that matters.* But she couldn't help herself. The Harts were part of the fabric of her hometown, and right or wrong, their side of the story had a certain contagion. The way Ruth and Sammie were acting—so hesitant to continue to be her friend—proved it. The last person she'd *ever* thought would join her side would be Cormac, the dude who'd harangued her at her locker the day the news broke. She hadn't even had to say much to him tonight, hadn't even really bothered to plead her case.

She'd assumed it would be futile...

Pulling out the front of the royal blue sweatshirt he'd lent her so she could look down at it, she studied the white "Duke" lettering. She'd been so stunned she'd forgotten her own shirt in the bathroom when she left his house. She figured he'd put it on the fence after the storm passed, just as he'd instructed her to do with his.

She considered taking off his sweatshirt so she could wash it right away. She didn't want to explain to her parents where she'd gotten an oversized Duke sweatshirt. But the storm wasn't due to move on until the day after tomorrow, so she had time; she wasn't prepared to give up the comfort it provided. The fleece was thick and warm, but the fact that this particular sweatshirt belonged to Cormac made it special. It served as proof of what'd transpired tonight, and she wanted to live in that moment as long as possible.

"At last," she muttered as she let go of it and fell back onto her pillows.

Curious to see if Cormac was still up, she climbed off the bed and went to the window—only to find him standing at *his* window, staring out at her.

Dropping the curtain, she jumped back. Had he seen her? If so, had he noticed she was still wearing his sweatshirt? Would it seem weird that she hadn't been more anxious to get out of it?

She had no clue what he might be thinking. She hadn't known him that well even back in high school. He was a year younger, had been a particularly good baseball player who'd come to a few of her Banned Books Club meetings. That was all.

She thought of the get-together she'd arranged this weekend. Considering the strain in her relationship with Sammie and Ruth, she was tempted to cancel it, but there were a lot more people from the club who were coming.

Besides, she didn't want to look like a coward. That would only make them believe she was guilty. Because she respected how he'd handled this evening, as well as the incident at his office, she decided to invite Cormac. She couldn't imagine he'd ever be willing to come. That'd be taking a stand against his own flesh and blood. But an invitation would probably be nice…

Edging forward, she peeked out through the crack in the drapes. He was gone.

Telling herself she was silly to keep wearing his sweatshirt, she finally pulled it off and put on one of her own. But she took it to bed with her and kept looking at it as she got out her laptop. Over the years, she'd tried not to spend much time dwelling on Cormac and his sisters. That only made the past more painful, because then she'd wonder if she could have spared them had she not come forward. The therapist said she'd done the right thing, that someone had to put a stop to that kind of behavior, but she wasn't convinced he would've gone on to victimize other students. What'd happened with her could've been the perfect storm.

She glanced at Cormac's sweatshirt again. What kind of man had he become? He seemed fair, just, kind, honorable. And he was obviously smart.

After navigating to Instagram, she searched for his account, which was filled with pictures of his dog, an old motorcycle he was restoring and various members of his family. She didn't see any photographs of women, except in a few groups that contained both sexes, which seemed to confirm what Sammie had said—he wasn't currently dating anyone.

He was thirty-four. Why hadn't he settled down? He had a lot to offer a woman. He was an educated professional in a town of mostly blue-collar farmers. He already had a home. He'd inherited his mother's height and regal bearing—her bone structure, too, which made him even more attractive.

He probably wasn't ready to settle down...

As she surfed around, she found a separate account for his clinic. From the differences between what she found posted there versus his personal account, Gia guessed Louisa handled the clinic's social media, which was filled with darling pictures of various pets and their owners, Louisa at the front desk or with her kids coming into the clinic, fun facts about animals and memes encouraging people to neuter: *Balls are meant for catching—neuter your pets.* The Hart Veterinary Clinic also promoted a local shelter and featured a dog or cat that needed a new home on "Adoption Fridays."

Since there was more to be found on the clinic's account, Gia took her time scrolling through and eventually found a picture of a slightly younger Cormac, standing shoulder to shoulder with Dr. Tomlin and announcing the fact that he'd be taking over the practice "after working together for almost a decade."

Bottom line, Cormac had made good, despite what'd happened with his father. She couldn't help feeling proud of him—for that and for being open-minded enough to consider the situation from various viewpoints. Too bad he hadn't done that seventeen years ago, but better late than never.

I wish...I wish he didn't do it, Cormac had said, but he certainly wasn't the first person to wish that.

With a yawn, Gia closed her laptop, scooted down in bed and pulled Cormac's sweatshirt up to her nose. It smelled wonderful—like his cologne—and served as proof that he believed her.

For tonight, anyway. She had no idea what would happen tomorrow.

A few days after Gia's visit, Margot found herself parked down the street from Cece's house, far enough away that she needed Sheldon's hunting binoculars, which she'd gone home to get. Anything closer risked exposure, and there was no way she was going to allow herself to get caught spying on him. She *wouldn't* be spying on him if she hadn't tried to drop off the lunch she'd made him—that he'd once again forgotten on the counter—and learned from one of his employees that he'd left claiming he was meeting *her* for lunch.

He'd never said anything about getting together today. She'd been planning to spend what time she could, until the boys got out of school, with Gia and her mother. She wanted to be with them as much as possible before she had to leave town for good, because she didn't know how long it would be before she'd feel safe to contact them after. Once she drove out of Wakefield, no one could know where she was. She was too afraid they wouldn't take the threat she felt seriously.

Her parents, especially, wouldn't be able to understand why she and Sheldon couldn't simply separate and then get a divorce. After all, that was what most other couples did. And she didn't know how to convince them that something about Sheldon was different from other men. The level of control he demanded over her. The complete domination. And how quickly he could lash out for the slightest infraction. He frightened her in a bone-deep way, but she doubted anyone who hadn't lived with him as she'd lived with him would believe her. Too many people in Wakefield thought they knew him, including her family. And she'd been complicit in making him look better than he was. She'd thought it was her duty as his wife not to criticize him to others, and she knew how he'd react if she didn't keep up appearances. That meant Ida and Leo would not only be shocked—they'd probably be skeptical. This would seem liked it was coming out of nowhere.

Gia would believe he was an asshole, of course. She'd seen him for what he was from the beginning. But her sister wasn't afraid of him. Gia's approach wouldn't be to run and hide, and anything short of that risked a severe backlash. In the worst-case scenario, Sheldon would use his money and his family's influence to gain custody of the boys.

Margot was afraid that if either her sister or her parents thought she was going too far, they might feel sympathetic to his parents, who would no longer be able to see their grandchildren, and insist she coordinate visitation with Sheldon and his family for the boys. And if she refused, and they let even the smallest piece of information slip, that would enable Sheldon to find her…

She shuddered. He'd be livid, embarrassed on top of everything else. She knew how vindictive that would make him. He'd do all he could to get revenge.

The only way to avoid having her family and friends make decisions she didn't want them to make was to keep her whereabouts a secret.

She peered through the binoculars again. She could see her husband's truck parked down the street, but it wasn't right in front of Cece's house. He probably thought he was being sly, that no one would notice and make the connection. But she knew he had no reason to be in this neighborhood—no reason other than his former girlfriend.

She was about to get out so she could creep a little closer. If she could snap a picture of them together, it could possibly help her in the future. She was hoping to slip through the gate into Cece's backyard and get a picture through a window using her zoom lens. But her phone rang, causing her to hesitate just as she was reaching for the door latch.

It was Gia.

Margot almost sent the call to voicemail. But she was nearly an hour late arriving at their parents' house for lunch. If she didn't give them an excuse soon, it wouldn't be easy to justify why she hadn't been courteous enough to check in.

"Hey, sorry I'm late." She sounded winded. Her heart had been pounding since she left Sheldon's office. But that was okay. She knew she probably came off as rushed, which was what she wanted. "I've had so many errands. The line was *really* long at the bank."

"Food's growing cold," Gia complained. "And Mom's tired. She needs to eat before her nap."

"I'm sorry, but I'm still fifteen or twenty minutes away. Why don't you eat without me? I'll get there as soon as possible and help with the dishes and do laundry. I'll even clean the bathrooms or whatever you need."

"You're offering to clean the bathrooms when you have me on the hook to do it?"

She'd say anything to make Gia happy so she could focus on what she was doing. "I'm the one who's late. Consider it my peace offering."

"Fine. You're forgiven. But hurry. Dad's been caught up at work, and Mom sleeps most of the time. I'm getting lonely and bored in this town, and you need me to stay."

"I do," she admitted. "Just...hang on. I'm coming."

As she disconnected, she started to get out again but looked up in time to see Sheldon emerge from Cece's house and jog across the street on a diagonal to his truck.

He was leaving? Already? Depending on which direction he decided to go, he could pass right by her...

"Shit," she muttered, but she knew she'd only draw more attention if she tried to drive away. All she could do was duck and hope he didn't notice their Subaru. A lot of people had gray Subarus, but—

Fortunately, she didn't hear his motor drawing closer, and when she dared to peek over the dashboard, he was no longer there. He must've whipped around and gone the other direction.

She was just pressing a hand to her heart, trying to settle her pulse, when her phone went off.

Assuming it was Gia calling to nag her again, she muttered, "I'm coming." But it was Sheldon.

She stared at his picture on her screen, wondering what she should do. If he'd seen her, he'd be banging on her door— wouldn't he?

Taking a deep breath, she squeezed her eyes closed and let her head fall back on the seat as she answered. "Hello?"

"Where are you?" he demanded.

Opening her eyes, she sat up straight. "I—I'm on my way to my folks'."

"With my lunch? I got a text from Racine a few minutes ago saying you'd stopped by the office."

That was why he'd left Cece's in such a hurry. Now it made sense. "I thought you might want it, but she said you were already out to lunch, and I promised my family I'd be over, so..."

"We must've passed each other," he said. "I just went home to pick it up."

What a liar! There was no way he'd had time to do that. He'd peeled away from the curb and called her almost immediately. "Why didn't you text me?" she asked.

"Why didn't you text *me*?" he countered.

"I assumed you were taken care of."

"Well, I'm not. Can you come back?"

She didn't want to see him. She was still trying to determine how his affair might figure into her future plans. Was there any chance he'd let her go? That she *wouldn't* have to take the boys and try to make a new life somewhere else, completely on her own? "Sheldon?"

The change in her tone must've alerted him to the fact that she was about to ask a serious question, because he sounded somewhat defensive when he said, "What?"

"If...if you'd rather be with Cece, I'll give you a divorce. You can have the house and the business. I would...I would just need a little money to get a new start—until I can find a job. That's all."

Silence. She curled her fingernails into the palm of her free hand, hoping and praying that Cece—and not some desperate attempt to go into hiding—would prove to be her salvation.

"We could share custody of the boys," she added, to make it even more appealing. She didn't want to resort to what she'd planned—not if she could do it in a way that would enable her to stay in the community with her family and friends.

"Are you telling me you don't love me anymore?" he asked. "That you could walk away from me that easily?"

What did love have to do with their marriage? He hadn't loved her for years; he treated her as though she was the dirt under his feet. "I'm saying I want you to be happy," she replied, trying to be as diplomatic as possible. "And if *I* can't make you happy, maybe she can."

She held her breath. If she said the wrong thing, he could suddenly decide to call off his trip to go to marriage counseling or do something else, and she was well beyond trying to save what they'd once had. In her view, their marriage had already burned to the ground.

"I'm happy with you," he insisted. "I would never break up our family. You know how I feel about divorce, what it does to the children. Marriage is forever. That's how I've always viewed it."

Each thump of her heart seemed deafening. *Forever*, he'd said—and she didn't feel as though she could survive another day! "What about Cece?"

"I told you. Cece and I are just friends."

In other words, he intended to keep Margot pinned under his thumb, taking care of his house, his meals and his kids, while he had an exciting sexual affair with his former girlfriend. He didn't think he should have to choose between them; he believed he should have it all.

"Okay."

He didn't speak right away. She got the impression her response—that she'd given in so easily—had shocked him. "Do you want to go to lunch and talk about it?"

"Not today," she said. "My family's expecting me. I'm sitting in their driveway right now." She wasn't at the house quite yet, but she wanted to make him believe she was so he wouldn't press her to meet him.

"Our marriage doesn't mean that much to you?"

How many times had she asked him the same question? But when she'd asked, she'd been sincere, hadn't been trying to manipulate him. "Of course it does," she said, scrambling to add some emotion to her voice even though she no longer felt anything. She had to hold her world together for just a little while longer—even though it felt like her life was crumbling through her fingers.

"We'll talk about it tonight," he said. "And don't you dare tell your folks or anyone else that I'm having an affair," he added, "because I'm not."

The sight of him emerging from Cece's house just a few minutes earlier played in her mind like a video. "I would never do that."

"You would if you thought you could get away with it."

The things she'd said before—a couple of comments to his mother—were desperate attempts to get some help with him. She'd thought if anyone could encourage him to be a good husband, it would be the woman who'd raised him. But in Peggy's eyes, Sheldon could do no wrong. So all she'd done was tell him what Margot had said.

"I have to go," she said and meant more than just getting off the phone. The brief flicker of hope she'd felt when she saw his truck parked near Cece's was gone. Once again, she saw her options dwindle down to one—disappearing while he was out of town. The only way to protect herself and be sure he wouldn't take her children away from her was to take them away from him first.

When her phone rang, Gia was shocked to see that Ruth was trying to reach her and immediately thought of Cormac. She was dying to tell both Ruth and Sammie that even Mr. Hart's son believed her now, but she hated the idea of him suffering a huge backlash just because he was finally willing to open his heart and his mind to her side of the story.

Assuming Ruth was calling to say she wouldn't be attending the Banned Books Club reunion, after all, Gia started toward the back door. She'd just made vegetarian chili with corn bread and served a bowl to her mother and sister for lunch, so they were within hearing distance, and Gia didn't want them listening to the conversation. She'd rather not have either one of them pick up on the fact that her friends were deserting her.

Telling them she'd be back in a minute, she walked out by the pool. "Hello?"

"Gia, it's Ruth."

Gia already knew that, of course. But she supposed it was a place to start. "What's going on?"

"Listen, we've been friends for so long. I—I don't want Edith or Louisa to come between us. So… I'm sorry I said what I did at the restaurant."

"I appreciate the apology, Ruth, but if you think I'd destroy a man's life over a grade—even at seventeen—you can't hold too high an opinion of me, so I'm not convinced we could ever be friends again."

Ruth seemed taken aback that she wouldn't simply accept the apology. "Well, I just think… I think no matter who was to blame, what happened was unfortunate. I'd rather not even form an opinion on it."

She was still trying to maintain a connection to both sides; her words made that clear. "Meaning you don't know who to believe."

"Meaning I don't care either way, G. If Mr. Hart did what you said, he's been punished, okay?"

Gia walked to the fence and peered over. She assumed Cormac was at the clinic, but she couldn't help looking at his house periodically during the day. She was so stunned by what'd happened there and the sudden shift in her feelings toward him—resentment to relief in minutes. "Because you think there's a chance I'm lying, and I'm not! How would you feel if you were in my shoes?"

"I have no doubt I'd feel terrible. But have some sympathy

for the rest of us. We weren't there that night, G. We have two people we care about—in my case, you and Louisa—telling us very different stories. I think you're expecting too much if you think we should base a decision like that on who we love the most. Isn't that what you're accusing Edith, Louisa and Cormac of doing? Being blind to the truth because of their love for their father?"

She had a point, although Cormac was no longer doing that. Maybe she *was* expecting too much of her friends, especially when they had to continue living in Wakefield and bump into the Harts at spin class and other places in town after she returned to Coeur d'Alene. "Fine," she said. "We'll leave it in the past."

"Thank you. I'm sorry that...that I can't give you more support."

She could live without Ruth's belief and trust, she told herself. She was strong enough on her own. She just needed to be able to get along with everyone while she was here; she was all for anything that made that easier. "No problem."

"I appreciate you trying to understand. But...that isn't the only reason I called."

Gia rolled her eyes. "Let me guess, you can't make the Banned Books Club reunion..."

This response met with silence. Then Ruth said, "I'm still coming to the reunion, G."

"Won't you have to answer to Edith at spin class if you do?"

"I'm trying to be fair to both sides," she reiterated.

Maybe she was. But Gia knew it was going to cost her. She no longer felt as close to Ruth as she did before, and if Ruth attended the reunion and continued their friendship, Edith would no doubt feel the same way. It was sad that what'd happened so long ago still had such an impact on the present. The ripples seemed to go on and on, which was exactly the reason Gia had been loath to return. "Got it. Okay. Sorry. So...what's the other reason you called?"

"I hate to tell you this when you're already going through so much, but...I think your sister's husband is having an affair."

Gia had heard the same thing from her own mother. Tongues had to be wagging all over town for news of it to have reached Ruth. She was hoping for an opportunity to broach the subject with her sister, but so far, they'd just been visiting with Ida and having lunch.

Hoping for more information, Gia acted surprised. "You think that idiot's cheating?"

"That's what I hear."

"With whom?"

"Cecelia Sonderman."

The same name her mother had given her, of course.

"He used to date her when we were in high school, remember?" Ruth went on. "She married some dude who was a friend of her cousin's. They moved to Chicago, where he's from, but have since divorced, and now she's back with her son, Ashton, who's in sixth grade at Wakefield Elementary."

Where Ruth taught third grade... "Do you have any idea what caused the divorce?"

"Apparently, Ashton's father decided he'd rather travel the world than support a family. He's in Thailand or Tibet or somewhere else far away. That's what Linda Pugh, Ashton's teacher, told me. She also said he came to school in a Wakefield Trucking cap the other day."

"That doesn't mean he got the hat from Sheldon. At least twenty people work for Wakefield Trucking—"

"But none of them have been seen in the car with Cece when she comes to pick up her son from school. He has."

Gia tightened her grip on the phone. Sheldon had so little respect for Margot he'd make it that blatant? His own boys went to Wakefield Elementary! "How often has that happened?"

"More than once, I take it. He thinks he's being cautious by having her park a block away and staying in the car, but Linda is good friends with another parent who lives nearby. Maxine McConkie has seen him twice and mentioned it to Linda."

Gia kneaded her forehead as she tried to decide what she should do. Did Margot know? Was she ignoring it, hoping it was only a brief affair that would go away on its own when Sheldon grew bored? If so, where was her self-respect? Or was Sheldon's involvement with Cece what Margot was about to confide the other night? "I'm surprised Ashton isn't the one talking about it. If he's in sixth grade, he's got to be…what… eleven? That's old enough to know something's going on."

"Ashton's autistic, only spends one day a week in Linda's class. The rest of the time he's in special ed."

"I see. So as long as they fool the neighbors, they don't have to worry about her son."

"Exactly."

Gia cursed under her breath. No wonder Margot had wanted her to come home and take care of Ida. She was dealing with some serious issues in her own life.

But then…why was she always defending Sheldon? Insisting he was wonderful? "Thanks for telling me," she said to Ruth.

"You bet. I'm sorry to be the bearer of bad news."

"I'd rather know the truth."

"Me, too. So what are you going to do? Are you going to tell Margot?"

Gia wanted to confront Sheldon, blast him for being the douchebag she'd assumed he was when he married Margot. He'd just proven her right. Maybe she'd tell him that eventually. But first, she needed to talk to her sister.

14

Normally, Cormac loved his work. By Friday, he found himself just going through the motions while trying to decide what he should do now that he felt it was Gia who'd been telling the truth about what'd happened in high school. Since he'd joined his mother's side, the family was split down the middle. His sisters would be upset that he'd defected—Louisa was already upset with his earlier uncertainty—and he didn't want to put them through any more grief.

But he also felt bad that his mother had been the only outlier for so long. That couldn't have been easy on her, especially with the public humiliation and embarrassment she'd suffered, along with the betrayal. No wonder it'd taken forever for her to start dating. Right after the divorce, she'd been busy trying to earn a living so she could finish raising her children, which she'd had to do without much help from Evan, who'd lost his job and couldn't seem to get back on his feet. Then she'd had two weddings to pay for—alone—and grandchildren to welcome. After what she'd been through, she probably had deepseated trust issues when it came to men.

Over the years, Cormac had taken his mother's strength for

granted, he realized. He'd even blamed her, on occasion, for breaking up their family right when her husband needed her most. Louisa and Edith had said things that led Cormac to believe they'd done the same.

But now he saw the situation in a whole new light and understood how hard it must've been for her. She hadn't even been able to rally her kids around her! They'd all chosen to believe their father, despite the fact that *she* was the only one who was still coming through for them.

Shoving what remained of his sandwich to the side—he was eating in his office so he could be alone, since Louisa still wasn't really talking to him—Cormac rubbed his temples. He'd not only been unfair to Gia, he'd been unfair to Sharon. His mother could've tried to enlist his support long ago by sharing what she'd told him this morning, of course. Maybe he would've listened and changed his mind much earlier.

But there was an equal chance it wouldn't have done any good. Had she tried to persuade him and failed, it would only have created a greater division between them, which was why he wasn't prepared to take what she'd told him to his sisters. Sharon didn't actually *know* if Evan was guilty; he'd never admitted anything. Cormac only believed the way she did because he was finally open to the other side. His sisters would have to be of a similar mind, and he wasn't convinced they'd ever get there.

He glanced at the clock. His next appointment was due in ten minutes.

Figuring he might as well get on with his day, he started to gather up what was left of his lunch so he could return it to the small fridge in the breakroom when his phone went off.

Tyler Jenkins, an old friend he'd known since elementary school, was trying to reach him. They'd been talking about setting a date to go fishing, but they'd both been too busy to make it happen.

"Hello?"

"Hey, what's up?"

Cormac wiped the crumbs from his desk. "The usual. Taking care of the dogs, cats and horses in the area—and maybe a few other animals. What about you?"

"Oh, man, the kids have been sick. Some sort of flu. What a nightmare."

"I'm sorry to hear that. I hope they get well soon."

"Fortunately, I think we've seen the worst of it."

"Good. You still want to go fishing?"

A child started to cry in the background. "I'd love to go somewhere, *anywhere*—even if it's just grabbing a drink. But I don't know when I'll be able to do it. At the moment, I'm not only dealing with sick kids, I'm building a new house while juggling two remodels."

Tyler was a general contractor, so he was probably racing to get the new house roofed before the weather could turn ugly. "Too much work is better than too little, I guess," Cormac reminded him.

"Don't try to be positive. I'm complaining right now."

"Sorry." Cormac laughed. "Then...poor you."

"That was weak, dude. Fortunately, gaining your sympathy isn't why I called. You've probably heard that Gia's back in town..."

"Of course."

"Figured word would spread quickly."

"How'd you find out?"

"She went through Mel's checkout line the other day."

Tyler's wife worked at Higgleston's. She was the same age as Edith and had been over at the house quite a bit when they were growing up, so Cormac had known her fairly well even before she married Tyler. He doubted Gia would've had any reason to associate with her, though. She probably didn't even realize the woman running the register at the grocery store knew who she was. "She came back to be with her mother, who's dying of cancer," Cormac told him. "Do you know Ida or Leo?"

"No. I never even knew Gia very well. But I got invited to the Banned Books Club reunion."

That must've been a mistake. He couldn't imagine Gia meant to invite him. She knew he and Tyler were friends. "You did? Are you going?"

"Hell, no. I only joined because you twisted my arm."

Cormac hadn't wanted to stand out too much. There hadn't been many boys in the club and even fewer athletes, so he'd talked Tyler into joining with him.

"We were only in it for the girls, remember?" Tyler went on. "You had a thing for Gia until—well, until she did what she did, which is downright evil. I'm guessing you didn't get an invitation, but you're going anyway, right?"

Cormac blinked in surprise. "No. Why would I be going? Like you said, I wasn't invited."

"Well...neither were your brothers-in-law."

"What's that supposed to mean?"

"Dan told me that he and Victor and Louisa and Edith are going to confront Gia. They want to get a retraction out of her at last—in front of everyone."

Cormac came to his feet. "Wait...*what?*"

"You didn't know? They're sick and tired of what their wives have been going through. It's been so long. They figure it's time they did something about it."

"Dan told you this?"

"Yeah. He and I ride dirt bikes together. He asked me if I'd received an invitation to the Banned Books Club meeting."

"And..."

"And when I said I got an email about it, he asked me to forward it to him, so I did. I know how much you want to reach the truth, too. I figured you'd be going with them."

"Oh, my God..."

"What?" he said, obviously confused.

"They're planning to gang up on her? Four against one?"

"I guess you could say that," Tyler said, suddenly sounding unsure. "They want to make her fess up at last."

"What if she's not lying, Tyler?"

He didn't seem to know how to respond. "I didn't even consider that because...well, we know she *is* lying, right? And she's never been held accountable for it."

Cormac dropped his head back to stare up at the ceiling. What was he going to do? He had to stop this before it turned into a train wreck. "When's the meeting?"

"Tomorrow night."

"Where? Can you forward me that email?"

"I can if you want, but..."

A sour-faced Louisa stuck her head into the room. "Cormac, your one o'clock is here," she said curtly before immediately closing the door.

"I have to go," he told Tyler. "Just...send it to me."

"Is everything okay?" he asked. "I thought you'd be happy that you finally have the chance to—"

"To what?" he broke in. "Hurt her even more?"

"Dude!" he said. "I thought *she* was the one who hurt *you!*"

The door opened again. "Cormac, are you coming?" Louisa asked. "We can't get behind. Maybe you don't care what time you get home, but *I* have a family."

"I'm coming," Cormac told her and said to Tyler, "I'll have to talk to you later."

Because she hadn't wanted to confront Margot when Ida was around, Gia waited until Margot had left and Ida had gone into the bedroom for a nap. Then she tried to call, but Margot didn't answer, and she didn't call back. It was after three o'clock before Gia was able to reach her.

"Why haven't you been picking up?" she asked when her sister finally said hello. "I've called at least six times."

"I was volunteering in Matthew's class and didn't have my

phone on me. Why? What's the emergency?" Her voice grew tense, worried. "It isn't Mom, is it?"

"No. Mom's been resting peacefully. We're planning to watch an old movie this evening."

"That's what you said at lunch. So why would you call me six times when I was just there? Don't tell me you're *that* bored."

She hadn't been bored today; she'd been agitated, worried and angry. When she couldn't reach Margot, it'd been all she could do not to call Sheldon and give him a piece of her mind. "Ruth called earlier."

"So? What'd she want?"

Now that she had her sister on the phone, Gia wasn't quite sure how to approach the fact that everyone believed Sheldon was cheating with his ex-girlfriend. "She's...concerned about you."

The tension returned to Margot's voice. "Why would she be concerned about *me*?"

"Because of Cece."

Silence.

"Margot? Do you know that Sheldon and Cece have been seen together around town several times?"

"They're just friends, G."

There was no shock or surprise, which took Gia aback. "Friends? Margot, sometimes he's with her when she picks up her son from school!"

"You would do that with a friend."

Shocked, Gia began to pace in the kitchen. "In the middle of the day? When he's supposed to be at work? He doesn't even help out with his own kids!"

"That's not true. He...he provides for all of us."

"He does what he wants to do and grudgingly pays the bills so you'll continue to serve him. But that's beside the point. What is he doing hanging out with his ex-girlfriend?"

"There's nothing going on, G."

"Nothing going on," she repeated. "You're letting this asshole betray you and make a fool of you in front of everyone you know, and you won't stand up to him or do anything about it? What's wrong with you?"

"My life is exactly how I want it," she insisted. "It's fine. Especially now that you're here to help with Mom. That's what I needed. That was...crucial."

Gia found this an odd choice of words. "To..."

"What do you mean?"

"What is it crucial to?"

"My peace of mind, okay?"

Gia shook her head. Clearly, there was something going on that wasn't quite right. "You were about to tell me something the other night before that caveman you're married to so rudely interrupted and ordered you to bed. What was it?"

"I don't remember," she said. "And I can't talk right now. The bell just rang. I have to get Greydon from class."

"If you won't handle it, I'll have to say something to Sheldon, Margot. You've put up with a lot. The least he can do is remain faithful."

"Don't say anything to him!" she said. "Please! I'll call you tomorrow after Sheldon leaves on his hunting trip. We can discuss it then."

Gia pivoted at the stove and started back across the kitchen. Having Sheldon in Utah for a week might give her the chance to make some inroads with her sister, get Margot to see how unfairly she was being treated and make her demand more. "Fine. Okay. We'll talk then."

Margot disconnected without a goodbye.

Cormac had almost forgotten that he had plans for Friday night. A patient who had a single niece had set him up on a blind date. Amy Floccari was a nurse, like his mother, who'd just moved to the area and worked at the same regional hospital. He'd seen a picture of her—and she was just as pretty in person—but he was so preoccupied when he took her to dinner that he couldn't imagine he was very good company. He kept checking his phone, wondering if one of his sisters or their husbands would contact him to tell him they were planning on showing up, uninvited, to the Banned Books Club meeting tomorrow night.

But that message never came. When he dropped off Amy where she was staying, he hadn't heard from anyone, and it was getting late enough that he could only assume he wouldn't. No doubt Louisa had mentioned his sudden change of heart, so they weren't including him. Now he didn't know whether he should warn Gia, which *would* really seem like a betrayal of his family, or try to convince his sisters and their husbands not to follow through.

Talking to his sisters seemed the better course—the more conscionable course given his sudden reversal—and since he knew Louisa was mad at him, he tried Edith. She didn't answer, but before he could call Louisa, Edith called him back.

He hit the talk button as he was pulling into his garage. "Hello?"

"You called?"

"Yeah, I wanted to talk to you."

"About what?"

"Tomorrow night."

The slight hesitation that followed his response told him she was surprised he knew they had something planned. "What about it?"

He could sense her defensiveness and it concerned him. He could almost see her walling him out, and he needed her to be receptive if he was going to derail his family's attack. "There's no way any of us should show up at that meeting, Edith." Even though he'd actually been invited. He'd found the email when he checked his inbox at lunch today.

"It's at a public place, Cormac. We have as much right to be there as Gia does."

"It's a restaurant, and I'm sure the staff, not to mention the people who'll be dining there, won't appreciate a screaming match. Think, for a second, about how tomorrow could go down."

"She won't be able to say or do anything. She's been gone for so long, everyone there will know us better than they do her. It's time she got the reaction she deserves—instead of an outpouring of sympathy. The fact that she doesn't care about what she's destroyed makes me *so* angry."

"She cares, Edith."

"How do *you* know?"

Because of the way she'd acted when she was at his house, for one. She hadn't been gleeful or smug; she'd been afraid to trust him. If she were manipulating everyone, he would've gotten an entirely different vibe. At least, that was his take on it. And then she'd invited him to her meeting after. He was sure that was just a gesture of goodwill, but it was one she didn't have to make. "Dad already had his day in court."

"That doesn't mean the judge got it right. It's time we have *our* day."

"Edith—"

"Stop! I know where this is coming from. Louisa told me you're growing sympathetic to her. She said you've always had a thing for her."

"That's not true," he said. Then he realized it wasn't that far off base. "Well, I mean… I wanted to date her in high school. But that's not what's informing this decision. Until recently, I was as angry as you are."

"So what's changed?"

"I stood back and started looking at the situation more objectively—taking in how Dad's turned out, what Mom did and how she feels about what happened, what Gia's done since then and how she acts these days. If she was lying, I feel like she would've admitted it by now."

"You don't know that."

"What would be stopping her?"

"The hate she'd receive for lying about something like that in the first place!"

Because of what their father had done, she'd had to see a therapist. He doubted she would've thought to say something like that if she'd been lying. And there were so many other little things. The problem was they were subtle. Nothing he felt would convince his sisters. "Fine. If you want to approach her, do it privately. But don't gang up on her in public."

"We'll take that under advisement."

It sounded more like she was flipping him off than listening to what he'd said. "Edith—"

"You've said your piece," she interrupted, cutting him off again. "We'll either take your advice or we won't. But that's our decision. You may be our big brother, but you don't get to tell us what to do. Not anymore."

Cormac sighed as she gave him a curt goodbye and disconnected. Louisa and Edith were all worked up—too worked up to listen. And their husbands were standing behind them, supporting them in this fool's errand. He could only hope that once Edith calmed down and had a chance to think about what he'd told her, she'd change her mind, especially because he tried calling Louisa next, and she wouldn't even pick up.

15

Sheldon was leaving, after all. He'd pretended—until the very last minute—that he might not go. He liked keeping her unsettled and off-balance. But he'd really had her going this time. Margot had been afraid he was seriously considering missing the trip, not because he was worried about letting her spend time with Gia, as he claimed, but because he was so caught up in his clandestine relationship with Cece.

In the end, his friends had prevailed upon him not to cancel—they had their lodgings and everything else in place—and Margot had acted disappointed by the fact that he wouldn't be around to "support" her while she was "going through so much with her mother." That made him angry, of course. *It's just one week, Margot—for Chrissake! Why do you have to make me feel guilty about it?*

At least he didn't seem to realize how she really felt.

While he loaded the truck, she made chicken salad sandwiches for him and his buddies and cut vegetables for the ranch dip she'd made last night. It felt like she'd run the gauntlet to get to this point, as though she was nearing some sort of finish line. And yet...this was just the beginning. What happened from here would be anyone's guess—where she'd end up, if she'd be able to get a job, whether Sheldon would come after her and what she'd do if he did. He was taking the shotgun with him, so if she didn't take the Glock, and he ever found her and got violent with her, she'd only have pepper spray with which to protect herself.

But she didn't want to have a handgun around the boys. She'd have to make do with less, even though she hadn't even purchased the pepper spray yet. Sheldon often complained about what she was spending on basic household items and went over the receipts. She didn't want a purchase like that one raising a red flag. From what she'd heard, it was widely available; she figured she'd just get some at one of her first stops. But when she imagined his rage once he realized she'd left him and taken the boys—not to mention the fact that she was about to drain their joint checking and savings accounts to be able to survive until she could establish an income—she didn't feel pepper spray would be enough.

She could only hope he'd never find her...

"Mom, can we go to the park today?"

It was still very early, barely six o'clock, but when she glanced over her shoulder, she saw her oldest standing in the doorway, rubbing his eyes. All the commotion of Sheldon trying to get off on the trip must've awakened him. "It's Saturday, so you don't have school," she replied. "I don't see why not."

She'd packed some of the items and clothing she felt they'd need and stored it under the house, filling boxes that'd once held holiday decorations—after secretly throwing away the decorations, bit by bit, in the school dumpster. She knew Sheldon would never go near that section of their storage. He was an absolute Scrooge when it came to Christmas. She could barely get him to help her drag out the tree. And once he did, she had to decorate it by herself—until the last couple of years, when the boys were finally old enough to help with the lower branches.

As soon as Sheldon left, she was going to grab those boxes, throw them in her Subaru and take off herself. She wouldn't waste a single minute. She wished she could stop and say a final farewell to her family, especially her dear mother. Her heart ached at being unable to do that. But she knew she'd break down if she did. Or Gia would start in on her about Sheldon and the rumors of his affair with Cece. She didn't have time for any of that. She had to think about her children, put them first, and get out while she could.

"Now?" Matthew asked excitedly.

She chuckled. "It's too early for the park, honey. I'm going to help your father get on the road. Then I'll make you some breakfast. Why don't you watch a few cartoons while I finish up in here?" She figured she could make good on her park promise by pulling over somewhere once she felt they were far enough away. She'd been studying maps she'd taken from the closet in her mother's house; she didn't dare search the internet for fear Sheldon would be able to bring up her browsing history. The last thing she needed was to create a trail of breadcrumbs leading right to her. She was going to leave her cell phone behind with the computer. She'd seen too many true crime shows where a victim or suspect could be traced using cell towers.

"I think that's it," Sheldon announced, coming up behind Matthew.

Matthew craned his neck to look up at his father. "Are you leaving, Daddy?"

"Yep."

"Can I go with you?"

Margot knew Sheldon wouldn't take him, but if he did... She couldn't even consider that.

"You're not old enough. I'll take you when you're fourteen or fifteen."

"Go turn on the TV," she told him. "I'm about finished with Daddy's lunch. I'll start on your breakfast next."

As Matthew slipped past him to go to the living room, Sheldon came to the counter and snagged half a sandwich before she could put it in a baggie. "Are you hungry?" she asked. "I thought you said you had cereal."

Stuffing most of the sandwich into his mouth, he talked around it. "I did, but there's no reason I can't have this, too."

As she watched him chew, she thought about having shared almost fifteen years of her life with him. She'd borne his children. She should feel more of a sense of loss... But there were only nerves, the butterflies in her stomach that made it so difficult to eat. She was going to turn her whole life upside down, do something he'd never expect from her.

"Here you go," she said when she'd packed the rest of the food in a cooler. "I cut up some apples, too."

"I doubt anyone will want an apple."

She drew a deep, steadying breath. "You can leave them here, if you want. I'll feed them to the kids."

"Naw," he said with a shrug. "I'll take them just in case."

There was no gratitude, just entitlement. But this would be the end of it, she promised herself. "Okay." She lifted the cooler for him. "Have a good time."

He gazed down at her. "What? No goodbye kiss?"

Unless he wanted sex, he'd pretty much quit touching her. He'd never been a particularly demonstrative person, but even the small amount of affection she'd been clinging to early on was nearly nonexistent these days. "Oh, of course."

She rose up on tiptoe, but he held her off. "What's going on with you?"

Her heart leaped into her throat as she dropped her arms instead of putting them around him. "What do you mean?"

"You're acting weird—remote, like a fucking robot."

"I—I'm going through a hard time with...with my mother," she stammered. "I'm just...trying to keep functioning."

He squinted slightly as he stared down at her. "And that business about Cece? Asking me if I'd rather be married to her?"

She focused on her mother, on the fact that she'd very likely never see Ida again, which made it easy to conjure up tears. They were already just below the surface today. "I thought... I thought you didn't love me anymore."

He shocked her by pulling her into his arms and resting his chin on her head. "Of course I still love you. I'd never give up on us. It's *you* giving up that I sometimes worry about."

The lump in her throat grew so big she couldn't speak. She *had* given up; she'd given up months ago. But that didn't mean she didn't mourn the loss of what they could've had—and had almost achieved in the early years.

After a few moments, he held her away from him so he could look into her face. "Are you going to be okay while I'm gone?"

A tear slid down her cheek, and he actually smiled at her as he wiped it away. "Everything's going to be okay. You'll see."

She nodded. Then he grabbed the cooler and carried it out.

She stood in the kitchen, listening to his truck as he pulled out of the drive and headed down the street. Even after the sound had grown so dim she couldn't hear it anymore—so she knew he was gone—she felt frightened, unsteady. Once she left, there'd be no coming back. Was she equal to the challenge of all that lay ahead?

It didn't feel like it. But that was why she had to go now. In a week, a month, a year there might not be enough of the old Margot left.

Wiping the tears that were still streaming down her face, she called out to Matthew. "Matthew! Go wake your brother. You two need to get dressed right away."

He met her as she was coming out of the kitchen, on her way to throw their clothes and toiletries into suitcases and gather the extra bedding, pots and pans, plates, silverware, towels and even toilet paper she'd hidden in storage.

He gave her a funny look when he saw her red-rimmed eyes. "What's wrong, Mommy? Did Daddy make you sad?"

"Yes," she said. "Daddy has made me sad for a very long time."

Stepping forward, he attempted to comfort her by hugging her leg, and she squeezed her eyes closed as she took far more solace from that gesture than he could ever know. "Thank you, baby. Mommy's going to be okay. We're all going to be okay. Run and get dressed."

He pulled away. "Are we going to the park now? What about breakfast?"

"We'll get McDonald's. How's that?"

"Yum!" he cried and ran ahead of her down the hall yelling, "Greydon! Get up! We're going to McDonald's!"

As she heard Greydon's voice and the boys started to get dressed, Margot ran her fingers lightly down the wall—her way of saying goodbye to the house she'd tried so hard to make a home.

Gia grabbed a sweater and helped her mother into it. The rain had stopped, but it was chilly out, and Ida constantly complained of being cold. "How's that?"

"Better," her mother replied.

Ida had just taken a nap. She had to do that often. "Want to watch what Dad's watching in the living room or have me turn on the TV in your bedroom?"

"Neither. Not right now. While I feel strong enough, I'd like to spend an hour working on our genealogy in the office." She started down the hall but turned back. "What time is it?"

"Nearly three," Gia told her.

Her mother frowned. "Margot must be busy with the boys today. I thought once Sheldon left on his hunting trip, she'd be over."

Gia had assumed the same thing. She'd tried calling her sister, but Margot hadn't picked up. "Maybe Sheldon's running late. Or he decided not to go."

"That's possible, I guess. She doesn't generally come over when he's home on the weekends, so that could explain it. He wants...family time."

Or total control, Gia thought.

"But it's weird that she's not answering my calls," her mother continued.

"You've been trying to reach her, too?"

"I have. Three times."

Gia checked the clock again. "I'm sure we'll hear from her before nightfall."

"Maybe you should drive over there..." her mother suggested.

Since Leo was home today, Gia didn't feel quite so tied to the house, and she thought paying Margot a visit might give them a chance to talk privately. "Good idea," she said, but once she reached her sister's house, both Sheldon's truck and Margot's Subaru were gone, and no one answered the door.

She called her mother from her sister's front stoop. "No one's here. I'm guessing Sheldon went hunting, since his truck is gone, and Margot's out grocery shopping or running other errands."

"So why isn't she picking up?"

"Maybe she forgot her phone here at the house."

Her mother seemed to accept that, so after peering through the window to make sure everything was as it should be, Gia drove to Delia's Big Buns on the main drag and ordered a burger. When she was living in Wakefield, half the high school hung out at Delia's, either at lunch, while ditching class, or after the final bell. She'd loved the food and was just unwrapping her favorite menu item—the barbecue bacon cheeseburger—when she happened to glance up and see a man staring at her as he drove slowly past.

That was Mr. Hart, she realized, sitting up straighter. He'd aged, lost some hair and gone gray, but she'd know that face anywhere...

The car behind him honked, wanting him to speed up, so he gave the aging Blazer he was driving some gas. But a few minutes later, he drove by again, going in the opposite direction.

Gia ignored him. He was trying to get a better look at her. Or upset her. Or both. She tried to keep her eyes averted, but before she could even finish her burger, she saw him come by yet again.

Of course this would happen on her first chance to get out of the house...

Shoving the rest of her burger and fries back into the sack, she tossed the food in the wastebasket as she made her way to her father's SUV. She was done letting Evan Hart gawk at her.

Besides, she had to help her parents with dinner and get showered before the Banned Books Club meeting. Since she'd heard from Ruth, she wasn't quite as nervous about attending as she'd been a few days ago, but she still wanted to look her best.

Gia was just climbing into the driver's seat when the vehicle Mr. Hart had been driving turned into the burger joint. A chill ran down her spine the moment she saw him. He wouldn't say anything... Surely, he knew better than to do that.

Stopping immediately behind her, he glared at her via her side mirror.

Incensed that he'd made it impossible for her to leave, Gia got out. "What do you want?" she yelled.

It was cold enough that there weren't many people eating at the outdoor tables, but there were a few. They looked up in surprise, but Gia didn't care. Mr. Hart was obviously trying to intimidate her, and she wasn't going to put up with it. "Well?" she demanded, resting her hands on her hips.

His window slid down. "I want to know how it feels to ruin a man's life," he yelled back at her. "I want to know if you're proud of yourself."

"How dare you!" she said. "*You* ruined your life—and you nearly ruined mine!"

"I'm happy you suffered *some* consequences!"

"You know I'm not lying about that night!"

"Hey!" A mountain of a man stood up from where he'd been eating and motioned for Mr. Hart to move along. "I won't tolerate a man accosting a woman. If you have a legitimate beef with her, you'd better handle it somewhere else, when you're not around me."

Mr. Hart didn't respond to the man directly. He shook his head, said she should be ashamed of herself and drove off.

The man held his soda in one hand as he watched the Blazer go around the drive-through and turn onto the street. "You okay?" he called over to her when Hart was gone.

Initially, Gia thought it might be someone she'd known from high school—someone who understood what was going on. But she was glad, once she had a chance to look more closely, to see that her Good Samaritan was a total stranger. That made things a little simpler. Encountering Mr. Hart had been enough of a blast from the past. "Yeah, I'm fine. Thanks for...thanks for getting rid of him," she said and climbed into her father's SUV as he returned to his meal.

Cormac hadn't been able to reach Louisa or either of his brothers-in-law. They must've decided among themselves that he was now part of the enemy camp and closed ranks. That they would exclude him instead of considering what he had to say stung—and made him angry at the same time. These were his little sisters. Louisa worked for him; he was the reason she had a job that was flexible enough to allow her to take off when she wanted or even bring her kids to the clinic. But she, along with Edith, had fully embraced their father's side of the story for so long they'd indoctrinated their husbands. He was the one who'd changed; he could see why that would upset them.

Finally, an hour before the reunion was supposed to start, Cormac called his father. He wanted to know if Evan was involved, if he knew what was going on and was possibly even behind it. If so, maybe he could get his father to listen to reason and call off the others. Evan had to see how a confrontation, especially a public one, would just dredge it all back up and continue to split loyalties and keep people talking.

When his dad's voicemail came on, Cormac thought maybe Evan wasn't speaking to him, either. But five minutes later, his phone lit up with a picture of his father.

"You called?" Evan said when Cormac answered.

"I did. Are you at work?"

"Not anymore. Just got home."

"You must be feeling better."

"I told you I would be, that you were worried I'd miss more days for nothing. What do you need?"

Cormac sat on the edge of the couch and scratched behind Duke's ears while he talked. "Louisa and Edith and their husbands are going to a reunion Gia planned for the Banned Books Club tonight."

"They are? Why would they go there?"

It didn't seem as if he knew about it. "They plan to confront Gia, to humiliate her in public, I guess, because nothing else will come of it. They haven't told you about this?"

"No. Haven't heard a word about it. But more power to them. It's about time someone stood up for me."

Cormac grimaced at his father's response. "You were a grown man. She was just a girl."

"Which is why all the sympathy went her way. You think that's fair?"

It was more than fair—*if* he'd done it. "I don't think it's a wise idea to start a fight at a restaurant, Dad. I'm hoping you'll call them and get them to change their minds."

"Why would I do that?" he asked.

"Because it's in the past, and we need to let it go! We've been over this."

"It's not in the past for me, especially now that she's in town and everyone's talking about it again and…and looking at me as if their young daughters might be at risk. That's a terrible feeling. You have no idea because you still have a great reputation here in town."

He had a great reputation because he hadn't done anything to sully it.

Dropping his head in his hands, Cormac tried again. "Dad, if they want to talk to her, they need to do it privately. Ganging up on her, especially in public, isn't right."

"She'll be fine. I just saw her in town a couple of hours ago. And you know what she did? She started screaming at me. That was at a restaurant, too. All I was doing was turning in to the drive-through to grab a burger—and she made a big scene. I don't feel sorry for her. She deserves whatever she gets."

Cormac had a hard time picturing the woman who'd come to the house doing what his father had just described. Was it true? He was beginning to doubt everything his father said. "So…you won't step in and stop them?"

"No! I've been miserable for seventeen years. Maybe it's time *she* feels a little pain."

"Dad—"

"You need to call *them*, not me. I'm not getting involved." The line went dead.

"Damn it!" Cormac muttered. Was his father's reaction due to righteous indignation? Or something else?

A snippet of Gia's testimony seventeen years ago came back to him: *He said he held all the power, so no one would believe me if I tried to challenge him.*

But she had challenged him. Did his father want to see Gia punished because she was lying—or because he'd thought he could get away with what he'd done, and she'd fought back and proven him wrong?

★ ★ ★

Gia couldn't help being nervous. She showed up at the restaurant thirty minutes early just so she wouldn't have to walk into the room after it was full. Even then, she wished she'd asked Margot to accompany her. She'd been a lot more confident in her friendships when she'd planned this event, hadn't felt as though familial support would be necessary. The Banned Books Club had lasted when almost nothing else from high school had.

The waitress showed her to the room Sammie had reserved. It had two long tables going down each side, so Gia chose a seat at the far end, where she could watch the door as people arrived. She'd checked in with Ruth and Sammie after she left the drive-through, just to be sure the whole thing was going to come off, and they'd both assured her that there'd been a good response to the email.

We're expecting eighteen people, which is huge, considering some members haven't been active for a long time, Sammie had said, and she was probably right. Coming to the online Christmas party once a year wasn't quite the same thing as being an active ongoing member.

Fortunately, Sammie showed up a few minutes after Gia. Then Ruth came. The others started dribbling in at seven. After her encounter with Mr. Hart, Gia had been tense and uneasy—she hadn't felt like socializing, not in her hometown where opinions of her were so polarized. But she slowly started to unwind and enjoy herself and was talking and laughing as the waitress delivered the food. It wasn't until she was halfway through the meal that she heard a murmur that caused her to look up. Then she saw Louisa and Edith stalk into the room, looking grim and determined, followed by two men she could only assume were their husbands.

16

Cormac could see the Suburban Louisa drove at the edge of the parking lot and hoped he wasn't too late. He'd argued with himself for too long, trying to talk himself out of coming. It was none of his business. He shouldn't get involved. His sisters had a right to their own opinions and could decide for themselves how they wanted to act. It wasn't his job to police them, especially since he still didn't know *for sure* that they were wrong about what had gone down with his father.

But in the end, he couldn't bear the thought of Gia being confronted in public, couldn't allow his sisters to go after the woman he'd seen crying in the backyard. Gia had been through too much already—and she was going through a lot now.

As soon as he could find a spot to leave his truck, he jammed the gearshift into Park, turned off the engine and jumped out, cursing his father as he jogged in for putting him in this untenable situation. Protecting Gia against his own family would cause a rift he'd have to live with long after she was gone. Louisa would probably quit the clinic, which would leave him in the lurch. And if she and Edith got mad enough, it could be quite some time before they were willing to speak to him again.

If he had to bet, he'd say even his mother would advise him not to get involved.

But he hadn't asked his mother for her opinion. Since Louisa and Edith wouldn't listen to him, and his father wouldn't try to stop them, he felt he had no choice.

The hostess at the restaurant looked startled when he threw open the door and marched past her without a word. But he didn't have a second to waste. He was familiar with the restaurant. They hosted parties in the back room, so he knew exactly where to find the Banned Books Club.

Because of his own loose association with the group, and how long it'd been since high school, he was surprised to find so many people there. But Gia had always been popular. For a moment, he thought he should've left it to one of her many friends to stand up for her. There might be a little shouting, then his sisters would leave. No big deal. Gia didn't need him.

He could still get out before anyone saw him...

But what if it *didn't* go down that way? What if no one stood up for her and Gia felt attacked from all sides? What if she was further traumatized and had to go back to therapy? She'd only come to town to say goodbye to her dying mother, for God's sake!

He couldn't let his sisters do what they had planned. So instead of grabbing hold of that final excuse and turning around, as he desperately wanted to, he entered the room just as Louisa was pointing at Gia while yelling at someone else, "I know her mother has cancer! I'm just sorry it isn't her!"

There was a collective gasp. Even Louisa's husband, Victor, turned to gape at her. That was when Cormac's eyes locked onto Gia's face—and he saw the blood drain out of it. "You're a truly nasty person," she said to Louisa, and even though she'd spoken quietly, she'd spoken into absolute silence, so everyone heard it.

Louisa burst into tears but continued to point at Gia while trying to excuse what she'd said. "She destroyed my father's life! She broke up my family! She's been lying all this time! Can you imagine being fourteen years old when a fellow student accuses your father—a respected English teacher—of sexual misconduct? Talk about embarrassment and humiliation! You have no idea!"

Cormac pushed his way through those standing between him and his sisters. "No, Cormac," he heard someone say. An arm even came out to stop him. But he knocked whoever it was away. He wasn't here to gang up on Gia as that person probably thought.

"Louisa, Edith, that's enough," he said. "You don't know what you're talking about. Why do you think Mom divorced Dad? Because she knew things we didn't, right? She had a reason to believe that Gia was telling the truth, and I believe that now, too. I'm only sorry it took me so long to figure it out. If I'd listened sooner, with an open mind and heart, maybe I would've had the chance to convince you that it's Dad who's been lying, and you wouldn't be so set on this stupid confrontation."

"Cormac, you need to stay out of it." Victor came to his wife's defense, but Cormac whipped around to face his brother-in-law and challenge him in return.

"If *you* can get into it, I can. And I don't think coming here was the right thing to do. You need to help me convince your wife to go home."

Louisa had been so distracted by the battle she was waging that it took a second for his presence to register. To him, in this moment, most of the people around them were nameless and faceless, except Gia. Maybe it was the same for his sister, because when she saw him, *really* saw him, the fight seeped out of her like a balloon that'd been filled but not tied. "I can't believe you'd do this," she murmured. "I can't believe you, of all people, would turn on me!"

"I'm not turning on you," he clarified as gently as possible.

"I'm trying to stop you from making a terrible mistake. You're hurting someone who's been hurt enough!"

"And what about me? Haven't *I* been hurt enough?" she demanded, once again finding her full voice, then ran from the room.

Edith looked from their departing sister to the many faces staring back at her to Cormac and started to cry herself. "What have you done?" she said to him and ran after Louisa.

Victor and Dan quickly followed their wives, leaving Cormac facing a roomful of shocked Banned Books Club members and a stunned Gia.

"I'm sorry," he said to everyone at large. "I should've come sooner. Maybe I could've headed them off at the door or something. I was... I don't have a good excuse. But please don't blame my sisters for this. It's my father's fault. *Everything's* his fault."

"So he *did* do it?" someone called out, seeking the confirmation they'd all, no doubt, craved for years.

Cormac was tempted to say he didn't *know*. That was the truth. He hadn't been there that night. But he couldn't equivocate now. He'd only make Gia hate him again—and possibly cause more anger and division—by trying to remain in the middle. "*I* think he did."

"Then you did the right thing," someone else said. But there were obviously those who didn't agree. Ruth Stinson looked as though she'd been struck before she walked out of the room, presumably to see if Louisa and Edith were okay.

Cormac's gaze landed on Gia once more. "I didn't want this to happen," he told her. "Again, I'm sorry." He didn't wait for a response. He'd done all he could. He'd taken a stand—publicly—against his own father and sisters, which, hopefully, had saved Gia the pain she would otherwise have felt. But he'd upset Louisa and Edith. He'd always been close—and united—with his sisters.

But he couldn't see that he'd had any other choice.

★ ★ ★

After she got home from the Banned Books Club meeting, Gia sat out by the pool. The lights were on at Cormac's house and she was hoping he'd come out so she'd have the chance to speak with him. But he didn't. She wondered if he was too busy being harangued—on the phone since he didn't seem to have company—by his sisters, their husbands or his father. His mother, if she'd heard about it, might not be happy with what he'd done, either.

Without him, the Banned Books Club meeting would certainly have gone much worse. There was no telling where the fight the Hart sisters had started would end.

She still couldn't believe he'd shown up and defended *her*. It'd been such a relief just to know that he'd finally realized she was telling the truth; what he'd done tonight was well beyond her expectations. She was grateful to him, of course, but she was worried about the repercussions. What would his father do? What would his sisters do? Would this cause him to be estranged from the other members of his family? And if so, how long would it last? *Years?*

She winced at the thought of that, especially since she wouldn't be in Wakefield for much longer. They were the ones building their lives here.

He probably shouldn't have gone to the restaurant. But she couldn't help admiring the fact that he had. That had taken guts.

She remembered him confronting her the day his father was fired and had to admit he was the type, right or wrong, to stand up for what he believed.

Her phone rang. It was Eric. Soon, he'd be shutting down Backcountry Adventures and heading to Glacier National Park, the trip she'd been looking forward to taking with him but would now have to miss.

"Hey, how's your mom?" he asked when she answered.

Gia glanced at the dark house. Her parents had been asleep

by the time she returned because she and Sammie had gone out for drinks afterward. Ruth had never come back into the room where they were having the reunion and wasn't answering her phone, so Gia had no idea what'd happened to her. "She's fragile but hanging in."

"And your sister? She still glad you're there?"

Mention of Margot reminded Gia that she hadn't heard from her all day. She'd been planning to drive by the house after the party tonight, but then the confrontation with Louisa and Edith had occurred and thrown the rest of the evening off course. By the time she and Sammie were ready to call it a night, she'd been so distracted she hadn't even thought of Margot. It would've been too late to knock on her door, anyway. Maybe Ida had heard from her. "I think so. She's taking some time off and letting me handle things on this end."

"She probably needs the break."

"I should've come sooner," she acknowledged.

"You're there now. Make the most of it, okay?"

She smiled. He was thirty-eight going on fifty-eight. She always told him he was the oldest, wisest soul in the room. "I am, for the most part."

"So...it's not as bad as you anticipated?"

"It's every bit as bad. But..." She stood up to peer over the fence into Cormac's backyard before sitting down again. "There've been some welcome surprises, too."

"I'm happy to hear it. Just wanted to let you know that everything's going well around here. You don't have to worry about the business. We're closing out our biggest season ever. I still wish you could go to Glacier with me, but I'll send you the pictures I take so you can enjoy the sights along with me."

She was afraid that would make her more jealous than happy, but it was such a kind gesture that she couldn't say no. "Thank you. Give my love to Coty and kiss Ingrid for me."

"Coty and Ingrid send their love right back," he said and disconnected.

She checked her watch. It was nearly midnight. But she was tempted to call Margot anyway, just in case she could reach her sister. She wanted to talk to someone who would actually understand the significance of what'd happened tonight. She was still so shocked by Cormac's appearance.

Again, she got up and looked over the fence. He was definitely still awake. She saw him pass in front of the kitchen window, but it looked like he might be shirtless, which meant he was probably preparing for bed.

She told herself to leave him alone—leave the whole thing as it was—but she didn't know if she'd have a better opportunity to thank him and to tell him that she didn't expect him to stand up for her. She actually preferred he didn't so she wouldn't have to worry about the impact on his life. It was enough that he believed her; she didn't want him to go to war with his family.

She went back inside to get the Duke sweatshirt he'd loaned her. He'd put her shirt on the fence last night, but she'd been hanging on to his, secretly hoping for the chance to speak with him again. Now she was glad she'd held off returning it for a day or two. She could go to his place under the guise of returning it and thank him for what he'd done tonight at the same time.

The temperature seemed a lot colder once she stepped back outside. She knew she probably shouldn't go over so late—he certainly wouldn't be expecting company. But she knew she wouldn't sleep well if she didn't get the chance to say what was on her mind.

Once she let herself through the gate and walked around to his front door, she knocked softly and heard his dog bark as she shifted nervously on her feet.

A curtain moved; he was looking out at her. She dug her fingernails into her palms because she felt awkward. She couldn't imagine he'd be happy to see her.

He held his dog back while opening the door. "Hey."

She cleared her throat. "Sorry to bother you so late, but... Well, the light was on..."

"I'm up. No problem. Would you like to come in?"

She almost refused. She felt terrible barging in on him so late. But he was having to hang on to his dog, and she felt what she had to say might be better received if he didn't have to worry about that. "Sure. For a sec."

"Duke," he said to his dog as he encouraged him to move out of the way so she could get inside. Then he closed the door and straightened while his rottweiler smelled her feet and legs.

"This has been washed," she said, handing him his sweatshirt. "Thank you for letting me use it."

"No problem. I left your shirt on the fence last night. I assume you got it."

"I did."

"I'm sorry about what happened at the restaurant earlier. Once I became aware that Edith and Louisa were planning to crash the reunion, I did what I could to talk them out of it. But they wouldn't listen to me. Showing up probably made an even bigger scene, though. I just...didn't know what else to do."

He could've let it play out. Instead, he'd come to stop his sisters, despite what it would cost him on a personal level. "What you did was...courageous. I'm grateful. But I also want to make it clear that you should never do that sort of thing again."

He blinked in apparent surprise. "Why not?"

"Because I don't want to leave you in a worse place than you were when I came home. I'll be in town only until... Well, you *live* in Wakefield, are building a life and a business here. It'd be better for me to just weather the storm, you know? I'd rather not get in the way of your relationships, especially with your family."

He looked slightly baffled. "Even with my father?"

"Of course. It was never my intent to strip him of every-thing he had. I just... I wanted to get out of his class. I couldn't be comfortable there after...after what he did. And it was only fair that I get the grade I deserved on that paper so I could go to college."

"But you dropped out, anyway."

"I was too messed up at that time. I couldn't function like the other students."

He frowned but she continued before he could comment.

"It wasn't as if I had a big vendetta or something against your father. People make mistakes."

"Let me get this straight." Cormac scratched the back of his neck. "You're worried about what will happen to *me* in all this?"

"I know what it feels like to be the person your sisters hate," she said with a laugh. "I wouldn't wish that on anyone."

She was hoping he'd laugh with her and let it go at that. She'd delivered her message, told him to stay out of whatever happened so he wouldn't get hurt and returned the sweatshirt he'd loaned her. Her job here was done. But he didn't thank her for coming by and move to open the door. He continued to look at her as though he could see right through her.

"What is it?" she asked, growing self-conscious again.

"What my father did was terrible, Gia. We should've stood behind you."

She waved a hand. "That was a long time ago. I just want to forget and move on...if he'll let me."

"If he'll let you?" he echoed.

"He's so afraid I'll destroy the cover he's created that he's trying to make things difficult."

"Now? How's he making things difficult *now*?"

She'd made a mistake speaking in the present tense. She didn't want to tell him about the incident at Delia's Big Buns, didn't want to make him feel as though he had to continue to protect her. "I meant...in the past."

Hoping to get out of the house before she could blow it even more, she turned to go but he caught her arm. "You haven't heard from him since you came back to town, have you?"

"No," she said immediately but spoke with a little too much force and couldn't meet his eyes. She hated to lie to Cormac, of all people. She'd been called a liar by Mr. Hart and certain members of his family for so long, she understood the value of credibility.

His eyebrows knitted. "What'd he do?"

When she didn't answer, he gave her arm a slight squeeze. "Gia, you're not nearly as good a liar as I once gave you credit for."

Just the word *liar* made her flinch—and tell the truth. "He... he saw me at Big Buns earlier today and kept driving past— back and forth, back and forth. That would've been okay. It's a free country, after all. But he pulled in before I could pack up and leave. Blocked me in, actually, rolled down his window and started yelling at me in front of the other people who were eating there."

Cormac's jaw hardened. "What'd he say?"

"The usual."

"He was trying to intimidate you and discredit your side of the story."

"Yes. He feels personally betrayed. He thought he should be able to get away with what he did, that I shouldn't have outed him. Maybe he even believes the punishment was way worse than the crime. And that could be true. How much punishment is enough for something like that? Does anyone really know? The actual encounter didn't last long. From that perspective it seems the punishment might've been too great. But the repercussions have gone on and on, so from *that* perspective... I don't know. All I can tell you is that it was terrible trying to defend myself with him twisting the truth like he did."

Cormac shook his head. "Because this isn't just about what he did. It's about what he did after. And to think I was part of that..."

"You didn't know any better."

"I do now," he said.

"I won't be in town long," she reminded him. "At this point, let's just let it go. Maybe screaming at me while I was there satisfied his anger." She said that but didn't really believe it. Somehow, Mr. Hart had made himself the victim in this situation and still seemed to believe *she'd* wronged *him*.

"He'd better not bother you again," Cormac said. "I won't allow it."

She gave him a pointed look. "We've been over this. You can't get involved."

"But I will," he said.

And he'd proved it tonight.

17

Before she left, Cormac got Gia's number. He wanted to monitor the situation better than he had in the past and knew it would help to be able to reach her even when she wasn't sitting at the pool.

He was tempted to call his father. He didn't care how late it was. Evan was still twisting the truth; he'd said Gia had attacked *him* at the drive-through. Maybe he thought going on the offensive would make him appear innocent—that showing others he still felt strongly enough about his reputation to continue to fight Gia's accusations would finally convince his skeptics.

But he was making Cormac angry. While his trust in his father's side of the story crumbled, his trust in Gia's grew stronger. Her insistence that he stay out of the fight solidified his belief in her basic goodness. If she were the one lying, she'd encourage him to stand up for her. And who better than Evan Hart's own son?

Gia, the true victim in this situation, seemed to care more about what might happen to him as a consequence of getting involved than his own father, who'd bent his ear and complained for close to two decades.

Evan's selfishness was becoming more and more apparent.

Cormac went to the window to see if the light in Gia's room had gone on. He expected her to be getting ready for bed. But when he saw no light, he looked more closely at the pool and spotted her sitting in the hot tub.

He checked his watch. It was nearly one. Even if he called his father, Evan probably wouldn't pick up. Chances were he'd be drunk if he did. But Cormac was too wound up to sleep and saw no point in going to bed only to toss and turn for the next few hours.

With a sigh, he peered out the window again. Then he put on his swim trunks, grabbed a couple of beers and went out the back door and through the gate between the houses.

Gia looked up when she heard him coming.

"Would you mind some company?" he asked, lifting the beers to show he had a peace offering and hesitating politely before approaching her.

"Not at all." Her smile was genuine and natural—and therefore easy to return. It was nice to feel she was receptive to his presence and no longer tensed up or watched him with distrust.

He walked over and handed her one of the beers. "Here you go."

"Thank you." She popped the top and took a long drink.

After opening his own can, he got in and sat opposite her. "Do you always stay up this late?"

"It's an hour earlier in Idaho," she replied with a shrug.

"That's right. But still, it's getting late."

"I've had a lot on my mind since I got here."

"No doubt. I'm sorry about what you're going through with your mom and…and everything else. It also can't be easy to leave your business behind."

The steam was causing water to bead on her face, arms and bare shoulders, making her skin look dewy and moist. Although she had her hair pulled up, small tendrils clung to her neck and forehead. "Fortunately, the business is in good hands. My partner knows what he's doing."

She obviously had a great deal of respect for the man she was in business with. Was there more than business between them? "Are you two...seeing each other?"

She chuckled. "No. Eric's happily married, with a young daughter."

He took a drink of his beer. "If my father hadn't done what he did in high school, do you think you would've settled here like so many of us?"

"There's a good chance of it. When I dropped out of college to head to Alaska, it was sort of a fluke. I'd met some other students who worked on fishing boats there during the summer and made some good money, so I went with them when they left in the spring. I just didn't come back, like they did, in the fall."

"How'd you like it?"

"Loved it. There's no place like Alaska."

"It didn't get lonely—not even during the winter?"

"Not really. At the time, I needed the peace, the quiet, the space. Those years were very therapeutic for me."

"So what took you to Coeur d'Alene?"

She told him how excited she'd been to learn to fly, how her current business partner had once been her flight instructor, how she'd pushed Eric to start a business with her and how they'd ended up in Coeur d'Alene because he'd just met the woman who was now his wife on the internet, and she was from there. "Did you always want to be a veterinarian?" she asked.

"Pretty much," he replied. "I've always loved animals, knew I wanted to contribute to the community in some way. Growing up, the old movies where doctors made house calls made a big impression on me."

"You make house calls?"

"When we're talking about a horse, a cow or a pig, I do," he said with a grin. "And I would do it for any animal, if it became necessary. Do you have any pets?"

"No. I don't want to leave an animal alone in my condo all day while I'm working. I might get a dog at some point, though, if and when I marry and start a family."

"You'd like kids?"

"One day. You?"

"Definitely."

"You'd have to settle down with someone for that," she said wryly.

"I'd be happy to settle down if only I could find the right woman."

Finished with her beer, she set the can aside. "From what I've heard, you have your pick."

He hated the reputation he was getting, wished the people of Wakefield would mind their own business instead of showing so much interest in his love life. "Who told you that?"

"I think it's the general consensus."

"I'm sure you've had plenty to pick from over the years, too, and yet you're still single," he pointed out.

She eyed him through the steam. "I have a hard time falling in love."

Cormac was willing to bet that what she'd been through in high school played a role. During the years when most people fell in love for the first time, she'd probably been too traumatized to experience it. That made him feel even worse about what'd happened. "Look at us," he said, gesturing between them with his can. "Did you ever think we could be friends?"

She tilted her head as she studied him. Then the prettiest smile spread across her face. "Never."

He finished his own beer. "Just goes to show...anything's possible."

Margot peered through a crack in the curtains of the cheap motel room she'd rented in Billings, Montana. What with bathroom breaks, food breaks and a park break so the boys could play for a bit, she'd been on the road for sixteen hours. When she'd first left Wakefield, she'd considered traveling east. There were so many more people on that side of the country. It felt safer somehow, as if she might need that big a melting pot in which to hide.

But that was panic talking. There were plenty of good towns and people in the other direction, too. Thanks to the weather, north wasn't an option, but she could go south…

In the end, she'd decided to go where her heart led her and since she'd always wanted to live on the West Coast, she'd plotted a course through Montana and Idaho to Washington. If she didn't find a place she liked there, she's drive down into Oregon or even California. The coming months were going to be hard enough. Why not trade a cold, snowy winter for a warm one? At least she wouldn't have to shovel the walks.

The back parking lot, which was all she could see from the second-story room, was almost empty. She couldn't say what she was looking for, anyway. She was just checking her car. Besides the few boxes and bags of belongings she'd brought and the suitcase full of cash she'd wheeled into the room with them, that car was all she had. She needed to sell it and get something else—the sooner the better—but she wanted to put more distance between her and Wakefield first.

Stretching her neck to ease the tension headache that'd come on around dinnertime, she wandered into the bathroom and stared into the mirror. A wan stranger stared back at her. She couldn't believe she was really doing this. That she'd felt desperate enough. She'd taken what money she could, her children, their clothes and a few toys and left most everything else, including her dying mother. She didn't even have a computer or a cell phone to make things easier. She was so used to technology making it possible to search the internet, provide directions, give weather forecasts and keep her abreast of what was going on in the world—all at the touch of her fingertips—that she felt helpless without those tools.

She knew she should get some sleep. The boys would probably be up at the crack of dawn. If she wasn't well-rested, it would be hard to cover very many miles.

But she was too uptight, too fidgety. She'd used some of the cash she'd withdrawn from the bank for gas, but they wouldn't let her rent a room without a credit card. Before she left Wakefield, she'd opened a new account with a card exclusively in her name—and created an email address Sheldon wouldn't know about for the digital statements—but even that left a trail. People could be tracked so easily these days.

Would the police get involved? She didn't think so. Not from everything she'd seen on the internet. And if they didn't, she should be okay. The average person, like Sheldon, wouldn't be able to access her credit card data.

Besides, he and his buddies would be in the wilderness, out of cell phone range, much of the time he was gone. It was once he got back that she had to worry. Then he'd probably get a private investigator involved if the police wouldn't help him, and she had no idea how far a professional might be able or willing to go to find a runaway wife.

Maybe to avoid using a credit card and creating that paper trail, she and the boys would have to start sleeping in the car. Or go to a women's shelter—at least until she could buy a new computer. She was finally feeling enough panic to brave the dark web, where she'd heard she could purchase a fake ID. A simple Google search explained how, but so far, she'd been hesitant to venture into such a dangerous space.

Probably the worst that would happen was that she'd get ripped off by paying for something she never received. But it was a risk she was going to have to take.

Leaving the mirror, she wandered back into the hotel room

and covered up her sleeping children. Had Sheldon already tried to call her?

Typically, he didn't call home that often, not while he was hunting. With Cece back in his life, maybe he'd be calling her instead. The longer it took before he realized something was wrong, the more time she'd have to get situated and prepared.

Stepping back, she watched her boys. She'd figure everything out. She had no choice.

She just had to take it one day at a time.

Something was wrong. Gia hadn't heard from Margot at all on Saturday, even though she'd said she'd call after Sheldon went hunting. And she wasn't returning Gia's many calls and texts Sunday morning. Given their mother's situation, Gia would've expected Margot to call her back regardless of what she was doing.

So, after breakfast—and at her mother's urging—Gia went back over to Margot's house only to find both cars were still gone. And the view in the window hadn't changed one bit. If Margot had been home since Gia last stopped by, the boys would've left out a toy or their shoes or *something*. Although Margot kept a clean house, children were children. They made messes.

But if Margot had been gone since yesterday, where was she now? She wouldn't take the kids and go hunting with Sheldon, would she?

Gia got out her phone, searched for her brother-in-law's contact information and nearly called him. She wanted Sheldon to allay her fears. But the memory of her last conversation with Margot gave her pause. Margot had asked her *not* to call Sheldon. Gia had assumed she was just trying to protect him from the dressing-down he deserved—she was all about keeping the peace—but...what if there was more to it?

Because of the possible affair, Gia decided to hold off to see what she could learn on her own and walked around to the backyard.

The back door was locked, too. So were the windows. If she wanted to get in, she was going to have to break some glass. She hated to go that far, but she was feeling enough panic that she decided it'd be worth paying for any damage she caused— just in case.

After removing the screen, she used a rock from Margot's backyard and smashed the laundry room window. Then she took off her sweatshirt and wrapped it around her arm to keep from getting cut as she reached through and opened the latch so she could climb through.

"Margot?" she yelled as soon as she'd managed to get down off the dryer.

With the Subaru gone, she wasn't likely to get an answer, but she kept trying. "Margot? Matthew? Greydon?" she called.

Silence greeted her. The house was eerily quiet as she walked toward the bedrooms. Surely, Margot hadn't confronted Sheldon about the affair and—

She wouldn't even think it. There was no way he'd physically harm his wife.

Except, under the right circumstances—and if he thought he could get away with it—maybe he would. He was a controlling bastard. A self-absorbed one, too.

"I swear to God I'll make sure you rot in prison for the rest of your life," Gia whispered, and held her breath as she reached her sister's bedroom to find the door standing halfway closed.

As she gave it a push and it swung inward, the first thing she noticed was that the bed wasn't made. That was unusual. Margot prided herself on her homemaking skills; that was the only thing she had to feel good about since Sheldon wouldn't let her do anything else.

"Margot?" After poking her head in, Gia moved on to the

boys' room. She was moving fast. She could take the time to look closer on her second pass, if a second pass proved necessary.

The boys' beds weren't made, either. And their drawers were hanging open.

Gia moved closer. Not only were they open, they were empty. What was going on?

Adrenaline pumped through her system as she hurried back to the master bedroom to check her sister's dresser. Those drawers were closed, but when she opened them, she found the same thing. Margot's closet was empty, too. And all of her makeup and toiletries were gone.

The strange thing was… Sheldon's stuff was still there. His side of the closet was so full Gia couldn't even tell that he'd taken anything with him when he went hunting.

Needing answers faster than they seemed to be coming, she lifted her phone to call him—and once again forced herself to hold off.

Instead, she tried to reach her sister. If Margot didn't pick up this time, Gia would leave a message stating that she needed to hear from her or she was going to call Sheldon.

"You have fifteen minutes," she said aloud as she waited for the call to go through. But once it did, she could hear the jingle of her sister's peculiar ringtone in the house with her.

Closing her eyes, she listened carefully. It was coming from the kitchen.

18

"What do you mean she's gone?" Ida sat at the kitchen dinette with Leo at the other end, looking absolutely bewildered as Gia paced.

"I mean she's gone," Gia said. "Her car's not there. The kids aren't around. Everyone's clothes—except Sheldon's—are gone. And Margot's purse was nowhere to be found, so I'm guessing she took that, too." She held up her sister's phone, which she'd brought back with her. "And yet her cell was right there in the kitchen in plain sight."

Ida's eyes rounded in her gaunt face. Covering her mouth, she spoke through her fingers. "Why would she go anywhere without her phone?"

"I'd say she forgot it, except...except I think if she'd meant to take it, she would've gone back for it. We rely on these little computers too much these days. It's not something you'd be happy to leave behind."

"That makes sense," Ida agreed.

"Not to mention that everything seemed so...purposeful," Gia added after searching for the right word.

"How so?" her father asked.

She turned at the end of the kitchen and came back toward them. "Well, first, there were the rumors of Sheldon being involved with another woman. I got the impression when I brought up the subject with Margot that she was well aware of what was going on. Since she wouldn't let me confront him, I assumed she was simply letting him get away with it—like she has with so many other things. But maybe she put me off because she had something bigger planned..."

Ida dropped her hand. "Like what? A divorce? Where has she gone? And how are we supposed to reach her if she doesn't have a phone?"

Gia didn't want to say it, but the obvious answer was that they *couldn't* reach her. No one could. "I think...I think she's left him."

Her family, too. Gia didn't add that. But Leo obviously understood the implications because he came to his feet as he said, "Margot would never leave her mother when...when she's battling...what she's battling."

Ida's eyes brimmed with tears. "And even if she would, she'd never take the boys away from us, not to mention their father."

Gia couldn't see her sister crossing that line, either. Margot had never stood up to Sheldon. So then to do something so drastic... It seemed out of character. But nothing else explained the facts as Gia knew them. "I think that's exactly what she's done. When I let myself out of her house, the neighbor was watering his lawn. I asked him about Margot, and he said the last time he saw her was early yesterday morning. He said he was changing the oil in his truck as Sheldon loaded up to go hunting. They spoke for a minute, then Sheldon left, and about an hour later, Margot dragged several suitcases to the Subaru."

"Did she say anything to him?" Leo asked.

"No. When he yelled a hello to the kids, they said they were going to McDonald's and then the park, but she was so busy making trips to and from the house, he didn't get the chance to say anything to her. He said she looked 'tense.'"

"Should we call Sheldon?" Her mother reached for her phone, which was on the table next to her. "See if he knows what's going on?"

"No." Gia moved quickly to stop her. "We can't include him."

"Why not?"

Gia thought of the voicemail she'd planned to leave Margot, giving her fifteen minutes to get in touch before Gia approached Sheldon. She'd never left that message. Once she'd found Margot's phone, she'd assumed it would be futile. But she'd realized after that there were ways her sister could check her voicemail remotely—if she knew how. "Because we all know how level-headed Margot is. If she left, she did it for a reason."

"Without telling us?" Her mother couldn't seem to comprehend the sudden desertion, and Gia understood. Margot had never done anything like this before.

"She must've thought it was necessary," she said.

"Sheldon's infidelity has to be at the bottom of it," Leo said. "She must be brokenhearted, poor thing. But spouses cheat all the time. She can't just take the kids and disappear."

"Most people don't go that far," Gia agreed. "No one wants to walk away from everything they know and love. And she's always been close to Mom. That tells me she must've felt she had no other choice."

Ida wiped an errant tear. "This is so hard to believe."

Gia wished she knew the passcode to her sister's phone. She wanted to see whom Margot had called and texted last. Maybe there'd be some clue as to where she went—if she was involved with another man or whatever. But she'd already tried several combinations—Margot's birthday, her boys' birthdays and several other guesses—with no success. "Could there be another man in her life?" she asked hesitantly.

"No way," her mother replied.

"You haven't heard her mention anyone? There's been no new name that's cropped up?"

"None," Leo replied. "She hasn't been seen with anyone, either."

Now Margot's insistence that Gia return home made sense. Gia could even see why her sister would call her return "crucial." She'd needed someone in Wakefield she could rely on to support Ida so she could leave in good conscience.

But why would she disappear without saying goodbye? Especially to Ida? That was the piece of the puzzle Gia couldn't understand.

"What do we do now?" Ida asked. "Go to the police?"

"Not yet," Gia told her.

Her mother's voice went up in pitch. "You don't want us to call Sheldon *or* the police?"

"From what the neighbor said, she left of her own free will, Mom. And she did it the day Sheldon went hunting—almost as soon as he was gone. Think about the timing."

"She didn't want him to know she was leaving," Ida said.

Gia nodded. "That has to be it. If we want to help her, we need to trust that she knows what she's doing."

"So...now what?" her father said, also looking confused. "We just wait?"

"Wait and hope she reaches out to let us know she's okay."

"What if she doesn't?" Ida asked uncertainly.

Gia shook her head. "I don't know. Just...give me some time to break into this phone and see what I can find."

Cormac had tried calling Louisa and Edith. Neither of his sisters would pick up. He did get Victor to answer, but Victor said that Louisa was devastated he'd turned on her, especially in public, and when Cormac pointed out that he'd done everything he could to speak to his sisters in private *before* they crashed the Banned Books Club reunion, Victor had snapped that he didn't feel Cormac had any right to get involved either way and hung up.

As Sunday afternoon turned into Sunday evening, Cormac began to wonder if Louisa would even show up for work on Monday. And if she didn't, what was he going to do? Hold her job? Cajole her back? Would that even be possible?

He could hire a replacement, of course, but he'd hate to do that. They had always enjoyed working together. Besides, training someone else would take time and effort. And then what would he do if Louisa wanted to come back?

He was worried about the clinic, but he was even more worried about his niece and nephew. Surely, she wouldn't try to keep him from interacting with the kids.

At about eight o'clock, he called his mother.

"I've heard," Sharon said the moment she picked up. "My next-door neighbor's daughter was at that book group meeting, and she just brought me a pumpkin from her garden and gave me an earful."

"And you haven't called me?"

"I'm trying to stay out of it. You're all my children. It wouldn't be fair for me to choose a side."

"But you believe the same way I do—that Dad did it."

"*Believe* is the key word, Cormac. I made it clear the other morning that I don't know for sure, and I don't want to be responsible for leading you and your sisters to a conclusion that could possibly be wrong. Not when it comes to a relationship as important as that of a child with a father. You asked me what led me to form *my* opinion, and I told you because…because you're a man now and should have all the facts. If Louisa and Edith ask, I'll tell them the same. That's all I can do."

"What about Gia?" he asked.

"I feel bad for Gia. But—" she hesitated before continuing, obviously choosing her words carefully "—as terrible as it might sound, I have to put my family first. Do what I think is best for the three of you."

"Even if it means letting Dad destroy her life?"

"Don't be overly dramatic," she replied. "She's moved on."

"She's having to put up with all kinds of bullshit about the past when you and I know she was probably an innocent victim."

"I don't 'know' anything," Sharon said. "That's the problem."

A knock interrupted. Hoping it was Gia—they'd had such a good time talking in the hot tub last night that Cormac had been thinking about her all day—he told his mother to hang on while he checked to see who was at his door.

A glance through the window showed him it wasn't Gia; it was his father.

"Dad's here," he told his mother. "I'll let you go."

"Cormac…" Sharon said, her voice a warning.

"What?"

"Be careful. You're risking a lot for a woman you'll probably never see again—after a month or two."

But he didn't understand how he could do anything different. He had to stand up for what he believed, didn't he? Had to protect the people—or person, in this case—who was innocent. He wouldn't be able to live with himself if he didn't.

There was no time to explain that, however, and he wasn't convinced she'd understand even if he tried. Ever since it happened, she'd managed to remain neutral—beyond what could be inferred from the divorce. But she didn't know Gia as well as he did. Or care about her the way he did. And if he said that, she'd want to know *why* he cared, which was a question he couldn't answer, because *he* didn't know. "I understand. I'll talk to you later."

He hit the end button and swung open the door. "Hey, Dad. What's up?"

A muscle moved in his father's jaw. "I need to talk to you," he replied curtly.

Apparently, Sharon wasn't the only one who'd heard about the debacle at the restaurant. But Cormac thought it took some gall for his father to show up angry. According to Gia, Evan had even lied about what'd happened at the drive-through. *He'd* confronted *her*, gone so far as to block her escape while he harangued her. Last night in the hot tub, she'd explained the whole thing in greater detail. The guy who'd stepped in sounded like Grizzly Bowman. He owned the shooting range about five miles out of town, and his pit bull was a patient of Cormac's. If it was Grizzly, Cormac would be able to corroborate her story—unlike what'd happened before. "Come on in," he said.

His father had gone to the trouble of combing his hair and shaving. That was nice to see. The scruffy look wasn't flattering on him; it made him appear too unkempt.

"Is it true that you went to the restaurant last night and told everyone there that I've been lying about Gia all these years?" he asked as soon as he'd slammed the door behind him.

"Haven't you?" Cormac said.

His father's face turned beet red. "You really did. Louisa and Edith were right. I can't believe this! I could take it from almost anyone else, but not from you."

"You lied to me about what happened at Delia's," he pointed out.

Evan spread his hands. "What'd I say?"

"You said she started screaming at you and made a big scene."

"That's true!"

"No, it's not! *You* were the one who saw *her*. You kept driving past, glaring at her and trying to intimidate her. Then you turned in, blocked her car and said some very nasty things."

"That's not true—"

"It *is* true!" Cormac interrupted. "Grizzly was there! He saw the whole thing. He told you to leave her alone, didn't he?" It was a bluff to pretend he'd already spoken to Grizzly. But he was dying to *finally* hold his father to the truth.

Evan's eyes went flat, devoid of feeling. "How'd you know Grizzly was there?"

"She told me."

"When did you talk to her?"

"I've talked to her several times. She's staying in the house right behind this one, for God's sake."

"She doesn't know Grizzly. He moved here after she left."

"Is that what you were counting on?" Cormac demanded.

"She deserves whatever I say to her and then some," he replied, suddenly changing his story.

Cormac froze. "So you *were* lying…"

He threw up his hands. "Are you even listening to me?"

"I'm listening. I just don't like what I'm hearing."

"She destroyed my life!" his father shouted. "And for what? What I did—it was hardly *anything*!"

Cormac gaped at him. Had he just admitted to molesting her seventeen years ago? "Making a sexual advance on one of your students is a very serious offense, Dad."

"I barely touched her!"

"But you *did* touch her. First, you set her up. You gave her a bad grade, so she'd come to you to get it changed. Then you tried to use the power you held over her to coerce her into having sex with you. Isn't that true?"

His father straightened. "No."

"You just said you 'barely' touched her. 'Barely' is still touching her."

"I didn't do anything wrong," he insisted.

He was only taking it back because Cormac wasn't accepting his justification, and Cormac could tell. "You've been lying all along," he said, feeling stunned. "You know it, and I know it!"

"Quit putting words in my mouth!" his father snapped and bolted from the house without even bothering to close the door.

Cormac watched as he got into his old Blazer and tore out of the drive, nearly hitting the neighbor's car, which was parked on the street. What had just happened? Evan had admitted the truth but then taken it back?

That *had* been an admission, though, hadn't it?

What was Cormac supposed to do now? Would his sisters even believe him if he told them what'd just happened?

He didn't shut the door even after his father was gone. He stared out into the night for several minutes, letting the chill wind ripple through his hair and clothes. All this time his father had been saying and doing anything he could to avoid responsibility for what he'd done to Gia. And until very recently Cormac had stood by him.

The whole thing was so disgusting!

"Hey."

He blinked and focused. Gia had come from around the back. Had she heard Evan leave?

He didn't get the impression she even knew Evan had been here. Fortunately, she'd missed him, but only by a matter of minutes.

He tried to answer her but couldn't speak. The rage that filled him tightened his throat to the point that he didn't have a voice.

"What's wrong?" she asked, looking alarmed.

He shook his head. He didn't want to see her right now. He was too upset. But he didn't know what to do to make her leave, not without also making her feel bad.

"Cormac?"

He opened his mouth to speak, but once again couldn't squeeze any words past his throat. Then, inexplicably and without warning, his eyes began to fill with tears of anger and frustration.

That was the last thing he wanted. Embarrassed on top of

everything else, he started to close the door. He had to get away before she could tell he was breaking down. But the next thing he knew, she grabbed hold of his arm and turned him toward her.

"What is it?" She searched his face for answers with those stunning eyes of hers, but when he couldn't provide her with an explanation, she put her arms around him and pulled him in for a hug. "It's okay," she murmured. "Everything's going to be okay."

Gia had been worried about how Cormac's family would respond to what he'd done last night. Now she knew she'd had good reason to be concerned. Something significant must've happened with them—or, much less likely, something else had upset him—because his whole body was rigid. "It's okay," she murmured again, rubbing his back. "What happened?"

"My father... I've just...lost my father," he said as if everything he was thinking and feeling could be summed up in that one simple statement.

"What do you mean? Has he been hurt?" She started to pull back, but he buried his face in her neck and continued to hold her.

"No. I..." When he'd had a moment to compose himself, he lifted his head. "I just realized that he's not the man I always believed he was. I mean...since you've been back, I've had to face the idea that he was probably lying about what happened in high school. That's shameful enough. But harassing you at the diner, too, and the way he characterized it afterward, and how he's been using Louisa and Edith—and wants to continue to use me—to give him false credibility..." He shook his head as if that was the best he could do to explain what was going on.

"I feel terrible," she said. "I don't want to be the cause of this. For nearly two decades, I've been blamed for destroying your family. I hate the thought that just by coming home, I'm responsible for more pain."

He stepped back, breaking the contact between them. "That's just it. *You* care about the damage that's being caused. That says it all right there."

"Your father's a proud man, Cormac. He's embarrassed that he was caught doing something so far beneath him. So he's still fighting to shore up the lies he told. I think he'd do anything to reclaim some of the respect he had before. It's not right, but... it's understandable."

"Not to me," he argued. "If he'd just told the truth, I could've forgiven him! You were almost an adult and *so* beautiful, even back then. I could understand wanting you. I've *always* wanted you. It's what he's done since—all the lying and the total disregard for how it affects everyone around him—that's shown me who he really is. And I don't like what I see. I can't admire it. I can't—"

He stopped. The way she was looking at him let him know he'd said something completely unexpected.

"What?" he said, taking another step back.

"You've always *wanted* me?" she echoed.

Squeezing his eyes closed, he rubbed his forehead. "I shouldn't have said that. I can't talk right now. I have no filter. I'd better—"

"Cormac," she cut in.

Dropping his hand, he looked at her.

"I can't thank you enough for your inherent honesty and... and goodness. I admire it—admire *you*—and hate that it's costing you so much." She meant to give him another hug, a brief one, and leave. She'd come at a bad time, caught him in an emotional moment that should've remained private. But what started out as a hug quickly turned into a heated kiss.

They pulled away, seemingly at the same time, both of them

breathless. "Sorry about that," Gia said as he said the same thing, almost in unison.

Gia would've laughed, but there was nothing funny about that kiss. She could still feel the heat of it all the way down to her toes.

What'd just happened? She'd never had a thing for Cormac Hart. And yet…she was beginning to see him in a far different light. "That was incredible," she said on a long breath. "Possibly the best kiss I've ever had."

His eyebrows slid up. "You're not mad at me?"

"I'm not even sure you're the one who instigated it. Are you?" It'd felt spontaneous, as if they'd each made a move at exactly the same moment.

"To be honest, I don't know, either," he said. "I just assumed it must've been me because I've wanted to do it for so long. And I couldn't imagine *you*… Well, I was absolutely convinced I'd be the last man on earth who—"

She didn't wait for him to finish. Stepping closer, she rose up and pressed her lips to his once again.

His arms went around her, and one hand came up to support her back as she parted her lips for his tongue, simply giving herself over to him and what she was feeling. Since she'd come home, there'd been so much angst and upset—not to mention futile but Herculean efforts to outdistance the past. That was probably true for him, as well. But this was pleasurable in the most exciting way.

All she could feel, smell and taste was Cormac, and in this moment, that seemed to be all she needed.

19

Cormac had never dreamed he'd make love to Gia. He'd spent years blaming her for something she didn't do and was shocked she didn't hate him for the past, regardless of how he'd behaved in the present. But she seemed relieved just to know he finally believed her.

The thrill he felt touching her and being touched by her created such a stark contrast to everything else that'd happened since she returned to Wakefield that he could only close his eyes and enjoy the moment as he ran his hand up her bare leg.

She was even more stunning without her clothes. Tall, slender and firm in that tomboyish way of hers, with long limbs, she had the softest, smoothest skin he'd ever felt. Her breasts weren't particularly large, only the size of his cupped hand, but he thought they were perfect. And her smile was mesmerizing.

"What are you doing?" she asked when he stopped and simply stared down at her.

He lifted his gaze from her wide, sexy mouth to her thickly lashed eyes. "Admiring you."

This was a big step to take so suddenly. Living in a small town, it was especially imperative not to create romantic expectations he couldn't fulfill—not unless he wanted the women of Wakefield to hate him—so he'd been cautious his whole life. There were things he should probably be saying before getting this intimate, things he always said. But he didn't want to ruin the moment. What was happening seemed special, almost fragile, and he planned to treat it as such. There was no way he wanted to do anything that might break the spell that'd propelled them upstairs, dropping their clothes behind them as they went. She understood this wasn't a commitment. She wasn't even going to be in town for long. This was merely an escape, a welcome release for two beleaguered souls who desperately needed a time-out.

Besides, she'd already told him she had trouble falling in love, and that created an understanding of sorts. He knew the situation going in, and so did she. He didn't need to worry that he was setting her up for future disappointment.

If anything, he was setting *himself* up for future disappointment. He was afraid that after today, he'd never be able to look at her again without wanting her.

"This is crazy, right?" she said, showing the first hint of uncertainty.

"It's crazy," he agreed. "Crazy *good*, in my opinion. I don't think I've ever wanted anyone quite so much. But if you're asking me to stop—"

"No," she broke in. "I just… I hope we don't regret it later."

"I have condoms, if that gives you any reassurance," he said. "Or is it something else? Have you changed your mind about that guy you were dating in Idaho or—"

"No, none of that. Sex can make things complicated. That's all. But it's too late now." After pushing him onto his back, she kissed his mouth, his jawline, his neck and his chest.

"Oh, God," he said as her mouth continued to move lower and finally closed around him. "I don't think you'd better do that. Not yet."

She knocked his hands away when he tried to draw her up but lifted her head so she could talk. "What if I like seeing what it does to you?"

He laughed. "You can do whatever you want. But first, let me do what I can do for you, or it'll end far too soon."

Rolling her beneath him, he nuzzled her neck, then kissed her deeply while teasing her with the promise of penetration without actually pressing inside her.

"Are you ever going to do it?" she asked, growing impatient.

He grinned at her. "You bet I am. Just...not quite yet."

Giving himself permission to really let go and make love to her as boldly and confidently as he craved, he kissed her as many times as he wanted—touched her, too, and entwined his limbs with hers. But the more he touched and kissed her, the more he wanted to touch and kiss her. He seemed to be chasing something elusive, something he couldn't quite catch. It was that buildup, together with the anticipation, that made his time with Gia unlike anything he'd experienced before.

Lifting her legs over his shoulders, he licked his way up her right thigh, inhaling the musky scent of her as he went. Everything about her appealed to him, he realized. He wanted to continue to experiment and become more familiar with her body and figure out what she liked.

Eventually, he located the spot that would bring her the most pleasure. She jumped when his mouth settled there, so he knew he'd found what he was looking for, and that success brought him such an exquisite feeling. She was so engaged and responsive; it made their intimacy that much more fun.

Too bad this couldn't last forever, he thought.

Maybe it was the fact that when it came to each other they had nothing to worry about except what happened tonight that made the sex so remarkable. Gia didn't have to be concerned about getting into a relationship that might be difficult to escape, didn't have to wonder whether she'd like Cormac next week, next month or next year, whether she'd hurt him in the end, or he'd hurt her. None of that played a role because they had zero expectations of each other. It had to be the absence of all the things that normally hung over her head that made it so good.

Their peculiar history made it more than a little surprising that they'd ended up in bed together, but making love with Cormac felt cathartic, as if they were dispensing with all the pain and negative feelings they'd had concerning each other in one big cataclysmic event. The emotional release added to the physical release; it was the combination that made it so powerful.

As the tension built, she tightened her legs around his hips and told herself to quit thinking. She wanted to be completely present in this moment, wanted to concentrate solely on the feel of him—his lower body pressing into hers, the muscles that stood out on his arms and shoulders as he bore the bulk of his weight to avoid crushing her, the smell of his bedding and the scent of his warm body, and especially the intense expression on his face.

When he closed his eyes, she knew he was getting close to climax and thought he might beat her there. Especially when her phone started to ring outside the room, somewhere on the stairs where Cormac had dropped her jeans after helping her peel them off. The sound caught her attention for a split second, but she resisted the distraction just long enough to achieve her release.

When she groaned, he said something unintelligible. She guessed it signified relief, especially when he stopped trying to hold back and drove into her more powerfully until his body jerked and he shuddered before slumping over.

"Wow," he said, breathing heavily as he shifted his weight to one side.

She didn't get the chance to respond. Her phone was ringing again. Apparently, someone *really* wanted to get hold of her.

Her first thought was of her mother. This wasn't the moment she'd been dreading, was it?

Her stomach knotted at the mere possibility. But then another thought struck her, and this one somehow seemed more imminent and therefore more likely, despite her mother's fragile health.

Margot.

"I have to get that!" she exclaimed and climbed over Cormac as quickly as he could let her go.

"Hello?"

Margot caught her breath when she heard her sister's voice. She'd promised herself she wouldn't reach out to *anyone* after she ran away. She knew it could ruin what she was trying to do by leaving clues as to where she was and where she might be going. Sheldon could find out she was in Spokane and start searching from there.

But she was leaving Washington in the morning. And she'd had to use her credit card again for the room. That would probably provide him with just as much information. So the fact that she'd use a stranger's phone at this particular time seemed worth the risk, especially since she'd blocked the number. She'd felt she had to speak to her sister. The magnitude of leaving the way she had—what it would mean for her and her children—had become overwhelming. All she could think about was her family, especially her mother.

"Hello?" she heard Gia say for the second time. "Margot, is it you?"

In a sudden panic, she hung up.

Unsure and self-conscious, she looked over at the woman whose phone she'd borrowed to make sure she wasn't being watched too closely. The kind-faced, middle-aged brunette was still checking in and didn't seem to be worried that Margot might run off with her phone. But Margot didn't have much time. When she'd come to the lobby to purchase trail mix—she'd been too riddled with anxiety to eat dinner—she'd left Greydon and Matthew sleeping in the room a few doors down the hall and needed to get back as soon as possible, just in case one of them woke up.

Margot told herself she should return the phone to its owner, purchase the trail mix and stick to her original plan. But the thought that her mother might die without any word from her prompted her to call back.

When Gia answered for the second time, Margot said, "It's me."

"What phone are you calling from?"

"A stranger's."

"A stranger's! Margot, what are you doing? Where have you been? Please tell me you're on your way back home."

She ducked her head so her words wouldn't echo across the lobby. "No, I can't ever come back. And I can't tell you where I am. I—I just wanted to check on Mom. I need to hear that she's okay, and I was hoping you'd tell her that...that I'm sorry and I'll always love her."

"Why don't you call and tell her yourself?"

"Because it's too late for tonight. I don't want to wake her. And I only have this phone for a few minutes."

"What's happening?" Gia asked. "Why'd you leave without saying a word? Is it Sheldon? Is he really having an affair? If so, you don't need to give up the house, the town you grew up in and associating with your family. Divorce the bastard! I'll help you do it. You know I will."

"That's just it," she said. "I don't want to drag you into this. It's not your problem. Besides, you don't understand. He's not like you or me or most other people. I don't want anyone to get hurt."

"I can take care of myself, Maggie," she said.

Maggie had been her childhood nickname. Gia had called her that all through grade school and middle school, even after she'd asked everyone to call her Margot. Margot missed the trusting child she'd once been, missed the sheltered existence she'd known before she'd become responsible for children herself. "You don't know that."

"We can take him on together," her sister insisted.

As Margot had expected, Gia was all for fighting. But she didn't understand how vicious Sheldon could be or how far he'd go to avenge even small slights. "No, G. He'll win in the end."

"Win *what*?" she asked, sounding confused.

How did she explain what was at stake? That was the problem. The verbal abuse she'd suffered had been terrible, but no one considered verbal abuse debilitating—not until it grew bad enough that it finally turned physical. And she could feel it drifting in that direction, wasn't willing to wait that long. By then it'd be too late. "The battle between us for...for the understanding and support of our family and friends. And for custody of the boys. He'll use the money he makes, the business he owns and the influence of his parents to discredit me. Make me look small and insignificant next to him—unworthy of what's rightfully mine. And if that would only cost me my reputation, I'd risk it. But I *won't* risk my children."

"You're afraid he'll take the boys?"

"I know he will."

"But...how could he?" her sister demanded. "You haven't done anything wrong."

"Doesn't matter. He'll paint me as unstable or unfit or unable to provide for them or...or something. It's so hard to fight him on anything. He's *always* right. And once he learns I've left him and won't stay in the marriage any longer, there won't be anything holding him back. He'll let me have it any way he can. I had to get out, G, had to save myself. You understand, don't you?"

There was a brief silence during which Margot imagined her sister being stunned as she tried to absorb this news.

"I understand that you married the wrong man," she said when she spoke again. To her credit she didn't say anything about having known that all along. "I need to help you get away from him. And I can do that. Come back. You and the boys can stay with me, Mom and Dad while we navigate this thing. We'll look after you."

"No! If Sheldon knows where I am, he'll find ways to torture me. And since he can hurt me the worst by using the boys, that's what he'll do. I refuse to let him tell them terrible lies about me and try to destroy our relationship. I won't put myself in that constant tug-of-war."

"What's your other choice?" Gia asked. "Hiding? Going off to live alone? Is that any better? You don't even have a phone!"

"Maybe not. But I have Greydon and Matthew. There's no way he can threaten my relationship with them if he can't even find us."

"How will you get by?"

"I took all the money in our checking and savings. I'll be okay for a while."

"You *what*?"

"I drained our accounts. Took it all." Saying that both empowered her, because it was the punch she'd been longing to throw at Sheldon for years, and terrified her, because she knew how enraged it would make him.

"How much are we talking?" Gia asked.

"Nearly forty thousand. That should be enough to get an apartment and a car and carry us over until I find work."

There was another long silence. Then Gia said, "Margot, he won't let you run off with the kids."

"I think he'll care more about the money. But I've earned

that money. I've worked so hard over years, and he's been so damn stingy with me. I'm leaving him much more. Think about the equity in the house and business and all our furnishings. This money is mine and so are the boys."

"Margot, come back! We can fight him."

"*You'd* be able to fight him, G. I can't. I'm not strong like you. I have to deal with this my own way. And that's by getting out and disappearing." Margot glanced up in time to see the hotel clerk hand the brunette her key. She was going to have to relinquish the phone. "I have to go."

"Wait!" her sister said. "At least tell me where you are. Or how I can reach you. Or where you're going."

"I wish I could, but I can't. Tell Mom I'm sorry, and I love her. Tell Dad I love him, too," she said and disconnected.

Gia heard a creak behind her, alerting her to Cormac's presence.

"Is everything okay?" he asked as he sat down beside her.

He was still naked, but she was, too. She hadn't taken the time to so much as grab her panties. She'd merely stepped over them as she ran to find her phone. She was afraid Margot—or whoever was calling—wouldn't try a third time. And she was glad she'd made the effort. At least she understood a little more about what was going on with her sister. She just couldn't believe it. It was so unlike Margot to do anything this drastic. "I don't know," she said, staring off into space.

"That wasn't about your mother, was it?" he asked gently.

She shook her head.

"That's good, at least. Something with work, then?"

"No." She turned her head to look at him. "It was Margot."

"Your sister's awake? Isn't it getting late?"

"Saturday morning, she left town without telling anyone— just drove away as soon as Sheldon went hunting."

"You're kidding."

"I wish I was."

"I know Sheldon. I thought they were happy together."

"So did I—until recently."

"Then…what does it all mean?"

"She's leaving him," she said simply.

He seemed unsure of what to say next. "Is that a good thing or a bad thing overall?"

"He's a douchebag. On that count it's a good thing. But what a way to go about it. The situation inside their marriage must have been much worse than I ever dreamed. I feel bad for getting so caught up in my own life. I've sort of walled her out, I guess. Otherwise, surely I would've seen this coming." It was self-preservation, a defense mechanism she'd perfected years and years ago that'd made her keep her distance. But she didn't go into that.

"If she didn't come to you for help, how would you know?" he asked.

She raked her fingers through her long hair. "We've always been different—never looked at the world in the same way, which has made it hard for us to be close. But… Jesus! With what's going on with my mother and now my sister, it feels like the whole world's burning down around me."

He took her hand and curled his fingers through hers. "You're strong," he said. "One of the strongest people I know. You're going to get through this."

She drew a deep breath. "The fact that you're the one sitting here comforting me is also nothing I ever would've expected."

"Me, neither." He made a clicking sound with his tongue as he shook his head. "The fact that we just made love and are both sitting here naked is also a little shocking," he added, and something about his quizzical expression made her laugh in spite of everything.

20

Cormac was at his desk with Duke by his feet on Monday morning an hour before he normally opened the clinic. He'd showered as soon as he got up and, after notifying Mrs. Wood that he wouldn't be able to take her to the park, he headed to work. He'd been up so late with Gia he didn't have the energy or the will to go running. He was too busy marveling over everything that'd transpired since she came back to town, especially the part where he'd taken her to bed, because that added yet another element to an already complicated situation.

He kept telling himself their encounter had been a fluke—that the stars had aligned just for that one moment. It wasn't as if he could actually have a relationship with her. But making love to Gia was all he wanted to think about. It'd been raw and passionate and so incredibly satisfying. Remembering how she touched him, how good she felt beneath him and the taste of her kiss beat the hell out of dwelling on the rift in his family. He had no idea what he was going to do about that—or if Louisa would even show up for work today. If she didn't, and they couldn't get past their recent disagreement, what was happening in his personal life would spill over into his professional life, and the next few days would get bumpier still.

He was amazed by how quickly everything he'd taken for granted and relied on for years could be turned on its head...

His phone signaled a text. He was afraid to look at it for fear it was his sister telling him to figure out how to run his own front office. But if that was the reality of it, he had to find out sooner or later, so he picked up his phone.

Do you want to tell me what happened with your father?

He'd been on the phone with his mother when Evan came over. He'd said he'd call her back but never did.

He started to type a reply but decided it would be easier to call.

She answered on the first ring. "I'm assuming things didn't go well last night."

"He admitted the truth to me, Mom," he said. "He took it back right after, but he *did* admit it."

"What do you mean?"

"When I told him I believe he molested Gia, he said, 'I barely touched her' as if it wasn't a big thing—but he *did* do it. He's mad at her for outing him. That's all."

She didn't respond.

"Mom?"

"I believe it, but...what are you going to do now?"

She hardly sounded jubilant, and he could understand why. Just because they were right in what they believed didn't make things any better. "I'm going to tell Louisa and Edith. That's what I'm going to do."

"What makes you think they'll believe you? Especially if he's already denying it again?"

"They would never think I'd lie about something like that..."

"I don't know," she said skeptically. "People can be pretty resistant to the truth, especially when it hurts." She paused. "I hate what this is doing to our family. There's got to be a better way to handle it."

Like she had before? By standing back and saying nothing? Not trying to persuade anyone either way? Cormac didn't believe remaining neutral was the answer, either. "How? This can't be easy for Gia. And it's all because of Dad."

"People make mistakes—"

"Don't offer that as an excuse, Mom. It's not the mistake so much as the way he handled it—trying to blame it on *her*. You've said so before—that it was the lies that make it so hard for you, too. I'm sure an admission and an apology would've gone far toward helping her through the years right after it happened. That sort of thing would probably be a relief even at this late date."

"I don't know what to say, Cormac. I've tried my best to keep our family together despite what he did, and now…"

"And now it's falling apart because of me?"

"I'm not blaming you. I just—I wish the past didn't have to rear its ugly head again."

"I think we should deal with it once and for all."

"Despite the damage it'll cause?"

"We have to face reality. Call the girls and get them to come over. Let's have a family meeting."

"With your dad, too?"

"No, without. But I'll tell them what he said last night."

"He'll just deny it when they ask him."

If that happened, Cormac would feel a lot like Gia had back in high school, he supposed. He'd be swearing things had gone one way; his father would be insisting they hadn't. The irony didn't escape him. "He can try, but if the rest of us are unified, maybe we can hold him, and he'll finally realize he has to change."

He heard her sigh through the phone.

"What?" he said. "You don't like that idea?"

"It's hard to take someone's good opinion of their father away from them."

"Trust me. I understand that. But if he doesn't deserve their good opinion, maybe he shouldn't get it."

It took a moment, but she finally said, "Okay."

"Wait...did you just say that Margot called you last night?" Ida asked.

Gia stood at the stove making oatmeal for breakfast. Her dad sat at the kitchen table, reading the news on his phone, and her mother stroked Miss Marple while waiting to eat. But Gia was exhausted enough that she kept leaning against the counter. After leaving Cormac's house, she hadn't gotten much sleep. She was worried about her sister and kept trying to break into Margot's phone. After talking to her, she doubted it would tell her much, but it gave her something to concentrate on. Because the second she lost focus, she'd have an *Oh, my God, what have I done?* moment as thoughts of Cormac managed to intrude. She hadn't even slept with Mike, and they'd gone out together a number of times. So she wasn't sure exactly how she'd ended up in bed with Cormac. She supposed she'd been feeling vulnerable enough to grab hold of someone she probably shouldn't have.

But the sex had been incredible. She could never claim otherwise.

"Gia?" her mother pressed.

Shoving the image of a gorgeous and very naked Cormac out of her mind for probably the hundredth time since she woke up, she turned off the stove and reached into the cupboard to get three bowls. "Yes, she finally called me."

Her mother nudged Miss Marple to encourage the cat to leap down. "And? What's going on?"

Her father put his phone aside so that he could listen, too.

"She's left Sheldon."

"We guessed as much," Leo said. "When's she coming back?"

Gia knew her parents wouldn't like the answer. "It didn't sound as if she plans on coming home anytime soon."

"What about the kids?" Ida asked. "They'll miss school. And she doesn't have any way to support them. How will she get by?"

"She has enough money for now."

"How?" her father asked.

"She took what they had in their savings." Gia didn't mention the amount. If Margot was leaving everything else to Sheldon, he'd gotten the best end of the deal, but the amount sounded shocking and taking the money without getting his agreement would hit her parents wrong.

"So…she's moved away from Wakefield permanently?" her father said. "Where'd she go? And why did she feel it was necessary to take such a drastic step?"

"She didn't say as much as I wanted her to. She was on someone else's phone and wouldn't tell me where she was or what she plans to do—except that she's worried about the two of you and wanted me to tell you how much she loves you."

"She couldn't call us to say that?" her father asked, clearly offended.

"She doesn't have a phone, and she's traveling. But that doesn't mean she won't call when…when she can."

Ida pulled the shawl she'd brought from the bedroom tighter around her shoulders. "Did she say when she's coming back?"

"I don't think she plans on it. She's done with Sheldon, and she's afraid of what he might do when he finds out she's gone."

"Oh, my God," her mother said. "What will his parents say? They'll be furious to think she'd do such a thing. Those boys are their grandkids, too. *I'd* be furious if I were them!"

"He's clearly having an affair, Mom. They have only their son to blame."

"I agree. Margot's been a great wife," Ida said. "But she needs to come back and take care of their property and custody issues legally, just like everyone else."

"She can't," Gia said. "At least, that's what she says. I told her to come home, that we'd help her. But she was too terrified."

"What is she so scared of?" Leo asked. "Has he been violent with her?"

"I don't get that impression. He hasn't yet, anyway. She did tell me that he'd discredit her and take the kids, and she won't allow that to happen—won't allow him the chance to even try."

Her mother dropped her head in her hands. "Oh, dear."

"Let's call her," Leo said.

Gia dished up the oatmeal and carried two bowls to the table. "How?"

"You have the number she called from, don't you?" he asked.

"It came in as an unknown number. Which means she blocked it," Gia explained.

Her father looked as though she'd struck him. "So there's nothing we can do?"

"Not right now," she confirmed. "I can't even break into her phone, so that's useless to us. But the fact that she did call is a good sign. I'm hoping she'll calm down and try again in a few days."

"But for now…she's out there…somewhere…with the family car," her father said.

"And everything she could take out of their checking and savings," Gia added.

Ida lifted her head. "That can't be right. This…this just isn't like Margot."

Gia brought her bowl to the table, too. "Which is why I think we give her the benefit of the doubt. She knows Sheldon much better than we do. There must be something he's done—or she thinks he'll do—that has made this whole thing necessary."

"But it's unsustainable," Leo said. "Sheldon and his family

aren't going to sit back and let her have Greydon and Matthew. They'll search for her and probably find her, and when they do, they'll force her to recognize their legal rights. Where will she be then? At that point, he might even have a case for full custody because she's already proven she's a flight risk."

"I know, Dad, but—"

Her mother's phone went off, and Ida's face turned ashen when she looked down at it.

"Who is it?" Gia asked.

Ida looked up. "It's Sheldon."

Cormac breathed a sigh of relief when he heard his sister come in and greet Herman Wise, the owner of their first patient of the day. Louisa was ten minutes late, but at least she'd shown up for work.

He waited until she was settled behind the desk in the reception area before gathering his clipboard and strolling out of his office. "Morning," he said to the room at large.

She didn't respond, but Mr. Wise, an elderly gentleman who owned three labradoodles but had only one with him today, stood and came forward to shake his hand. "Morning, Doc."

Cormac squatted to give Bella a scratch behind the ears. "You didn't bring Tweety and Tinkerbell?" he asked.

"No, the wife's got 'em. I told her you'd want to say hi, but she said we didn't need to fill your whole waiting room."

Cormac straightened. "They're always welcome to tag along. But what's going on with Bella?" He checked the clipboard that listed his appointments and the reason for each visit. "Something about a sore leg?"

"She's favoring this one." He lifted his dog's left hind leg. "I'm wondering if she has a fracture or something."

"Bring her on back and we'll take a look." Cormac motioned for Mr. Wise to follow him and glanced at Louisa as he turned to go into the examination room. But she wouldn't meet his eye. She was obviously bent on ignoring him, which was how she behaved all day. Even at lunch, she slipped out of the clinic without saying a word and went elsewhere to eat, returning only after their first afternoon appointment had arrived.

It wasn't until she was packing up to leave for the day that he finally went into the lobby to confront her.

"Is it going to be like this from now on?" he asked.

When she shot him a dirty look and marched past him, he assumed she wasn't even going to answer. But she turned back at the door. "I can't believe what you did at the restaurant on Saturday night, Cormac. I'll never forgive you. I just want you to know that."

"I'm sorry," he said. "But if you'll remember, I tried to stop you well before it got to that point."

"You had no right to get involved."

"Says who?" he demanded. "I had more than a right—I had a duty."

She gave him an astounded look. "What's gotten into you? Do you have a crush on Gia again...or what?"

He opened his mouth to deny that he felt anything for Gia. But visions of her naked body entwined with his had been parading around on the stage of his mind since he woke up, and he could still smell the heady scent of her soap or shampoo or whatever it was on his sheets. Normally, he enjoyed his work; today, he couldn't wait to get home because he knew she'd be close by and might come out to the pool again. "It isn't that," he insisted.

She slung her purse over her shoulder. "Then what is it?"

"I told you! I don't want our family to be responsible for hurting anyone. Especially Gia. She's been through enough."

"You don't know that our family's been responsible for *anything*."

He opened his mouth to tell her he *did* know. Waiting until his mother called a family meeting no longer seemed prudent. He had to work with Louisa every day; this couldn't go on. But Victor walked in at that moment. "You ready?" he said the second he saw his wife holding her computer bag, purse and water bottle.

Louisa shot Cormac another dirty look. "Yes, I am," she replied and walked out with Victor.

Cormac sighed as he shoved his hands into the pockets of his lab coat. Maybe his mother was right, and Louisa wouldn't believe him no matter what he said. Then what?

"Are we there yet?"

Matthew and Greydon were getting tired of riding in the car. Margot had bought them new toys, extra snacks and loaded plenty of movies and games on her iPad to help entertain them. She'd also stopped at various parks to let them stretch their legs. Still, three days in a car was a long time for any child. "Not quite," she mumbled, leaning forward to see the sign overhead.

"Are we going to Disneyland?"

Margot figured they might as well. They were in southern Oregon heading to California, and it was something she'd always wanted to do. She'd asked Sheldon a number of times if they could go as a family—most recently for Matthew's birthday—but he'd claimed it was a waste of money. He could spend on guns, racks, fishing rods, camping and hunting gear, even the gold and silver coins he liked to collect. But anything anyone else in the family wanted, he often deemed too frivolous.

Although she knew she should conserve the cash she had, the kids deserved a reward for suffering through three days in a car and doing it mostly without complaint, especially since she was uprooting them from their home and taking them from their father. They didn't understand the full repercussions of what she was doing. How could they? "I don't see why not," she replied.

Greydon clapped his hands. "*Really?* Last time we asked, you said 'maybe.'"

"Well, I've decided," she told him. "The answer is yes."

"Is Daddy going to meet us there?" he asked.

"No, stupid," Matthew said. "Dad's hunting, remember?"

"I'm not stupid," Greydon said, and Margot heard a *smack* as he hit his brother.

"Stop it! Both of you!" She adjusted her rearview mirror so she could see what was going on. But that didn't prevent Matthew from slugging him in return.

"Ouch!" Greydon yelped and started to cry. "He hit me!"

"He hit me first!" Matthew snapped, obviously feeling thoroughly justified.

"I guess we won't be going to Disneyland, after all," Margot told them. "I thought it would be a fitting reward for how well you've behaved but look at you now. You're *hitting* each other? You both know better than that!"

"I'm sorry," Matthew said. "I won't do it again. I promise."

"Me, too." Greydon's words were muffled as he wiped his face. "But... I want to get out. When can we stop?"

"I'm thirsty," Matthew said before she could respond.

She glanced into the back seat. "You have your water bottles."

Matthew lifted his, then dropped it again. "Mine's empty."

She shook the one beside her. It felt as if it was at least half full, so she pulled over a safe distance from passing traffic and got out to give it to him and stretch her back at the same time.

As soon as she opened Matthew's door, Greydon pressed his hands together in a heartfelt appeal. "Can we still go to Disneyland? Please?"

A semi whizzed past, creating a huge gust of wind that blew Margot's clothes around and caused her hair to fly into her face. "If you're both good until I can get to the next city and rent a motel room," she said, using one hand to hold her hair back.

"Can you get one with a swimming pool this time?" Matthew asked.

The others had had pools. They'd just checked in too late to use them. But it was earlier today, only dinnertime according to the clock on the dash, and she didn't see any point in soldiering on. The boys had obviously endured all they could take of being in the car. So had her lower back. "Yes. I'll stop in the next town, and we'll get a room with a pool."

Matthew's expression darkened with suspicion. "Wait... Can we still go to Disneyland if we swim tonight?"

"I think so."

Greydon broke off drinking from his own bottle. "Tomorrow?"

"No, it'll take another day of driving just to get there," she told him.

Matthew groaned. "*More* driving?"

"Yes, but then that's it." And if they had Disneyland waiting at the end of the trip, she just might be able to encourage them through another long day in the car.

Once again, Greydon leaned forward to see around his brother. "We're stopping at Disneyland?"

"Yes, we're stopping at Disneyland, and we'll rent a house in LA."

Matthew handed her water bottle back to her. "What does that mean?"

It meant she saw no reason to go any farther. There were four million people in Los Angeles—she could certainly get lost in a place like that. The weather was gorgeous most of the time, an improvement over the cold they would've experienced had they stayed in Wakefield for the winter. And there were plenty of fun things to do to keep them all busy.

Rent would be high. But hopefully, there'd be plenty of job opportunities, too.

"It means we're going to stay there for a bit and see how we like it," she said.

He looked even more confused. "What about Dad?"

"I think he's going to be hunting for a while." She left it at that, and they didn't seem to have a problem with it. But then... they didn't understand that he'd be hunting for *them*.

21

Gia had refused to let her mother answer Sheldon's call, but he wasn't giving up easily. He'd called Ida probably five more times throughout the day. He'd tried to reach Leo, too. When he couldn't get either one of them, he'd finally deigned to try Gia. Like her parents, she let the call transfer to voicemail. Although he'd left both her parents a message asking them to call him, he'd left a much longer one for her.

Hey, do you know where Margot is? Is she staying there with you and your folks? I've been trying to check in with her the last couple of days, but she's not picking up. I assumed she was just busy and would get back to me when she could, but then the school called, asking why the boys weren't in class. Can you go over to make sure everything's okay?

Gia had just finished the dinner dishes and was folding towels in the laundry room off the kitchen as she listened to that message. She played it three times, trying to decide how to respond. She didn't want to alarm him. Then he might cut his hunting trip short and come home sooner than Margot was expecting, and Gia guessed that wasn't what her sister would want. It stood to reason that she'd left when Sheldon did because of the lead it gave her.

But maybe Margot had only needed a few days. She'd already had the chance to get far away from Wakefield...

Still, just to be safe, Gia was about to call him back and try to buy more time by claiming she'd drive over and check first thing in the morning, when there was a knock at the front door.

The volume of the TV went down as voices floated to her ears from the living room.

"I've been over there twice. It didn't look as if anything had changed, so I asked some of the neighbors if they'd seen her, and the guy in the white house told me she left right after Sheldon did and hasn't been home since."

That was Sheldon's mother. Gia easily recognized her voice. Apparently, he'd gotten his family involved, too. And why wouldn't he? It made sense that he'd rope in whomever he could to check on his family.

"I don't know what's going on," Gia heard her father say and hurried out of the laundry room to find that Peggy hadn't come alone. Ron, Sheldon's father, was standing next to her.

"Hey," Gia said to them.

Sheldon's parents turned toward her, but neither one of them offered her a smile or moved to embrace her. That didn't surprise her, though. She never got a very warm greeting from Sheldon's family, not since she'd called him out at the wedding. "Have you seen your sister?" Peggy asked.

"Not for a few days," Gia replied.

"Do you know if your mother's spoken to Margot more recently?"

"Maybe." Gia shrugged. "But Mom's already taken her pain pills and gone to bed. We'll have to ask her in the morning. Why? Is something wrong?"

"She's gone," Peggy replied.

Trying to come off as authentically surprised, Gia looked questioningly at her father before returning her gaze to Sheldon's mother. "What do you mean she's gone? Where'd she go?"

Ron was obviously as agitated as his wife. "That's just it," he said, jumping in. "We don't know. You haven't heard from her?"

"Not lately."

"Do you have a key to the house?" he asked.

Gia pressed a hand to her chest. "*I* don't. But then, I don't even live here, so I'd be unlikely to have something like that."

"We don't have one, either," Leo volunteered, speaking for himself and Ida.

Peggy reached into her purse and pulled out a key she showed them. "Sheldon gave me this years ago when they were going to be gone and he needed to me to take care of the hamsters— before they became class pets at school. But it hasn't worked for months."

Gia knew why. Margot had mentioned that her in-laws would let themselves in at will, even if she wasn't home. Usually, it was to leave food or return something Sheldon or the boys had forgotten at their house, which was a nice thing, but the invasion of privacy made Margot uncomfortable. Gia would've simply asked for the key back, but Margot had been afraid it would start an argument, so she'd prevailed upon Sheldon to change the locks. She'd been proud of that win, since he hadn't wanted to do it. He'd seen no need for it, thought she was being ridiculous. But she'd said he'd grown tired of her complaints. "Maybe they lost a spare and had to change the locks," she suggested.

Peggy dropped it back in her purse. "Regardless of the reason, this key no longer works, and I need to get in."

Gia had broken a window, but if they hadn't noticed that yet, she wasn't about to make them aware of it. She intended to impede their search, draw it out as long as possible, to give her sister time to think things through and, hopefully, come back before this situation got any more out of hand. "I wish I knew how," she said. "Have you tried calling Margot?"

"Many times," Peggy replied. "So has Sheldon. Even the school has tried. The boys didn't show up for class this morning, and Matthew had a book report due."

Gia had her sister's phone in a drawer in her bedroom, but that was her little secret. "It's not like Margot to let him miss something like that."

"Exactly," Peggy said. "Something's wrong. I hate to say this, but...I think she's run off."

"Run off?" Gia echoed, her stomach cramping as she realized that it was probably already too late to have this end peacefully.

Peggy pursed her lips, moving them only slightly as she said, "I think she's leaving Sheldon and taking the kids."

"Why would she do that when he treats her so well?" Gia knew even as she said it that she was going too far, and the hostile expression on Margot's in-laws' faces told her they'd picked up on the sarcasm.

"He *did* treat her good," Ron insisted. "He's worked his ass off to support her and those boys!"

Gia couldn't help coming right back at him. "She never asked him to be the sole breadwinner. That was *his* idea of what a marriage should look like, not hers. If you ask me, she needed to work, needed an outlet where she associated with other adults on occasion and she could earn a little money of her own. But he was determined to retain absolute control— of her and their finances."

Peggy's eyes flashed with anger. "You know where she is, don't you? You're behind this. You're the reason she finally got the nerve to go."

Gia felt her jaw drop. "I had nothing to do with it! I didn't even know she was going to leave. And I don't know exactly why she did, *if* she did, but it could be because of the affair he's having with his ex-girlfriend, right? Have you heard about that?"

"What affair?" Ron asked, grimacing to show his skepticism.

"You *haven't* heard?" Gia asked. "He's been seen all over town with Cece Sonderman. Everyone's talking about it."

Peggy touched her husband's arm to let him know she wanted the floor. "I've heard those rumors, too. And I've spoken to Sheldon about them. He's assured me that he and Cece are only friends."

"And you believe him?" Gia scoffed. "You think he'd tell you if he was cheating?"

Peggy's glower darkened. "My son has never been a liar. He's not a cheater, either. And Margot needs to believe that. That's why we have to find her—to tell her she's making a big mistake. So...where is she?"

Gia threw up her hands. "I don't know!"

"She can't just leave!" Ron said.

"I guess she can, since it looks like she has," Gia said. "But there must be a good reason for it. No woman—not someone like Margot, anyway—takes her kids and runs away because it sounds like fun."

Rob's eyebrows knitted into one long, scruffy gray line. "You have no idea what you've started."

His threatening tone sparked Gia's temper. "I haven't started anything! But I know my sister. She would not have left unless she felt she had no other choice—and if you try to make this all her fault or hurt her in any way, you'll find out very quickly that she's got family to support her. It's between her and Sheldon. It has nothing to do with you."

Peggy gritted her teeth. "It has *everything* to do with us," she argued. "Those boys are our grandchildren. She'd better bring them back, or she'll have hell to pay!"

She whirled around to leave, and Ron followed her out without so much as closing the slider behind them.

"Oh, my God," Leo said. "This can't be happening. Not right now."

Gia closed and locked the door. "I know, but it's about time

Margot fought back. Now that she's left Sheldon, we'll help her through it. I'm not going to let that bastard get away with anything else."

He hardly looked comforted. "You think the marriage is over?"

She frowned. "Don't you?"

Gia wished Margot would call again. She wanted to warn her sister that the school had alerted Sheldon to the fact that the boys weren't in class and that his parents were now involved and had probably notified him about what the neighbor had said. But she didn't hear from Margot that evening. It was nearly eleven before she gave up pacing and monitoring her phone, just in case, and went to the pool.

It was cold outside, but she was too agitated to sleep and pre-occupied with checking Cormac's house, as she'd been doing for hours, to see if he might be at his window, possibly looking for her.

Was he even around?

She'd seen a light on at his place earlier, but it'd been dark for the past couple of hours. He was probably asleep. She didn't know his schedule, but she guessed he'd had to work today and would most likely have to work tomorrow.

She sat on the chaise and called Eric to check on their business.

"How's it going out there?" he asked after reassuring her that all was well.

Did she tell him her sister had run away with her nephews? That her gun-loving braggart of a brother-in-law would probably be showing up on her parents' doorstep mad as hell in the next day or two? Or that she'd gone to bed with the son of the man who'd caused so much trauma in her life seventeen years ago? Those things were certainly noteworthy. She'd had no idea that coming back to face what her mother was going through would mean getting embroiled in so many other complicated situations.

Still, she was glad she'd come home. She understood now that Margot had been hanging on by a very thin thread and her parents had desperately needed her. But she had a funny feeling that what was happening here would affect the rest of her life, which certainly wasn't something she'd anticipated when she caught her flight out of Idaho.

Actually, she'd realized she'd lose her mother, which would affect her life. But what was happening here went beyond that. It was changing a lot of her relationships—with her sister, her friends, even Cormac. They were no longer enemies. That dramatic of a change, along with everything else, made her uneasy.

She'd finally felt settled and at peace in her life, which was why she decided to keep everything that was happening in Wakefield to herself. These were her problems, not Eric's. He had enough to deal with running the business so she could take care of her mom.

"Everything's...great," she said but shook her head as she stared up at the stars.

They talked about Ingrid losing another tooth and Coty screwing up as the Tooth Fairy and forgetting to put money under her pillow. They'd had to fake their daughter out by acting as though she hadn't searched hard enough, at which point they'd planted a twenty—guilt money—while helping her look.

Gia laughed in all the right places, said all the right things and acted as if all was well. But after she hung up, the fact that she missed the simplicity of her life in Coeur d'Alene didn't stop her from looking at Cormac's house, wishing she could at least talk to him. That didn't entirely make sense since she'd just counted him as a complication she didn't need, but she couldn't help feeling a jolt of excitement when she saw movement at his bedroom window.

Seconds later, her phone pinged with a text.

You look lonely.

She smiled at his message.

I am lonely.

Regardless of anything else, that much was true. She'd been lonely for years, and yet, despite all the men she'd dated, no one had been able to fill that void.

I can fix that. ☺

Knowing he was there looking out at her, she glanced up at his window.

I think you might be part of the problem, she wrote but added a smiley emoji to take the harshness from that statement.

Me? I'm harmless.

It's late. Why aren't you asleep?

Honest answer? I can't quit thinking about you.

Well, in the spirit of full disclosure, you'd probably be smart to keep your distance. I have a lot of crazy things going on in my life right now. I'm like...radioactive. LOL

What if that doesn't scare me?

Falling into Cormac's arms sounded far more appealing than it should have, so appealing she found herself writing, I admire a risk-taker. Front or back door?

He directed her to the back door, where he met her and pressed her up against the wall to kiss her as soon as she came in.

The feeling that swept through Gia in that moment was charged with excitement. She liked Cormac—his manner, his voice, his smile, the way he touched her—more than anyone she'd ever been with.

Not him, she thought. *Anyone but him.* And yet…as he led her upstairs and stripped off her clothes before pulling her into his bed, she told herself she didn't have anything to worry about. She'd never fallen in love before. She didn't think she *could*. Chances were much greater that this was just another relationship she'd enjoy for now but wouldn't make a meaningful impact.

When Cormac's alarm went off the following morning, he was loath to move. He could feel Gia in the bed next to him and wished he could roll over and make love to her again. Instead, he kissed her neck, her jawline and then her lips before, with a regretful groan, forcing himself to climb out of bed.

"Don't tell me it's morning," she mumbled, clearly not any happier than he was to find the night already over.

"It is for me. I promised to take one of my clients to the park to walk their dog. Then I have to get to the clinic. But it's pretty early. You can stay and sleep if you want."

She shoved the hair out of her eyes. "And if my parents realize I'm gone?"

"I doubt they'll come looking for you over here," he said with a chuckle.

She gave him a wry smile. "I can only imagine what they'd think to see me walking back through the gate looking this disheveled. They'd definitely be able to tell I spent the night here."

"What *would* they think about that?" he asked. "Would they be upset?"

Her smile disappeared. "Who knows? They've been through so much lately."

She pushed up onto her elbows, which inadvertently caused the sheet to fall to a tantalizing level—where it barely covered her breasts. Having her in his bed made it that much harder for him to fulfill his word to Mrs. Wood, but how could he cancel on her again? He'd already sent her a text in the middle of the night saying he'd be thirty minutes late.

"I wouldn't want them to find me gone in the first place," Gia added, "especially given that their other daughter is missing."

After they'd made love, she'd told him what was going on with Margot while lying in his arms. It was arguably his favorite part of the night because it was so...*companionable.* That she'd trust him with information about her family and her concerns, and wasn't eager to get up and hurry home, came as a welcome surprise. "You think Sheldon will show up today and cause trouble?"

"He might. If his parents were able to get hold of him, I bet he's already on his way home."

Cormac got a pair of jogging shorts out of his drawer. "Where do you think Margot could be?"

"I can't even venture a guess. After three days of travel, she could be anywhere. I still can't believe she took off like that on her own."

"Maybe she'll call again."

"I hope so. I really need to talk to her."

He dug through a stack of T-shirts. This time of year, he started out with a sweatshirt, too, but he usually peeled that off after the first mile. "I'm afraid of what Sheldon will do when he realizes she's taken their money."

Gia grimaced. "Yeah, something tells me he might care more about that than the kids."

Cormac looked back at her. "Are you serious?"

"Not entirely," she said. "Although he's left taking care of them almost completely to her."

He imagined the desperation Margot must've felt to do what she'd done. "You don't believe he'd ever get *violent* with her… or with you?"

"Your guess is as good as mine. She's obviously afraid of him, but maybe it's mostly a fear of losing the children. He's been large and in charge for so long, I don't think she has a lot of confidence in her ability to defy him, which is why she left him the way she did."

She got out of bed, and he couldn't help admiring what he saw. "God, you're gorgeous," he said. "I've always thought so."

She looked slightly startled by the compliment, and he thought the smile that spread over her face as her gaze briefly met his was more beautiful than any other part of her. "I've got a heart of gold, too," she joked. "After all, I was just about to offer to make you breakfast."

"Don't you have to get home before your parents realize you're gone?"

She picked up her phone, presumably to check for any texts or calls she'd missed. "They won't be up for another hour. I think I'm okay."

"Then I'll gladly let you make breakfast." He grinned. "That's the nicest offer I've received since…well, since what you gave me last night."

She laughed and tossed the clothes he'd left on the floor at him. "Go ahead and finish getting ready while I fumble my way through your kitchen, hoping to find the groceries I need."

"What do you plan to make?"

"I'll figure it out once I see your pantry."

"I'll let you surprise me then." He stopped to kiss her one last time—and allowed himself to linger over her lips and tongue for a few extra seconds—before going into the bathroom.

By the time he got out, he could hear her moving around downstairs and the smell of bacon wafted up to him. He wasn't looking forward to another tense day working with Louisa, but it was hard to worry about that when he had Gia here.

After he got dressed and went downstairs, he found that she was wearing one of his sweatshirts, which she must've found tossed across the chair in his room. It hit her at midthigh, making him wonder if she was wearing anything underneath.

"I hope you don't mind me borrowing this," she said, lifting the soft fleece in the front. "But it's getting chillier and chillier as the days go by."

"No problem. I'm not sure how you managed to withstand the cold last night, coming out in a T-shirt and no jacket."

"I was too agitated to worry about the temperature. But I wasn't prepared for it this morning, not after leaving the warmth of your bed."

He poured himself a cup of the coffee she'd brewed. "You can take it with you, if you like, and bring it back tonight."

She sent him a quizzical glance. "You think I'm staying over again?"

He raised his eyebrows. "Why not?"

"I could name several reasons, but let's start with the fact that you're going to need some sleep at some point!"

"I'll manage," he said. "Having you stay over again will be worth the trade-off."

She'd fried eggs as well as bacon and made toast. She said she was waiting to eat with her parents, since she'd have to make them breakfast when they got up, too, but she sat down with him, drinking a cup of coffee while he ate, and they talked about his work. He told her how uncomfortable it was at the clinic these days with Louisa and that he planned to tell his sisters his father had basically admitted what he'd done as soon as his mother could arrange a family meeting.

"How do you think they'll react?" she asked.

"I have no idea."

She set her mug on the table. "Are you sure you should even

tell them? At this point, it might be kinder just to let them believe what they believe."

She had the most to gain from the truth coming out. But he was already starting to understand that she was more emotionally mature than most people. That was one of the things he admired about her—what drew him beyond her beauty. "Except that it's not the truth."

"There's that," she agreed.

He reached over to take her hand. "It's time everyone knows you weren't the one who was lying."

"If you say so," she said, her face pinched with worry. "But I hate that you and your sisters—and your mother, of course—are victims of his behavior, too." With a sad smile, she slid off her stool. "I'd better get dressed."

"Okay. Thanks for breakfast."

He rinsed off the dishes while she started toward the stairs, but as soon as he turned off the garbage disposal, he heard the four beeps corresponding to the combination that offered an alternative way to unlock his front door.

He turned in surprise, and Gia did the same from the stairs, as his father stepped inside. "Cormac?" Evan shouted as he closed the door behind him. "I knocked, but—" He fell silent as he lifted his gaze, and they all gaped at each other. Then, blinking several times as if he couldn't believe his eyes, his father said, "You're *sleeping* with her?"

22

The seventeen years that'd passed since her former English teacher's trial hadn't been good to him. Gia had been able to tell that much when he'd accosted her at Delia's Big Buns. But with a bright sun overhead and the shadowing inside his vehicle, she hadn't seen the deep lines in his face; those were much more apparent when standing in the same room.

Of course, she'd gotten only a glimpse of him before turning and running upstairs—although she was covered, she wasn't fully dressed—but that brief moment was enough to tell her he wasn't in a good state. His clothes were rumpled and dirty, his hair was uncombed and had outgrown any style or shape it once had, and the gray in his scruffy beard growth added even more years.

Because she didn't feel as though she had any right to say anything—*she* was the interloper here—she was leaving whatever unfolded downstairs to Cormac. But unless she was willing to pass through the living room and risk being drawn into the confrontation, she knew she'd be trapped in the house until the coast was clear.

She yanked on her jeans while their voices rose from below.

"How could you?" Evan yelled. "How could you act so morally superior, as if you would support me if only your conscience would allow it, when you were just trying to curry favor with her?"

"I wasn't trying to curry favor," Cormac said.

"Are you telling me you're *not* sleeping with her?"

"I'm not telling you anything, because it's none of your business!"

"She was wearing your sweatshirt and nothing else. I saw her fucking *panties* as she ran up those stairs, Cormac," Evan said.

Gia felt her face burn with embarrassment. She'd never dreamed they'd be so rudely interrupted, not this early.

"There's no question about what you've been doing," Evan railed. "And it *is* absolutely my business because it would color your judgment! I've been dealing with a deck that's suddenly been stacked against me. This explains everything."

"That isn't what influenced my opinion, Dad. If you want the truth, *you're* the one who convinced me by the way you've behaved. Can you even see yourself these days? Look at you! You never get up this early, so I'm guessing you haven't even been to bed. You probably read until you were too tired to see straight. Then you started drinking. You smell like you just crawled out of a bottle, for God's sake. Why wouldn't you sleep, shower and get ready for work like most other people? Please don't tell me you've called in sick again."

"I need a mental health day, thanks to you," Evan exploded. "How do you expect me to work when you're going around telling everyone that I admitted to inappropriately touching one of my students?"

"That's molestation, Dad. You molested Gia when she was your student. Let's finally call it what it is. And maybe you could quit lying while we're at it!"

"You'd better not tell Louisa and Edith I admitted to anything, because I didn't!"

"Wait, hold up," Cormac said, his voice changing tone. "You've talked to *Mom*? Did she call you, or—?"

"We're still friends, you know," Evan broke in.

"Friends?" Cormac echoed. "Since when?"

"She's older and wiser than you and understands how nuanced life can be."

"I won't argue that there are a million shades of gray in life, but trying to get one of your students to sleep with you isn't the least bit nuanced. It's just plain wrong. So tell me, did Mom call you?"

Gia could tell that having Sharon go to Evan felt like a betrayal to Cormac. That his mother would contact her ex-husband made it appear as though she was siding with him. Gia could understand why that would upset Cormac, and yet Evan was also right. It wasn't just life that was complicated—it was relationships. Sharon had married him once. She had three kids with him. Maybe she still cared about him or was acting for some other reason.

"She came over when she got off her shift at the hospital an hour or so ago," Evan said. "Apparently, she feels more loyalty to me than you do."

Now dressed, Gia hovered in Cormac's bedroom, out of sight and watching the clock on her phone nervously as it drew closer and closer to the time her parents normally got up.

"That's why she came over?" Cormac asked. "That's what she said?"

"She's worried about what this could do to our family, Cormac, and so am I."

"You're worried about what this could to do *you*," Cormac corrected. "That's what you've always been worried about, why you would never admit the truth, even though that would've been far better for Gia and the rest of us. That way, we wouldn't have continued to defend someone who's guilty and who doesn't deserve it. That way, we couldn't be split in our opinions on the matter and end up exactly where we are today!"

"Cormac, listen to me," Evan said. "Please don't say anything to Edith and Louisa. Why would you want to destroy their good opinion of me? It's the last thing I've got left!"

At this, Gia couldn't help herself. Throwing the bedroom door open, she walked out onto the landing, which overlooked the living room below. "Don't tell them, Cormac," she said. "Just...leave it. The past is the past. And I'll soon be gone, so hopefully you won't feel you have to continue to defend me."

When Evan looked up at her, he seemed taken aback that *she'd* show him such mercy, but he was quick to take advantage of it by turning supplicating eyes on his son. "Come on," he said to Cormac. "Even she says you shouldn't tell them. Whatever you think, I've been through enough. After the horrific public ordeal of that trial, I lost my job, my reputation, my marriage..."

"And you've done nothing to try to build it all back," Cormac said. "That's my point."

"But I will," Evan insisted. "If you let this go, I'll pull myself together and put it behind me at last."

Cormac looked from Gia to his father and back again. "But it's not fair."

Gia sighed. "If we can stop this thing from continuing to hurt people, I think we should."

"That's just it," Cormac said. "*You* haven't hurt anyone. And yet you're having more compassion for him than he is for you."

Gia's parents got up at seven. She wanted to be home and in her own bed well before that.

She checked the time again, saw that it was edging closer to six thirty, and jogged down the stairs. "The people who matter most believe me. I've got a thriving business to go back to, where none of this really affects me anymore. I can forget and move on, but—" she jerked her thumb at Evan "—he may never be able to repair his relationships with Louisa and Edith.

Just…let them think they're right. Maybe it's better if they believe *I'm* the bad guy."

Cormac scowled. "It goes against my sense of justice, but…"

"But?" Evan echoed hopefully.

Ignoring his father, he kept his gaze on her. "I don't want to hurt my sisters."

"Then patch things up with them and let it go." Gia squeezed his arm as she passed him on her way to the back door. "I'll talk to you later."

She walked out without so much as looking back at Mr. Hart. What he was thinking or feeling no longer mattered to her. This moment was about what *she* was feeling, and she was feeling a new kind of vitality. The past hadn't beaten her. Although there were moments since she'd come back when it felt as though a frightening specter was reaching out and trying to drag her back into the swamp she'd escaped seventeen years ago, she was no longer frightened. She'd finally slayed that swamp creature, put the past to rest.

Now she was facing a future free of the anger and upset, even the bitterness, caused by the injustice of Mr. Hart's actions, because it simply didn't matter to her anymore. By telling Cormac to let what his father had done go, *she'd* finally been able to let it go. She was writing it off as a loss, perhaps, but it was a loss she was now confident she'd fully recovered from.

She was finally unencumbered, wasn't hauling around old grievances.

And that meant everything.

Thanks to his father's unexpected visit, Cormac ended up having to skip his run, but he got Mrs. Wood and Astro out for a half hour walk, which was better than nothing. After he dropped them off at home, he went straight to the clinic.

Louisa wasn't there yet. She was still punishing him, he supposed—letting him feel her extreme displeasure.

He heard the bell over the door and Dorothy Backus's voice, speaking to her two kittens. Their first appointment had shown up before Louisa—a repeat of yesterday. But, fortunately, the sound of an engine rose to his ears only two or three minutes later.

He peered out through the blinds in his office to see her truck pull into the back lot. "Talk about waiting until the last minute," he grumbled.

Telling himself everything would soon be put right, he pulled on his lab coat while she finished parking and got out. He was planning to meet her as she walked in and ask her to come into his office for a quick chat. As much as he hated to do a mea culpa when he wasn't really the one who was wrong, he'd decided to take the pass Gia was offering him and his family. If she could be that generous, he figured he might as well accept the kindness for the sake of his sisters, especially since he believed his mother had been colluding with the enemy. He'd never seen that coming.

But when he left his office, said good morning to Mrs. Backus and saw Louisa step through the door, he could tell she'd been crying. Her red-rimmed eyes made it all too apparent.

"Mrs. Backus, would you mind giving me and Louisa a few minutes?" he asked.

The stout, gregarious woman who owned a small card and gift boutique downtown, in which almost everything was cat related, gave him a look that indicated she'd noticed the evidence of tears on Louisa's face, too. "Not at all."

Louisa waved a hand. "There's no need to make anyone wait," she said, her words clipped, and kept her head down as she rounded the counter to stow her purse.

"It'll only take a moment." Cormac was wearing a smile but knew she'd heard the steel in his voice when she removed her sweater, draped it over the back of her chair and followed him, reluctantly, into the office.

"What's going on?" he asked as soon as he closed the door.

Her voice sounded choked when she responded, "I don't even know where to start."

"Does this have to do with Dad?" He was hoping she'd say yes so that he could go into his apology and get it over with. But she surprised him.

"When were you going to tell me, Cormac?" she asked, bursting into fresh tears.

He was at a complete loss. "What are you talking about?"

"You know what I'm talking about."

His mind grappled for how this might fit into his current understanding of the problem, but he came up empty. "I don't. Is this related to what happened at the Banned Books reunion? Are we going back to that? Because I've been thinking about that…um…situation, and I'm willing to say that I certainly didn't mean to hurt you. I don't know *exactly* what happened back when Dad was teaching, so…you should just go on believing what you've always believed. For all I know…"

He'd meant to say something like *For all I know, you could be right*. But he knew she *wasn't* right and couldn't conjure those words. "Never mind. Believe whatever is easiest for you, and I'll go along with it."

She gaped at him. "If that was supposed to be an apology, it sucked, especially because I know that you've been sleeping with Gia. I was right when I asked if you were interested in her, yet you denied it!"

Cormac nearly missed his chair when he sat down. He was so stunned he hadn't bothered to look behind him. Why would his father go and blab to the girls when he'd been given a "get out of jail free" card he didn't even deserve? "Dad told you that?"

"Yes, he did." She sniffed and wiped her nose with the back of her hand. "He said he went over to your house this morning to talk to you, and there she was, half naked in your kitchen."

Cormac had just shaved and yet he could hear the rasp of fresh beard growth as he rubbed his chin. "Louisa—"

She put up a hand. "And before you go after him, insisting he really did molest Gia, I know that now, too. Mom set me straight."

Another surprise. He sat up taller. "When did you talk to Mom?"

"She came by early this morning, said she didn't want me to be mad at you when you were right."

"But she also went over to Dad's—"

"To ask him if he really admitted what you said he did."

Cormac scratched his head. "And he told her the truth?"

"No. But she was hoping he would. She wanted to do away with every last shred of doubt, has always tried to reserve judgment—just in case he was being falsely accused."

"And?"

"He denied admitting anything to you. But she said she could tell he was lying. And she'd take your word against his any day."

Cormac struggled to piece together the events of the morning. "So...after Mom got off at the hospital, she stopped by his place, then went over and told you not to be mad at me because I'm right? What about Edith?"

"Mom's probably talked to her, too. She told me we couldn't let this tear our family apart, that we had to be mad at the right person and you're not the one. But when I called Dad to tell him I'll never speak to him again, he said of course you'd believe Gia—you're sleeping with her."

That was the missing link right there. Their father had tried to defend himself by throwing Cormac under the bus, even though it was Cormac and Gia who'd been kind enough to agree not to tell Louisa and Edith the truth. He'd known his mother had visited his father, but he'd assumed that was it, had no idea she would finally go into action and take a firm stand.

Laughing mirthlessly, Cormac shook his head.

"You think it's funny?" Louisa asked.

It *was* kind of funny that the truth had come out, anyway. But Cormac wasn't going to say that. "I think our father doesn't have nearly the character I once believed he did," he said instead, which was also true.

Blinking her tears back, Louisa dashed a hand across her cheeks. "Yeah, well, thanks for destroying any admiration *I* had for him." She got to her feet to leave the office, but he called her back.

"*I* didn't do that, and you know it," he said. "Sure, I was going to let you know he was guilty—I thought it was only right that we all accept the truth—but you know who talked me out of it? Who said I should let you believe whatever was easiest for you to believe so you wouldn't be hurt any worse?"

She didn't look as though she cared to guess but was curious enough to say, sullenly, "Who?"

"Gia," he replied.

When Sheldon's call came in, Gia told herself to ignore it, to maintain her silence for a little longer, in case she heard from her sister and could get some idea of how Margot wanted her to handle the situation. But she was afraid she wouldn't hear from Margot—and maybe he could provide some answers. She wanted to know what had gone wrong, why Margot had left without saying a word to anyone and where she might've gone. Whatever he could contribute might prove helpful.

Besides, Gia was curious to find out how he was reacting to the fact that his wife had finally wised up and left him. At this point, she figured more information was better than less, so she quickly closed the door to her bedroom and answered before the call could transfer to voicemail. "Hello?"

"What the fuck's going on?" he demanded without preamble.

That answered one question. He was as furious as she'd expected him to be. Gia guessed she was about to see the worst of her brother-in-law—and she'd never liked him much to begin with. "That's what I'd like to ask you."

"You and your parents won't even answer my calls!"

It sounded as though he was in his truck, probably on speakerphone since it was an old vintage Chevy, which wouldn't have Bluetooth. She could hear road noise as well as country music playing in the background. "I just answered this one."

"Is it true?" he demanded. "Has Margot taken the boys and left?"

"That's what your parents are saying, but... I have no idea."

"Bullshit!" he shouted. "You have to have some role in what's happening. If there's trouble, you're always behind it."

She wanted to say that even at her worst she couldn't be as bad as he was, but she was afraid he'd just hang up, and she hadn't gotten any information yet. "I'm telling you—honest to God—I don't know where she is."

"She just happens to pick one of the rare moments when you're in town to pull this shit?"

"Wait a minute! You happen to be having an affair. That could have something to do with it, right?"

"Oh, my God. For the last time, I'm *not* having an affair!"

"Even if that was true—and with the rumors that are going around I highly doubt it—you were going out of town for a week, which gave her the perfect opportunity to gather whatever she needed without you knowing a thing. I bet she made her plans around your hunting trip more than my return, although I do believe I played a role, since she needed me to come home to take care of Mom."

"You're saying you didn't know this was going to happen? That you didn't encourage it, didn't help with it?"

"That's exactly what I'm saying! There's no way I'd suggest she run off, not considering what's going on with my mother!" When she passed the window, she couldn't help but stop to look out at Cormac's house. It'd become a terrible habit. "I'm not going to lie, though," she said when she didn't see any evidence that her backyard neighbor was home. "If she *had* come to me and told me she was unhappy, I would've encouraged her to leave you. I knew she was making a mistake marrying you in the first place."

There was a brief silence. Then he said, "No way..."

She'd just insulted him. Gia had expected him to come right back at her with something even more scathing, so this two-word, somewhat restrained reply took her off guard. "No way... what?" she asked uncertainly.

"I believe you. Somehow, I thought for sure you'd engineered this, but I think she knew I'd assume you were involved, which is why she left you out of it."

"From what I can tell, she left *everyone* out of it. Took no chances." Margot had even abandoned her phone, but Gia was never going to volunteer that piece of information. Sheldon would just demand she give it to him, and she wasn't about to do that in case he could do what she hadn't been able to and get inside it. "So...what are you going to do?"

"I'm on my way back right now to figure out what the hell's going on. She won't get away with this, I'll tell you that much."

Gia wanted to ask what he thought he could do about it, but she knew they'd end up in a fight if she did. Trying to keep calm long enough to pump him for as much as he could tell her, she asked, "Do you know where she might've gone?"

"I have no clue."

"In the past few months, you haven't heard her mention a certain place she'd like to visit? She hasn't been looking at travel brochures or surfing other towns or cities on the internet?"

"Not that I've seen."

He'd probably been too busy with Cece to notice what his wife was doing. "Could she be involved with another man?"

"She'd better not be," he snapped.

An ironic response, considering Gia was almost certain he

was lying about his ex-girlfriend. But for the time being, she let that go. "So what do you think's going on?"

"I think people have been sticking their noses into my business and gossiping about me all over town, and it has her freaked out. If I could just speak to her, everything will be fine."

"You think she'd come back?"

"I know she would. She has no way to survive. She *has* to come back."

Gia passed the window again—and checked to see if Cormac might be home from work even though it'd only been a minute or two since she'd done it last time. "I don't think so, Sheldon."

"You don't know that," he said.

She resumed her pacing. "Except... I do."

"What do you mean?"

Should she tell him? He was going to find out anyway, so she didn't see where it would make any difference. And maybe it was mean-spirited, but she was sort of eager to be the one to deliver the news that Margot had taken all their money. "She called here once."

"You lied to me, after all?"

"No. I said I don't know where she is, and I don't. I also said I didn't know she was going to do it, and I didn't."

"So...what'd she say? She didn't tell you where she was?"

"No, she wouldn't. She just wanted me to give my mom and dad her love."

"What about the number she called from. Maybe that will tell us something."

"She blocked it before she called me."

"And you couldn't hear anything in the background that might give her away?"

"Nothing."

"Well, there's only so much money in her account."

"She has her own account?" Gia asked in surprise.

"It's for gas and groceries—the household account—and she's

always complaining there isn't enough in it. But right now, I'm glad I didn't raise her budget. That money won't last long."

"Sheldon…"

No doubt he heard the ominous tone in her voice, because he hesitated before saying, "What?"

"She told me she has enough to get an apartment and a new car."

The volume of the radio went down in the background. "Where would she get that kind of money? And why would she want to get rid of the Subaru? That's a great vehicle!" he said, but the answer to that question must've dawned on him immediately after. "Wait, she wants to get rid of it so the police can't trace the license plate?"

"See what I mean?" Gia said. "She's not coming back."

The phone went dead quiet, which scared Gia more than if Sheldon had exploded in rage. "She must've taken our savings, then."

Gia winced. *Bingo!* "Maybe that's it."

His voice dropped an octave, at least, and grew threatening. "If she did, she'd better hope I never find her."

A chill ran down Gia's back as he disconnected. She was used to standing up to people. And she'd never been afraid of Sheldon before. But she was beginning to believe Margot: there was something missing, something wrong with him.

23

Disneyland was everything Margot had imagined it would be. She refused to worry about the expense of the tickets or the food. She let the boys buy almost whatever they wanted, and they had an absolutely marvelous time riding rides, eating at Goofy's Kitchen, taking pictures with the various characters who were stationed throughout the park and buying matching T-shirts along with Mickey Mouse balloons and caramel apples rolled in M&M's on Main Street. Despite what was going on in her life, she was so far away from Sheldon and Wakefield that she felt safe and free for the first time in ages and wondered if this was how it would be in the future. Could she truly escape him? Make her own money and spend it however she wanted?

She couldn't even imagine what it would be like to live without his cutting rebukes when she didn't put enough ice in his Thermos, or she spread too much mayonnaise on his sandwich. It was always something—there was no way to be perfect enough.

She felt bad she'd had to leave her parents and Gia, but she was so happy in this moment she couldn't regret it. *This* was what living was supposed to be about. *This* was building the kind of memories she wanted to have with her children—where they could relax and have fun without the anxiety that ruined even camping when Sheldon was around.

"This is the best day ever!" Greydon exclaimed as he and Matthew raced to meet her after coming off Mr. Toad's Wild Ride.

She was smiling broadly, standing with the strollers parked near the exit of the ride, and holding their balloons. "I'm glad we came."

"Can we come back tomorrow?" Matthew asked.

"Not tomorrow," she said. "But we'll do other fun things over the next few months. There are a lot of sights to see in Southern California, including the San Diego Zoo."

"The zoo?" Greydon said. "Can we go *there* tomorrow?"

"I'm afraid not. We need to start looking for an apartment. And I have to put the Subaru up for sale. I should probably start job hunting, too. That might take a while."

She hadn't used her degree since she'd graduated, which would most likely make job hunting more difficult. But she didn't mind living lean and pinching pennies as long as she could feel safe and free, like she did in this moment.

"I'll miss Disneyland," Greydon said as they walked toward the Jungle Cruise. It was Margot's turn to pick a ride, and she'd selected that one.

"We'll come back here if we can—once a year."

The boys paused as they saw the character Belle taking photos with some little girls who were dressed up in the same costume.

"Do you want to go over and get another picture?" she asked.

"No, I like the Beast," Matthew said.

"And we already got one with him," Greydon added.

Margot chuckled. They'd liked Gaston the best, once the young man playing the character started doing one-armed push-ups while showing off for the crowd. "There will be other opportunities. After all, we'll be fairly close to here, so, like I said, we'll get back."

"We can save up!" Greydon volunteered.

"Exactly," she told them. "We'll do what we can. And if we can't afford it, we'll go to a regular park, which is free, and play Frisbee. Or we'll go to the beach, which is also free, and build sandcastles and collect seashells. Or we'll simply make popcorn and watch movies at home. We'll make the most of every day."

"I've never been to the beach," Matthew said.

"Neither of you have," Margot told them. "I've only been a few times myself. But now we can go whenever we want."

"Even in the winter?" Greydon asked.

"If it's warm enough. It doesn't snow here, so we can do things outdoors for most of the year."

"After the Jungle Cruise, can we go on the Peter Pan ride?" Matthew asked.

"You bet. It's your turn to pick the next attraction." Margot slowed them down while searching the crowd for someone who would meet her gaze. "But wait just a second. I want to get a picture of all three of us before we get in line for the Jungle Cruise."

She'd had to purchase a disposable camera to be able to take photographs, and she knew they wouldn't be nearly the quality she could've gotten on her phone. But at least she was able to document this day.

After she stopped a man and asked if he'd take the shot, she squatted down, an arm around each of her boys.

"Thank you," she said afterward, as the man handed her camera back to her. She was just putting it in her bag so she wouldn't lose it when Matthew, squinting against the glare of the sun, looked up at her curiously and said, "You're so different today, Mommy."

"How am I different?" she asked in surprise.

"You're smiling all the time!" he said and gave her an impromptu hug.

She pulled Greydon into the embrace and held both boys tightly. "Because I have a new lease on life," she said. "You're going to get to know the real me at last."

Louisa hadn't been quite as hostile today as she'd been yesterday, but Cormac noticed that she went about her work without having much to say. She was acting like a robot, just going through the motions, and he felt terrible for her. He understood what a blow it was to realize—with the level of certainty he'd come to feel—that Evan wasn't the man they'd always thought he was. It'd hit him hard, too. He'd experienced a profound sense of loss, compounded by humiliation for allowing his father to manipulate him in the first place and embarrassment for ignoring the results of his father's trial and doggedly defending him, anyway. Gia had offered him the commiseration that'd made it a little easier—and the excitement of being with her in such an intimate way. But his sisters didn't have anything with that kind of power to distract them. So he tried to give Louisa the space she needed to come to terms with this latest blow. But even by the end of the day she wasn't quite herself.

"I'm heading home," she said flatly, poking her head into his office.

"Louisa, wait…" He was sitting behind his desk, annotating various patient files and calling to check in on the animals he'd treated in the past few weeks. "Why don't you come in and sit down for a minute so we can talk?"

She looked tired, even defeated, when she shook her head. "Not right now, Cormac. I think I've heard enough for one day."

She was still mad at him for choosing Gia's side over their father's. When she first arrived this morning, she'd insisted he'd done it for the wrong reason—because he'd wanted to get in Gia's pants. But he'd figured out the truth before he'd ever touched Gia. Louisa just wasn't ready to hear that. She preferred to take her hurt and anger out on him because she still felt betrayed that he would show up at the Banned Books Club meeting and support the other side.

"Okay, see you tomorrow," he said and listened as she walked out and locked up behind her.

Cormac had tried calling his mother on his lunch break, but she hadn't answered, and he'd been too busy since. After being at the hospital all night, she was probably sleeping and had her phone turned off, but he was hoping he'd be able to talk to her now, and breathed a sigh of relief when she answered almost immediately.

"You told Louisa that Dad admitted to touching Gia?" he said.

"I did," she replied. "I told Edith, too."

"Why?" he asked. "What happened to calling a family meeting?"

"After some serious reflection about what I could do to make this better—at last—for our family, I decided I didn't want the news to come from you. Because of what happened at the restaurant, I was afraid they'd be tempted to shoot the messenger and would be much less likely to do that if *I* was the one to step forward."

"I appreciate you taking the heat, especially because Dad is definitely fighting back by trying to discredit me."

"I heard."

Cormac switched the phone to his other ear. "He told you, too?"

"No, I'm guessing he knows better than to try that with me. But he told Louisa and Edith. They both called me in tears afterward, insisting I must be wrong."

He shoved the files he'd been working on away from him. "They did? Because Louisa seems to have accepted the truth…"

"It didn't take me long to convince them. Your reputation speaks for itself, Cormac—and so does his."

That he'd established some credibility made Cormac feel a little better. "I don't know about Edith, but Louisa will hardly talk to me."

"They're both upset. Give them some time. They'll come around. Accepting that they were wrong about their 'loving father' isn't easy."

"You realize you're preaching to the choir, that I've had to accept the same thing?"

"I do, which is why I also implored them to go easy on you—even though you're sleeping with the enemy," she added with a laugh.

"Gia didn't do anything wrong."

"I know, honey. I'm just teasing. But…considering the close connection you have to the man who caused her so much pain in the past, it *is* a little surprising."

"*I* had nothing to do with what happened back then. And, fortunately, she recognizes that."

"Not many women could. Even if they didn't hold you accountable for anything, you'd remind them of the past."

"She's not like other women. She's strong, opinionated, feisty."

"She must be pretty special," his mother conceded. "First my husband destroyed his life wanting her, and now my son is sleeping with her. I admit, since the truth has finally come out and it didn't go our way, we've all had to swallow a bitter pill. I'd rather she be out of our lives, so we can go on and forget. Maybe I'm the one who can't handle the reminder."

"You don't have anything to worry about," he assured her. "She won't be in town very long. After Ida's funeral, Gia will be heading back to Coeur d'Alene and her helicopter business."

"And you'll be okay with that?"

"Of course. I'm not likely to fall for someone I know from the beginning I can't have," he said as if that should be obvious.

But even as he brushed off the question, he felt a frisson of concern.

Gia put the pan she'd used in the kitchen sink and left it there so she could focus more fully on the telephone call she'd just answered. When she'd seen Sammie's name appear on caller ID, she'd assumed it was a follow-up to the text she'd received this morning: **Robert Cormier's We All Fall Down is a thriller for young adults?**

When Gia had confirmed that Sammie had the right read, she'd received a second message: **So what's wrong with it? Why was it banned?**

Gia had explained that some parents didn't appreciate the tough issues Cormier tackled or how he went about it. They considered the book too hard-hitting for its intended audience.

It'll be interesting to see if we agree, Sammie had written back, and Gia had thought that was all she'd hear from her friend for the day—until she'd had dinner with her parents, and they'd moved into the living room to watch TV while she did a little food prep for tomorrow. Then Sammie had called her and, in lieu of hello, had said, "Is it true?"

"Are you talking about Margot?" Had the news about her sister running away with Greydon and Matthew already gotten out? If so, Gia had no doubt it would spread like wildfire, adding to the drama surrounding Sheldon's affair.

"I'm talking about Cormac," Sammie said.

Gia had been about to put the bread custard she'd made for breakfast in the oven along with a second pan she planned to take over to Cormac's tonight. But at this, she straightened. "What about him?"

"Are you really sleeping with him?"

Gia could see why her friends would find that shocking. It certainly wasn't anything she'd anticipated, either. But neither had she expected it to become public knowledge. "Who told you that?" she asked tentatively.

"Ruth. She said Edith called her, very upset that you're now involved with her brother."

"We're not *involved*," Gia said. She'd been so focused on her mother and what was happening with her sister that she hadn't even considered how the people in Wakefield would react to having her name coupled with Cormac's in a romantic way. She'd never even thought they'd find out.

"So…you *haven't* slept with him?" Sammie asked, trying to clarify.

Gia moved back to the sink to fill the pan she'd used with water and grimaced at her reflection in the window. "We've become…friends."

"Oh, my God! It's true? I don't believe it! How could that have happened? You two have always hated each other."

"We've never *hated* each other. He thought I was lying, so maybe he hated me for a while, but now he knows I was the one telling the truth."

"He's Mr. Hart's son!" she cried. "How can you even look at him without thinking of our former teacher?"

"I don't know. We've both been affected so deeply by what Mr. Hart did that instead of pushing us apart, it started pulling us together, I guess. We began to commiserate, and one thing led to another."

When Sammie didn't respond, Gia held the phone more tightly to her ear. "Hello? Did you hear me?"

"I heard you," Sammie replied. "I'm just…jealous. And so is Ruth. We've both done everything we can to draw Cormac's attention, and he's nice but never shows any real interest."

"There's nothing to be jealous about," she said. "It's not like

I live here. I'll be heading back to Idaho after—" She couldn't bring herself to continue.

"Then it's not serious."

"Absolutely not! There's something wrong with me. I can't fall in love."

"Does *he* know that?"

"I'm pretty sure he does. But I don't see whether it matters. You told me he hasn't shown any signs of wanting to settle down."

"That's true, but...all it takes is one."

"Stop. If he decided he wanted a girlfriend, it wouldn't be me." He might already have decided to move on, she thought. She'd texted him when she saw his light go on two hours ago to let him know she'd be willing to come over, as he'd asked her to do this morning, and bring some bread pudding, and he hadn't responded.

"Okay, so...at least tell me what he's like in bed," Sammie said with a laugh. "Is he as good as we'd hope?"

She laughed, too. "Honestly? He's probably even better."

Once he got off work and was paying more attention to his phone, Cormac realized he'd missed several calls and texts from his friends today. And more were coming in, but he wasn't answering at the moment. All of them were asking if it was true that he was sleeping with Gia.

Cormac had never intended for his relationship with her to become public. That his father would tell his sisters—who must've told their husbands and/or friends, who must've told the people they knew and so forth—made the hurt and betrayal he'd felt toward his father the past few days harden into something much different. Not pity or compassion. Not even frustration or disappointment. Those emotions were far too mellow and belonged to years past. Now Cormac was feeling downright contempt.

Ignoring all the other calls and messages he'd received, he sent a text to his father.

I can't believe the lengths you'll go to.

It was his father's fault Gia had been abused in the first place. It was his father's fault that it was still an issue seventeen years later. And it was his father's fault that the whole town was now talking about what should've only been his and Gia's business.

You're the one who turned on me, his father texted back.

No remorse. No apology. Stunned, Cormac shook his head.

You're a child. You know that? A selfish child.

You're thinking with the wrong head, Cormac. I'll never understand how you could take Gia's side over mine.

I'm taking her side because you did it, you freaking narcissist! We're not in grade school! This isn't about choosing sides. It's about standing up for the truth.

And that includes fucking her?

Cormac flinched. Evan was trying to make the intimacy Cormac had shared with Gia sound tawdry.

At least I had her permission, he wrote back. Why did his father keep putting the people around him through so much bullshit?

Because he didn't care about the people around him, Cormac decided. And that was what hurt the worst.

"What a mess," he muttered.

Duke was lying at his feet. The dog lifted his head off his paws and cocked it as if to say, *What's wrong?*

"Everything," Cormac said and scrolled back to the text that'd come in from Gia two hours ago.

Let me know when you get home. I'll bring over some bread pudding. If you haven't had it before it might not sound very good, but this was my grandma's recipe, and it's delicious. Trust me. ;)

He told himself he needed to respond. It was growing late; she had to be wondering what was going on with him. But he didn't want to tell her that his father had caused yet another scandal and the whole town was talking about her. She'd definitely regret becoming friends with him, and maybe she wouldn't know if he didn't tell her.

Putting down his phone, he got up to get a beer while he tried to think of a nice way to put her off. He couldn't keep spending time with her, anyway. As soon as her mom passed, she'd be gone.

24

Gia hadn't slept well. She'd been disappointed by the text she'd gotten from Cormac saying he was exhausted and asking for a rain check on the bread pudding. Something about how long it took him to get back to her as well as his less-than-enthusiastic answer led her to believe he was pulling away. She knew a little about that type of thing, since she was usually the one doing it.

She kept telling herself she didn't care—she didn't know him all that well, anyway—and yet, strangely, she kept checking her phone hoping he'd sent her something else.

Her mother called her name. Her parents must've had a rough night, too, because they never slept late, and yet she hadn't heard anything from them until now.

"What is it?" she asked, concerned that maybe Ida wasn't feeling well. Her mother had been so fretful since Margot left. And knowing Sheldon had to be home by now only compounded the worry. No one could say what would happen next, what he would do, but his last words to Gia on the phone had certainly been ominous.

All of the anxiety had to be taking a toll—but, fortunately, Ida looked fine.

"I think it's Margot," Ida said as soon as Gia entered the room.

Stopping a few feet from them, Gia glanced at her father, who was wearing a pair of slacks and pulling on a shirt. He obviously already understood what Ida was talking about. "She called you?"

"No, look!" Her mother turned her phone so that Gia could see a beautiful picture of a beach at dawn. Neither Margot nor the boys were in the photo, but someone had drawn a huge heart in the sand.

"What's this?"

"Someone just sent it to me. It's Margot, don't you think?" Tears filled Ida's eyes. "It came in as a text from a number I don't recognize, but it has to be her. This is her way of letting me know she's thinking of me and she's okay. Just look at that glorious, hopeful picture!"

Gia felt a measure of relief—but also a flicker of the old jealousy. She'd grown closer to her parents since she'd been home, mostly because she'd quit holding them so accountable for the mistakes of the past. She'd made her own mistakes and forgiveness was necessary on both sides.

But she'd never be what Margot was to them. Margot had been the perfect daughter. She was also the one who'd stuck around the last seventeen years. That was something Gia was just going to have to live with.

"I think so, too," she said. The other good news was that her sister had used SMS instead of calling, which meant she hadn't been able to block the number. "Here, let me see if we can get someone to answer."

Using her mother's phone, she called the number from which Ida had received that picture, and a man answered. "'Lo?"

"Um, yes, this is Gia Rossi. My mother just received a text from your number."

"The picture of the beach?"

"That's it."

"Yeah, a woman and her kids drew that heart in the sand, then asked me if I'd take a picture of it and send it to this number. So I did."

Gia arched her eyebrows as she stared back at her parents, who were clearly hanging on every word they could hear. "You're obviously on the coast, but...where exactly?" she asked the man.

"Can't say," he replied.

Gia blinked in surprise. "Why not?"

"The lady who asked me to send you that pic paid me twenty dollars to keep my mouth shut. She said she just wanted to send a little love to her family and leave it at that."

"That's great, but...is she there with you now? If so, can you get her? This is her sister. I need to tell her something."

"Sorry, she's already gone."

Gia sank into the chair in her parents' room even though it meant sitting on top of the clothes her dad had discarded there the past few days. "How long ago did she leave?"

"Right after she had me take the pic."

Her mind racing, Gia began to knead her forehead. How could she turn this into something that could help them? There had to be a way. "Listen, I'll Venmo you fifty bucks if you'll tell me where this picture was taken. Since my sister's not there anymore, it doesn't really matter, right? You're not giving away anything."

"She made me wait until she was out of sight to send that. I don't think she'd like it if I told you where she was."

"She'll never know!"

He didn't answer.

"Do we have a deal?" Gia pressed.

He covered the phone while discussing her offer with someone in the background—it sounded like a woman. "Okay," he said when he came back on.

"You'll do it?"

"For fifty bucks? Why not?"

"What's your Venmo?"

"I'll text it to you."

She sent the money. Then, as soon as he said he got it, she asked him again. "So...what beach are you at?"

"Huntington," he said and disconnected.

"Huntington," she repeated to her parents. "Do you know where Huntington Beach is?"

They both shook their heads, so she asked Google. "Orange County, California," she read aloud. "Margot went to Los Angeles!"

"That's so far away," Ida said.

"And LA's a big place," Leo added, sounding discouraged. "How are we ever going to find her there?"

Gia shook her head. "I have no idea, but it's a start. It feels better knowing even that much, doesn't it?"

Ida took her phone back, looked at the picture of the heart drawn on the beach and smiled as she pressed the screen to her chest. "It certainly does."

Over the next few days, Gia felt she was waiting for the other shoe to drop, but she wasn't sure exactly what that would look like. She and her parents were hoping for some new word from Margot while fending off calls and texts from Sheldon and his parents, who were getting angrier by the day and beginning to accuse them, once again, of knowing more than they did.

Of course, they didn't tell the Nelsons that Margot had been in Southern California. Since they had no idea whether she was still there, even if they were willing to share that information, which they weren't, they doubted it would help.

In the middle of the tension growing between the two families, friends and neighbors who'd heard about Margot were stopping by to console Ida. That gave her some extra support, but it also meant she heard what Sheldon's family was telling everyone—that Margot had been a terrible wife and mother and he was the stable one of the two, with a home and a job, and thus deserved custody of the boys.

As upsetting as that was, at least the constant flow of people kept Ida so busy Gia felt safe leaving the house. She needed a break.

She went for drinks with a handful of members from the Banned Books Club on Saturday night and enjoyed it; this time there was no drama. Then she met Sammie at Wakefield Pub & Brewery on Sunday for brunch. But her time with Sammie wasn't proving to be quite as fun. Her friend kept asking questions about Cormac, and that was the last thing Gia wanted to talk about, because she hadn't heard much from him. Since he'd put her off on the bread pudding, she'd received only one cursory text. It'd come the next day, while he was at the clinic, she assumed, and simply said he hoped she was doing as well as could be expected considering what was going on with her sister.

It was nothing that had even invited a response.

He seemed to have backed away from their friendship.

She told herself she didn't need him anyway; she'd never been unable to get over a man. But even though they hadn't spent a great deal of time together, she missed him. He'd been the one bright spot amid all the problems she'd been dealing with since returning to Wakefield, and thoughts of the way he smiled or kissed—or teased her by rubbing his beard growth on her neck when they were cuddling in bed—intruded despite her best attempts to bar those memories from her mind.

She felt they'd made a meaningful connection, that he'd overcome who she was and she'd overcome who he was to get to know the person behind the name and reputation. So she didn't understand why he'd suddenly bailed out.

Maybe cutting ties with her gave him a better chance of reconciling with his sisters…

"You're making too big a deal out of it," she told Sammie. "Cormac and I are just friends, which is monumental enough, considering the past, right?"

"Absolutely," she agreed. "He's just so picky when it comes to women. Ruth said he's never even given her a second look, and yet he wants to get involved with his family's mortal enemy. We can't help wondering how you two got together in the first place."

"I get it. Like I said, it started out as commiseration and sort of went from there. So…what's going on with Ruth these days?" Gia was interested in the answer to this question, but she was also hoping to change the subject.

"You haven't heard from her?"

"Not since right after the Banned Books Club meeting. I think she's become too close to Edith to be friends with me."

"I didn't realize they knew each other that well, but I think you might be right. It's too bad she can't be friends with both of you, especially now that everyone knows it was Mr. Hart who lied about that incident in high school."

Gia wiped her mouth with her napkin. "*Everyone* knows that?"

"Yeah. You haven't heard?"

Gia picked up her strawberry lemonade. "I've been almost entirely out of circulation. Why don't you fill me in?"

"Cormac didn't tell you?" Sammie said. "I heard Mr. Hart more or less admitted to him that your version of events was the right one."

That'd happened right before Gia had slept with Cormac for the first time. But she'd thought Cormac had agreed *not* to tell Edith and Louisa—or anyone else so that it wouldn't get back to them. Why had he gone ahead? "Does that mean they're finally willing to accept the truth?" she asked.

"I don't think they really have a choice—although Mr. Hart's saying he didn't admit to anything." She rolled her eyes. "He

claims Cormac is just saying that because he's become infatuated with you. But they know Cormac wouldn't outright *lie*,
especially about that, so, yeah, they have to believe it."

She took a sip of her lemonade. "I'm sorry they had to be
disillusioned about their father." She'd tried to let them go on
just as they had been, but she doubted anyone other than Cormac would believe that.

"Thank God the truth has been established once and for all,"
Sammie said. "Mr. Hart has been *so* unfair to you."

Gia put her lemonade back down. "He's hardly apologetic,
even now. Because he didn't 'hurt' me physically—or really
get anywhere sexually—he thinks there shouldn't have been a
penalty, especially such a harsh one."

Sammie grimaced. "Ew. He's so gross. It was more than the
fondling. It was that business with your grade, right? At least
now everyone knows that the court got it right and maybe
those involved, like you and your family and Cormac and his
family, can get some closure."

"I hope so. I'd like to put it all behind me and forget about
it at last."

Sammie was about to say something else when her eyes fas-
tened on a spot over Gia's right shoulder and she put down her
fork.

Gia twisted around to see what had caught her attention and
saw Sheldon sitting with Cece in a corner booth. Apparently,
since Margot had left town, he wasn't particularly concerned
about being seen out and about with his other woman.

"That's brazen," Sammie whispered.

Gia curved her fingernails into her palms to help contain
her anger. "He thinks he's untouchable, that once Margot is
found, he'll get his money and his kids back and toss her aside
with nothing."

"Do you think he'll ever find her?"

"That's a good question," Gia said and glared at Cece until

she noticed and touched Sheldon's arm, who looked back and locked eyes with her.

Sammie leaned in. "I wonder what he's thinking."

Sheldon gave them a defiant "kiss my ass" grin before turning back to his girlfriend, and that was when Gia vowed that she wouldn't let him get the best of Margot, no matter what it cost her.

Why did you tell Louisa and Edith, after all?

That text came from Gia on Sunday evening while Cormac was watching a football game he'd recorded earlier. The Jets were playing. They were his favorite team, had been since he was a kid simply because his best friend's father had been a Jets fan and watched game after game with them. His own dad had shown more interest in books than sports.

But Cormac had been having trouble paying attention to the game even before Gia texted him. Just knowing she was so close, right in the house behind him, had made for a long week. He'd forced himself to stay away from her, but whenever he was home, he had to fight the impulse to go to the window every few minutes to see if she was in her parents' backyard.

He couldn't understand why he wanted to see her so badly. They'd had a good time together, and he knew she was a nice person. But there was no way they could ever get into a serious relationship. If she was leaving town, he'd have to say goodbye to her eventually. It made sense not to get *too* close.

Besides, his family had accepted the truth about his father, and his sisters were slowly beginning to speak to him again. Louisa had acted more like herself on Friday than she had in over a week. Part of it was because he'd told her he wasn't involved with Gia anymore, that whatever had flared up between them was already over. If letting go of her a little early helped to placate his sisters, he felt that was probably the best way to go.

But that approach sounded better during the day when he was working with Louisa than at night when he was home alone and could be seeing Gia. And now she'd sent him a direct text, so of course he had to respond:

You mean about my dad admitting what he did? Long story. But they've been told. And as hard as that was for them—especially with my dad acting like such an ass and still trying to deny it— I'm glad everyone knows *you* aren't to blame for anything.

He set his phone aside and went back to watching the game, but he found his mind drifting almost immediately. He was waiting for her to respond.

Five minutes passed, then ten minutes, then fifteen. When all he got was a mere thumbs-up an hour later, he realized that was probably all he was going to get, and he couldn't blame her. He hadn't invited further conversation. He'd purposely held back so he *wouldn't* spark more interaction.

"Just hang on and see it through until she leaves," he told himself when he was tempted to send a follow-up text.

Turning the channel to a sports news program he could listen to while cutting up vegetables to take to work with him in the morning, he moved into the kitchen. But it was only a few minutes later when he saw the porch light snap on over at the Rossis' and found himself running up the stairs to look out his bedroom window.

Sure enough, Gia was getting into the hot tub.

Cormac knew Gia had to have heard the gate open when he came through it, but she didn't look over. "Hey," he said.

She continued to stare up at the stars as if he hadn't spoken.

He'd taken the time to throw on a pair of sweats before coming outside. It was growing colder by the night. "How are things going with Margot?" he asked, walking to the edge of the hot tub.

She still didn't look over at him. "They aren't going," she said. "Nothing's happening there. We haven't heard from her, don't know where she is."

She'd said it mechanically, as if she'd repeated it a dozen times, which let him know that was the official statement she was giving everyone. He wondered if it was true. "I'm sure you're worried about her. I'm sorry."

"We'll manage."

With that simple two-word response, she'd already dismissed him. He should leave. After all, he was the one who'd put this distance between them with how he'd behaved this week and how he'd just responded to her text, which might've been her way of trying to reestablish communication with him.

But he'd always been attracted to her, and that hadn't changed, so he couldn't help trying to engage her again. "Sheldon's been saying a lot around town—about how he's going to find her and take custody of the kids."

"I've heard that."

"You're not concerned?" he asked.

"He wasn't a great father to begin with. Those boys are better off with their mother."

He shoved his hands into his pockets. "But you won't be the one who gets to decide, right? He'll take her to court if he finds her. It'll turn into a battle."

"With any luck, he *won't* find her."

"She plans to stay gone indefinitely?"

"*I* think so."

He whistled. "Wow. She's serious."

"We obviously didn't understand how truly unhappy she was. I feel bad about that."

"Gia…"

At the change in his tone, she finally looked at him. "Is this where you tell me you still want to be friends, Cormac?" she asked.

He stared down at his tennis shoes, trying to figure out what he really wanted to happen from here. He knew he'd be a fool to go back to what they'd started. She had a life somewhere else. That was why he'd backed away to begin with—but it didn't hurt that it helped patch things up with his family, too. "I honestly do, you know."

"Fine. Consider us friends," she said and grabbed her towel as she got out and went back inside.

Margot was so excited her hands were shaking. Getting a new identity opened up the world. She could sell the Subaru, buy a new car, get a phone, rent an apartment, apply for jobs— *start over.* So much had depended on a new social security number and driver's license. And it hadn't been that hard to get. She'd had to brave the dark web and pay in Bitcoin, and she'd had to trust the unnamed person on the other side of the transaction to deliver with authentic-looking documents. But what she got looked real. Amazingly so.

"Did that come in the mail, Mommy?" Greydon asked from the back seat, where he was watching a movie on her iPad with his brother. "What is it?"

Margot set the torn envelope on the empty passenger seat. She'd rented a PO Box on the other side of LA and had the documents sent there. She wasn't about to give anyone she didn't know the address of their motel, and she certainly wasn't about to meet a stranger in person, especially one involved in illegal activity. She didn't have anyone to watch the boys and couldn't risk taking them into a potentially dangerous situation. So she'd had to trust that the person she'd paid would actually send the items she'd purchased and, after driving in two hours of traffic for three days straight and finding nothing, was infinitely relieved that he'd finally followed through. "It's what

I need to be able to get us into an apartment," she told him. "Won't that be nice?"

"What's an apartment?" he asked.

"It's sort of like the motels where we've been staying," she told him.

He clapped his hands together. "Can we get one with a pool?"

"Maybe," she said. "We'll have to see what's available."

Greydon went back to the movie while she continued to marvel at the quality of her new documents. "Margaret Lane…" she said aloud in an effort to get used to her new name. "Margaret *Lane*… Hello, I'm Margaret Lane… This is Margaret Lane. I'm not available right now, but please leave your number at the beep."

"Why are you saying 'Margaret Lane' over and over again?" Matthew asked.

"I've decided to go back to Margaret," she told him.

"Go *back* to Margaret?" he repeated, obviously confused.

"That's my real name. Margot was just a nickname." She'd chosen her new last name from Lois Lane in the *Superman* movies. Not only did she like the way the two names rolled off her tongue, "Lane" was short and easy to spell.

"Oh," he said as if it wasn't particularly remarkable—and that was it as far as probing questions from her children.

She smiled. Kids were so flexible. She felt she'd gotten away from Sheldon just in time, before the boys were old enough to know what she was doing and to tell other people about it.

She dug deeper into the file she'd taken from the envelope and found the three birth certificates she'd also purchased. One was for her, in case she ever needed it. There was no way she wanted to have to go onto the dark web again. The other two were for the boys, so their last name would still match hers. They'd need birth certificates when she enrolled them in school. She didn't think there was any way Sheldon, his fam-

ily or even the cops could track every child who went to public school. There was no big repository of information on all
American students, no computer search that could be done,
so she could've let them keep Sheldon's name and simply explained to anyone who asked that she was divorced and was
using her maiden name.

But it would be so much more difficult to change their sur-
name when they got older, if she wanted to, that she'd decided
to make the switch now and keep it clean and consistent. With
enough time, they probably wouldn't even remember that anything had changed. She'd let them keep their first names, which
was about all they identified with at this point. Changing those
would be far more impactful.

With a relieved sigh, she put the documents back into the file
and set it on the passenger seat on top of the envelope. Then
she adjusted her rearview mirror to be able to see her children
in the back seat. "You boys still buckled up?"

"Yep," they said, and she put the Subaru in Drive.

"Who's hungry?" she asked as she pulled out of the post office. "Should we get some lunch before we drive back to the
other side of town?"

"Can we have pizza?" Greydon asked.

"I don't see why not. And after that we can go look at a few
apartments."

They didn't respond. The movie must've hit a high point
because they were both glued to the iPad. They'd had way too
much screen time lately. She had to get them back in school,
hated that they'd already missed two weeks. But she had what
she needed, so she'd get on top of everything.

It was only a matter of time.

25

The next week passed slowly, mostly because Gia had to fight herself on contacting Cormac every day. She'd never been in this situation, where she missed a man and longed to hear from him. It was especially annoying that she'd gotten hung up on Mr. Hart's son. But she supposed she was struggling because this was the first time someone had walked away from *her*.

"I just want what I can't have," she kept telling herself. "And I'm getting bored because I can't work at anything more mentally challenging than cooking and cleaning." She didn't mind helping her folks and was glad it had set Margot free. But the fact that she wasn't always busy, like she was at home, made it so much more difficult to cope with wanting someone who seemed to have turned his back on her. Cormac came to his window almost every night and looked down into her folks' yard, but she'd quit going to the hot tub. She didn't want him to think she was hoping he'd come out again—even though, deep down, she knew she would be. She also didn't want to put herself in the position of wanting him to come out and having him not do so.

Besides wrestling with herself over Cormac and trying to put

the two nights she'd shared with him behind her, she continued to hope that Margot would check in. Ida kept asking her if
she'd heard anything. But there were no more beach pictures or
calls from blocked numbers. The only person who kept trying
to reach them was Sheldon. Several things had come to light that
he hadn't expected—namely, the reaction of the police. They'd
told him that since there was no divorce pending, Margot could
leave the state and take the boys with her, and they weren't even
going to look for her. An attorney confirmed their response. He'd
said that until there was a court-ordered plan, Margot could do
whatever she wanted, which had sent Sheldon off the deep end.
He'd gotten so nasty that she and her parents had stopped answering their phones. He behaved even worse when he was drinking.

It got to the point that Gia finally blocked him from contacting her parents. They needed a break from the constant
upset. She would've blocked him from contacting her, too, except she felt it might be important to hear his rambling, angry
messages. Then if Margot checked in, she might be able to tell
her what to watch out for.

While Gia was sitting on her bed, surfing through Instagram, she noticed that the lights had gone on at Cormac's. Unable to stop herself, she got up and went to the window. She
was standing to one side of it, hoping to catch a glimpse of him
when her phone lit up—once again—with her brother-in-law's
name and number.

She almost answered. The phone was already in her hand.
But she decided not to. She had nothing more to tell Sheldon.
Why continue to take his abuse?

Once the call transferred to voicemail, she could see that
he'd left a message, so she played it back.

*Where the hell is she? You and your parents have to know some-
thing. You'd better tell me where my kids are and make her return my
fucking money. If you don't and you're playing some sort of game with
me, you're going to be sorry,* you bitch!

He'd screamed the last two words before ending the call.

"He's losing it," Gia muttered. At this point, she was afraid Margot would decide to come back, and he'd show them all why she'd felt she was in sufficient danger to run away in the first place.

Just the thought of him scaring Margot to such a degree made Gia call her brother-in-law back.

"It's about time!" he snapped when he answered.

She didn't respond to that comment. She had a short and sweet message to deliver, and that's what she did. "You'd better not ever do anything to hurt me, my sister or my parents, or you'll be the one who's sorry," she said and hung up.

Still seething, she began to pace. Obviously, he'd never dreamed Margot would get the best of him, which was why Gia couldn't help applauding her sister's well-executed escape. She'd left him before he could get any type of court order to stop her, and according to what Gia had been reading on the internet, if she stayed gone long enough, Greydon and Matthew would be considered under the jurisdiction of their new state, which would only complicate matters and make it more difficult for Sheldon to gain custody and bring them back. Margot had completely hamstrung him, and he never saw it coming, which was why he was flying into a blind rage. "You're getting exactly what you deserve," she grumbled, remembering the cocky grin he'd given her while eating out with Cece.

Her phone dinged with a text message. She thought for sure it would be Sheldon responding to her call, but it was Cormac.

What's wrong? Are you okay?

She peered out her window to find that he was standing at his own window and had probably seen her marching back and forth across the room.

Should she tell him?

No. He was the one who'd cut her off. Why put herself in a position where he could do it again?

It's nothing, she wrote and lowered the blind.

He'd blown it. Instead of pushing Gia away, Cormac should've been spending time with her while he could. The more days that passed, the more he regretted his decision.

But she obviously wasn't open to giving him a second chance.

He frowned as he stared at her drawn blind. He'd gotten spooked, plain and simple, and now he was paying the price.

He was just contemplating whether he should try to call her and formally apologize, whether that would change anything even if she answered, when his father texted him.

I hear you're not seeing Gia anymore. Was it worth it—what you did? You ruined our family for nothing.

Closing his eyes, Cormac shook his head in disgust. He was getting along better with his sisters, but he doubted he'd ever be able to have a relationship with his father.

Until you're ready to take responsibility for your own actions and apologize, don't ever contact me again.

After he typed that, his thumb hovered over the send button. Could he really cut Evan off? He'd been trying to maintain a relationship with him for so long it'd become a habit to justify and excuse his many shortfalls. And they lived in the same small town, which meant they'd run into each other here and there—at a restaurant, the gas station, the pharmacy. If they weren't speaking, it would be awkward. But would Evan ever change if Cormac didn't demand it?

You ruined our family, he added to what he'd written before and sent it before blocking him.

★ ★ ★

Halloween was hard on Ida. She cried because, after spending every Halloween with her grandkids since they'd been born, she couldn't even see them this year, let alone get the traditional picture of them in their costumes.

Gia tried to cheer her up by making the caramel apples she'd given out since Gia could remember, and stationed her at the front door so she could be the one to greet the trick-or-treaters. They had plenty of them in this neighborhood—a steady stream, unlike the condominium complex where Gia lived in Coeur d'Alene.

"How are you holding up?" Gia asked after about an hour and a half, when traffic began to wane. "Are you getting tired?"

With a nod, Ida allowed Gia to help her from the chair by the door to the couch, and Leo handled the last of the cowboys, superheroes, doctors, Disney princesses and dinosaurs.

Once the apples were gone, Gia turned off the porch light to signal that they were done for the night and sat down with her parents to rest for a few minutes, too. "That was fun, wasn't it?" she said in an effort to keep their spirits up.

"It wasn't the same," her mother replied. "I can't believe we haven't heard from Margot."

Gia had also thought they would've received something else by now. Margot had been gone for two weeks. But she was probably afraid that any type of contact could get her caught. "She must realize that this would be the worst time to take any risks."

"Why?" her mother asked.

"Because Sheldon's finally realized she's gone for good, unless he can find her, and he can't find her. He's reached maximum frustration and fury and has been getting increasingly threatening and aggressive."

"He has?" Leo asked.

Gia hadn't been showing them the stuff Sheldon had been

sending her, but today he'd texted her a Halloween gif featuring the Grim Reaper cutting off someone's head. "He is," she confirmed. He certainly hadn't sent that to her as a joke.

Ida's eyes filled with concern. "Should we go to the police? Get a restraining order against him?"

"We might have to," Gia said. "I haven't done that so far because I want to hear what he has to say just in case some small piece of it turns out to be meaningful—something I can pass on to Margot, if I ever get the opportunity."

"Did you hear Sandra Richey tonight, when she came with her kids?" her mother asked.

Sandra was Ida's hairdresser and had been in business for so long she had quite a long list of clientele. "No," Gia replied. "What'd she say?"

"His folks are hiring a private investigator."

Shit. "That makes me nervous," she admitted. "See? Margot is smart not to leave a trail for Sheldon—or anyone he hires—to follow."

"It's probably for the best," Leo concurred.

Fresh tears slipped down her mother's cheeks, but she nodded. "I'm exhausted. I'd better get to bed."

Gia cleaned while Leo helped Ida up the stairs. She'd just finished and was about to go to bed herself when a vehicle turned into the drive. She couldn't see the make or model or who was driving it—the headlights were glaring through the kitchen window, blinding her—but it was easy to guess when the lights flashed brighter and the vehicle just sat there.

Gia picked up her phone and punched in 9-1-1 in case she had to call for help. And she almost pressed Send when Sheldon revved his engine, then popped the transmission into Drive and the truck lurched forward as if he'd smash right through the wall.

He slammed on his brakes at the last second only to back

onto the grass and spin out, leaving deep ruts through their front lawn.

Determined to get a video that showed his license plate number so she could use it to get a restraining order, Gia ran outside. But the only thing she captured was his red taillights as he rocketed away. "You bastard!" Gia yelled. "No wonder she left you!"

Since it was Edith's birthday, Cormac had agreed to meet his sisters and their husbands for a drink at Vivian's, a local restaurant, while Sharon watched the kids. Cormac was tired. He'd been up late last night at a Halloween party with Tyler Jenkins and some of his other buddies, and he had to work in the morning. So he wasn't really excited about going out again. But this was the first time they'd all be together since they'd realized that their father had indeed molested Gia, and he felt they could use the chance to smooth over some of the cracks that'd developed in their relationships.

So far, most of the conversation had revolved around his niece and two nephews. Cormac ordered a beer and simply listened until Dan started telling him he thought their Corkie was getting another cyst. Cormac told him to bring the dog to the clinic so he could take a look, then slid over to make room at the table when Ruth showed up. No one had told him she'd been invited to join them, but it was Edith's birthday—she certainly had the prerogative to invite who she wanted—and he considered Ruth a welcome addition when she brought up Gia almost straightaway. He was far more interested in a conversation that involved her than any other topic.

"Have you heard the latest with Gia?" Ruth asked.

Louisa sent her a baleful look. "Whatever it is, please tell us it has nothing to do with our dad…"

"No, nothing to do with him," Ruth said.

"Then what's the latest?" Edith asked.

Ruth lowered her voice. "She's trying to get a restraining order against her brother-in-law."

Cormac hid his surprise. He knew better than to say anything about Gia—or show much concern in front of his sisters.

Fortunately, Louisa responded the way he wanted to respond himself. "Why would she need a restraining order? What's he been doing?"

Ruth sent Cormac a tentative smile. He could tell she was trying to read how he felt about this information, probably because she'd heard from Edith that he'd been sleeping with Gia. Over the past couple of years, Ruth had made it obvious that she was attracted to him—so obvious it sometimes made him uncomfortable—so he conjured what he hoped was a neutral smile, trying to walk the thin line between being nice and giving her false hope.

"I guess he's furious about Margot running off and won't believe they don't know where she is," she replied as she returned her gaze to Louisa. "So he keeps harassing them."

At this point, Cormac couldn't resist speaking up. "In what way?"

"Damaging their lawn. Texting threatening messages. Shooting up their garbage can—"

"He shot up their garbage can?" Victor broke in.

"Well, no one actually saw him do it," she said. "But Sammie told me Gia's convinced it was him. She saw him peel out on their lawn last night."

Dan put down his soda. "Why doesn't he just focus on finding his wife instead of making trouble with his in-laws?"

The waitress arrived to check on them, and Ruth ordered a blended margarita before answering. "From what I've heard, his parents have hired a private detective, but he isn't turning up many clues. Not yet, anyway. It's as if she just dropped off the face of the earth."

A horrified expression descended on Louisa's face. "I'd be

frantic without my kids. Can she do that? Legally, I mean? Just...take the boys?"

Ruth shrugged. "I guess she can. I work with a teacher whose husband is on the police force. She told me he says there's really nothing they can do, since there's no court order to prevent her from leaving."

Edith clapped a hand over her mouth. "That's unbelievable! Taking your kids and disappearing into another state without the permission of your spouse—isn't that kidnapping?"

"Apparently not," Ruth said. "But if he can find her and file for divorce, he could change that eventually. He might have a much better chance of gaining full custody after what she's done, too. But my friend's husband said it's important he find her fast. If she moved to a different state, the longer she's there, the harder and stickier it'll be."

Edith tucked her hair behind her ears. "Why's that?"

"Something about jurisdiction," Ruth said. "And, of course, the judge would have to consider what's best for the boys. If they've settled into their new place and are thriving, he or she might be hesitant to uproot them. Not only that, but if it goes on for another five years or so, the boys will be old enough to speak for themselves and say where they'd most like to live, which could have significant influence."

Louisa shook her head. "The way he's acting, if he finds her, he might not wait for help from the courts."

"That's just it," Ruth said. "I wouldn't want to be her."

Edith toyed with the condensation from her water glass. "Margot's brave. I'll give her that."

Cormac was equally impressed. He never would've expected *her* to do something so gutsy. Gia was the spunky one. She'd always lived her life unapologetically.

"Why do you think she ran away?" Victor asked the table at large.

"Her husband was cheating on her, and everyone knew it—even you," Louisa said. "I'm the one who told you."

He scowled at her. "I know, but a lot of people have affairs without their spouse taking the kids and running off."

"Well, if you're going to cheat, that's a risk you take, so let that be a lesson to you," she joked.

Everyone chuckled. Then Edith grumbled, "And we thought we had drama in *our* family..."

"Hopefully, the business with your father and Gia is finally over and done with," Dan said.

"Whoa!" Victor pointed at the entrance. "Speak of the devil."

They all turned to see that Gia had walked in. She was standing at the hostess station, waiting to be seated, looking down at her phone, so she didn't notice them. Otherwise, Cormac believed she would've walked out. And he wouldn't have blamed her. Why would she stick around when she was outnumbered by his family—not to mention Ruth, who'd defected from her side and joined theirs.

"Unless she's meeting someone who's late, it looks like she's here alone," Dan said.

"That doesn't surprise me," Ruth said. "I don't think she's getting out much, what with taking care of her mom and then this thing with Sheldon. She certainly hasn't called *me*."

The hostess approached and Gia exchanged a few words with her before being taken to a table not far from where they were sitting. She'd already sat down and stowed her purse in the empty chair next to her by the time she saw them all staring at her.

She blinked as though she couldn't quite believe her eyes. Then she reached for her purse as if she'd get up again—probably to head right back out to her car. But the waitress stood over her already asking for her drink order. Either Gia felt penned in, or she decided she wouldn't let anyone chase her away, because she let go of her purse once again and ordered a drink. Then, acting as if they weren't even there, she went right back to doing what she'd been doing on her phone.

"I wonder how her mother's feeling," Edith whispered.

"I don't know." Ruth kept her voice down, too. "Like I said, she hasn't called me since…since before the Banned Books Club meeting."

Cormac didn't find that to be even slightly surprising, given that Ruth had been more supportive of Edith. But he didn't say anything.

Louisa looked over at him. "Do *you* know?"

He shook his head. "I haven't talked to her, either. That was part of our peace agreement, remember?"

Louisa had the good grace to look slightly abashed before getting to her feet.

"Where are you going?" her husband asked, but she didn't answer. She just started over to where Gia was sitting.

"Louisa, it wasn't just you!" Cormac hissed, feeling as though he'd put whatever was about to happen in motion because of his last dig. It was easier to blame her and Edith than himself for cutting off his relationship with Gia. But he shouldn't have done it. He didn't want either one of them to bother her ever again. "Come back here!" he added.

He knew she'd heard him because she glanced at him—but kept on going.

Gia was going through the photos on her phone, selecting images that would be good to put on social media to promote Backcountry Adventures, when a shadow fell across her table. Sammie had originally agreed to come with her tonight, but something had come up at the last minute and Gia had decided to get out of the house, anyway. Wouldn't you know she'd have to face Cormac and his sisters when she was completely alone and looked friendless and rather pathetic?

Bracing for what could be an emotional encounter—she'd

known almost nothing except emotional encounters when it came to Mr. Hart and his kids—she looked up to find that it was Louisa who'd walked over.

"Can I...help you?" she asked uncertainly when Louisa didn't speak right away.

Cormac's sister began to dig at her cuticles. "I just wanted to say—" She cleared her throat. "I wanted to say that I'm sorry. I misjudged you and...and I know you were going through a difficult time as it was. When I put myself in your shoes and try to imagine what it must've been like, I feel terrible. I hope you can forgive me."

Gia had never expected an apology. They'd been enemies for so long she figured at some point that sort of thing just became set in stone, because even if they finally believed her, they could still wonder, deep down, if she'd done something to entice their father. It had to be hard to completely give up on the idea and not simply look for different reasoning.

"I appreciate that," Gia said. "Of course I forgive you. You weren't in a good position to determine the truth, not with everything your father has said to discredit me."

Louisa blinked, seemingly surprised that her apology had been accepted so readily. But Gia didn't see any point in holding grudges. She was just glad the truth had finally come out, and she knew Cormac was responsible for that, so she couldn't be too hard on those he had to cross to make it happen. "Thanks." Louisa smiled. "I appreciate it."

Gia smiled, too. "No problem."

Louisa started to go back to the other table but turned almost immediately. "Hey, is there any chance you'd like to join us?" she asked. "We're celebrating Edith's birthday."

Looking over at all the faces that were turned in her direction, Gia swallowed hard. "Um...that's okay. I wouldn't want to intrude. But I hope she has a wonderful birthday and...and thanks for coming over." She thought that would be the end of it. She couldn't believe Louisa *really* wanted her to join the party. But then Edith got up and came over, too.

"I also owe you an apology. I'm sorry—on behalf of me and my father," she said. "I hope you'll come have a drink with us and that we can...start over."

Gia assured her she harbored no hard feelings, then tried to decline again. But Victor and Dan joined their wives and pressed her to accept.

"Come on over, really," Victor said.

"We'd love to have you," Dan added, and the next thing she knew, Gia found herself sitting by Ruth at one end of the table, with Cormac on the other end and his sisters and brothers-in-law in between.

"I never dreamed *this* would happen," Gia joked as they signaled the waitress that she'd moved.

Cormac caught her eye and smiled. She could tell he was looking for some type of forgiveness, too. But the way she felt when she looked at him, she knew that would only lead her right back to his bed.

26

Cormac couldn't keep his eyes off Gia. He kept looking for some sign that she wasn't angry since he'd cut her off, but he couldn't tell. At least she was sitting at the table with him and his sisters were being kind. He was so proud of them for apologizing.

It was easy to see Gia didn't feel as though she belonged in this small family celebration, and Cormac could understand. They ended up ordering some appetizers as well as drinks, and after a while, as they all told stories and began to laugh, she seemed to relax and start having fun, too. Then the waitress carried out a big cake—thanks to Louisa, who'd had the foresight to make it happen.

Eventually, Louisa asked Gia about Sheldon, and she told them what Ruth had already said—that he was becoming a persistent problem. Louisa followed up by asking if she'd heard from Margot. She insisted that she hadn't, but Cormac wasn't sure he believed that. He wouldn't tell anyone whether he'd heard from Margot, either, if he were in Gia's place.

They were all a little tipsy when they walked out, except Dan, who was the designated driver since he was raised by an alcoholic and had sworn off drinking. He took the birthday girl, Louisa and Victor home. Then he came back for Cormac, Ruth and Gia.

Cormac was hoping to sit in the back with Gia, but Ruth insisted he take the front seat since his "legs were longer." He tried to tell her he was fine in the back, but she was so insistent that he got the impression there was more behind it than mere courtesy. She didn't want him to sit by Gia. It didn't ultimately matter that much, though, because Dan dropped Ruth off before driving Gia and Cormac home.

Cormac wanted to get out with Gia, so that maybe they'd have a chance to talk. But she didn't invite him. As soon as Dan pulled into her drive, she thanked him, told them both goodbye and got out. That was it.

Cormac wished she'd been more encouraging, but when he got home, he texted her, anyway.

Is there any chance you'd be willing to come over so we can talk?

She answered right away: I'm not sure I want to get involved with you again.

I'm sorry, Gia. You have to admit things were going pretty fast. I just needed to slow us down for a second. I won't change my mind again.

When she didn't text him back, he assumed the answer was no, so he was stunned when he heard a distinct knock on his back door fifteen minutes later.

Gia told herself she was being a fool. She and Cormac had already quit seeing each other. The hardest part was over. She should leave it there.

She wished she could be just that logical, knew it would be

for the best, especially when it came time to leave Wakefield. But she couldn't.

"Are we going to lay down any ground rules?" he asked hesitantly as he let her in.

She closed her eyes for a second while she tried to decide. But nothing came to mind that would help the situation. He was all she'd been able to think about since they'd first kissed, and she wasn't going to miss the opportunity to be with him again.

"We'll play it by ear," she said and stepped into his arms.

"I know I've asked you this before, but you don't think Sheldon would ever really hurt you, do you?" Cormac asked as he got ready for work the next morning.

Gia was still in his bed and barely starting to stir, but he knew she had to get up soon to make it home before her parents started their day. "I'm not so convinced."

He scowled at himself in the mirror while combing his wet hair. "Maybe I should have a talk with him."

She shoved into a sitting position. "No, don't. He's looking for a target right now, and I don't want you to become a focal point. This isn't your fight."

"But maybe it'll take some pressure off you. I'm afraid of what he might do if he thinks he can get away with it."

She shoved a hand through her hair. "It'd help if I could get the damn restraining order…"

"Why can't you?"

"The police say I don't have enough grounds. He insists he wasn't the one who shot the garbage can to hell the other night. When I showed them the gif he sent me, he claimed it was just a Halloween joke. And they don't give out restraining orders because he peeled out on the front lawn. The officer I spoke to chuckled and said the grass will grow back. But *I* think it's that everyone in this town knows him and his family and can't believe he's truly dangerous."

Cormac put his comb away and walked out of the bathroom. "So where do you see this going?"

She covered a yawn as she looked up at him. "I have no idea. If he can't find Margot, maybe he'll snap."

"But you'll protect your sister even if she comes home."

"Of course."

"Have you really not heard from her?" he asked with a skeptical expression.

She gave him a secretive smile but that smile quickly faded. "Nothing meaningful."

"She can't come back now, you realize that. I mean…not until the kids are of age. Even then… I don't think I'd want to be in the same town as Sheldon and his folks."

"That she felt desperate enough to do something like this is upsetting. I keep wondering what that would be like. To want to escape someone so badly you leave your family and the town you grew up in and go into hiding."

"That's the thing. She would know whether Sheldon was dangerous more than anyone else."

"I know. I think about that, too," she said.

When he bent to kiss her, it felt like the most natural thing in the world, which made him slightly uneasy. A voice in the back of his head said, *You can't get used to this.* But how could he unravel what had already transpired?

He couldn't. Neither would he back out on her again.

"I'll call you later," he said and left.

Gia came home at least thirty minutes before her parents typically got up. She thought she'd have no trouble slipping into her room unnoticed. And yet she found both Ida and Leo sitting in the kitchen when she came through the back door—her mother still in her nightgown, which she never wore out of the bedroom.

"Oh, my God!" Ida exclaimed and burst into tears.

"What's wrong?" Gia glanced from her father to her mother and back again.

Her father motioned her to the living room, where she could see what was wrong. The picture windows had been shot out. Glass glittered like crushed diamonds all over the furniture and carpet. "When we heard the gunfire in the middle of the night, we were terrified. We didn't know what was happening. And it wasn't just a few shots, like with the garbage can. Whoever did this fired again and again—must've used more than one gun because he didn't take time to reload."

"Whoever did this?" she echoed. They knew who it had to be.

"It was terrifying to be awakened like that," her mother said from behind her. "And then…when you were gone…we thought…"

Gia looked back to see Ida bury her face in her hands. "You thought I'd been kidnapped or something?"

"Or worse," her father said. "Come here." He guided her through the family room slider to the front yard where she could see that someone had spray-painted "Fuck you, Gia!" on the front of the house in bright red paint.

"That son of a bitch!" she muttered. "If I can't get a restraining order, why aren't the police at least keeping an eye on our house?"

"I don't know," her father said. "I've called them. They're on their way."

She glanced up at the eaves. "We need to get some cameras up so we can at least document anything in the future."

"Who would have thought we'd need that in a town like this?" He shook his head. "We've lived here all our lives."

He looked tired, with the lines in his face more pronounced than usual and his hair standing up on one side. "Don't worry," she told him. "We'll get through this."

"It's not right," he murmured. "Your mother's suffered enough."

"Maybe we should take her to my place in Coeur d'Alene for a while," Gia said. "Get away and give her a chance to unwind."

"She wouldn't want to die there," he said.

He *never* said the D word. Neither did she. Hearing it reminded her of the inevitability of what they were facing and made her that much angrier at Sheldon for creating so much fear and upset in her mother's last days. If he was mad at Margot, that was one thing. He didn't have to take it out on them. They'd just become a handy stand-in, a target for his rage. "I'll order a surveillance system right away."

"How much will that cost?" he asked wearily.

"Not much. I'll take care of it."

They walked back inside to find that Ida had dried her cheeks and composed herself. "Where were you last night?" she asked Gia. "When we looked in your room, your bed was untouched." She gestured at the clothes Gia was wearing. "And didn't you go out in that last night?"

Gia was tempted to tell her she'd slept in the chaise by the pool, but with everything that had just happened that wasn't believable. She would've heard the gunfire. And with the way gossip circulated around town, anyway... "I was with Cormac," she admitted.

Her mother's jaw dropped. "*Mr. Hart's* son?"

She winced at Ida's reaction. "Yes."

"You're *seeing* him?" her mother pressed.

Was she seeing him? There was nothing official between them. They were just going day by day with what they felt at the moment. At the same time, she was sleeping with him, so... that was definitely something. "Sort of."

"What does that mean?" her father asked. "Do you care about him?"

That was a much easier question to answer. She *did* care about him, or she wouldn't have been drawn back to his house. But having feelings for him would only make it harder when it came time to leave, so she wasn't particularly happy about it. "I do."

Her father gaped at her. "Since when?"

"Since I've been home."

He scratched his neck. "Who would ever have thought Margot would disappear with our grandchildren, and you'd come back to Wakefield and fall in love, especially with Cormac Hart."

She opened her mouth to say she wasn't *in love* with Cormac. She'd never been in love before, couldn't believe it would happen now, of all times. But as she pictured him—his smile, his touch, the way he laughed—she knew she was in far deeper than she felt comfortable with. "We aren't putting a label on it," she said.

Her father's eyebrows went up, but he didn't say anything else. The police had arrived.

It'd been three weeks since she ran away. That wasn't very long, and yet Margot had accomplished so much. After Sheldon had called her stupid for years and treated her with disdain, as though she couldn't get anything right, she was proud of herself. It felt wonderful to have put so many important pieces in place for her future and that of her children. Not only had she driven all the way to California on her own, she'd gotten an apartment in Burbank and enrolled her boys in school, so now she had more time to focus on getting a job. She hadn't secured one yet, but she had several interviews this week—one with Starbucks, which was in a couple of hours, one as an office manager for a small accounting firm and one at an independent bookstore. They weren't prestigious positions. She could hear Sheldon in her mind, mocking her for not being able to do better. But she had to start someplace, needed to get a stream of money coming in so she could save as much of her nest egg as possible.

She missed her parents, worried about her mother constantly and pored over her sister's social media posts for Backcountry Adventures as a way to feel like a part of them. She was curious what Sheldon and his family were doing. He had an Instagram account, but he didn't post very often—unless he wanted to show off a picture of a buck he'd killed or something like that. He had taken the time to put up her picture—and so had Wakefield Trucking, on their Facebook page—asking anyone with information as to her whereabouts to contact him or his parents.

That had made her paranoid at first, but there were so many people in LA. She couldn't imagine those posts had enough reach to endanger her in any way.

As she put her makeup in the drawer, she realized she was as happy to be in Los Angeles now as the first day they'd arrived. Moving to a place like this was something Sheldon would never have been willing to consider. To be fair, he couldn't have left the business. But the story would've been the same even without the business. He blamed Californians for ruining the country, complained about it all the time. So it was nice to finally have the freedom to choose where *she* wanted to be. Living in such a warm, gorgeous place, with so much to do and see, was the perfect antidote to the miserable years she'd spent trying to make Sheldon happy—and losing her own happiness in the process.

"I'm me again," she said to herself in the mirror. She was scared she'd live to regret what she'd done, was afraid she wouldn't be able to provide a life as good as the one her boys would've known in Wakefield. But she'd been so desperate, she hadn't seen any other way. And she couldn't go back. All she could do now was put the past behind her and give it her best shot.

She put on the taupe dress she'd bought yesterday at a discount store with a pair of low heels and turned to the side to examine the fit. It wasn't too dressy or too casual. It didn't scream "discount store," either. Hopefully, whoever handled the interview this morning would think it was just right.

The color was back in her cheeks, she noticed before she turned away from the mirror. Even though she was nervous about whether she'd get the job—was afraid she'd be turned down across the board—she'd felt so hopeful these days and that wasn't something she was used to experiencing.

"You can do it," she told herself and grabbed her keys.

Something had to be done; this couldn't go on.

As Gia listened to her parents talk to the officer who'd come out to take the police report, she realized nothing was going to change. The officer didn't show much alarm. He shrugged it off by saying someone was probably just drunk and acting out. He didn't feel the malevolence behind Sheldon's actions like Gia did. After all, the town was generally safe, and they were talking about the son of one of Wakefield's most prominent families, a hardworking business owner they'd never had any problem with before.

Even the words that'd been spray-painted on the house didn't seem to rattle him—and that afternoon around three, Gia understood why when Cormac called to see how her day was going. She was sitting on her bed with her computer in her lap, commenting on responses to her posts on behalf of Backcountry Adventures while she told him about the windows, the graffiti and the lack of any real response from the police.

"What was the officer's name?" he asked.

"Pratt."

"Waylan?"

She "liked" a comment about how fair their prices were given the value of the experience. "I don't know. His first name wasn't on his badge, and I'd never met him before."

"Has to be," Cormac said. "He's a good friend of Sheldon's. I see them at the bar together all the time."

She rolled her eyes. "No wonder, then. Sheldon's family is too well-connected. I doubt we'll be able to get the help we need. And that is so unfair to my parents. They haven't done anything wrong. They don't know where Margot is. Neither do I, for that matter. But at least *I* made it clear from the beginning that I don't like Sheldon. That gives him a reason to hate me. *They* welcomed him into the family with open arms."

"Maybe I should spend the night on your couch tonight so I can keep an eye on things."

"And get shot because Sheldon doesn't expect anyone to be there? No way." And she couldn't go back to his place, either. She wouldn't leave her parents again.

"Then I'm going to call him and ask what the hell he thinks he's doing."

"That'll only make him mad at *you!*"

"If it'll get him to leave you and your parents alone—"

"No," she interrupted. "I ordered some security cameras. That should help."

"When will they come?"

"Email confirmation says tomorrow. He'd be stupid to come back tonight, anyway. He has to know after what he did to the windows we'll be on pins and needles, so he'll be much more likely to get caught."

"This has gotten way out of hand," Cormac said.

She "hearted" a comment from a customer who'd posted a picture of a mountain lion taken while on one of her tours. "Because Sheldon is used to getting his way," she explained, agreeing with Cormac. "He's never had anyone stand up to him, and he didn't think Margot had the nerve to be the first. If I'm being honest, neither did I. She's never done anything this gutsy before."

"What if we approach his folks? Ask them to see if they can

get him to calm down? It's in their best interest, too. He could wind up in jail if he doesn't."

She remembered their behavior the night they came over and knew they were probably helping to fuel their son's anger—not mitigate it. "I might have to try that approach—get them to see reason since I know he won't. But I don't have a high degree of confidence it will work. Where he's concerned, the apple didn't fall far from the tree."

"I take care of Johnny Maine's bulldog. He's on the force. I'll call him and see if he can do something to help."

Gia didn't answer. She hadn't even comprehended what she'd heard. His words had merely turned into a background rumble as her eyes zeroed in on a comment she'd just found on a post. It was from someone named M. Lane, and it was simply a heart.

She wouldn't have thought anything about it. The pictures she'd posted were gorgeous, meant to entice more bookings. This person could simply be showing some love for the beauty of Mother Nature. But something about it was familiar; the same person had put a heart on all her recent posts.

"Gia?"

She drew her attention back to their conversation. "What?"

"Did you hear me?"

"I'm sorry. It's just… Give me a minute." She scrolled back through the last several posts and searched the comments. Sure enough, M. Lane was putting a heart on everything. And on the most recent post? He or she had gone a bit further and written: I'm so excited! I think I just got a job!

Why would a stranger want to tell her that?

And then it occurred to her. When they used to play together as children, Margot's doll was always named Margaret Love, which morphed into Margaret Lane after she saw *Superman*.

M. Lane. Margaret Lane. That had to be Margot.

"Cormac, can I call you back?" she asked.

"Is everything okay?"

"It's fine," she replied. "It'll just be a minute."

She disconnected so she could concentrate on what she was doing as she navigated to Messages. She had to "like" M. Lane's account in order to be able to DM her, but she was accepted almost immediately.

If this is who I think it is, be careful. The evil empire has a private investigator, and I'm sure he'll be watching my pages if he's not already.

She didn't get an immediate response. Just when she was starting to wonder if she'd made a mistake, and M. Lane was Mason Lane or something like that, an answer appeared—simply another heart.

It was Margot. It had to be.

Gia called Cormac back right away.

"What's going on?" he asked.

"I think Margot's been following the Instagram account for Backcountry Adventures."

"What makes you think so?"

"She's commented quite a bit lately under a name she used when we were children. Only I would recognize it."

"She must be okay, then."

"Must be. Sounds like she just found a job."

"You'll have to tell your mother."

Ida was under too much strain. Gia was afraid she'd break down and tell the wrong person—a cop or a friend of Sheldon's or his family—in some misguided attempt to justify Margot's actions. "Not yet."

"Why not? She's worried."

"Because I don't want her saying anything to someone she thinks she can trust—but who ultimately tells the wrong person. No one else is going to fix this for us."

"What does that mean?"

Gia set her laptop aside and slid down in the bed, so she was staring at the ceiling. "It means that *I'm* going to have to be the one."

"To..." he prompted, sounding concerned.

"Put a stop to it."

"How?"

"The only solution I can come up with is to push Sheldon just a little further..."

"What?"

"I need to bring him out in the open, make sure other people know how dangerous he is. Then Margot would be safe to come home, or at least visit. I want my mother to be able to see her again before she dies."

"What will you do?"

"What I'd do with any other bully."

"Now I'm *really* scared," Cormac said. "What's that?"

"Stand up to him."

"Gia, no! This guy's liable to come after *you*."

"Exactly," she said. "Let him try."

27

Gia sent a message to Sheldon almost as soon as she hung up with Cormac.

Hey, nice job on the vandalism at my parents' house. The spray-painting was an especially nice touch. I didn't know you knew how to spell.

She knew him well enough to believe he wouldn't be able to resist gloating over what he'd done, and he didn't disappoint. While he didn't take ownership of the damage—then she could've taken that as proof to the police—he wrote back with a winking emoji.

"You're so predictable," she murmured, but she considered that to be a good thing. She was relying on how predictable he was—hoped it might make all the difference.

Heard from Margot, by the way. She's met someone who's actually attractive, and they're having a blast spending all your money. 😊

Gia nibbled on her bottom lip as she awaited his response. She was willing to bet he wouldn't come off quite so smug.

Do you have a death wish or something?

Yep. She was right. Not so smug.

I'm not afraid of you.

Her door opened, and she quickly set her phone aside as her father stuck his head into the room. "Are you going over to Cormac's tonight?"

"No, I'm not leaving you and Mom."

"If Sheldon comes back, there's nothing you can do."

"I can keep an eye out so you two can sleep."

He jerked his head toward her computer, which was sitting to one side of her. "So…what have you been working on?"

"Just some social media stuff for Backcountry Tours." That was a while ago, but there was no way she was going to tell him she was giving Sheldon the fight he'd been asking for. Leo wouldn't like the risk. But she couldn't sit back and let her brother-in-law continue to torment them. Someone could get hurt even if she tried to lay low. So why not stand up and throw a few punches herself? Her mother deserved peace in her final days. And Margot deserved better than to live in fear that Sheldon would eventually find her.

The more she thought about it, the more Gia realized that doing nothing was probably the worst option. Since Sheldon held every advantage—he was bigger, stronger, more comfortable with weapons and was willing to take things further—and the police and his parents weren't making much of an effort to rein him in, her only option was to prove just how dangerous he really was. Otherwise, he could make their lives miserable indefinitely, or at least long enough that Ida would die without even knowing where her daughter was.

She was fairly certain he'd take the bait. The only thing that remained to be seen was whether she'd be able to get away once he sprung the trap.

★ ★ ★

Cormac had left a message for Johnny Maine, but it wasn't until after eight that he received a call back.

"Hey, hate to trouble you," Cormac said. "But I'm wondering if there's something you can help me with."

"Sure, what is it?" Johnny asked.

Cormac explained the situation with Gia's family and Sheldon. "He's being a real asshole," he said when he finished.

There was a brief silence, then Johnny said, "Well, his wife ran away with his kids, right? I'd be pissed off, too."

"That isn't the point," Cormac said. "The point is that he's harassing her family, and they had nothing to do with it."

"He's convinced they know where she is and won't tell him."

"That isn't against the law. What he's doing *is*. You can't vandalize other people's property." Cormac couldn't believe *he* had to be the one to say this.

"He'll settle down," Johnny said dismissively.

"Is that what everyone else on the force is saying?"

"For the most part. It's not as if we don't know Sheldon. Waylan's his best friend."

"I've seen them together on several occasions. So…you're not going to do anything to stop him?"

"There's nothing we can do, Doc. He insists he wasn't responsible for the vandalism, and we don't have any proof that he was."

"Who else could it have been?" Cormac asked. "Who else would have the motivation?"

"Do you really want me to answer that question? Because *you'd* have sufficient motivation, right? You've hated Gia Rossi for years for what she did to your father. Your sisters hate her, too. I heard they crashed the Banned Books Club meeting recently."

"That was a mistake. And if you heard about the meeting, you probably also know I showed up to stop them."

"Then it could've been your father who shot out the windows. He tells everyone Gia ruined his life, and he's been pretty deep in his cups when I've seen him around town lately. He'd probably like to spray-paint a few things about Gia on the Rossi house, wouldn't he?"

Cormac couldn't help gritting his teeth. "It wasn't him."

"I'm supposed to take *your* word but not Sheldon's?"

"Jesus, Johnny! Thanks for nothing," he said and hung up.

Johnny called him right back and backpedaled a bit, saying he'd keep an eye on Sheldon, that he'd just been playing devil's advocate to show the situation wasn't as cut and dried as Gia and her family might be representing it. He ended the conversation by saying he took his job seriously and wanted to keep everyone in the community safe, but Cormac was so put off by his arrogance it was all he could do not to tell him to find a new vet for his dog.

After listening to him make that rather pathetic attempt at public relations, Cormac tried to call Gia to let her know Johnny wasn't going to be any help. But she wasn't answering his calls or texts. He would've thought she'd gone to bed, but it was too early for her. It was even early for him. And the words she'd said when he'd last spoken with her were far too concerning to automatically assume such a benign end to the evening.

To reassure himself that all was well, he went outside and walked through the back gate into the Rossi yard. The house was dark except for a slim glimmer of light that looked like it was coming from the kitchen.

He tossed a few small pieces of gravel up at Gia's window. Several bounced against the pane but still didn't evoke a response. Where was she?

Just in case Sheldon had come back to cause trouble again, he went around to the front. Sure enough, there was a light on in the kitchen, but he couldn't see anyone through the window.

He started to pull his phone from his pocket to try calling

again when it occurred to him that Mr. Rossi's SUV wasn't in the drive. If Gia was just running an errand or something, he was fairly certain she would still answer her phone.

He could be wrong, but he had a feeling she was up to something, and if it involved Sheldon, it definitely wasn't safe.

Margot looked in on the boys to find them sleeping soundly on the air mattress she'd bought. They seemed to be adjusting to their new surroundings. They hadn't asked to go home yet, probably because it felt like they were on vacation. Instead of being stressed and unhappy, she was smiling and relaxed, and no doubt the joy she was feeling trickled down to them.

They'd gone to the park after school, and she'd sat at a picnic table and read a book while looking up every few minutes to check on them. It'd felt unbelievable to know there was no one waiting for her at home who'd be upset that she'd spent too much time away or didn't have dinner on the table. They could stay as long as they were enjoying themselves. And when they left? It would be her decision as to what they'd eat. They could get In-N-Out if they wanted, and in celebration of Starbucks calling her back right after her interview to offer her the job, they'd done exactly that.

She'd found work. The pay wasn't anything that would put them on Easy Street, but it was better than she'd expected, and the hours were perfect. She'd drop off the boys at school, go to the coffee shop and work until four. Greydon and Matthew would spend a mere forty-five minutes in an after-school program until she could pick them up, and then they'd have evenings together. No babysitter required—at least until summer. But she wasn't going to worry about that quite yet.

She was starting her new job next week, had already canceled her other interviews. There was no way those positions could match the hours. Besides, the Starbucks location where she'd be working was close to the school. If there was a problem, she could get there in minutes.

After turning off the light in the hallway, she went out to the living room. They didn't have a lot of furniture yet—just the couch and TV she'd been able to buy. She was sleeping on an air mattress, too, and their clothes were simply piled in the closets. But she'd get everything they needed eventually and turn this place into a real home.

The only thing that was bothering her now was being unable to speak directly to her parents. Worry for her mother, knowing she was missing Ida's last days and wasn't there to comfort her, broke Margot's heart.

She'd done what she had to do, she reminded herself, and pulled the pepper spray she'd purchased a few days ago from her purse. While she was researching how to use it and why it worked, she'd watched a video where a police officer had suggested she spray herself to see what it was like. She hadn't gathered the nerve to do that quite yet—and certainly wasn't going to do it in the house, where the boys could come in contact with the solution. But she was glad she had a can. Gia's message on Instagram made her nervous. She'd tried to cover her trail well enough that even a professional couldn't find her. But had she thought of everything?

She'd sold the Subaru, so that didn't create a link to her any longer. She'd purchased her new vehicle, a Toyota RAV4, with cash using her new identity. The apartment was in her new name. She'd gotten her job under her new name. And she'd left her old cell phone behind so it couldn't be used to trace her and purchased a prepaid one, also using her new name. Even the Instagram account she'd created to be able to comment on Gia's posts, which she'd deleted after Gia warned her, was under her new name.

So she was pretty sure she was in the clear. She had the pepper spray, just in case she was wrong. But she knew if Sheldon ever found her, there was no way that would ever be enough.

Gia followed Sheldon from his house to the bar and sat at a table not far away. He didn't see her at first, but once he did, he kept turning around to glower at her.

Cormac kept trying to reach her, but she couldn't respond. She didn't want him to know where she was or what she was doing, wouldn't draw him into the fight. She didn't want to create a feud for him to deal with after she left town. And she knew that with someone like Sheldon, who was basically a coward, she'd have a better chance of drawing him into the open if he thought the odds were stacked securely in his favor.

He wouldn't be afraid of a woman. He felt too superior.

She ordered a Coke and watched him as he had a beer, got up and went to the restroom, then walked over to throw a few darts before finally returning to his table.

She wondered if he really had any interest in the basketball game he was watching here and there, or if he was just reluctant to go home to an empty house and be reminded that Margot had gotten one over on him. But then Cece walked in, and she knew he'd been waiting for his girlfriend.

Gia spotted her right away and tipped her head, and Cece had the good grace to look slightly abashed. She said something to Sheldon as soon as she reached the table, and he looked back at Gia again.

Gia grinned at him.

He narrowed his eyes and, after a glaring contest Gia refused to lose, got up and came over to her table.

"What are you doing?" he demanded.

She lifted her Coke. "Having a drink."

"You don't have to do it here."

"I like this place," she said.

His face reddened and his hands curled into ham-like fists. "You're flirting with danger," he warned, his jaw clenched.

He looked mean—and dangerous—which was unsettling. She wondered if this was what Margot had seen whenever he got angry, if she had to live with someone who looked as if he was about to choke her to death and throw her in a river. It was frightening enough to make Gia reconsider her plan. But he was trying to scare her and she wouldn't concede. Backing away would only mean she'd have to continue to worry about her loved ones indefinitely.

She shrugged as if she wasn't remotely concerned and took a drink of her Coke. "It's a free country."

Calling her all sorts of names under his breath, he returned to Cece but didn't sit down. He paced around the table like a caged panther, throwing a few peanuts in his mouth every now and then, ordering another drink and looking back at her again and again with that malevolent expression.

Eventually, he must've suggested they leave, because he threw some money on the table and escorted his girlfriend out.

Gia hurried to pay her bill so she could go, too.

Cece's car followed directly behind Sheldon's truck, but she was in third place as they drove through town. As they stopped at each of the two stoplights, she could see Cece's worried eyes as they glanced nervously into the rearview mirror.

Once they arrived at Sheldon's house—the house Margot had lived in for probably ten or twelve years—they pulled into the driveway, and Gia parked at the curb.

When Sheldon saw that she'd had the nerve to follow him home, his eyes widened in disbelief. It looked as though he was going to come over and say something to her again, but Cece grabbed his arm. Although Gia couldn't hear what was said, she guessed the other woman was pleading with him to just ignore her.

After a few seconds, he reluctantly allowed his girlfriend to lead him into the house. But Gia knew the fact that she was sitting out front was bothering him, because he kept peering out through the blinds to see if she was still there.

At ten thirty, she received a text message from him.

Why are you doing this? What do you hope to accomplish?

If the police won't keep an eye on you to stop you from damaging my parents' property, I will.

If I wanted to damage anything, you'd be the last person who could stop me.

I guess we'll see about that.

You have no idea what you're doing.

Are you saying you're going to make me sorry? 😁

She knew the emoji would enrage him. The last thing a fragile ego could withstand was being laughed at.

Just you wait.

Until I'm asleep and can't fight back? Is that the plan?

I'm not remotely scared of you.

"I hope that's true," she murmured. "Because then you'll be much more likely to underestimate me, and that's what I'm banking on."

Does the woman you've been cheating with know what kind of man you really are?

She never got a response. But it wasn't long after that Cece came out and sent Gia a self-conscious look while hurrying to her car.

Before she could get too far, Gia opened her door and stepped out to yell, "A woman doesn't go into hiding with her kids without good reason, Cece—especially someone like my sister. Margot would never leave our dying mother unless she felt she had to. I hope you're taking that into account as you get involved with this asshole," she said, gesturing at the house.

Only then, when Cece lifted her face so that Gia could see it in the halo of the streetlight, did it become apparent that she was crying. "I just told him I don't want to see him anymore. I'm done." She craned her neck to check the front stoop and continued only when she knew he hadn't followed her out. "He's got an anger management problem. I think you need to be careful and leave him alone," she added, the last of what she said coming in a rush before she got into her car and drove away.

A trickle of alarm ran down Gia's spine. Her plan was working far better than she'd expected—almost too well. No doubt Sheldon would blame her for Cece's defection, which would further stoke the fire of his rage.

She was about to get back into her car and leave. She'd done enough for one night, she told herself. But then he came out of the house with a rifle.

28

Cormac had guessed where he might find Gia. As soon as he turned the corner that led to Sheldon's house, he saw her father's vehicle parked at the curb and felt a measure of relief—until he noticed Sheldon standing on his front porch *with a rifle.* In a panic, he pumped the gas pedal, which revved the engine and must've drawn Sheldon's attention, because he lowered the gun.

Slamming on his brakes, Cormac skidded to a stop in the middle of the street next to Gia's car. "What's going on?" he shouted as he jumped out. "What the hell do you think you're doing?" he asked Sheldon.

"Me?" Sheldon pressed a hand to his chest. "I'm just protecting my hearth and home. I have a legal right to do that. *She's* the one who's causing a problem. She's trespassing, has no right to be here."

"I'm parked in the street!" Gia yelled. "You don't own the street!"

Cormac motioned for Gia to get into her car. "Go home before you get hurt," he said.

"I can park here," she insisted. "He can't do anything about it."

"Gia, please. He's got a gun. That's enough."

The light came on at the house next door, and the neighbor poked his head out. "What the hell? What's all the yelling about? People are trying to sleep, for God's sake, people who have to work in the morning. Do you want me to call the police?"

"Please do," Gia said.

"Gia, you don't want the police to perceive *you* as the problem," Cormac said before raising his voice to speak to the neighbor. "That won't be necessary. I've got it now."

"Cormac, I want this over and done with," she said. "I want my sister to be able to come home and see my mother. This prick is standing in the way of all of that."

"We'll figure it out, but nothing's going to change tonight," he said. "Please go."

When she scrubbed her hands over her face, he wasn't sure she'd cooperate, but eventually she nodded. "Okay, maybe I got a little carried away," she admitted. But then, only a second later, she looked over at Sheldon and yelled, "See you tomorrow!"

"We'll see each other sometime," he responded. "That I can promise you."

Cormac followed Gia home and parked behind her. "What was that all about?" he demanded as he got out. "Are you trying to get yourself shot?"

"An angry person is a reckless person," she replied, coming right back at him. "They make mistakes. And that's what I need Sheldon to do—make a big mistake that I'll be able to capitalize on."

"You're pretty angry yourself," he pointed out. "How do you know *you* won't be the one to make a mistake *he* can capitalize on?"

She jutted out her chin as though she'd continue to argue, but then he could see her start to blink rapidly and knew she was battling tears.

"I know you're going through a lot," he said, gentling his voice and pulling her into his arms. "But you're trying to do too much. You need to take a deep breath and get some sleep, regroup."

She didn't say anything. She just buried her face in his chest.

"Are you okay?" he asked a few minutes later, dropping a kiss on top of her head.

He wanted to stay angry with her for being so reckless. He didn't know one other woman who would've done what she'd done. But he couldn't help admiring her spirit. She'd been the same kind of fighter in high school. Few people had her grit.

"You scare me," he murmured. "I'm terrified you're going to get hurt."

She leaned her head back to gaze up at the stars while he continued to hold her. "Standing up to a bully always comes with risks, Cormac. That's why no one wants to do it. But I can't live with the alternative—won't let him *make* me live with the alternative. I'm going to fight back. And whether I win or not?" She met his gaze. "Well, that remains to be seen."

Margot turned to look at the man who'd followed her into the thrift shop from the nearby park, where, after dropping the boys off at school, she'd been reading a book while drinking a latte. She couldn't remember ever being able to simply relax in a park by herself—not while she was with Sheldon. She'd always had a list of things she had to get done before he returned home that she was afraid she wouldn't be able to complete in time. But she didn't have to start her new job until Monday, she was in a gripping part of her novel, and it was a beautiful fall day. She'd given herself an hour to read before continuing to furnish their new apartment and had been thoroughly enjoying herself—until she'd spotted a middle-aged man with a drawn face and a thickening waistline watching her from another picnic table. He didn't have a book or a cup of coffee or any children with him. He hadn't come to run or anything like that, either. He was just sitting there, dressed in black slacks and a white button-up shirt, doing nothing.

Who was he? she wondered. And what did he want? Despite the circumstances, she'd felt pretty secure since coming to California. This was the first time she'd been notably uneasy. Could it be Sheldon's PI? Had he found her somehow, maybe from those comments she'd posted on Gia's Instagram page?

She didn't see how that could be the case. The only thing required to create an account on Insta was an email address. But maybe that was all a good investigator needed. She'd seen movies where people could be traced using an IP address or something like that—she didn't completely understand what it was or how it worked. Or maybe she'd left some other trail she wasn't aware of. She didn't have any experience with trying to drop out of sight.

Fear gripped her as she moved around the shop, putting various dishes and a toaster in her basket while watching him surreptitiously through the shelves. He didn't seem to be actively shopping, just like he hadn't been doing much of anything at the park, but he *would* pick up an item here or there if she glanced over.

She slipped her hand into her purse and felt for her phone. She'd entered Gia's number into it. Her parents' too. But she hadn't dared call them. It just felt better, more normal, to have her contacts in place, especially the numbers of the most important people in her life.

She was tempted to text Gia to tell her about the man who was following her. Her sister may have heard something, could know more than Margot did. Whoever this guy was, he had a great deal of interest in her. She felt his gaze on her whenever she wasn't looking at him.

As he meandered closer, she couldn't resist sending her sister a message.

Have they found me?

Her heart pounded against her chest as she waited for Gia's reply, which came only seconds later.

Why? What do you mean?

There's a man here, following me.

There is? I don't see how they could've found you.

You haven't heard anything?

No.

"Excuse me."

Margot jumped when she looked up to find him standing right next to her.

"I'm sorry," he said, lifting a hand as one might to a calm a spooked horse. "I didn't mean to startle you. I just... I saw you in the park and... Well, my wife died recently—not quite a year ago. I visit the park every now and then because it reminds me of her. She liked to go there and read, just like you, and while I was sitting there, missing her, I looked up and...there you were, so serene and pretty." He cleared his throat, obviously feeling awkward. "It's been a long time since I've done any-thing like this, and I was never very good at it," he said with a self-deprecating laugh. "Obviously, I've only gotten worse. But I was wondering if... I thought... Well, if you'd be willing to give me your email address, we could try to get to know each other that way, and if things go well, maybe one day you'll feel comfortable enough to go out to dinner with me."

Stunned, Margot blinked at him. He wasn't an investigator.

He wasn't even asking for something as intrusive as her phone number. He merely wanted her email address.

The expression on her face must've made him think she was going to turn him down because he started to move away.

"Never mind. I shouldn't have bothered you. I'm sorry. You could be married or seeing someone or just want to be left alone. I'm not sure what compelled me to follow you in here…"

He turned, obviously eager to get away as fast as possible. But he'd been so respectful and sweet—and authentic. It was the authentic part that got her. "Wait… What's your name?"

He seemed surprised that she'd stop him. "Max. Max Schwartz. I'm an eye doctor here in LA."

"Well, Max, my name is Margaret Lane, and you can have my email address," she said. "Since we're strangers, I don't feel safe giving you anything else. Not yet. But…I'm new in the area and could use a friend, too."

A smile spread across his face, and for the first time, she thought he was kind of attractive. He had thick dark hair, long eyelashes, brown eyes and amazing teeth. And he wasn't as old as she'd first thought, she realized.

He pulled out his phone and had her type in her email address. "I hope it's okay if I write you tonight," he said and started to laugh.

Margot laughed, too. "That would be fine."

"Have a good day, *Margaret*."

"Thank you!"

Dazed, she stared after him as he left. She hadn't really considered what her future love life could be like. She'd thought only of escape—the chance to find peace while raising her children. Meeting someone else could add a whole new dimension. Although she wasn't ready to move forward on that front quite yet, this guy didn't seem to be in any hurry.

She glanced down at her phone and a new text from Gia.

What's happening? Are you okay?

Drawing a deep breath, she typed a response. I was terrified for a minute. But it was a false alarm. Everything's fine.

Who was it?

Just a guy who finds me attractive, I guess.

Be careful. Just because he's not connected to Sheldon doesn't mean he's safe.

She smiled as she remembered how deferential he'd been. Max seemed like the total opposite of Sheldon. And the depth of feeling he'd had for his wife, the sorrow that was still in his face after losing her, told her he knew how to love.

She'd learned that not everyone did.

He's nothing to worry about. I'm actually glad I met him.

So you're safe? Do you have enough money? Do you need anything?

I'm happier than I've been in ages. I just wish I'd listened to you and never married Sheldon in the first place. How're Mom and Dad?

Hanging in there. I'm taking good care of them.

I knew you would come through. I doubt I've told you this before, but I admire your strength.

I'm going to make sure you and the boys can come home and see Mom again before... Well, soon!

Could that really be possible? Margot didn't see how. But she smiled as she put some cooking utensils into her cart. If anyone could do it, it would be Gia.

Gia's phone chimed and she read Sheldon's text message twice.

Going to the same bar tonight. Thought I'd be courteous and save you the trouble of having to follow me.

He was telling her where he'd be—as if he wanted her to come join him? He was up to something. She could feel it. And she wasn't going to be stupid enough to fall for it.

"What is it?" Cormac asked. He'd come over for dinner as soon as he'd gotten off work—she'd made lettuce wraps—and they were playing a game of liar's dice with her parents.

"That's not Margot, is it?" Ida added in a hopeful voice.

The dice clacked as Gia poured them back into her cup. "No, it's the bozo she married."

The blood drained from her mother's face. "Why is Sheldon texting you? I already told Peggy there's no way I'll ever put him in contact with Margot, not after what he's done to us since she left—shooting up our property and spray-painting profanity! He should have to pay for the damage."

"Except he claims it wasn't him," Leo said. "And the police believe him."

"When Peggy insisted her son would never do anything like that, I started to laugh," Ida said. "We all know it was him."

Leo jerked his head toward Gia. "What does he want with you?"

"There's no telling," she said. "He's playing some sort of game. Just wanted to let me know he'd be at the bar tonight, if I'd like to join him."

"Why would you ever want to join *him*?" Ida was suitably

put off, but she also had no frame of reference, didn't know about last night. She was getting so fragile; Gia tried not to tell her anything that might upset her.

"He's just taunting me," she said. "Trying to get a response."

Cormac lowered his voice, which imbued it with more meaning. "Surely, you're not going..."

"No." Now that she had the security cameras in place—Leo had helped her install them this afternoon—she didn't feel as though she had to keep such a close eye on Sheldon. If her brother-in-law came over and tried to cause any more trouble, he'd be caught on video.

"Thank God for small miracles," Cormac grumbled, and Gia gave his foot a slight kick under the table to let him know she didn't want him to say anything else for fear her parents would get suspicious that there was something she hadn't told them.

When he yelped, obviously on purpose because she hadn't kicked him that hard, Ida and Leo looked up in surprise. He excused it by claiming he'd accidentally bitten his tongue, then he shot her a grin to let her know he could've paid her back for that kick but had chosen not to.

She chuckled to herself. Cormac was fun and engaging and so damn easy to be around. Too easy. That she liked having him hang out with her and her parents was sort of alarming. Usually, once she got to this stage of a relationship, when whoever she was dating felt they had a spot in her life and could be part of even mundane daily activities, she was ready to run the other way.

But that wasn't the case with Cormac. She liked having him with her no matter what she was doing and was grateful for his support. She admired him in so many ways. He stood up for what he thought was right—even when he'd had to turn on his own family. In her opinion, that was the definition of integrity.

They were nearly finished with the game when Ida slumped lower in her seat and nearly dropped her cup of dice. "I'm sorry," she said as she managed to get the cup safely onto the table. "I just… I don't have the strength to continue." She offered them a feeble smile. "Maybe tomorrow."

Alarmed, Gia stood up and came around the table. "Can I get you something? More painkillers? A drink of water?"

"No, I… I don't need anything," her mother said. "I just… I think I'll go to bed a little early tonight."

Leo exchanged a concerned look with Gia. "I'll help you to bed, honey. I'm tired, too. Why don't we put on a movie, and you can drift off to sleep in my arms."

Ida's gaze met and locked with his as a faint smile curved her lips. "I'm so glad I married you."

Gia's eyes filled with tears as she watched her father help her mother up the stairs. Ida was fading fast. Gia didn't see how she was going to bring Margot home before it was too late.

Cormac came up behind her and slid his arms around her waist, pulling her against him. "I've got you," he whispered in her ear. "It's going to be okay."

But it wasn't going to be okay. Because of Sheldon, Margot couldn't be here, couldn't say a proper goodbye to the woman who'd borne and raised her.

29

Gia heard a noise in the middle of the night. Was Ida sick? Did she need help?

Gia was just trying to come to full consciousness when her bedroom door swung open. She lifted her head, but the shape coming toward her was too big to be her mother or her father.

"What—" she started to say, but that shadow suddenly rushed forward and clamped a hand down tightly over her nose and mouth.

"Where's your phone?" a harsh voice rasped.

Sheldon! Her mind, still sluggish from sleep, seemed to trip over itself in an effort to catch up. And once it did, she had so much adrenaline pumping through her body she had no strength, felt as limp as a wet noodle. How'd he get inside the house?

She couldn't shout. She couldn't even breathe. And he seemed to realize that at the same second and to take great pleasure in continuing to cut off her air supply.

"You think you're tough, bitch?" he gritted out, bringing his face down to hers. "You think you can take *me* on? Huh, do you? Well, let's see what you can do now."

Gia began to buck and try to fight him off, but that only enraged him further, especially when she managed to bite his hand. He pulled back, cursing, and she started to scream, but he cut the noise off only a second later by wrapping his hands tightly around her throat. She could feel him crushing her windpipe as she fought. He was heavier than she was, and because he was above her, he had the advantage of being able to use his weight.

"Is that all you've got?" he taunted, breathing heavily in her ear. "There's nothing you can do, bitch. How does it feel to get exactly what you deserve?"

Her eyes began to burn and water, and the dark image he made above her blurred. She knew she had only a matter of seconds before she passed out.

She *couldn't* let that happen, couldn't be defeated so easily. She just hadn't been prepared for this, had never dreamed he'd be bold enough to come into the house. Striking when he had an open escape route was more like him. But she'd obviously pushed him beyond his normal boundaries, made him so mad he'd risk almost anything.

She was scratching at his arms, but that proved ineffectual. She had to reach a more vulnerable part of his body. She tried to knee him in the groin, but the blankets got in the way, and the attempt only made him laugh. "Look at you," he said. "I could do anything right now."

For a moment, she was afraid he'd act on that threat in a sexual way. She could tell he was trying to decide if he had the nerve to go that far. And that moment of hesitation, of brief indecision, was all she needed. Summoning every last bit of strength she had, she pressed her thumbs into his eyes and heard him yelp in pain.

He let go of her neck to pull her hands away—and she gasped for air, hauling in one lungful, then two. But still, she couldn't scream. He was trying to get his hands around her throat, trying to return to the position that'd given him so much leverage when she managed to kick free of the bedding and knee him.

As he gasped in pain, she found her phone, which was under her extra pillow because she'd fallen asleep texting Cormac, and started pounding him in the head with it.

She wouldn't have thought such a small device could do much damage, but he put up one arm to fend her off. Then he grabbed her wrist, trying to wrest her phone away. She was afraid he'd run off with it—and Margot's contact information.

She had to relinquish it but letting go paid off. Grabbing the phone tied up one of his hands, and she was able to squirm out from underneath him by essentially falling out of bed.

He jumped off the bed to come after her, but she sprang to her feet and started throwing everything she could at him. A jewelry box. A figurine. A bookend. A book.

She didn't realize she was screaming to high heaven until her father came running into the room and turned on the light.

"Oh, my God! What's going on?" he shouted.

Gia thought Sheldon was planning to take her phone and run right through her father. She already knew he didn't care if he hurt someone. But she stuck out her foot just in time. As she tripped him, he went down like a felled tree, and the lamp she hit him with next knocked him out cold.

She was breathing so heavily she thought she might throw up as she stood, wavering, still holding the lamp like a bat in case he tried to get up. "Call...for...help," she managed to say to her stunned father, and he picked up her phone, which had gone skidding across the carpet almost to his feet.

After coming into the room and turning it toward her face to unlock it, he dialed 9-1-1.

"Gia? What's going on?" Her mother came into the room, but she was so weak she had to cling to the door frame to remain standing.

"We got the son of a bitch," Gia said. "We got him, Mom."

"He broke in?" Ida said.

"He sure did. And he assaulted me." Gia dropped the lamp and gingerly touched her throat, which hurt so much she could barely speak. "The police won't be able to ignore this."

Her mother looked stunned. "What was he trying to do?"

"He was after my phone, but he didn't mind doing a little damage at the same time."

Her father left the room and came back holding a kitchen knife. "He'd better not try to get away."

Sheldon was starting to come to, but he wasn't getting up. It didn't appear that he could. He was rubbing his head where she'd struck him and writhing in pain, and he was bleeding. It looked as if she'd nearly cost him an eye.

Still, she wasn't confident her father would be able to stop him if he got to his feet. But Leo had apparently called Cormac as well as the police, because only a couple of minutes later, Cormac came running down the hall, calling her name.

"What happened?" he asked. "Are you okay?"

She was trembling from all the adrenaline as she nodded. "It's over," she whispered hoarsely and sank back onto the bed. "Give me my phone. I want to call Margot to tell her she and the boys can come home."

The police insisted both Sheldon and Gia go to the hospital. It didn't take long for Sheldon to be examined, bandaged up and released into police custody, but the doctor made Gia stay a little longer for observation. While she was there, the police sent a photographer over to take pictures of the bruises that were starting to show around her throat.

"Sheldon's in *such* big trouble," Cormac told her. He'd been with her since it happened, had called and had his sister cancel all his appointments, which was well beyond anything Gia had expected. She kept telling him she was okay, but he didn't want her to be alone after something that traumatic. Her parents had been there with her earlier, but Leo had taken Ida home so she could rest.

"He should be," she said. "The vandalism was bad enough. But breaking and entering? Assault? He tried to choke me!"

"I know that, and so do the police. I heard someone talking about possible charges, and attempted murder was on the list."

"I don't think he was trying to *kill* me. At least, I hope he wasn't. But his rage was certainly boiling over."

"Regardless, depending on the charges they ultimately go with, he's probably going away for five or ten years, maybe longer."

"I'm happy for Margot, because that gets him out of the picture. But I'm sad, too. If only he'd been a decent human, it wouldn't have had to be like this."

"You can't get someone like Sheldon to play fair. Did you hear what his buddy Waylan said to him?"

"The cop?" She shook her head. "When was this?"

"At the house. He was one of the officers who came to arrest him. I heard him say, 'I tried to warn you to leave her alone. You just wouldn't listen.'"

"The police gave him the benefit of every doubt."

"There's no way they can smooth this over."

"Cece should be glad she broke things off as early as she did," Gia said. "Poor Margot."

"Have you had a chance to talk to your sister?"

"Not yet. Mom and Dad told her what happened. But the doctor was here with me at the time, so I couldn't get on the phone, and then the police photographer showed up."

"Want me to call her?"

Gia had been up almost all night, and the flood of adrenaline that'd kicked in during the attack was taking a toll. "I'm not sure I can do it right now. I can't keep my eyes open."

"Okay. Sleep," he said. "I'm right here, and I won't leave you. When you wake up, I'll take you home."

She forced her eyes to remain open long enough to look over at him, and he brought his chair closer, so he could hold her hand. "What am I going to do with you?" she mumbled.

He blinked in surprise. "What do you mean?"

"I'm afraid...I'm afraid I'm falling in love for the first time."

That slightly crooked grin she found so charming curved his lips, and he stood up to drop a peck on her lips. "Would that be so bad?"

"Maybe. What if...what if you're not falling in love with me?"

He smoothed the hair out of her face. "Gia?"

Her eyes were starting to close despite her efforts to keep them open. She was pretty sure the doctor had given her a sedative to get her to sleep, because she couldn't seem to avoid the darkness that was quickly swallowing her up. "What?" she managed to say, trying even harder to stave it off.

"I tried *not* to fall in love with you—but it proved impossible."

Santa Monica Pier was crowded. This could easily be the last weekend with such warm weather, so everyone was out to enjoy it while they could. But Margot didn't mind the company. The babble of voices and laughing children around them only added to the festive feeling.

While the boys played in the sand next to her, trying to dig a moat for their castle, Margot turned her face up to the sun. She loved California. If the situation were different, she wouldn't leave it. But she was going home on Monday. She'd already called Starbucks to tell them she couldn't accept the job, after all, but she planned to keep her apartment until the lease was up. Depending on what happened with her mother, she might bring the boys back for the summer.

She wouldn't miss the last few weeks or months of Ida's

life, wouldn't keep her kids from being with either set of grandparents—providing Sheldon's folks proved to be decent and fair with her and with them. She had yet to see how Peggy and Ron had reacted to their son's arrest. She hadn't talked to them. She was willing to bet they blamed her for everything. But she'd do what she could to be fair, if and when they were ready. She was just glad she no longer had to live under the yoke of fear and negativity that'd plagued her marriage. Now she could heal, grow stronger and live free and happy right in Wakefield.

Her phone rang. She dug it out of the beach bag to see that it was Gia and answered with an eager smile. "Hey! How are you feeling?"

"Much better."

"Did they let you out of the hospital?"

"They did. I told them Cormac would take care of me."

"Cormac again, huh? That name keeps coming up," she teased.

"He's a good guy."

Margot laughed. She could tell that was the understatement of the year. Gia really liked the town vet. Ida and Leo thought he was "the one," which was pretty ironic, given that he was Mr. Hart's son.

"Are you sure you won't mind having Mr. Hart as a father-in-law?"

"Whoa!" Gia said. "Take it easy. We just started dating."

Margot pressed a hand to her hat so that it wouldn't fly away in the breeze kicking up. "The fact that you didn't say it will never happen tells me this guy is different."

"He might be," she admitted with a laugh.

"Your voice sounds better. It was so raspy after what Sheldon did to your throat. How's the bruising?"

"Not pretty. Looks like I'm wearing a purple scarf."

"I'm so sorry that happened."

"Don't be. I'm just glad you're able to come home. Mom and Dad have missed you and the boys so much."

"I've missed them, too."

"What are you doing today?"

Margot gazed out to sea. "Just relaxing on the beach."

"I wish I was there with you."

"I wish you were, too. You'll have to come back with me in the summer and spend a couple of weeks."

"Maybe I'll do that," she said.

Margot hadn't expected this answer. "Won't you be in Coeur d'Alene running your business?"

"I might be able to squeeze in a vacation," she said. "A girl's gotta live."

After they hung up, Margot checked her inbox. Sure enough, she'd received another email from Max. They'd exchanged several so far, and this morning he'd sent her a darling picture of his dog curled up with his late wife's cat and told her about going to the symphony last night.

He was so different from Sheldon. But that was what she found appealing.

She hit the reply button and wrote a response.

I'd like to give you my number. I have to go back to Iowa to be with my family for a while. It could be months, depending on how my mother fares, but I hope we can continue to get to know each other.

She added her phone number and sent the message. Then she took the boys over to the pier for some rides and cotton candy. She was nervous about how Max would respond, wondered if he might end the relationship since she was no longer going to be in the area.

But when she checked her inbox again and read his message, a warm feeling washed over her.

I'm sad you have to leave, especially because this sounds health related. If it's serious, I'm sorry. But I'm happy to have your number and will text or call you from now on. ☺

I look forward to getting to know the beautiful woman I saw in the park.

Max

Under his name, he'd provided his number, too.

EPILOGUE

The funeral was on a blustery day at the end of March. Ida had lasted longer than the doctors had predicted by nearly three months—and had passed peacefully in her sleep only three weeks after Gia had to return to Coeur d'Alene to help Eric open Backcountry Adventures. She'd wanted to stay longer—until the end came—but no one knew when that would be, and life had to go on. Her mother had been the one to insist on that.

Gia felt awful now. She could've made it just three more weeks. But she'd checked in every day and laughed and talked with Ida about the good times they'd had over the holidays, playing cards as it snowed outside, watching shows and movies together with bowls of popcorn and eating all the meals she'd made—some that'd turned out better than others. Witnessing her mother's slow decline had been heartbreaking, and yet…she found a deep comfort in those five months. Gia was sure she would never have gotten to know her mother quite like she did without them. The resentment she'd carried around for so long before that—for the way things had gone when Mr. Hart did what he did, for constantly trying to rein her in when she wanted to run free and for giving Margot so much more approval—was gone. In its place was a newfound appreciation for the sacrifices and love of a good mother.

Cormac sat on one side of her, holding her hand and offering the same steady support he'd given her almost since they started dating, while the pastor spoke of her mother's many wonderful attributes. When it'd come time to go back to Idaho, it'd been difficult to leave him, too, but they'd never planned on being separated for long. He'd told her he'd sell his practice and move to Idaho, and she'd thought that was probably the best way to go, since she couldn't move her business to Wakefield.

But she'd since stopped him. It didn't make sense that his sister should be put out of a job when Gia wanted to come home, anyway. The year she'd dropped out of college, she couldn't seem to get far enough away from Wakefield. Now she preferred to be surrounded by the memories of her childhood—or most of those memories, anyway. She also wanted to be with her father, her sister and her nephews during this difficult time—and maybe well beyond that.

Coming home was what felt right, so she was selling her half of the business to a friend of Eric's and was going to use the money to open a bookstore. There was a redbrick storefront for rent not far from Cormac's clinic. It'd been a gift store until the owner retired, but Gia could easily imagine all the changes she'd make to turn it into an awesome bookstore. She even knew what she'd name it: The Banned Books Shoppe. She still had the club going. At Margot's request, the next book the Banned Books Club had decided to read was *The Patron Saint of Liars* by Ann Patchett.

"Are you doing okay?" Margot asked. She was sitting on the other side of Gia, and the boys were sandwiched between her and Leo.

Gia leaned closer. "I'm glad you talked me into coming home for the winter—I can tell you that. It changed my life."

Margot smiled despite the tears glistening in her eyes. She hadn't been the same person since Sheldon had gone to jail.

Although he'd only been sentenced to four years in the state penitentiary, it was enough to give Margot the chance to get a divorce and rebuild her life without having to worry about him, and she was thriving.

Fortunately, his legal troubles had shocked his parents, made them realize they'd probably overindulged him and excused his behavior way too many times. They hadn't been perfect to Margot since she came back, but they were treating her with enough respect that she'd been willing to work out visitation for the boys. Peggy and Ron were even at the funeral. So were Eric, Coty and Ingrid, Sammie and Ruth and Cormac's sisters and mother. Gia had seen several members of the Banned Books Club enter the church, too. The only person who wasn't there was Mr. Hart—and that was a good thing.

At least, that was the only person Gia thought was missing— until she heard a murmur at the back of the church and turned to see a man walking up the aisle, smiling apologetically at everyone he passed. Gia didn't realize who he was until he reached the front pew, where they were sitting, and Margot's mouth dropped open. "Max!" she said.

Cormac and Gia slid to the left immediately to make more room, and he sat in the spot they'd just vacated. "I'm *so* sorry I'm late. My plane was delayed by four hours. I wanted to surprise you, but not like this."

Margot pressed a hand to her chest. "You came all the way from California?"

"Of course," he said. "I would've come all the way from Europe if I had to. There's no way I'd let you go through this alone."

Margot blushed and smiled, obviously so happy Gia could hardly look away.

★ ★ ★ ★ ★

AUTHOR NOTE

The subject of banned books has once again become a passionate debate. The interesting thing to me is that, if you look back through time, some of the books that have moved and inspired people the most—like *The Grapes of Wrath* and *To Kill a Mockingbird*—have been banned.

It's the stories that make us the most uncomfortable that are often targeted; the ones that shine a light on things we'd rather not see. And yet exposure to these stories and the ideas they contain have the power to expand our understanding and make us more empathetic and better human beings. It's a closed mind that threatens society, not an open book.